ANITHIA

Ancestry of Creativity | Book One

LEE LEHNER

First Published 2022 by Kinslee Oak Publishing

ISBN: 978-0-6468617-0-8
Cover art by Hannah Linder Design.
Typesetting by Rack & Rune Publishing
rackandrune.com

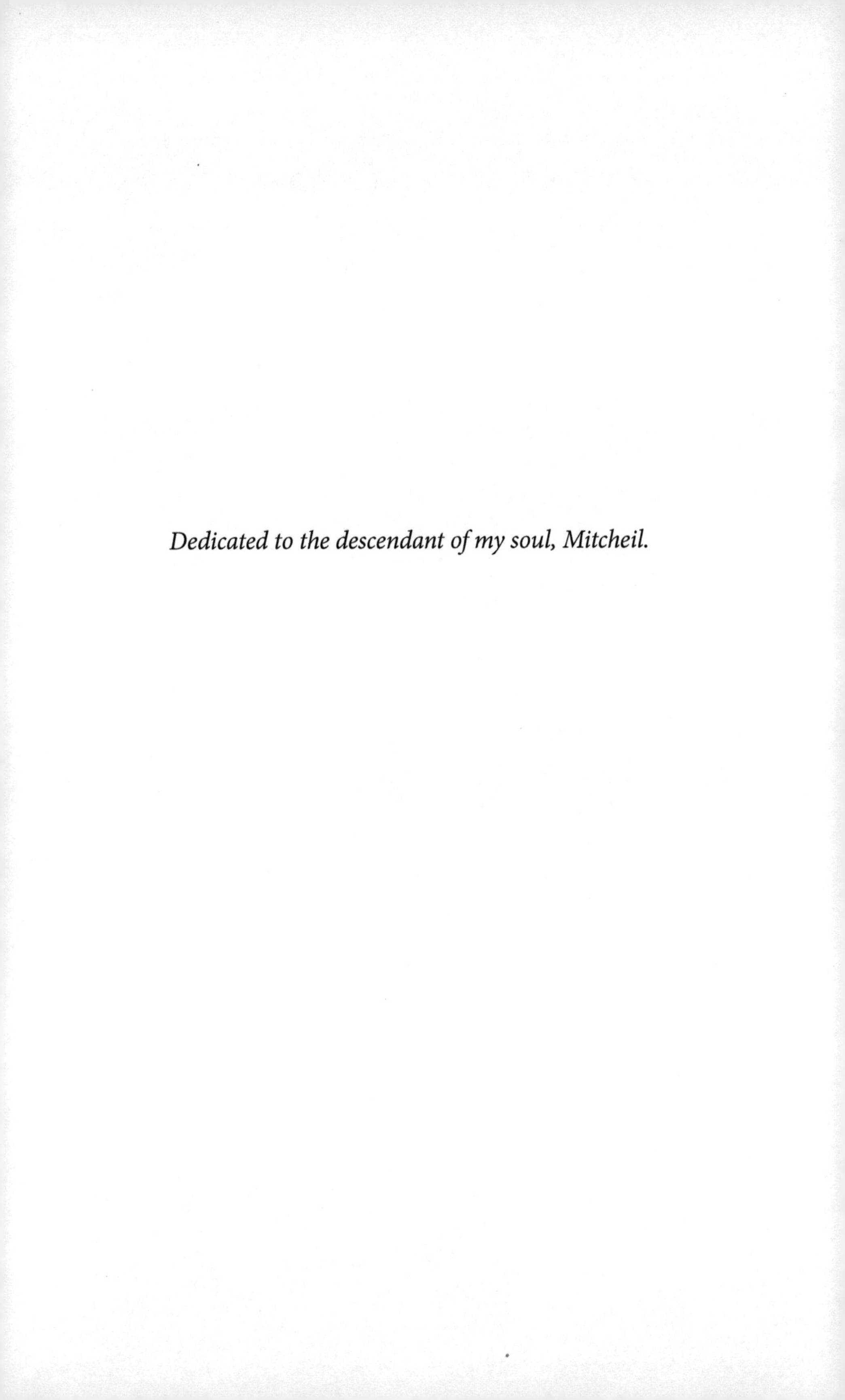

Dedicated to the descendant of my soul, Mitcheil.

Chapter One

Benjamin McCall, 2010. America.

Everyone has a story to tell. But I have a story telling me. It's time it was told.

Characters appear like illusion, seeking literary life through me. But why me, damn it? I'm not a writer. I hold power tools for a living, not pens. Yet despite my disinterest, Isola, the main character, insists I bring her story to life. A story unintended for humans, she explains, but then who else is there?

After multiple failed attempts, I call a writing tutor and ask, would she be interested unpacking the assemblage of characters inhabiting my head. Accepting the challenge, we pencil in an appointment.

A knock on the door kickstarts my nerves.

"Hello, I'm Benjamin. You must be Rose."

"No, I'm the fairy godmother, minus the wings." She charms me with a smile.

Her quirkiness is unexpected. So, too, her stylish clothing and bright red lipstick. She is far from the stiff-looking librarian I was expecting.

"How did you get here?" I glance at the empty driveway.

She points to her yellow pushbike, leaning against the oak tree. "I rode my bike, dear."

"Wow. Come inside, I'll grab you a drink." I open the screen door wider.

"First, lets walk the exterior of this odd-looking house." She beckons me with her hand to come outside. "Its nautical appearance would see it better suited to the sea, than an oak forest. What do you make of it?"

"It's my home, I guess." I shrug my shoulders, following her onto the lawn.

"It hasn't always been your home. This place was built long before your mother put wind in your chest."

"You're right. My uncle inherited it from his great-grandfather. His name was Elliott. But I'm baffled as to why he built a boat in a forest."

"Interesting." She runs her hands along the timber wall. "It looks like a brigantine. I bet she's watertight with all this oakum filling the cracks."

"She?" I give Rose a side eye.

"Every boat is of feminine nature and likened to a mother's embrace. As though she cradles the sailors, in her protective arms, rocking them safely across the sea, back to shore."

"Cool, I never knew that."

"Let's have a gander inside, or should I say, aboard the deck, Captain." She salutes.

Opening the door, the surprise on Rose's face is expected.

"Wow. Am I inside a house, a boat or a woodwork museum?"

"Take your pick."

"The craftsmanship of those waves carved in the wall is commendable. Even the portholes are meticulous. Oh, my goodness, Benjamin." She gasps. "Look at that tree. That's the last thing I expected."

"It caught me by surprise, too. It seems Elliott built the boat around the tree, then carved winding steps up the trunk."

"What's up there?"

"My bed."

"Up there?" She points, narrowing her eyes.

"Yes, the trunk acts as a ladder to the loft. It's quite embarrassing, though."

"How so?"

"Well, when I bring a woman home and she has to climb my tree house to get to bed, it kind of ruins my masculine image."

Rose giggles. "True, making love to a man who climbs trees isn't encouraging. Nevertheless, there is a Jane for every Tarzan." Rose strolls off, leaving me with the thought.

Running her hand along the joinery, and carved waves, she stops at the kitchen table covered in my laundry.

Rushing over, I clear a space for us to work.

"Okay, let's make a start. How much writing have you done?" She takes a seat, placing her bag on the floor.

My gut jumps into my throat. Now I'm too agitated to take a seat beside her. I feel like I'm back in fifth grade. "Apart from a hundred failed attempts, I've never written anything."

"Every book has a hundred draft copies come before it, don't you worry about that."

"Well, those attempts incite defeat. It's laborious trying to be something I'm not."

"Well, it's your choice. Do you want to write a book or not?" Her hands rest in her lap as she awaits my reply.

"I don't know. You see, I have this story telling me it's time to be told, but it's not my desire to write it. Texting a message is painful enough, writing a manuscript is unbearable."

Her subtle movement away from me fuels self-doubt. "Maybe I should have called a shrink, not a tutor. Hearing voices possibly qualifies for medication, not manuscripts."

"No, writing has fewer side effects, and you might even have fun." She pats the seat beside her, prompting me to sit.

"I don't appear to be having much fun," I chuff, pulling the chair out, sitting down.

"You wouldn't, with all that creativity bottled up."

"I don't have any creativity. That's the problem."

"Oh, yes, you do." She taps her finger on the table with certainty.

"I've tried to write this story. Believe me, I have."

"Have you tried letting go?"

"I've let go of my pen and sent it flying across the room multiple times." I replicate my pitch, smirking.

"Listen here, Benjamin. We all have a story to tell. Some people paint their stories, others sing them, and we write them. The world would be a dreary place without creativity, true?"

"I guess so," I halfheartedly agree.

"So, first things first. What genre is the story? Mystery, romance, crime?"

"Currently, it's a bloody mystery, but from what I gather, it starts as a love story set in the Sixties. However, getting to know the characters, I'm led into other eras and realms of life." I surprise myself with my explanation.

Her eyebrows rise. "Sounds like a love story, with a dash of fantasy."

"Fancy that. A guy in his twenties, telling a love story with a dash of fantasy. I must be going mad."

"Don't mock your manhood." She waves her disapproving finger at me. "How about you tell me a bit about your story?"

"Well, like I said, it's about a woman who falls in love and stuff."

Rose's face turns inert at my vague description, then she leans forward. "If I were to ask the woman in your story to describe it, what would she say?"

I, of course, know exactly what Isola would say. I've heard her description many times.

"She would say it's a love story traipsing back through the ancestry of creativity, to reveal her sacred gift."

Her eyes light up. "That's more like it. So, is she human?"

"She is, but she isn't." I struggle putting Isola's existence into words. "To me she is the original free-spirited hippie. Yet she possesses abilities from beyond this world."

"Mmm," she mutters, scratching her head. "So, is she the protagonist or antagonist?"

"I guess she's both. It's the tug-of-war between her humanness and her inherentness, where the conflict arises. If she doesn't surrender her human existence, she can't awaken to her inherent existence."

"Your muse has sacrifices to make. Are you sure you haven't written before? You have a promising imagination."

"It's not my imagination; they tell me their stories. I witness them as like a movie playing out in my head. It's really weird."

"It's your imagination allowing you to experience it."

"How can I possibly imagine all that?"

"How can you possibly question imagination?" Her statement moves beyond questioning.

"Well, then, how do I get my imagination onto paper? I've tried countless times, but all I get is frustrated. Really frustrated."

"Let me share a saying I heard many moons ago: 'Writers don't write great stories. Writers surrender to great stories, and the stories write themselves.'"

"So, I should get out of the way and let the story have its freedom?"

"Correct. Let it flow through your hands."

Running my clenched fingers over my skull, I begrudgingly accept responsibility for this story. "How am I going to do this, Rose?"

"The way every artist creates. We're going to get your hands and the heart of your imagination working as one, and from within the balance, creativity will flow to life. But first, we have to shut that head of yours up. Follow me outside, dear."

Walking out the door to a patch of lawn, Rose flicks the acorns to the side. "Come on over." She gestures with the flick of her head.

"What's this got to do with writing?"

"Everything and nothing," she says, without further explanation, then starts taking her shoes off.

"Right oh, Benjamin. Take your shoes and socks off and leave your ego in them."

Ego? I didn't think I had one of those.

"Listen up. You spend too much time in your head, thinking. Let's take your attention down to your tootsies."

Looking down at my toes, they resemble battered old war soldiers, leaning against one another in much need of a reprieve.

"Now, here we go. I want you to feel the soles of your feet making contact with the ground, then give your weight to the earth."

Is this woman serious? "If you start chanting, I'm out of here. I'm not into New Age self-help crap."

"This is no New Age crap. I'm simply guiding you back to your inherent nature." Rose takes an audible breath in, then exhales slowly. "Now, it's your turn. Take a few deep breaths in and out, pausing between the inhalation and exhalation."

"Okay." I do as instructed, relieved I live in the middle of nowhere and can't be seen acting strange.

"Good. Now close your eyes. On your next exhalation, imagine your breath flowing through the soles of your feet, into the ground, anchoring you on earth."

I close my eyes, take a deep breath, pushing it down through my body into the ground.

"Good work. Keep on breathing nice and slow, in and out. Now, feel the earth's energy rising up through your feet, nourishing your body."

Strangely, I'm starting to relax. I hate to admit it, but I'm getting into it. Rose's calm voice and chilled manner is working wonders.

"Now, in the same way you let your breath fall through your body, and out through your feet, I want you to let go of all your thoughts, good, bad and otherwise. Feel them falling, falling, falling down through your body, like water cascading down a waterfall. Freeing your entire body of beliefs, your childhood, your entire history, until all that remains is your inherent nature. From this place, the creative being you are will flow to life. Now breathe."

***

Sometime later, I come to and open my eyes. Has someone removed my head from my shoulders, tipped out the contents, and placed it back on my body? I'm so at ease, I could fall asleep.

Looking around for Rose, to see if she might be waiting nearby, fails. Her bright red lipstick and yellow pushbike are nowhere in sight. She's gone, and so too, has a ton of crap out of my head. It's time to have a proper crack at this story.

"Okay. Isola, I'm getting out of the way and giving you your freedom. Write away."

Chapter Two

Isola Destinn, 1963. America.

Nothing moves me deeply, or maybe I'm hard to please.

Being a teen in 1963 should be entertaining, right? James Bond movies have hit the screens. The first woman has entered outer space, and the Beatles are moving up the charts. Yet this teenage existence offers little substance. There has to be more. I know it.

One exception where I do sense a hint of belonging, of pleasure, is gliding weightlessly under the sea, while the sea effusively glides by me. It's the ultimate embrace of freedom. The sea and I hold one another, without holding on to one another. Here, and only here, I'm alive.

Luckily, I live on the Southeast Coast of America in a countrified beach town called Fortier, so the sea is never far from my ocean-loving heart. In the cooler months, my hometown turns into a sleepy hollow, but as summer approaches, so do Hobie surfboards, the surf-inspired songs of Jan & Dean, and now the fashionable Ursula Andress bikini.

One place maintaining a steady flow of life, year round, is Pattinson Pier. For as long as I remember, it's been the thoroughfare of Fortier. The pier is also where I catch the ferry to Reefers, a tropical island teenagers go to escape the parental eye.

I can be myself at Reefers. The island escapes time, society, fashion and conformity, making me feel right at home. The lush green mountains rolling into the turquoise sea does something for me—more than a Bond movie, anyway. Rumor has it the old lady who owns Reefers is inhospitable to visitors. However, I've never spotted a cranky old lady or been asked to leave. I'm more than happy for this rumor to circulate as truth. The fewer tourists at Reefers, the more room for me.

A group of friends and I caught the ferry to Reefers this morning. My friends are taking the evening ferry home, but as always, I have to catch the afternoon ferry. All because my father insists I be home before dusk. I constantly argue with him to let me stay out longer, but in his blunt, controlling tone he replies, "Either be home on the afternoon ferry or don't go at all." So, with all that freedom of choice, I bow to his oppressive domination and return home before night casts its evil tone on the earth.

I've run into a friend, Nick, on the ferry home today. We haven't seen each other since he moved away with his family two months ago. But in the scurry of passengers, I lose sight of him before I can say goodbye. I step onto Pattinson Pier and, instantly, I'm drawn to a guy walking in my direction. Each step he takes triggers sensations I've never experienced. By the time he passes in front of me, I'm in love.

As love becomes me, a new existence explodes to life. Finally, I can feel. But it's a little extreme. Way too extreme. Adrenaline coursing through my vains, constricting my airflow. *Breathe. Isola, breathe.*

Turning to the allure of his tropical-blue eyes, he stands at the end of the pier in a crisp white top. His hair is slightly untamed, as if washed in the sea. His skin has seen just enough sun and his hands look strong enough to hold the wildest of hearts, yet the softest of hands. Oh, but his eyes are the thieves I'd happily surrender all the days of my life.

Who on earth is this man, and how did he thrust my heart into sensory overload?

To my surprise, Nick reappears, shaking his hand. He spots me looking his way. Quickly, and might I add, nervously, I walk away.

"Isola! Isola!" Nick calls out over the noise on the crowded pier.

Trust me to have a name too original to ignore. Bravely, I turn and see them approaching.

"Isola, do you need a lift? My buddy, Sation, can give you one."

"I haven't got far to walk, but thanks, anyway."

"I don't mind driving you home, Isola." Sation adds.

The sound of my name leaving his lips makes me giddy. Shuffling my bag around, attempting to distract myself from being drawn back into his eyes, works. "Really, I'm good to walk. It was great to see you, Nick. Bye, guys." I turn to walk.

"No, no, I insist." Nick grabs my bag and rod out of my hand.

"Okay, then." I act cool, downplaying the neurotic adrenaline double-bouncing in my heart.

Sation and Nick walk ahead, making plans for tonight, while I purposely walk five feet behind, gathering air for the ride home. Reaching the parking lot, they approach Sation's truck. A pickup, with a bench seat. Seriously. Can this get any more challenging?

"Someone's got themselves a new Ranchero Falcon. Man, she's smokin'." Nick runs his hand along the hood.

"What do you think of the two-tone spray job?"

"The white and turquoise are outta sight. Don't you think so, Isola?"

"Yes, I like the turquoise." Although I'd much prefer a car with a back seat to burrow into.

Nick lifts my bag and fishing rod into the back, then holds the door open, gesturing for me to jump in. But I can't possibly sit next to Sation.

"Girls before guys."

"No, you go first, Nick. I have to get out before you."

"No, I'm being a gentleman." He smiles, waiting for me to be an obliging friend.

"Are you two getting in or not?" Sation calls out from the driver's seat.

I slide across the bench seat like an awkward schoolgirl. Normally, I embrace any situation with ease, but this man's got me all caught up.

Sation looks out the rear window to reverse. I feel his breath on the side of my face, inducing more hysteria. Please turn back around, else I won't make it out of this parking lot alive. I know I've yearned to experience emotions, but this amount is intolerable.

Sitting in the middle of Nick and Sation's conversation like a mute, I notice Sation is a man of few words himself. His relaxed personality is the opposite of Nick, the freedom rider. Nick's always been a playful extravert. Right now, he's saying a cheeky hello to every female we drive past. Acting like a real cat, with his jelly-roll hairdo, singing to Jackie

Wilson's track, "Baby Work Out."

"Get your head in the cab, Nick. You're scaring all the women," Sation jokes.

"They don't look scared to me. They're happy to see that Nick-sta's back in town."

"Right-oh," Sation scoffs at Nick's boastful ego.

I turn back towards the road and see the striking blue rim of Sation's eyes in the rearview mirror, staring at me. Oddly, he holds his glance.

"Where do you live?" he asks.

"Sycamore Street. Do you know where it is?"

"Yeah, I did some work on a house in that street, awhile back. It's a wonder I didn't see you out and about."

"I spend most of my time down at the beach."

"I gathered that from the tan and bare feet."

I look down at my sandy feet. Gosh, I hope I'm not making his new truck dirty.

"You always have been quite the bohemian beach babe, haven't you?" Nick adds.

"I can't think of any other place I'd rather be."

"I can't imagine you being at any other place. Actually, it's a wonder you two haven't crossed paths. Sation's a keen surfer. He's just spent the past eight months wave-sliding in Hawaii."

"Hawaii. That would've been boss," I add.

"Yeah, sure beats the surf here." He looks out to the flat swell.

"Did you go to Kauai?"

"No, just the Big Island. Have you been to Kauai?"

"I wish. I'm just a sucker for history and the sea, and Kauai is the oldest Hawaiian island."

"Cool. I never knew that." He nods.

Oh, my. Did I just make an idiot of myself?

"Here is close enough," I blurt out, still four houses away from mine. I need out, before my heart bursts over his windshield in every romantic shade of love imaginable.

Nick opens the door and we both hop out.

"It was great to see you again, Isola. You should come to Daniel's party tonight."

"I don't really know him well."

He shrugs his shoulders. "Come anyway. It'll be a gas."

"I'll see how I go." Although I know I'll never be allowed. "Thanks for the ride home, Sation." I glance into the cab.

"No worries, anytime." He lifts his hand off the steering wheel and waves.

Nick closes the door, then pokes his head out of the window as they drive off. "See you tonight, beach babe." He winks.

Standing barefoot by the curb, love beats against my ribs, making the sweetest sound. What on earth is happening to me? This isn't normal.

***

"Hi, Mom." I interrupt her date with *The Dick Van Dyke Show.*

"Good timing, Isola. We're on our way out to dinner soon. Go jump in the shower, love."

"I might give dinner a pass, if that's okay? I'm tired from swimming all day." Really, I'm too excited to sit down and eat.

She turns my way. "Look at those sun-kissed cheeks of yours. When are you going to stop hanging out at the beach and start acting and dressing like a lady?"

"Never," I casually affirm.

"You're probably right. You have a will all of your own. Go get changed and I'll get you something to eat before I leave."

"Thanks, I'm going upstairs for a shower."

"Put your swimsuit and towel in the washroom," she calls out as I make my way upstairs.

Oh, no. I've left my bag and rod in the back of Sation's pickup. I'll never get them back now… not unless I sneak out to the party when Mom and Dad leave for dinner. Maybe I can drop into the party and take another breathtaking plunge into Sation's blue eyes.

***

Mom, Dad, and my younger sister, Julia, leave for dinner. Wasting no time, I put my dusty pink dress on, some love beads, lots of jangly bangles, and my gladiator sandals, then step into the darkness. Dad would shoot me if he knew my whereabouts.

The party is in the older district of Fortier, where ornamental trees age graciously alongside colonial homes. This isn't something a person my age thinks, but my nostalgic personality has always admired how time defines nature and nature defines time.

One grand old home has always captured my attention. Its timeless beauty surpasses all the Sears kit-homes, built a few streets back. It sits on a large block, backing onto the beach, offering the best view in town.

Whoever lives here is the luckiest person in Fortier, although in all my years of admiring it, I've never seen anyone come or go. Which is strange. Someone has to be maintaining the impressive garden and lawns that I've wanted to run barefoot across all my life.

I turn into Daniel's cul-de-sac and my stomach knots, knowing there is a very special attendee, who sent my confidence flying over Pattinson Pier. Just as well I've only come to admire Sation from a safe distance.

Roaming around incognito through this older crowd, I enter a smoke-filled living room and spot Nick with a group of guys, telling a story and sassing it up with his lively personality.

"Boo," I say to Nick when he finishes speaking.

"Isola, you're here! And check your foxy threads out. What have you done to yourself?" He takes a step back.

"I had a shower and put on some shoes, Nick-sta."

"Love your wit, girl." He laughs. "You remember Sation, don't you?" Nick looks past my shoulder.

My body hardens, knowing Sation's standing behind me. Turning, I dive heart-first into the depths of his blue eyes. "Yes, I remember Sation."

But going by his baffled look and pause in his reply, I doubt I hold a place in his.

"It's Isola. Remember, you drove her home today from the pier?" Nick jumps in, noticing Sation struggling to place me.

"Oh, yes, of course. I didn't recognize you with your hair down. It's so long and blond. You're the fisherwoman?" he says just as the song ends.

Did the whole party just hear Sation call me the fisherwoman? Great. I remember him as the sea of love I happily drowned in, and he remembers me as the woman with the rod.

"Yep, that's me, the fisherwoman." I look around the room awkwardly, wishing the next song would start.

A guy walks over and interrupts our awkward conversation. He and Sation greet each other with a lively handshake, then both of them walk outside.

Half an hour passes. Sation still hasn't returned. Looks like I've bummed out. I ask Nick where Sation's pickup is, then we say our goodbyes. I'd like to linger longer, but I have to head home before Mom and Dad return. I spot Sation's pickup across the road. As I walk down the driveway I notice a man walking my way.

"Isola, is that you?"

Oh, no, it's Sation. "Yes, it's me. I left my things in the back of your pickup today. I'm just going to grab them before I leave."

"You're splitting already? You should stay longer." He nudges his head back towards the party.

"I should, but I have to call it a night, unfortunately."

"Well, let me drive you home, then."

"That's fine, it's not far. I'll let you get back to the party."

There will be a double homicide on Sycamore Street tonight if Dad sees me getting out of a guy's truck.

"Let me at least grab your things out of the truck bed."

Crossing the road together is delightfully strange. He hands my things to me, but now I'd rather lose the fishing rod.

"Thanks, Sation, I guess I'll see you around."

"Sometime soon, hopefully." He smiles.

"Yes, hopefully. Bye."

Walking away with his grin fresh in my mind, I reach the end of the road and look back to see Sation standing under the streetlight, looking at me. Oh my, I've held his attention.

The second I'm out of his sight, my calm, seductive strut turns into a clodhopping sprint, freaking out my father will be home. Burning blisters begin mounting on my heels, slowing me down. I lean against a fence, taking the wretched sandals off and realizing I've stopped at the grand old beach house I adore.

But in horror, I shriek, noticing a person moving in the yard. My piercing reaction frightens them, knocking them off balance. Into the garden they tumble.

"Blooming heck!" I hear a lady say, laying on the ground.

Running into the yard I see a Native American woman looking up at me, with her big brown eyes.

"I'm so sorry. I thought you were a creepy man in the bushes."

"You scared the crap out of me," she chuckles.

I didn't expect those words to come from her seventy-year-old mouth.

"I can't believe you're gardening at half past nine." I help her up.

"I'll tend to the garden whenever I like. I should be asking you what you're doing out so late." She dusts off her paisley dress.

"I shouldn't be. That's why I was leaning on your fence, taking my sandals off so I could run home quicker."

"Don't let me hold you up. Scram, before you get yourself into trouble."

She waves her hand at me to run along. I can't believe I've never seen anyone at this house, and now an old woman appears at nine-thirty, doing her gardening.

Turning onto Sycamore Street, the driveway is empty. Thank goodness. Sprinting up stairs, I change and fall into bed, knowing I'm wholeheartedly, inescapably, in love with Sation, Sation, Sation.

Chapter Three

For three weeks I hunt, without one glimpse of Sation, Sation, Sation. Now, casually walking with friends to get a soda, here he is, leaning against his pickup. He glimpses me, we both smile and walk in each other's direction. Hysteria, nervousness or weakened knees will not stop me.

"Hey, Isola."

"You remember who I am this time?" I playfully smirk.

"Sure do."

"I thought my name might have slipped your mind after three weeks."

"Has it been that long?"

"Thereabouts," I casually shrug, hoping he didn't think I'd been counting the days and minutes, like I have.

"Actually, I saw you last week when I was driving home."

I could kick myself, especially given I ransacked every square inch of Fortier to find him. "You should have stopped and said hello."

"I had my mom with me."

"That's okay. I could have said hello to her as well."

"True. She would like you too. You're down to earth, like her. Anyway, what have you been up to?"

"Not a lot. I'm just on my way to the diner with the girls."

"Looks like they have gone ahead without you."

"I told them I'd catch up with them later." I do my best to remain as easygoing as him, even though I'm trembling inside.

"Do you want to hang out? Maybe go for a spin?"

"Sure."

Driving alone with a male probably won't do my reputation any good, but that's only if I care about people's opinions of me.

"Wow, you accepted a ride from me." He bounces on his toes.

"Third time lucky." I smirk.

"You can say that again." He opens the door for me.

Driving off, Doris Troy's new song, "Just One Look," starts playing. The lyrics sing true to my heart. I did fall hard in love with him after just one look.

Out of town we drive, talking about nothing in particular, which suits me fine. The ease in my breath lets me know I've got this. Soon our small talk ends when Sation gives me a contemplative look, sparking my curiosity.

"What is it, Sation?"

"I don't know what it is about you, but I can't help but think we've met before. Maybe at a party or something?" His eyes narrow, looking directly at me.

"Not that I can remember." Oh, and I'd remember. "Maybe you saw me down the beach or at school."

"I didn't go to school around here, and I finished years ago."

"How old are you?"

"I just turned twenty. And you?"

"I'll be seventeen in a couple of months."

"Wow," he responds, shuffling around. "I thought you were older than that. You're more mature than women my age."

"I've been told that before. I guess I just don't care for the things women my age do, like makeup and stuff."

"That's not a bad thing, trust me. I've felt the same way most my life."

"You don't like wearing makeup either?" I inject my dry humor into the conversation.

His belly-laughing reassures me he enjoys my wit, along with my refusal to be like other women.

"You and I are going to get on well." He smiles, winding down his window, giving me some much-needed fresh air. "So, I'm four years older than you."

"Yeah, but it's closer to three years, and if you don't count, it's none at all."

"Let's not count," he laughs, "But if I have to, I'll run with three."

We park at the beach, chatting, laughing, and sending a few lingering smiles at each other. Sation tells me all about his time on the Big Island. Fascinating me with stories of the people he met and places he saw. Now I'm plotting out my future with him, living on an island, surrounded by eternal sets of waves, and his eyes looking back at me.

The tide makes its way to shore, with the sun setting behind it. I'm awfully close to my curfew, but too embarrassed to suggest we drive home. So, we continue talking until we can no longer see each other. Then make tracks and head home.

Awkwardly, I tell Sation my father wouldn't approve of me spending time with a man, requesting he drop me off around the corner from my house. Thank goodness it's dark and he can't see how embarrassed I am. I open the cab door, and just as I'm about to hop out, Sation grabs my hand, sending a burst of energy up my spine.

"I'm glad I ran into you today. Maybe we can go for a swim tomorrow, after I finish work?"

"That's music to my ears." I say, looking down to his hand on top of mine. "I'll meet you down by the pier at four."

"See you then." He smiles, letting go of my hand.

***

Stepping onto my dark front porch, acrimonious tension brews inside. I'm in a world of trouble, but I don't even care.

"Where have you been? We've been worried sick about you," Mom says in her harshest voice, which really isn't harsh at all.

"It's only eight o'clock."

"Your mother asked you a damned question. Now answer her." He slams his fist down on the kitchen table, spiking my anxiety with his spitfire voice.

"I've been at the beach."

"Well, you were down the beach two hours too long." He butts out his cigarette. "Now you have a month's grounding to remind you to be home on time."

"A month." I almost vomit up my punishment.

"Yes, a month."

My chances of seeing Sation sink lower than my dad's heart. "That's not fair. I'm not a child anymore. I'm practically seventeen."

"You know my rules." He gets up out of his chair, walking into the kitchen.

I look over to Mom. Her jaw has dropped in reaction to my father's disproportionate punishment.

"One month is a little harsh, don't you think?" Mom comes to my defense, but Dad's cold-hearted stare lets her know she's said too much.

"Seriously, Dad, you can't just ground me for that long." I follow him into the kitchen.

"I just did," he bluntly replies.

Bitter words fill my mouth, threatening to fly out and verbally attack him. But instead I walk away, knowing if I'm too audacious, one month will turn into two.

"Isola."

I turn, in hope he's changed his mind.

"No walking to school along the beach, either." He points his overriding finger at me.

I look him dead in the eye. In my head I yell, *I hate you so much for treating me like this. I hate you. I fucking hate you.*

***

Is it a bad dream? *Please, please, please let it be a dream.* The seconds tick by, reality kicks in, and I fall back onto my pillow, devastated it's not. I'm stuck in this house for the next month, all because I was born to an unreasonable bastard. I can't even contact Sation to let him know I can't make it. I'm locked inside this viper's nest without his phone number.

***

Days turn into weeks of torture. Dad and I spend the whole time snarling at each other. Socializing has been reduced to school hours or chatting with the Good Humor man when he drives up our street. Mom kindly brings home some magazines to help pass the time. After reading through *Seventeen,* I find myself comically amused by the articles. I've learned how to hold a boy, stay in fashion, and keep a conversation moving. Seriously, is this what women my age read? Or who my mom wants me to be?

Thankfully, twenty-seven painstaking days pass. One day remains handcuffed to my father's heartless existence. I just pray Sation hasn't met another woman.

Unfortunately, the last day of my grounding has fallen on the most eventful day of Fortier's calendar: March the seventh. It marks the anniversary of Fortier's founding, now known as Fortier's Botanical Birthday. Each year, a big carnival comes to town and locals gather in parks and down on the shore to celebrate the festivities. But this year I'm the only local not attending; I'm spending the day at the house of happiness.

The only good thing about being home today is having the house to myself, given the people I live with are at the carnival. After spending a solid four weeks with them, it's evident to me, and them, that I really don't fit into their Middle American existence. The only thing we have in common, apart from our surname, is a local restaurant we all enjoy. Tonight, the four of us are going to meet Dad's business partner, Bill, and his wife. We're celebrating the success of my dad's business in the steel industry. The only reason Dad's allowing me to come is to portray to Bill that we're a happy, wholesome American family. What a crock of shit.

***

The festivities in town create a lively atmosphere inside the restaurant.

Finishing my entrée, the atmosphere escalates when the one and only Sation walks in with a few friends. Should I run to him or hide from him. He may not even like me, after I'd stood him up. A few minutes later, Sation notices me. He smiles my way, dispelling my doubts. Thank goodness.

After the waitress takes his order, I notice him getting out of his chair. He motions with his head to follow him down the passage towards the bathroom. I excuse myself from the table, walk down the passage, and as I turn the corner, I smack straight into him.

"Well, hello."

"Oops, sorry," I say, feeling like a klutz.

"What happened? You never showed up."

"I'm so sorry."

"Did you get a better offer?"

"I forgot all about it," I say, too embarrassed to admit I was grounded.

"You forgot about me," he replies, as dumbfounded by my reply as I am.

"I mean, I forgot all about what time it was, thinking I had an hour up my sleeve. When I realized I'd stuffed up, I ran down the beach but you were gone. I'm really sorry."

"Fair enough."

"I really did want to see you."

"Me too. I was worried when you didn't show up. I drove down your street, but I recall you telling me your old man is a bit uptight about you talking to guys, so I didn't knock at your door."

"Yes, my dad is very uptight, unfortunately."

"He looks it." He nods in agreeance.

Bill, my father's business partner, walks around the corner. I get such a fright thinking it is my dad, I walk away from Sation and return to the table.

"We better make a move when Bill gets back. I've got an early start tomorrow," Dad says, finishing his wine.

"Aren't we having dessert?" I try stalling time.

"You hardly ate your dinner," Mom replies.

"I'm saving myself for dessert. You know I love their chocolate mousse."

"Is anyone having dessert? I could do with a coffee and cake," Bill asks, sitting back down at the table.

Thank you, Bill.

My chocolate mousse arrives. I have three mouthfuls and slide the bowl to my sister. I duck off to the bathroom, making sure Sation sees me out of my chair. Before I even reach the end of the passage, his hands grip the small of my waist. He pulls me towards the end of the passage, out of sight.

"This is to make sure you never forget me again."

His firm, yet soft, lips push up against mine, giving me the biggest rush of my life.

"You just kissed me," I say, breathless, touching my lips.

"And I want to again. When can I see you next?"

"Tomorrow," I reply, hoping I don't sound too keen.

"Where?"

"Down by the northern end of the beach."

"You know where north is?" He gives me a sideways glance.

"Yes, and south, east, and west."

He chuckles at my response. "You're funny."

"And you're cute." I smirk, boosted with confidence after one single kiss.

"I finish work at four. I'll see you then."

"I'll be there. I promise."

"Take this." He hands me a small piece of paper. "If you can't make it, call me." He kisses me one last time, then walks off, leaving me smiling deep down in my heart.

***

After two months of looking at Sation looking back at me, it's become, beyond a doubt, my favorite place to be. Upon this fleeting exchange of feelings that only he and I share, I contrive a future, grounded in love and happiness.

When my parents were out, entertaining business guests, I'd sneak out with Sation or else we caught up after I finished school. We laughed, listened to music, and made out together. Everything is working out perfectly.

That is, until yesterday. Unbeknown to Sation, I saw him leaning over a car, talking to the driver. A woman with long brown hair and skin that resembled porcelain.

I didn't need to see Sation's face to know what was going on. The look in her eyes said it all. I too had the same look in mine. Not long after, she started her car and drove off, waving goodbye with the suggestive twinkle of her fingers, then Sation left straight after. I stood up from behind the bush I was crouched behind with a feeling I'd never felt before. Jealousy.

Waiting on the beach for Sation to arrive, I'm unable to get the image of that woman out of my mind from yesterday. I turn and notice him approaching. He sits down behind me, wrapping his arms around me, which I awkwardly receive.

"Hey, babe. Have you been here long?"

"No, only a few minutes." Leaning back into him, I try my best to act as if jealousy is still a foreign emotion.

"Wouldn't it be cool if we could camp out here one night and wake up to this view?"

"It would be great, but unfortunately, it's not going to happen until I'm a little older."

"When are you turning seventeen?"

"In less than a month, on the twenty-first of June."

"So, I won't be kissing a sweet sixteen for much longer," he jokes, kissing my neck.

"In all honesty, does it annoy you I can't stay out later and do the things women your age do?"

"It would be cool to hang out longer and maybe at night, but I'll just have to wait until we can." He shrugs his shoulders, unfazed.

"But don't you want to do those things now?"

"Well, sure, but I can't do much about your age. It is what it is. Not unless I meet your parents. Would that make things better? Then I could come to your place to hang out."

"No, no. That would make things worse. Trust me." I'm sure the panic shows on my face.

"Well, then, we'll just have to wait and watch submarine races until you're older. Why are you even asking me these questions?"

I look down at the sand, contemplating voicing my suspicions.

"Isola, what's the matter?"

"Who is the woman with the long brown hair?" I blatantly ask, cutting to the quick.

"I knew you were tee'd off about something."

"Should I be?" I turn and face him.

"No. She is no one. I met her a few weeks ago at a party, then I ran into her down the street yesterday, which is obviously when you saw us talking."

"Just like I thought. You met her at a party I can't go to." I turn my back on him, feeling the sting of jealousy spilling from my mouth.

"She means nothing to me." He places his reassuring hand on my shoulder. "Nothing at all. She might like me, but the feeling isn't mutual."

"Oh, I can tell she likes you." I pull my shoulder away from his touch.

"Jesus, Isola, why are you laying a trip on me? I'm here with you, aren't I?" The tone of his voice changes in reaction to me pulling away from him.

"Yeah, but as soon as I go home, then where will you go?"

"I go home, like you, and look forward to seeing you the next day. Yes, I do go to parties, but I'd rather be with you."

"So why haven't you told anyone about us?"

"Because you asked me not to, so your folks don't find out."

"Yeah, but…"

"No. No buts, Isola. If you want me to tell people we're going steady, then I'll happily do so. I've never met anyone like you before."

"Like me?" I screw my face up. What that's suppose to mean?

"Yes, like you. You're intriguing. Not many women know where north is, or that the moon affects the tides. Heck, you wake up to swim in the sea to catch the sunrise. You're so attractive in so many ways, and yet you don't even know it."

"I am?" Wow, I'm taken by his opinion of me.

"I don't want a woman who wears makeup to impress me. I've found a woman whose hair smells like the sea. The sun colors her face, and her interests aren't out to impress me."

"I like that even more." I grin.

From out of nowhere, the sky darkens, unleashing a downpour of large raindrops. Racing for the car makes no difference, we're saturated by the time we close the doors. I can't help but laugh, looking at our dripping wet clothes. But Sation's laughter is short-lived.

"I'll never hurt you, Isola. You're the one I want," he raises his voice over the rain pelting on the roof.

"I believe you."

My wet dress slides along the vinyl seat with ease, as he draws me near. Our lips inseparable, as his weight bears down on my hips, swooning me in manliness.

But then he stops and sits back up. "I'd better get you home."

I pull him back down. Not wanting him to go anywhere.

"Isola, I can't." He pulls away again.

"I want you."

"You've got me, but let's continue this when the time's right and not in my front seat. We're saturated. I couldn't get them off if I tried."

I reckon I could.

Chapter Four

Bolting from Sation's pickup, I barge through my front door to escape the lightning. Mom and Dad look up, from the kitchen table, surprised.

"Isola, you're drenched," Mom states the obvious.

I'm sure my face is stricken with paranoia, knowing I've been kissing a guy three years older than me, less than five miles away.

Mom hands me a towel to dry off. "Go change, then come back downstairs. Your father and I want to have a word with you."

I freeze, wondering what that word is.

"Well, don't just stand there," Dad barks. "Go and get changed like your mother asked."

Heil Hitler, I want to reply, with the power-hunger salute from my forehead, or better still, my erect middle finger.

A long list of thoughts runs through my mind while drying my hair. Did someone spot Sation and me down on the beach? Did my sister Julia find out and tattle on me? Or could it be good news, like they've conscripted Dad to the Vietnam War.

Returning to the kitchen table, I take a seat across from Mom and Dad.

"Your father and I have some good news."

"Oh. Okay. What is it?" I pull my chair in closer, feeling a sense of relief.

"Your father's company is doing so well he's decided to expand into the overseas market. So your father will be going to work in England."

This isn't good news; this is the best news. Hiding the joy on my face isn't so easy.

"So, you're going to England, are you, Dad?"

"We all are."

"We all are," I repeat, making sure I've heard correctly.

"Yes. The four of us are moving to England."

Their so-called good news annihilates my future. Rushing out of the room, I ignore both Mom and Dad's demands to sit back down. The larceny of my love life is way too heartbreaking to discuss with the thieves who stole it.

Minutes later, I hear a knock at my bedroom door. Mom walks in and sits on the end of my bed.

"Isola, please, can we talk?"

"Get out, Mom," I weep.

"There's a beach where we're moving, so you can still swim."

"Good. I can drown myself in it when we get there."

"Don't be like that. It will be an adventure, just you wait and see. We can visit all the sights of England, like Buckingham Palace, London Bridge. We can even visit my friend Trealla and her famous garden."

Her enthusiasm's nauseating. "Why in hell would I want to see Buckingham Palace or some famous garden? I'm almost seventeen, not seventy. I'm not going anywhere with any of you. I'll go to boarding school," I declare, putting my pillow over my head to block her out.

"Isola, your father has already made arrangements for us to leave in five days."

"Five days! No, no, no, no," I scream, sitting up in bed. Not only are they taking me away, they're virtually kidnapping me off the streets of Fortier. "I'm not leaving. This is my home. You can all go without me."

"We're going as a family."

"I'm not even part of this family. I'm not like any of you. I never have been and never will."

"Stop talking to your mother like that," Dad yells, entering my room.

"I'm not going, Dad."

"I tell you what you can and can't do, not the other way around. I've already bought a ticket with your name on it, so you're going."

He's the most depraved man I've ever known. I want to push his heartless body out of my room, down the stairs, and out of my life for good.

"This can't be happening to me." I drop my face into my hands.

"Well, it is, so stop being so difficult and start packing," he bluntly replies, then walks away, with Mom following behind him like an obliging wife.

***

No one has knocked on my bedroom door for days. They're ignoring the hostile woman I've become after hearing their so-called good news. The excitement and mass organization outside my bedroom is rife. Boxes are being packed. Suitcases zipped closed. But I haven't packed a thing, nor do I intend to. I haven't even met with Sation, I'm so bummed out. The thought of having to leave Fortier is devastating enough. Saying goodbye to the love I've found will be torturous. Avoiding it altogether is working best for now.

"Are you going to leave this room, Isola?" Mom barges in. "Heavens to Betsy, you haven't packed a thing and we're leaving in three days." She looks around my room in a panic. "Enough is enough. Get out of bed."

"No. I'm not going."

"Yes, you are. You're going to school to say goodbye to your friends."

"What's the use of going to school if you're making me leave in a few days? I'd rather save my energy to hate all of you."

"You've already missed two days of school lying in this bed, sulking. Now get up, get dressed, and get to school, and when you get home, you can start packing," she shouts, then slams my bedroom door.

I eat a piece of toast, to give me enough energy to continue hating them. I take a deep breath and call Sation, telling him to meet me after work at the beach and that I'll explain everything then. However, I'd much rather disappear without explaining a thing. I detest saying goodbye at the best of times. The emotional confrontation of ending ties is too awkward.

School's a blur. I fail to tell my friends I'm leaving. Their girly tears will irritate me, so I leave school like any other Friday. But rather than go home and pack my life into an England-bound suitcase, I wander around Fortier one last time while I wait for Sation.

I farewell the beach I've grown up on, hoping the beach in Bristol will be as equally beautiful. Making my way through the pretty old streets of Fortier, I pass by the grand old beach house, wishing I lived here more than ever before.

"It's you again," a lady says, interrupting my daydream.

"Oh, you startled me."

"We're about even then." She strolls barefoot across the spongy lawn towards me.

"You remember me from that night, do you?"

"I do. However, you've been walking past this house most of your life, admiring it."

Her comment surprises me. All this time, she must have been inside, watching me.

"Its location is perfect." I look around at the sapphire sea, the lush green garden, and this grand home set amidst them.

"I couldn't agree more, Isola. Its positioning was well thought out."

"How do you know my name?" She arouses my curiosity.

Stepping a little closer, she looks me in the eye. "I gave you your name."

"But you don't even know me." I shake my head.

She chuckles. "You might not know me, but I've known you for a very long time."

Her comment triggers the memory of mom telling me that the day I was born she didn't have a name for me, so the midwife sugested Isola.

"You're the midwife, aren't you?"

The slight grin from one corner of her mouth lets me know I'm right. Maybe now is a good time to ask what it means or where she got it from.

"Excuse me, before you go, can I ask, where did you get my name from?"

"From an old friend of mine. She would have called her daughter Isola, but she never had one, and neither did I. The moment I heard your mother didn't have a name for you, I suggested Isola. It's a beautiful name and suits you. However, you're not looking so beautiful today.

Your energy is very heavy."

"My parents are making me move to someplace in England."

"I'm guessing you don't want to go to Coronation Street?"

"You guessed right." I kick at a rock on the path, feeling so bummed out.

"You can always return when you're eighteen."

"Oh, I will be, the day of."

"I'm certain you will. I'll see you in a year, with a smile on your face."

Without saying goodbye, which suits me fine, she walks inside the house. Maybe she hates saying goodbye as much as I do. That is the strangest conversation I've had, but what can I expect from an eccentric old lady who gardens at nine-thirty at night?

***

My emotionally battered appearance urges Sation to grab hold of me.

"Babe, what's wrong?" He consoles me as I sob. "Come on now, it can't be that bad."

"Oh, it is." I whimper, burrowing deep into his chest.

"Tell me what's wrong." He lifts my chin to meet with his eyes.

"My family is moving and I have to go with them."

"That's okay. I can come see you. I do have a car."

"You can't drive to England."

His beautiful blue eyes merge to black as his pupils widen, pinning me with his stare.

"When are you leaving?"

"In three days."

"Three days." He stomps off, clasping his hands around the back of his head. It's the first time I've seen him lose his cool.

"They can't just take you away from me like that. This is bullshit, Isola, goddamn bullshit. Doesn't your old man have enough bread?"

"My greedy father will never have enough."

"The jerk." He kicks at the ground. "Please tell me this is temporary."

The drop of my head answers his question.

"This is infuriating. If you were older, you could stay in America with me."

"Please don't go down that track. I've run all the 'what if's and 'how to's through my mind a million times. Nothing can be done, they're making me leave." I break down again.

"Come here, babe." He pushes my hair behind my ears and wipes the tears from my cheeks.

"Listen to me. This isn't the end. In one year, you can come back home and we can be together again."

"The day I turn eighteen I'm coming home. I'm not spending one day longer than I need to."

"That's it. Let's pretend you're going on a vacation or I've been drafted to Vietnam for the time being."

He attempts to dilute our reality to make me feel better, but unfortunately my brain's too shrewd for me to lie to it.

"It's more like I'm going to war and you're going on the vacation."

"Not being able to see you isn't my idea of a vacation, but it won't be forever. In one year, you'll turn eighteen."

"I guess we can write to each other and talk over the phone."

"Yes, we can, so dry your beautiful eyes. The sea can't separate us forever, babe."

"It's taking me away, but it will bring me back."

Hugging each other, we find hope for the distant future.

"If we only have this little time left, let's go enjoy it. Hop in the car. I'm taking you someplace special."

From this moment on, I'm focusing on the twenty-first of June, when I board a boat back to Fortier.

"Where are you taking me?"

"To a place my grandfather used to take me camping and fishing as a kid. It's a perfect place for a fisherwoman like yourself." He laughs.

"I can't believe you called me a fisherwoman that night at the party." I shake my head at him.

"Sorry, I was nervous."

"You, nervous? I doubt that."

"I'm serious. You looked so beautiful with your hair down, and that pink dress was outta sight."

"Sation, you didn't even recognize me."

"Well, yes, but only for a split second. You can't blame me. You wouldn't even look at me when we first met on the pier. You even walked ten feet behind me to my pickup."

"You're right, and that's because I was nervous. Your eyes did something to me that day. But at least I didn't call you a fisherman."

"I'm sorry. What do you want me to call you?"

I look out my window in thought, remembering back to a word I read in a book. "Ke aloha."

"What does that mean?"

"When we go to Hawaii together one day, you'll find out."

"I like the sound of that, my Ke aloha."

Around twenty minutes later, we reach a clearing in the ferns. A stream of clear blue water leading off to the sea trickles on past. All I can hear is distant waves crashing onto the shore and birds whistling in the trees.

"Oh, Sation, this is beautiful."

"I knew you'd like it."

"Oh, I do, I do. I never knew this place existed." I hop out of the pickup, hitch up my dress and walk straight into the water, feeling instantly calmer. "Why don't you come over and cool off with me?" I flick some water at him.

"What, in my work shorts?"

"No, in nothing." I lift my dress over my head and throw it onto the bank.

"Wow. I should have brought you here weeks ago." He smirks.

"Funny one. It's no different than if I were in my bikini. Now get those threads off and come over here. You're too far away from me."

Stripping down to his underpants, he pauses a foot away, looking deep into my eyes. I lean forward into his bare chest. I love that he doesn't wear cologne; the scent of his skin is pleasing, even after a day at work. This is another thing I can add to the list of things I'll miss.

"I'm not going home tonight, Sation."

"You're not?" He looks down at me confused.

"No, I'm staying with you. If I'm being sent to war, I want to make the most of our time together before I leave."

"I don't know if that's a good idea."

"It's a great idea."

"But what about your—"

"Stop." I cut him off before he says his name. "He's going to control me for the next year. Tonight, I'm in control. I'm choosing you."

"Okay then, but he's going to kill you and me."

"He already did when he bought me a ticket to England. Enough talk about me leaving. Let's get back to you and me." I snuggle into his chest again.

"How about we camp here on the beach, like we've always wanted to?"

"Sounds perfect."

Nothing is separating me from Sation tonight. No controlling father. No larceny. No ocean of water. No age difference. Nothing. Tonight, I'm in control of my life and the woman in me is going to freely engage with the man I love. I don't care that my father is going to ground me for the rest of my life. As far as I'm concerned, nothing he can sentence me to can hurt more than having to walk away from the love I've found in Sation's eyes.

I hope my dad goes out of his wits wondering where I am. I hope he experiences the same loss of control I'm having to endure. I hope it churns in his guts that I care so little for him, as he cares so little for me. And I'm deeply satisfied to know I'm at least doing this in the name of love and not inadequacy.

Lying in the back of the truck bed, I turn my head to Sation. "This is the right place."

"What do you mean?"

"Last time we were together, you said it wasn't the right place or time."

He turns to me. "Oh, I get you. It's definitely the right place." He looks back up to the beauty towering above us.

"And it's definitely the right time."

Sation turns his whole body in my direction, then places his forehead gently against mine.

"Are you sure?" His eyes search mine.

"I've never been this sure about anything my entire life."

***

Night falls. I lie for hours with my ear to his chest, immersed in the sound of his heartbeat, while he sleeps. I relive the passion from earlier, when Sation moved deep inside me. The sensation surpassed the exhilarating rush I get diving into the sea. My breath was momentarily stolen as he touched a part of me no man ever has. Now I have something else to miss, but something exhilarating to return too.

As my weary eyes begin to close over, and I realize I can no longer make this day last longer, I whisper to his heart what I've been wanting to say since the second I looked into his eyes.

"I love you. I love you so much."

Chapter Five

I drag my desecrated heart down Pattinson Pier for the last time. Reaching *Cybele,* the ship taking me away, a single tear falls, shattering like a pane of glass into hundreds of pieces. Then I step aboard.

Cybele pulls away from the pier. My wailing worsens, with every nautical mile I sail. Julia can't handle my distress for a second longer, and moves into Mom and Dad's cabin. Now I regret not saying goodbye to Sation this morning.

I've got to go back. I can't leave him, I can't. This jagged severance tearing away in my chest in unbearable. It might take an hour to swim back, but I can do it. Being in water is second nature to me.

Stepping onto the deck, I look to the dark blue sea, anticipating the rush of comfort I'll feel the second I break the surface. I put one foot on the bottom rail and climb the rest. Concerned passengers stare in horror, but I fear nothing under the water. My troubles exist above it.

Diving off the ship, I hear everyone gasp as I break through the surface, barely make a splash. "Ah."

Immersed in dark blue silence, momentarily appeased of reality, I float, at ease. But why aren't I itching to swim to the surface to breathe?

Something else captures my attention, a humming sound behind me. I turn, but can't see anything. Maybe it's the humming of a ship's propeller in the distance.

I turn back to Fortier and the fact that I've been under water for two or three minutes, without air. Years of swimming obviously built a mighty set of lungs. I start swimming home, but the sound behind me returns, stealing my attention again. Only this time it's easier to define.

From beyond the darkness, a dulcet sigh ripples my way, like a smooth satin wave of sound. Her voice summons my attention. The gentle ebb and flow sparks my curiosity. It's essential I follow her.

Then I hear a walloping sound above me. Someone's broken through the surface. They're coming for me. I don't need rescuing. I need to follow this beautiful humming. I'll hover silently, in hope they won't find me.

Snap! Someone grabs hold of my ankle, frightening the heck out of me. Frantically, I swim away from this rescue attempt.

My fleeing spikes the rescuer's determination. They grab hold of me again, only this time I recognize that they're a man and he's not letting go. He holds me around the waist and kicks with a propelling motion, shooting us towards the surface. I'm losing the fight, kicking and screaming, and so I sink my teeth into his arm. He flinches, but refuses to let go.

Once again, I've no control over where my life is going, and the fight in me turns to fatigue. My rescuer drags me back toward my heartbreaking reality, and my will to live plummets. I can't do this. I can't live this life.

***

I'm woken by the sailor's lips leaving mine, choking from his unnecessary breath forced into my lungs. I never drowned, I only passed out.

All the passengers cheer and clap, yelling, "Bravo, bravo," applauding the sailor for supposedly saving my life. He walks back and forth across the deck, shaking off adrenaline, while I sit with onlookers asking me if I'm all right. The sailor keeps looking over to me with a pensive look, rubbing his arm where I bit him. Any minute, he's going to question me about the whole scenario, but before he has the chance, the captain approaches and shakes his hand.

"I've been informed of the incident. Great rescue, Sailor Kipling." He gives him a firm handshake.

"Thank you, Captain. I really didn't do much."

"Nonsense. You dove into the ocean to save a passenger. It was a courageous act. Is the girl okay?"

They both look over to me.

"I believe she's perfectly fine, Captain," Kipling says.

"Your bravery will be rewarded in due time, and we will address her parents later. Right now, we have another serious matter to attend to. An unexpected storm's blowing in from the south. Send all passengers to their cabins immediately and ready the crew."

"Yes, Captain, right away." Sailor Kipling jumps straight into action in response to the storm warning. "All hands ahoy. All hands ahoy." His message spreads across the boat and a scurry of sailors run onto the deck in a semi-organized fashion. "Tie down the deck and have all passengers return to their cabins immediately."

Fearsome winds howl for hours as *Cybele* rises out of the ocean, then comes thumping back down. I lie alone in my cabin, unfazed by the storm. Heck, I couldn't drown under the water if I tried. I'm too consumed by my newfound ability, to breathe underwater, and the melody I heard humming to worry about the storm.

I can still hear her voice singing to me, like the sirens that tempted Odysseus with their humming melodies. Or was I simply delirious from a lack of oxygen and imagined it all? There is no probable explanation for today's mysterious events. Nevertheless, I'm happy for her beautiful melodic voice to remain with me. Its silky tones pacify my restless heart.

***

The roar of the storm subsides come morning. Never would I think a storm raged across this deck hours earlier. It is quiet and peaceful, apart from the footsteps I hear walking behind me. Turning, I see the sailor who pulled me out of the sea.

"Good morning, miss," he says, strolling along beside me.

"Morning."

"You're not thinking about taking an early morning swim, are you?"

His attempt at humor comes off as irritating. I still feel like hitting him for taking me out of the sea. But rather than leave more marks on his body, I'll just ignore him.

"Were you attempting to kill yourself?" he asks compassionately.

"Are you serious! I was trying to swim home."

"Wow, that's ambitious of you. Are you going to tell me how you held your breath for so long?"

It's obviously been playing on his mind, as it has mine. "I'm a mermaid."

"Really. Well, that explains everything. You're a mermaid with a good set of teeth."

"Yep, my secret's out."

"In all seriousness though, you had to be under the water for more than five minutes. How didn't you drown?"

"I did drown, remember? You saved my life, Sailor Kipling." Then I walk off to escape future questioning.

For the rest of the voyage, every time I see Sailor Kipling, I turn in the opposite direction. I've also done a great job of avoiding Mom. Every time I'm on the deck, she's no more than five feet away. I'd never attempt to swim home now though, I'd get lost. Instead I continue humming the sea's mysterious melody. It's proving quite therapeutic to my heart.

***

Bristol greets *Cybele* reverently as we sail through the kelp-green channel. *Cybele* might be severely weather-beaten, but she carried out her journey from Pattinson Pier to Bristol with grace.

Approaching the dock, I take one look at the littered water and become bitterly disappointed. It looks like dam water about to freeze. Turning to Mom, I don't have to say a word about the swimming conditions. The disappointment on my face says it all.

The harbormaster greets Sailor Kipling and awards him a bravery medal for his rescue of the death-defying young woman. Sailor Kipling hangs the medal around his neck, posing for a photograph to be published in the *Western Daily* newspaper. What a crock of crap. If anyone deserves a bravery medal, it's me for surviving the gut-wrenching severance of sailing away from Sation.

An English businessman greets us at the harbor, apologizing for the cold weather they're experiencing. He says it's normally a few degrees warmer. A few! He then informs us this winter is the coldest since 1739. This is going to be torture. Bristol's summer temperatures are equivalent to Fortier's coldest days. I've moved from the Sunshine State to the Monarchy of Cold.

Within fifteen minutes of arriving, Dad's business counterpart is in his ear about decisions that need to be made, and within minutes, Dad's changed our plans.

"I have to go take care of some business quickly," he tells Mom.

"Can't we go to the hotel first? It's been a long journey." Mom drops her arms by her side.

"This is important, Vivian. Why don't you have a look around town with the girls?" He doesn't even wait for Mom to repy. He simply walks off to bump up his bank account, leaving the three of us standing on the dock, on our own. Not that I'm complaining, although I know my mother wants to. Instead, she takes us shopping to fill in time.

It doesn't take long to form an opinion of Bristol. It's one big, functioning historical museum. Historical churches, monuments and theaters fill the bygone streets. Charming water canals act as the circulatory system of the city, pumping life around the streets. It's true to say, America and England are in stark contrast to one another. One is new, one is old, one is warm, and one is cold. Really cold.

We look so out of place, shivering our way along the cobble streets, well underdressed. After converting our American dollars into English currency, we head straight for the department store. Surprisingly, the English fashion is modern, especially for such an old-fashioned city. The simple lines and soft, warm fabrics, I'm taking a liking to. I feel the need to dress a little more ladylike, as opposed to my bohemian beach babe back home. So, I swap my bikini for a woolen blazer, my bare feet for Go-Go boots, and my shades for a beanie and gloves.

Julia is on an all-time high. England is one big adventure for her, and after the stormy journey across the Atlantic Ocean, she's more than happy to be walking on English soil. Mom's as excited. The new possibilities this country has to offer outweigh anything Fortier can. I also know this trip reminds her of the vacation she took in her early twenties, when she traveled to Europe with her friend, Trealla. I've listened to Mom tell stories about her vacation with her friend so many times, it seems like I was on the vacation with them. Now, twenty years on, Mom is here reliving that memory. Only now with her two daughters in tow or, as Mom likes to call us, her double D's.

The local Bristolian dialect has the three of us stumped, but also amused. Julia and I can't help but laugh, hearing the sales assistant identify the three of us as 'peepawl' from America. She asks if we are "on 'olides from across the pond or is Bristol our new 'ome." They seem to add L's and drop G's. I'm having so much fun mimicking the Brizzle slang, I forget to be my miserable self.

Julia and Mom enter a pet shop. I'm not a fan of seeing animals locked in cages, so I continue along in my new coat. A cobalt-blue shopfront further down the road draws my attention. I can just make out the faded block letters on the wall: Robust & Arabica. That's a different name. The shop front doesn't reveal much, apart from it being old and English-looking, with its large rectangular windows and fancy timber paneling. I'm curious to know what they sell.

I turn the big brass knob, push open the door, and feel the heat from inside rush at me, instantly warming my face. Next, the aromatic smell of percolated coffee smacks me in the face, but there's not a coffee bean in sight. What I can see, though, are hundreds of colorful books. I've found my way into my first English bookstore.

It's nothing like bookstores back home. The walls are full to the brim of gorgeous colored books, organized into color sequence rather than regimented alphabetical order. Yellow books blend into orange, orange fades into red, red into purple, and so on. The back wall has a cozy bluestone fireplace with amber coals crackling away. In front of it sits an odd-shaped, white couch, resembling the shape of a waning moon. It looks so comfy. I want to nestle into the fluffy cushions and snuggle up with a book for the rest of the year.

I walk over to warm my hands by the fire and a chilly breeze sweeps through the door. A lady wearing an adorable full-length ruby-red coat walks in, rubbing her gloved hands together. She looks my way and her raggedy brown curls bob around her face. Kindly she smiles and so do I. I turn back to the fire, not wanting to make her feel uncomfortable while she browses around the bookstore, but I could easily continue admiring her stylish appearance.

"That fire looks quite a treat. You'd never think it's summer out there," she comments in an English accent, minus the Brizzle slang which lets me know she isn't from around here.

"Yes, it's lovely and warm."

"It could do with a log, though." She walks over to warm her hands.

"I haven't seen anyone working here. Maybe they're off getting another log now," I say, inhaling the scent of her spicy perfume.

"No one works here, dearie. It's not a bookstore."

"Do you call it something else here in England?"

"Yes, it's called a residence. My private residence."

"Oh, pardon me." I step away from her fire. "I didn't mean to intrude. I thought I was in a bookstore. I'll leave straight away," I run for the door, bright-faced.

"You don't have to leave, dearie. You're not the first to wander inside, and you won't be the last." She chuckles as if amused by my intrusion. "It takes someone with a very distinct nature to discover this place."

"Distinct nature?"

"Yes, distinct. Do you know what is innate within your heart?"

The conversation pauses as I try my hardest to think what might be innate in my heart. It's the strangest question I've ever been asked. "Um, blood?" But going by the amused look on her face, blood isn't the answer she is looking for.

"You'll work it out one day, or better still, the innate will work its way out of you. What's your name?"

"Isola."

"Well, Isola with the dreamy blue eyes, I'm interested to know what brought you to England."

"Nothing willingly brought me to England. I was dragged here from America kicking, screaming, and crying."

"Don't be fooled. Part of you may have wished to stay in America, but another part of you desires to be in England."

"Oh, I doubt that." I firmly shake my head.

"Well, I know that."

"How do you know that?"

"Simply because you're here." She looks around her room, visually placing us here.

"No, not at all. I'm not here on my own account. Every part of me desires to be in America."

"If you say so." She shrugs her shoulders, giving in to me.

"The day I turn eighteen, I'll be on the first boat back home to America."

"And I'm sure there will be a boat waiting for you. If you're meant to leave."

Her 'if' holds the weight of a hundred dubious question marks. I know she's doubting I'll leave. However, she doesn't know the blue eyes calling me home.

She picks up the iron fork, stoking the fire, causing sparks to dart off. "You know it's quicker to fly?"

"Our family friend was killed in the New York plane crash last year. So, no thanks."

"I read about that crash in the paper. It was terrible."

"Yes, it was. I'd much prefer to travel on the sea. You can't fall out of a boat."

"Not unless you jump."

"True." I titter.

She places the fork back on its holder and dusts off her hands. "While you're in England, I suggest you make friends with her, rather than fight her. She really is lovely."

"I'll try and make friends with her." I go along with her peculiar request as if England is a female I could befriend.

"Of course, you will, dearie, she's on your path. You and England will be bosom buddies before you know it."

This lady is definitely different from most. Come to think of it, I don't even know her name.

"Sorry, I didn't ask your name."

"My name is Lizabeth-e."

"Don't you mean Elizabeth?"

"I meant what I said. Lizabethe is my name, which is the original pronunciation and spelling. That was until some fancy wordsmith grabbed hold of it centuries ago and recreated it into Elizabeth."

"Can I ask then, if your name is Lizabethe and this is your home, then who or what is Robust & Arabica?"

"This building was once a coffee emporium called Robust & Arabica. They are varieties of coffee beans, but that was a long time ago. Nevertheless, the aromas of the wine of the bean still linger." She smiles, inhaling the scent of coffee.

"The wine of the bean? I've never heard that before."

"It's an old Arabic saying."

"Well, the wine of the bean definitely permeated into the walls, given the scent is still lingering, not that you can see the walls past the books. It appears you like to read, Lizabethe."

"No, not at all. I just hate painting. They make do for lovely wallpaper, don't you think?"

"Um, yes, I guess so," I say, not knowing how to reply to such a bizarre reason to avoid painting.

"I'm only joking. I love reading. That's why every wall of my home is covered in books."

"You had me fooled for a moment. Well, I won't outstay my own welcome. I'd better get a move on. My mom is probably looking for me by now."

"If you must, but do come back."

"I'd like that," I say, taking one last look around this gorgeous room. "Next time I'll knock, though."

"My door is not for knocking on. Its only purpose is to keep out the cold."

"Thanks, Lizabethe with a capital e on the end. I'll come back and visit for sure. It was nice to meet you."

"You too, Isola. Toodle pip."

"Toodle pip," I reply, not knowing what it means, but it sounds cool. Toodle pip.

I step back onto Bramble Street, leaving behind this fascinating woman, her cozy ambience, and her massive collection of colorful books. What an experience. Come to think of it, I've engaged in a few of late. Now I have some distinct nature within me I have to work out, or it has to work its way out of me. Seriously. What the heck is going on lately?

Mom and Julia walk out of the pet shop. "You must have frozen out here waiting for us, Isola."

"Almost," I say, looking back down the road to Lizabethe's cobalt-blue residence, chuckling to myself.

"Now then, my double D's, we'd better make our way back to the harbor. Your father will be waiting for us."

"If we must." I roll my eyes.

"Yes, we must, Isola Destinn," Mom replies in the same bothered tone.

We catch the ferry back to the harbor with bags upon bags of clothes. After meeting back up with the commander of control, all four of us make our way to the hotel we are staying at until Dad collects the keys to our new 'ome tomorrow. I try calling Sation from a booth, but the call fails to connect. I'm obviously doing something wrong. Looks like I'll have to put pen to paper and keep in contact via the post for now.

One night turns into two nights at the hotel. The house we were supposed to move into fell through. Dad can't find another in Bristol so, unfortunately, we have to move to a village called Nolanberry, which is yet another thirty miles away from Sation.

Arriving in our new *'ome* town of Nolanberry, I soon learn how it got its name. Nolanberry trees ornament this mountainous town from beginning to end. We see their distinct shiny green leaves and clusters of round magenta berries everywhere. So much for moving to the city; it turns out we have moved to the boondocks. However, our house is rather modern and my bedroom is huge.

I'd say over ninety percent of Nolanberry is covered in forest, with flowing streams trickling from out of the mountains. The other ten percent is made up of a café, a grocery store, a gas station, and family homes.

***

We stay up late for nights on end, unpacking, finally settling in days later.

"Wake up, Isola. It's time to get ready to go."

Mom has organized for the three of us girls to visit Trealla and her "famous garden" called Avenlee. Mom takes one look at me and steps back from the sadness brewing.

"What's wrong with you? Didn't you sleep well?"

"No, I have a bed back in Fortier much more comfortable."

"Here we go again. The sad, intolerable Isola is back."

"She never left."

"I know a lot of things have changed for you, but please can you get up, get dressed, and leave whatever mood you're in at home? Trealla won't want to meet you in this mood, and Julia and I don't want to put up with it."

I pull the covers back down. "Well, maybe you can put me on the next boat back to Fortier and my mood will disappear. Then we'll all be happy."

"Get up, get dressed, and get in the car," she demands, walking out of my room.

Chapter Six

The weather's taken a turn for the better today. I can actually see the sun. Mom drives Dad's work car around our street a few times to get used to driving on the opposite side of the road. Julia and I nervously double-check every turn she takes, wishing she'd practiced driving with Dad and not us.

Stopping off at the local café, I run inside to ask for directions to Avenlee. The owner scribbles them down on a napkin and tells me to enjoy my day. We head north into the woodland, turn right at all the farmers' mailboxes, standing in a row. Cross over an old wooden bridge, turn left onto a dirt track, and wind around the mountain into paradise. Gaps appear in the treeline, teasing us with glimpses of the valley. Until, finally, the breathtaking view of Avenlee unveils itself.

Our mouths stop moving, the wheels stop turning, and our imaginations gasp with delight. Hopping out of the car, we stand on the side of the mountain, stunned by the most picturesque sight any of us has ever seen. Down in the valley, a botanical masterpiece flourishes to life, in every colorful tree, plant, and flower imaginable. It's so impressive it appears theatrical, like a valley of jewels has turned to seed and blossomed to life.

"Oh, my, it's magnificent," Mom says, stunned.

I step closer to the edge, unable to believe there are this many shades of green in the world. Then, a gust of Avenlee's ambience sweeps up the mountain straight to my senses, bestowing its charm to the core of my heart. Instantaneously, though, my heart begins to race, in much the same way as when I first saw Sation. It's pounding so vigorous, it's about to impulsively run down the mountain and chase after the view. Taking a discreet step back, I lean on the car, just in case my knees give way.

Mom and Julia seem taken by the view, but nowhere as overwhelmed as me. I can understand how Sation had this effect on my heart, but not a garden. This isn't normal.

"Mom. Let's drive down, I want to get closer." Julia bubbles with excitement.

"Jump in the car then, my double D's."

I let Julia sit in the front, relieved to have a back seat to hide in while my newfound love of Avenlee gushes through every extremity of my body. Attempts to calm myself fail. My heart's still pounding. Maybe humming the sea's dulcet melody might pacify my heart, like it has before.

"Isola, what's that song you're always humming?" Mom asks moments later.

"Yeah, I've heard you humming it too," Julia adds.

I'm amazed they've been paying attention to anything I do.

"It's just a song I heard a lady singing." Or possibly a siren from the deep blue sea.

"It sounds lovely," Mom says.

Resting my head on the top of the back seat, I look out of the rear window to the lush green trees sailing by. It almost looks like the sky's turned beautiful shades of green and I'm floating through it.

By the time we reach the entrance to Avenlee, my heartrate's slowed down to a relatively normal pace.

"Look, girls, it's Trealla." Mom waves, as Trealla opens the gate.

"She has no shoes on," Julia points out.

"Trealla's not like most women, Julia. Prepare yourself for that."

"Maybe she's a witch."

"Where on earth did you get that from?" Mom asks, looking across at Julia.

"The girls back home said there're lots of witches in England."

"Don't you listen to that nonsense."

All my life I've pictured what Trealla looks like, but I've grossly underestimated this woman's appearance. Her long, dark-blonde hair perfectly frames her high-set cheekbones and cocoa brown eyes. She looks naturally glamorous, with enchanting features, and the benevolent sparkle in her eyes has me besotted. Oh, but her imagination is what I underestimated the most. Only a genius can create a garden this ornate.

"Wait in the car, girls, while I take a moment to reacquaint with my long-lost friend."

We sit and watch their twenty-year absence dissipate in one rekindling hug. I wind down the window to hear them speak, but the invigorating aroma of the garden captures my senses, indulging me with floral, yet warm, earthy tones of the forest. Whoa, the scent is profound.

"Hello, Trealla," Mom says.

"Oh, Vivian, it's so wonderful to see you. You brought some sunshine from back home with you."

"It's a special gift from me to you." Mom smiles.

Trealla gives Mom a kiss on both cheeks and doubles up on the first side.

"Did you just see how many times she kissed Mom? Do you think she's a witch, Isola?" Julia tugs on my coat.

"Shh, Julia, I want to hear what Trealla has to say."

"My goodness, Trealla, you haven't aged a bit."

"You're too kind, Viv."

"I'm serious. You look great, and your garden smells and looks absolutely devine. Your wish came true, that's for sure."

"Yes, it did. However, I'm not sure if my wish came true or a lot of hard work paid off."

Even the sound of her voice has a smooth European consistency. I can barely hear her American accent. It's hard to believe Mom and Trealla are the same age. Trealla looks at least fifteen years younger. I guess living here at Avenlee, husband- and child-free, would keep you looking radiant and youthful.

"I can't believe I'm finally here."

"Yes, it took you a while."

"I've been busy nurturing two of my own little gardens for the past sixteen years."

"I can only imagine how busy those two little gardens have kept you."

"Would you like to meet them?"

"I'd love to, Vivian."

Mom motions with her hand for us to hop out of the car. I'm so glad I dressed up in my brand-new clothes and replaced my shitty mood with some love beads.

"Aren't you a beautiful ray of light?" Trealla smiles amiably. The warmth of her eyes draws me in like a lodestone. She has my full attention.

"Hello, Trealla. My name is Isola."

"Welcome to Avenlee. I hope you enjoy your visit."

"Oh, it's breathtaking."

"That's a lovely compliment, but it gives more than it takes." She says, sparking intrigue in me.

"Who is this little princess? Let me guess, you must be Julia?"

"That's right," Julia timidly replies. Which is odd, normally you can't shut her up. She must seriously think Trealla's a witch.

"Welcome to Avenlee. Would you like to come explore the garden and all it has to offer?" Trealla tries coaxing Julia out of her shell.

"Yes," Julia says, looking up from her downward gaze.

"We would all love to take a walk around your garden," Mom adds, with a little more enthusiasm.

"We won't get to all of Avenlee today. It's far too big. How about I show you the gardens I think you'll like the most?"

"I think I'm going to like all the gardens," I openly share my interest.

"I know you will, Isola. I can already see the effect Avenlee has had on your energy."

Obviously, the awestruck delight is radiating from within me.

"Let's not waste another second, ladies."

Trealla opens the gate to Avenlee as though she's opened the door to her beautiful imagination and invites us to step inside.

"Here we stand at *la via dell'amore*," she says in a smooth Italian intonation. "*La via dell'amore* translates to 'the path of love.' A path everyone should walk every day of their life, figuratively speaking."

Oh, my goodness. I'm mesmerized by this elegant woman.

"*La via dell'amore* is one mile in length and the huge trees lining either side are elm trees, all sixty-six of them. To me, they're more like gallant knights lined up in a guard of honor."

"What are they guarding?" Julia asks.

"Love, of course," Trealla modestly replies, then continues walking barefoot along her mile-long path of love. Her soft white dress flows with the breeze, so too does the subtle scent of her perfume. The long layers of her hair mold over her shoulders and fall down her back, slightly curling at the ends. Everything about Trealla is weightless and flowing, yet she's as grounded as her gallant knights and as earthy as the rich soil they grow in.

All of a sudden, the leaves on the elm trees come to life with hundreds of vibrant blue birds fluttering about the branches, cheerfully chirping as if singing to us.

"Calm down, little birdies. They're my friends," she says, looking up to the trees.

They settle back down as if they understand her. I've a feeling we are in for a few surprises today. Trealla stops a third of the way up the path and kindly asks us to take our shoes off, which I'm more than happy to do, but I know Mom will be horrified.

"Why do I have to take off my shoes?" Julia asks Mom, hesitantly.

"To neutralize and replenish you with the limitless supply of electrons rising up from the earth. That's why," Trealla explains, then continues walking.

I don't think any of us expected that response, whatever it meant.

"Now, ladies, some of the gardens at Avenlee are named after ancient goddesses, muses, and heroines. The garden to my left is named in honor of the Roman fruit-tree goddess, Pomona. She was a hands-on goddess and a generous woman indeed. Pomona spent her days in her orchard, nurturing her fruit trees whilst openly welcoming everyone to indulge in the nectar they provided."

I look to this grandiose garden to see hundreds of trees surrounded by pristine manicured lawns.

"The feature tree in the Pomona Garden is the crabapple tree, they're the ones with their fluffy pinkish-white flowers. The oldest is the maiden crabapple, just over there." She points to the left. "Her name is Queenee, and luckily for us, the seasons are late this year, so she is still in bloom. All the plants in this garden share the same symbolic meaning, and that is love, especially the apple tree. Everyone from the Norse to the Celts to the Etruscans believed the apple's core holds the most life and love. They built traditions surrounding those symbolic beliefs. My favorite tradition is from ancient Greece. In ancient Greece, if you were to pick an apple off a tree and throw it at a person's heart, it was an act of declaring your love for them, and if they caught the apple, it was a declaration of their love."

"That's a lovely tradition," Mom said. "Can you imagine all the ancient Greek women standing under apple trees waiting to be hit in the heart by one? Maybe that's where that song came from."

"What song, Viv?"

"You know, the Andrews Sisters song, 'Don't Sit Under the Apple Tree with Anyone Else but Me'?"

"Maybe, Viv," Trealla chuckles.

Looking over to the maiden crabapple tree, I think, Sation could throw a whole barrel load of apples at me and I'd catch every single one of them.

We continue walking, listening to Trealla explain the historical and cultural meanings behind all the plants in the Pomona Garden. No longer are plants green objects growing out of the ground. Now, they're living treasures, each blossoming with their own unique story, cultural significance and medicinal purpose.

We reach a garden within the Pomona Garden with a hedge of trees surrounding it. The entrance has a pretty gate painted rustic white. A timber sign hanging from it reads, "The Kissing Gate." My mind boggles with intrigue. What lies beyond its green walls?

"When I host weddings, some couples choose the garden of *La Lilliana* to take their first kiss."

"Who is La Lilliana?"

"In mythology, La Lilliana is the pink wildflowers, that grew in a place called Ilium, which was formerly Troy and is now in present-day Turkey. La Lilliana's love story is dearest to my heart. Maybe next time I'll tell you the story."

"Please tell us now, Trealla," Julia begs.

It seems Julia is as intrigued as I am now. "Yes, please tell us her story," I plead.

"I'll tell you the short version really quickly. Legend has it, for most of the year La Lilliana seeded herself throughout the forest. When it came time to flower, La Lilliana manifested into a woman and met with her lover, who patiently waited all year for her to blossom to physical life. He would wake in the field to see the curvaceous La Lilliana lying naked beside him. But as soon as the wildflowers went to seed, she stopped being human and disappeared back into the earth again."

"Now that's an annual love affair," Mom says.

"Where do you think the word *annual* originated from? That was her lover's name, Annualius. All year their love would lie dormant waiting for the one time a year when it flowered to life. Every time I see wildflowers growing, it makes me think La Lilliana and Annualius are very much alive and playing kiss-chasey all over the world. Now let me introduce you to the garden of La Lilliana."

Trealla unlatches the pretty white kissing gate and we follow her down a long aisle of trees. The path soon opens to an oval-shaped patch of lawn surrounded by mounted garden beds, much like an amphitheater, only the mounted walls are filled with thousands of blossoming flowers in every shade of pink imaginable. It looks like one big bouquet of pink flowers that perfume the air like pretty French eau de cologne. I've never seen or smelled anything this pretty in all my life.

"Oh, Trealla, it smells like the most exquisite florist in the world," Mom says.

"That would be the blend of jasmine, roses, clary sage and patchouli," Trealla explains.

"It smells like pink candy floss to me," Julia adds.

"To me it's the quintessential scent of love." Trealla describes its scent perfectly. "What do you think of the garden, Isola?" she asks.

"Avenlee bewitched my senses at first sight, now this garden's bewitched them even more."

"You have plenty more senses to get you through the day."

"We only have a few, don't we?"

Trealla steps towards me. "You've been led to believe there are only five, but there are plenty more to guide you on your path in life." She winks.

Trealla wonders off, leaving me to ponder what those senses might be.

"Mom, I want to get married behind the kissing gate. Can I? Can I?" Julia asks, desperate to plan her wedding even at age twelve.

"Let's get you through college before we talk about your wedding, dear." Mom pats Julia on the top of the head.

"Let's make our way up to the house to enjoy some lunch under the fig tree, ladies."

***

Trealla's English stone manor sits at the end of *la via dell'amore*. Trealla leads us around the back to a big old fig tree. It stands in the middle of the yard like the chief of the garden. Beneath its outstretched branches, we sit down to lunch at the table.

As we finish eating, a raft of ducks waddle out from one of the paths. As I turn to see them my chair gives an awful squeak.

"When the chairs squeak, it's of rain they speak," Trealla poetically says.

"What's that, Trealla?"

"When it's about to rain, wooden furniture, doors and windows absorb moisture from the air, causing them to swell, which results in sticking or squeaking. Therefore, it's of rain they speak."

"So, it's not about to fall apart?" I raise my eyebrows, concerned.

"No, your chair is just forecasting the weather."

"I'm learning so much about nature today."

"It will only serve you good."

"There is something I'm curious about, Trealla. Were all these trees originally here, or did you plant them?"

"That's a good question. The more established trees were planted by previous custodians and the woodlands, of course, existed long before anybody. But after I inherited this valley, I planted hundreds of trees I love, as well as the hazelnut orchard. I have a book in my library that explains the history of Avenlee. I can loan it to you."

"I'd love to read about Avenlee's history."

"You don't even like gardens, Isola," Julia comments, making me look foolish.

"I like them now." Julia is right. Gardens have never interested me, but Avenlee's changed my opinion. "What does Avenlee mean?" I ask.

"The purity of life," she says in an ethereal tone. "Shall we head inside and pop the kettle on, ladies? I'll try and find the book for you, Isola."

"Sounds good."

I soon discover that the English exterior of the manor ends outside. Inside is a spacious French affair. I'm waiting for a chef to appear and greet us with a linguistic *bonjour*, holding a tray of croissants. The decor is a mix of modern and antique furnishings. Fancy vintage lampshades dot around the living room, a large vase of lavender scents the room beautifully. Just before the hallway is a bookshelf, with tiny amber, green and cobalt-blue bottles on display. I'm intrigued to know what's inside them.

"Oh, Trealla, your house is delightful. I need a house as charming as this," Mom says in awe, busy looking around Trealla's kitchen.

"Would you like to come with me, Isola? I'll see if I can find that book in the library."

"Can I come with?" Julia asks.

"Sure, you can, hun." Trealla motions with her head to follow us.

"I'll put the kettle on," Mom calls out.

Julia and I follow Trealla down a long hall filled with paintings of distinguished-looking women, hanging in grand golden frames.

"What's in all those little glass bottles?" I ask as we pass them.

"Plant essence."

"Huh?" I respond, confused.

"These bottles contain oils from the plants, trees and flowers growing in my garden."

"Are they perfumes?" Julia asks, standing on her tippy toes, looking up to them.

"Yes and no. They're more like breast milk from the *Kingdom Plantae*."

"What do they do, or what do you do with them?" I ask, fascinated.

"Whatever the oils and my body decide. Some days I put them on my skin, some days I steam them, and other days I ingest them. Would you like to try one?"

"Okay, but you pick which one. I can't even read the names on the bottles."

"*Mmm*." She looks at me. "I'll pick *Citrus aurantium*, also known as neroli, or *Pogostemon cablin*, otherwise known as patchouli. Have a smell of each and let your senses decide."

"Can I smell them too, Trealla?" Julia asks.

"Sure, you can."

"They are both nice, I think I like the first one better. Neroli."

"Neroli is very uplifting, with its rich floral scent," she says, placing a tiny drop on my wrist and at my temples. "Which one would you like to wear, Julia?"

"I don't like any of them." She shakes her head, screwing up her nose.

"Fair enough." Trealla places the bottles back on the shelf.

Continuing down the hall, I smell my wrist, enjoying my new scent. Trealla stops at a timber door and attempts to push it open, but it's stuck.

"Let me guess. When the doors refuse to budge, the ground's about to flood," I make up my own saying, making Trealla giggle.

"Your wit is adorable, Isola."

Trealla gives the door a generous nudge with her shoulder and it opens. "Rain is definitely on its way."

Immediately, I'm taken by the number of books in her home library. However, going by the size of her house, everything is going to be on a grand scale.

"Do you have any books about animals?" the animal enthusiast, Julia, asks.

"I might have. Follow me and I'll have a look."

I wander around the rows of books, waiting for Trealla, and notice sunlight streaming in from another room. Peeping inside, it's just as I suspect: it's a sunroom with a pitched glass ceiling and walls. But what catches my eye are the large gilded frames sitting on easels all around the room. Each has a drawing of a tree inside that looks lifelike, as if they've grown on the canvas.

"Picturesque, aren't they?" Trealla says from the doorway.

"I've never seen anything like them."

"And I doubt you will again."

Taking a step closer, I'm surprised by the meticulous details in the bark. Then I realize the bark is some sort of ancient script. "Wow, writing is creating the effect of the bark. That's very artistic."

"It is indeed, Isola. You've a perceptive eye. This collection of drawings belongs to the Family Tree of Seeds. It's a very old recording of the seed's history on earth. And written within the trunks and branches are the names given to the tree from different countries and eras, as well as the tree's cultural meanings and its use in medicines and ancient rituals."

"It really is a family tree of the seed's history. What is this tree?"

"Its archaic name is Zelen. Now its botanical name is *Olea europaea*, commonly known as an olive tree." She points to the recording halfway up the trunk.

"Do these trees grow in your garden?"

"They sure do. All sixteen of them grow in the Kore Forest. I can take you to see them one day. They're spectacular."

"It would be great to see them in real life. No wonder why you have grown such a beautiful garden with all the history in these drawings."

"To be honest, there's not much to know, in regards to growing a tree. Come here, I'll let you in on a secret."

I step closer, excited she's going to share her knowledge with me.

"They grow themselves," she whispers.

What a letdown. I'm expecting to hear Trealla's secret to growing this breathtaking garden and all she tells me is they grow themselves.

"Trees don't need humans. They've been living long before humans have. A seed falls into the fertile earth, the rain falls on it, the sun shines on it, and from out of the rich, dark soil, a shoot breaks through the crust and grows towards the sun. *Voilà*, you have yourself a tree. No brains, education or humans required. Just the balance and flow of nature."

Trealla makes it sound simple, downplaying her part, but what she's created at Avenlee is far from simple. It would've taken a lot of hard work and creative talent to design and landscape a spectacular garden like this.

"There you are," Julia says, walking into the sunroom. "Can I please borrow this book about animals?" She hands Trealla the book, not even noticing all these amazing drawings around her.

"Sure, you can, hun. Now, let's go and find your book, Isola."

Trealla slides the library ladder across the face of the bookcase to a section of older books. Four steps up she goes, searching the entire row.

"Your book is either playing hide-and-seek, or I have loaned it to someone else. I'll have a look for it again tonight and hopefully it turns up."

"Okay," I say, a little disappointed.

"That's enough time spent inside, ladies. Let's head back out to the garden, where all the living is taking place."

Chapter Seven

Our visit unfortunately comes to an end. Mom and Julia walk ahead, while Trealla and I dawdle along behind.

"It was wonderful to finally meet you today, Isola."

"Likewise. Your garden is so pretty. It feels so good being here." I look around to the mass of color and textures growing all around me.

"I'm glad Avenlee has made you feel good."

"So am I. Especially after the way I've been feeling lately." Regretfully, the negativity slips out my mouth. The last thing I want is to come across as negative to the most uplifting person I've ever met.

"What have you been feeling of late?"

"A little homesick and lovesick, but I'm alright."

"Have you fallen in love?" she asks, turning her head my way, showing interest.

"Oh, I fell that's for sure. No one's mastered falling as grand as I. One minute I'm numb, the next, *boom*. He brought me to life. Now, four months after falling in love, I feel like I'm falling apart," I say, still mindful not to sound too negative.

"Did you say a man brought your heart to life?" Trealla asks, wide-eyed.

"The moment I saw him, my heart burst to life." I animate the explosion with my hands, bursting out from my chest.

"I was once brought to life just like you, but it wasn't love that caused this. Something much more innate created this awakening."

"Innate?" I ask, doubting her for the first time today.

"Yes, the essence within you is starting to awaken, hence why you no longer feel numb. You experienced an awakening, which is different from love."

"But I fell in love. He brought my heart to life." I try explaining again, looking over to her as she calmy strolls beside me, as if enjoying an evening stroll.

"You may have fallen in love with this man, but what awakened is an internal force, not an external one."

Lizabethe used similar words when she asked if I knew what was innate within me. Something strange is going on here for two people to have mentioned the same thing to me. Or could it be some sort of English saying that I'm not accustomed to?

"So, then what is innate within me that you think caused all this?" I open my mind to the possibility.

"It's the essence of who you truly are. Your energetic signature."

"What kind of essence?"

"It's not my place to disclose that. It's your purpose to awaken to it and become conscious of it. I received my first awakening in a garden at the Palace of Versailles. After that initial awakening, they kept on coming until I let go of the 'Trealla' I was brought up to be, to finally acknowledge my innate self. It's almost as if once I stopped thinking myself, I discovered my true innate self. Just as you will."

"But what if who I think I am is actually who I am?"

She stops walking and looks at me.

"What if who you truly are can only be found in the absence of thought?" She pauses. "Answer this, Isola. Have you ever not thought?"

"I guess I don't think when I'm asleep," I joke, knowing full well she knew not a second has ticked by in my life without a thought accompanying it.

"And how peaceful is sleeping? To be alive without having to think to be alive. Everything just functions naturally, just like the trees."

"Point taken, Trealla."

"When you stop thinking, you start knowing, and then you will truly start living. The question remains, whom might you be in the absence of thought, and how much are you willing to let go of to find out?"

I walk along, trying to figure it out. "You know, it would be a lot easier if you just told me."

"Well, yes, it would, but I don't want you to believe who I tell you you are. It is weakness to believe in another person's opinion of yourself. I want you to consciously know who you are. That's strength. And anyway, until you truly know yourself, you know nothing of importance."

"But how do you even know I have something inside me?"

"Because the nature in me can sense the same distinct nature in you."

"You can sense it?"

She looks across to me and pleasantly smiles. "Yes, hun, I have a gift to sense the energy of life in all living things."

"Wow, that's cool. You're the second person to mention this innate thing within me."

"You have met others, then?"

"It appears so, whoever 'others' are. I just wish I could see in me what you all see in me. I'm very confused by all this."

"One day you will awaken, and on that day, your life will never be the same again."

"It won't?" I'm not sure if I want my life to change in such a profound way.

"No, there will be significant changes. An entire new reality awaits you."

For the first time today, I don't like hearing what's coming from her mouth.

"But what if I don't want to change?"

"It's not a choice. Your path was decided before your first breath."

"But, but I'm not ready." I nervously chuckle.

"Well, given you've already had an awakening, hun, means your innate self is on the right path to being acknowledged."

"To be honest, I've had two awakenings. One when I first saw the man I fell in love with, and another this morning when I first saw Avenlee." I come clean, daunted by this path I'm not ready to walk upon. I've had enough changes to last me a lifetime.

"It's good to see Avenlee has the power to affect even the most stubborn of us." She grins. "Don't you worry, Isola. Your knowledge will awaken you when it sees fit. Its intelligence outsmarts our human ways."

Great. Now I'm going to stress about losing who I am, and Sation, because of some innate power I have no control over.

"Do Mom and Julia have this innate thing?"

"Oh, no, dear, it's not hereditary. You are a very rare entity, to say the least. Hence why we're having this conversation, away from them," she says, lowering her tone.

"I just knew I was never like them," I say, making Trealla giggle.

"You will have spent most of your life not fitting in with most. You may have even felt like something is missing in your life."

"I have. It's like a part of me is numb or missing."

She gently places her hand on the side of my arm, causing me to look back up to her. "That's because part of you *is* numb, the most spectacular part." Her ethereal tone makes her point even more intriguing.

"So, there's more to come?"

"My dear, what's yet to come is a whole new existence few get to experience."

I've gone from thinking Sation brought my heart to life, to Trealla telling me it's the innate within me awakening. One thing I know for sure is, I'll be on the right path when I'm on my way back to Sation. I'm not willing to change an ounce of myself, just in case it jeopardizes my future with him.

Trealla and I come to the end of the path after discussing a lot of mysterious things. This at least explains why I'm not like most people my age.

"Feel free to return to Avenlee whenever you like, Isola. My valley is always open, especially to someone like you."

"*Mmm*, whoever I truly am." A great big question mark looms over head.

We say our goodbyes. Well, the three of us do. Trealla blows all of us a kiss and walks back down her path of love. The second we drive off, all three of us burst into befuddled laughter, overwhelmed by the beauty we just encountered.

"Mom, look, it's raining, just as Trealla said it would." Julia points to the raindrops on the window. "See, I told you she is a witch."

"Oh, Julia, that doesn't make her a witch," Mom replies, rolling her eyes.

"And even if she is a witch, Julia, she's a good witch," I add.

"Enough about witches," Mom says. "We all learned a lot from Trealla today, didn't we, my double D's?"

"I already want to go back to see the rest of Avenlee," I say enthusiastically.

"That's funny. I thought gardens were only for sixty-year-olds," Mom replies, making sure I catch her direct gaze.

"I've changed my mind after being there. Avenlee is the biggest, most beautiful secret garden in the world, and Trealla's lovely."

"I agree."

"When we arrived at Avenlee, Mom, you said to Trealla her wish came true. What did you mean?"

"When Trealla and I were on our vacation in Europe, we went on a tour of Versailles. After taking in all the King's salons, we ventured outside to the beautiful manicured gardens."

"Was it more beautiful than Avenlee?" Julia asks, flicking through the pages of her book.

"No, nothing compares to Avenlee's beauty, now that I've seen it. Anyway, on the way out we came across the flora fountain and decided to make a wish in the pond. But then Trealla suddenly clutched her heart. I thought she was having a heart attack. She regained her breath, putting her heart palpitations down to drinking too much champagne the night before. Then we each flipped a franc over our shoulder into the fountain. I wished for love and Trealla wished to grow the most spectacular garden, which was out of character for her. I never even knew she had a passion for gardening. She was a stewardess."

"Her wish definitely came true," I say, smelling the ancient essence of neroli on my skin.

I think back to my conversation with Trealla when she told me about her first awakening at Versailles. It's exactly what Mom has just described, and also the same thing I experienced on the pier when I first saw Sation, and now at Avenlee. Maybe there is something awakening within me. It would be amazing to discover, especially if it means I'll be more like Trealla and live her enchanting lifestyle. But then my life will never, ever be the same again. Which means I may never, ever be with Sation again. Now it appears I have one year and two choices ahead of me, although Trealla has made it sound less of a choice and more of a sacrifice.

Chapter Eight

Julia and I sit around the kitchen table, eating breakfast in our new school uniforms, loathing the day ahead. The first day at a new school is challenging enough. Being foreigners makes this even harder.

"Before I forget, Isola, Trealla called to ask if you're interested in working at Avenlee," Mom says, packing our school lunches.

"Me?" I point at myself.

"Yes. Trealla needs help to prepare for the up-and-coming weddings."

"What about me?" Julia interjects. "Can I work at Avenlee, Mom? I can look after the ducks for Trealla."

"You're too young to work. You're only twelve," Mom replies.

"And anyway," I add, "Trealla didn't ask you, she asked me."

"Shush up, Isola." Julia slumps in her chair.

"Cut it out you two, before we wear each other's breakfasts. Have a think about Trealla's offer and let me know what you decide."

"I want to."

"You don't want to think about it first?"

"What's there to think about? It's Avenlee."

Mom takes a seat at the table beside me. "It's going to be a lot of hard work and you're in your second last year of school. Maybe you should give it more thought."

"I can do anything I set my mind to, Mom. You know that."

"That's true. There's a slight problem, though. I don't know how you're going to get there. I won't have the car to drive you, and it's too far to walk."

"You could buy me a bike for my birthday on Thursday and I can ride." Fancy me asking for a pushbike on my seventeenth birthday.

"I was wondering what to get you. That's a great suggestion. But do you remember how to get to Avenlee?"

"Yes, Mom. You head north towards the woodlands. Turn right at the farmers' mailboxes. Cross over the old wooden bridge, turn left onto the dirt track, then wind down the side of a mountain into Paradise."

"Wow, you were paying attention." Mom smiles, surprised.

"How could anyone forget the way to breathtaking Avenlee?"

Mom looks at me as though she'd forgotten the minute we got there, but then again, she doesn't have a good sense of direction. Look at the man she walked down the aisle to.

"I'm going to have coffee with Trealla on Wednesday. I'll let her know you're interested."

"I'm definitely interested."

"Good. Now that's sorted, it's time for school, my double D's. You don't want to be late on your first day." Mom stands back up, grabbing Julia's plate and mine.

***

My first week at school isn't so bad. There are twice the number of students here than at school back home. I meet a few girls to hang out with at lunch. Everyone seems to be rather academic and music-minded. The civil rights movement is just as active here as it is in America, especially at the moment with the Bristol bus boycott. Is it that hard to just treat everyone the same? I'll never get it.

Turning seventeen broke the week up. Now the big countdown's begun. In less than a year, I'll be boarding a boat and heading back to Sation.

Riding my new bike to Avenlee will take some getting used to. This last mountain's killing my legs. But I detect the scent of Avenlee now, so I'm spurn on.

Oh, my goodness, Avenlee's more beautiful the second time around. Bracing myself for another awakening, I pause for a moment. *Phew.* Nothing appears to be happening. I can breathe easy knowing my life isn't about to change forever. Not today, anyway.

I roll down the track with rousing excitement, although I'm a little skittish about what's expected of me. I know very little about gardening and I don't want to look foolish to a woman I admire so much, but I guess I'm bound to. I reach the open gate and her gallant knights. While no one is around to hear me make a fool of myself, I'll attempt to pronounce its name. "*La via. La via mora.*" Seriously, I suck. I can't even remember what Trealla calls it, and my *la via* sounds *la hideous.*

Melodic whistle resonates from one gallant knight to the next. Trealla is bound to know I am here now. I knock on the front door, but there's no answer. I doubt Trealla spends more than her sleeping hours indoors. Her garden is definitely her living room.

Looking out from the veranda, I notice numerous paths leading off into the backyard. Which one should I wander down to find her? Directly behind her grand fig tree, but further afield, a large entrance with two big earthenware pots on either side indicates a prominent garden. I'll venture down this path first.

Walking through the entrance, the brightest and boldest colors are present: burnt orange, golden yellow, and rusty red leaves sway with the breeze. What a botanical show of color.

"Hello, hello. Are you there, Trealla?" Again, I get no reply.

However, in the stillness, I hear a machine rotating in the distance. Following it down a large path, I come to a sign that reads *Kore Forest.* A few minutes later, the sound leads to a barn. I peep inside and see it's been converted into an entertaining area. The entire back wall is absent, so I can see out to the garden beyond the barn.

I spot Trealla in work overalls, shoveling sand into a concrete mixer. Now I know what's making the sound.

"Hello, Trealla."

"Hi, there." She waves with a big smile on her face, broadening her high-set cheekbones. "I wondered how long it would take you to find me," she says, turning off the mixer. She takes her hat off and kisses me on each cheek, then again on the first.

"Thank you for coming."

"Thank you for asking me to. I have to let you know though, I don't know anything about gardening, so I don't know how much help I will be."

"I'll teach you. We'll talk about why I asked you to come here later. Give me a hand here first. I'm almost finished."

"Okay. What are you building?"

"I'm hosting a festival next month, so I need to make a pizza oven to cook the pizza in. Now let's get those hands of yours dirty."

A little over an hour later, we finish. Both of us are thrilled with what we achieved.

"Who needs an apprenticeship in bricklaying?" Trealla stands back with both hands on her hips, smiling at what she has achieved. "A little initiative works wonders. You should never educate yourself too much. One must leave room for intuition to run wild."

"You need to tell my parents that."

"I think I'll leave that up to you, love. Haven't you almost finished school?" she says, starting to pack up.

"Next year is my final year."

"And what is your favorite subject?"

"The last one of the day."

Trealla giggles. "The quicker you get out of school, the better off you will be. Overcrowding your brain with the educational system's beliefs insults your intelligence, which is their intention. It's another way they control your creativity, by teaching you how and what to think. Then they grade you on how well you've let them brainwash you. Talk about indoctrination." She huffs, picking up the leftover bricks and putting them into the wheelbarrow. "Yes, reading, writing and math are necessary, and to some a privilege, but what you've come here to create is far more necessary," she says, waving her hand out far from her body, emphasizing our natural talents' importance.

"That's a different way to look at it."

"I'd love to see a school that has one class a day dedicated to nurturing a student's natural talent and creativity. Now that's how a child should be raised."

Hearing that just demonstrates how far outside of the box Trealla thinks.

"Anyway, that's enough of my opinion. Let's go wash up. Your mother will have a fit if she sees all that mess on you." Trealla picks up the handles on the wheelbarrow and starts wheeling it away in her dirty overalls and work boots, still looking as beautiful as ever. I'm convinced she could make a burlap bag look glamorous.

***

"They look yummy, Trealla," I say, waiting at the table under her grand fig tree, now clean and also hungry. She walks towards me with no shoes on, her hair twisted in a bun with a twig keeping it in place, a plate in one hand and a jug of juice in the other. "What kind of cookies are they?"

"Cookies. Wow, I haven't heard that word in a while. Cookies are called biscuits in England. These little delights are called *Nico biscotti alla nocciola*," she says in an eloquent Italian accent. "*Nocciola* is Italian for hazelnut. I grow the hazelnuts in my orchard. So they're homegrown and homemade, or as Italians would say, *fatto in casa*."

"What is Nico, then?"

"The man they're named after."

"Tell me more," I ask with a tone of intrigue.

"It's a story about a mother, her nuts, and her son."

"Wow, that's a combination of characters."

"Yes, it is. By the time my vacation with your mother ended on the Napoli coast, I had received two awakenings. Not that I knew what they were at that stage. But one thing was certain: I knew I couldn't leave Europe. The culture grafted to my feet and wouldn't let go, and so I settled into a seaside village called Santa Margherita in Italy. One weekend, I travelled to the Piedmont region to hunt for a tasty little treasure, Italians call *tartufi*. I ended up at a local market in Alba and came across a lady selling homemade *biscotti alla nocciola*. They were so tasty I cheekily asked for her recipe.

"In her broken Italian she replied, '*Ti darò la mia ricetta, ma prima devi uscire con mio figlio*?' What she was asking me to do was date her son first, and then she would give me her recipe. Which is odd because no Italian mamma ever wants her son to date an *americana.* Then she explained she needed my help to get her son out of the house, so she could invite her lover to stay."

"How old was she?"

"In her mid-sixties." She shrugs. "Or thereabouts."

I screw my face up, not wanting the visual to enter my brain. "That's yuck."

"Intimacy has no expiry date. Now, getting back to the story, as adventurous as I am, I met up with her son, Nico. One date turned into five months' worth. Before we knew it, we were in love. But I soon realized this *mammoni* was never going to leave his mamma. She had spoiled him so much, she ruined any chances of him leaving her *casa.*"

"What's a *mammoni*?"

"A mamma's boy. However, I had fallen madly in love with this *mammoni*, so I couldn't just walk away. That was until I unexpectedly turned up one night to discover my Italian lover had found himself another *americana* lover."

"Oh, Trealla, that's terrible."

"It was. He is a typical Italian, in love with falling in love, rather than staying in love. I can't blame him. There is something euphoric about the 'falling.'" She looks up to the sky as if it were a divine experience.

"What did you do, Trealla?"

"I went to the train station to return to Santa Margherita. But when I got to the platform, Nico's mother was there waiting to apologize for her son's hungry heart, pleading with me to come back, but I couldn't. She handed me an envelope with her *biscotto alla nocciola* recipe in it, as promised. I felt like ripping her recipe up and stomping on it, and her son's nuts. But in hindsight, I would have suffered a dozen broken hearts in order to get that recipe and the place it led."

"Wow, where did it lead you?"

"To my final awakening."

"You mean awakening like what we spoke about last time I was here?"

"Yes. It led me to the knowledge within me that longed to be acknowledged."

"How does a recipe do that?"

"When I read the ingredients, she stated to only use Sofia's *nocciole*, and at the bottom of the page was the address to Sofia's *nocciola* orchard. So, I went in search and found Sofia's highly recommended *nocciola* orchard and my life changed forever. I fell in love with the mesmerizing Sofia and ended up staying for over a year. It was the greatest year of my life because soon after I arrived, I awakened."

"Those hazelnuts definitely took you on a journey. They should be called awakening biscuits."

Trealla chuckles. "You're right. I might have to change their name. I went hunting for *tartufi* and ended up with a broken heart, but also an awakened one. You see, the innate within me was guiding me on my path with all sorts of highs and lows in order to put me where I needed to be to awaken. I learned some things don't work out in order for the right things to work out. Had I not stepped on my path, I would never have met the stunning Sofia, who changed my life in more ways than one."

Oh my God. Is Trealla trying to tell me she's a lesbian without coming straight out and saying it? She did say she fell in love with the mesmerizing Sofia, and she changed her life in more ways than one. Maybe that's why Trealla never married or had children.

Heck, if this is what is innate within her, does she think this is what's innate within me? Am I a lesbian and totally oblivious to the fact? Surely not, but I'd better ask.

"Trealla, are you a le, a les..." How do I say this without offending her?

"Am I a what, Isola?" She turns her right ear in my direction.

"Are you a... Do you prefer women over men?"

Trealla bursts out laughing. "No, no, I'm not a lesbian," she tries to say while laughing.

"I thought when you said you met the stunning Sofia, who changed your life in more ways than one, you meant Sofia and you were lovers."

"Isola, you're so funny. One day, you'll understand why I'm laughing so much. I love Sofia as a friend, not as a lover."

"I read that wrong, didn't I?" I scratch at the top of my head.

"You did. Sofia helped guide me on my path by creating the space I needed to figure out who I wasn't, so all that I truly am could energetically flow to life."

"Oh. So who flowed to life?"

"Nice try." She points at me.

"It was worth a shot."

"I don't mean to sound so evasive, as if I'm holding out on answering your questions. It's just not my place to take the place of the knowledge within you. It will inform you when it sees fit, not when I do."

"As frustrating as it is, I respect your evasive ways."

How couldn't I? She isn't preaching to me or asking me to believe in anything or become anyone. She is only asking me to be myself and trust in my natural intelligence. Therefore, I trust she can't answer my question for the right reasons.

"Well, then, I guess I'll just have to walk the path of the unknown for now."

"And what a beautiful path it is. Just look where it's led you so far." She holds out her hands to her garden.

"I can't argue with that." I'm surrounded by magnificence.

"So anyway, that's how these little hazelnut biscuits got their name."

Trealla hands me the plate of biscuits. I'm not sure if it's the story behind them, the quality of the hazelnuts, or the love Trealla had stirred them with, but the biscuits taste so good.

"Oh my gosh, they're yummy, Trealla."

"Have another." She gestures with her hand. Then pours me a glass of juice from a big glass jug. "Now, let's talk about why I asked you to come here in the first place. As you know, Avenlee hosts a number of weddings and special events. But it also hosts another type of celebration for people who walk the same path as us. We call it a *Sakrid* or 'Joining of the Hands.'"

"Okay." Where is this going?

"Normally weddings are legally bound in the eyes of God and the couple sign a certificate to seal their union. But at a Sakrid, the couples' love is bound in each other's eyes and sealed when they join hands, hence why it's also known as a 'Joining of the Hands.'"

"Don't witches have joining-of-the-hands ceremonies? I think I read that once."

"You mean witches with warts on their noses, that fly on broomsticks and cast malicious spells?" She over-dramatizes her response, then drops her chin, looking up at me.

"Yeah, kind of," I reply, not sure what to say.

Trealla giggles. "We will discuss what a witch truly is at a later date and remove the cinematic, fictional depiction you have in your head. Let's get back on track and talk about our up-and-coming Sakrid."

"Okay." I take a sip of my drink.

"So anyway, two dear friends of mine wish to celebrate their Sakrid at Avenlee on the nineteenth of June."

"That's two days before my eighteenth birthday." I light up knowing I'll be returning home then.

"Double the reason to celebrate." She picks up her glass and taps it on mine. "Cheers." She then takes a drink.

"Cheers to you too."

"This Sakrid will be Avenlee's event of the year, so La Lillianna will be too small for the number of guests. I need to create a new garden. This is going to be a huge project, and I'd like your help. Also, I'd like you to come up with the theme."

"I don't know any garden themes. And even if I did, the couple might not like what I come up with and I'll ruin their special day."

"Nonsense."

"I'm serious. They requested your imagination, not mine, and there's a big difference between them both."

"Your imagination is just as capable as mine, maybe even more exuberant, given it's been locked away for seventeen years. After all, it's a sense you're supposed to reinstate."

"You mean to say, imagination is a sense?" I say sliding my tall glass to the side.

"Yes, our kind call it *layleasta*. It's the most fascinating sense of them all. Well, at least it was, up until a few thousand years ago, before it was nullified from our sensory field."

"Why was it nullified?"

"To keep dictators in power. You see, imagination creates powerful possibilities that leaders fear people having. So, by diminishing imaginations, they weaken people's ability to create, which in turn produces workhorses for the rich and an energetically sick society."

"How could they just diminish a sense from our understanding?"

"Imagination can't be physically identified, like our sense of sight through our eyes, or our sense of smell through our nose. Therefore, it was easy to deny it exists and label anyone insane who thought outside of their control. Eventually, the sense of imagination was bred out of everyday use, along with all the other senses we once had to survive on this planet and stay connected to our source."

"That's a shame."

"Yes, but in the past few hundred years, people are getting back in touch with this creative sense."

"So, it's possible to reinstate it?"

"Of course it is. Just look at what I created when I stopped thinking and let my layleasta flow to life." She looks out to her garden.

How on earth could anyone contest the source of this garden's creation? And if I want Trealla to think highly of me, I need to rise to the occasion. Pushing my fears of inadequacy to the side, I send her an accepting smile.

"So that's a yes, Isola?" She grins.

"I don't know what my layleasta will come up with, but I'll try my best."

"Fantastic. You just stop that brain of yours from limiting your creativity, and all will be well." She takes another drink, instigating me to do the same.

"What kind of couple are these special friends of yours?"

"I'd say they're a sweet yet spicy couple who complement each other's differences and come together beautifully."

"Maybe you and I can complement each other's differences and create a beautiful garden together," I say, in desperate need of her help.

"There're not many differences between us," she replies, as if we're on par in the creative department, of which we definitely aren't.

"I would never put myself in the same category as you. The difference between your layleasta and mine is huge."

"One day, you will realize we're more alike than we aren't. The difference between us is: you think and I know."

"So, if I don't think, I'll become like you?"

She leans forward in her chair grinning. "You already are like me. You just think you're not."

"Well, I look forward to the day I think less and know more."

"So do I." She clasps her hands together with hope. "Now I have something rather important to share with you."

"What is it?" I ask, concerned by her serious tone.

"You will not quite grasp what I'm about to tell you. It might even sound odd, but I need you to trust me. There is knowledge within you that is sacred to you and should never be shared."

"Is this the innate within I must awaken to?"

"Not exactly. Our kind must awaken, but I'm referring to *sacred knowledge*. You know the ancestry of light, the stars that descend, and the legends they created on earth."

I'm sure the look on my face expresses my bewilderment. "I don't mean to undermine your insight, but I don't know what you're talking about." I shake my head, more confused then ever before.

"That's because you have temporary amnesia of this knowledge."

"Well, then, you don't have to worry about me sharing it. I don't even know what it is I know."

"True, but I'm also referring to obscure events or insights that will grace you on your path. I imagine some odd events have already taken place."

"You can say that again. I was comfortably under the sea for around five minutes the other day and could hear this humming sound. It was unreal. Oops, is this what I'm not meant to share?"

"It's the exact kind of events I'm asking you to refrain from sharing. It would be best for you to hold your wonder close to your heart until you make sense of it."

"So, I can't even share my experiences with you?"

"Not even me. There is wonder in the world for a reason, and when you remember the reason, you will be grateful you said not a word. If you ever need someone to talk to, the earth has the most trustworthy ears."

"You mean talk to the ground?" I say, not sure if I'd heard right.

"Yes, it will listen every time and never repeat a thing."

"You're obviously one of the few who knows this sacred knowledge, given you're telling me about it."

"There are seven entrusted with this knowledge and yes, I'm one of them. Now let's not speak of this until the sacred knowledge calls on us to."

Trealla is right about the obscure events taking place in my life. This conversation is one of them. "Wow, I didn't expect to hear anything like this today."

"Don't let it weigh heavy in your mind. Think of it as awareness you can reach for when the time comes. Until then, allow the sacred to remain a secret."

"I will. I've never been interested in other people's business or sharing my own."

"I didn't take you as much of a gossip girl. Now, before you leave, I have something to give you. Wait here a moment." She disappears inside.

I dust the biscuit crumbs off the table, thinking, what is the ancestry of light and the star that descend? I don't even know who I am, let alone what they are.

Trealla returns and hands me an envelope.

"Is this your *Nico biscotti* recipe?"

"Funny one. It's actually your birthday present."

"Thank you. You didn't have to get me anything," I say, holding it to my heart.

"It's just a little something, but please open it when you get home."

"Okay," I put in in my backpack.

"So, will I see you next Saturday and Sunday?"

"You sure will." I smile, reaffirming my commitment.

"Fantastic. You're welcome to stay here for the weekend as well. It will save you riding back and forth, but it's completely up to you and your parents."

"You're inviting me to stay at Avenlee?" I think she can tell by the enthusiasm in my voice the answer's yes.

"There are eight guest bedrooms to choose from, so I have the space. Check with your parents first. I don't want to step on any toes."

"I'm riding straight home to ask," I say, hopping on my bike.

"I'll see you next weekend, then, love."

"You definitely will."

Chapter Nine

"Looks like you've put in a hard day's work, Isola," Dad says as I walk inside. I can't believe he's sitting on the couch watching Benny Hill.

"I did. I mixed sandy-slushy mud in a mixer to help Trealla construct a pizza oven."

"It looks like it. You had better put your clothes in the wash before your mother sees them in this state," he says, giving me two seconds of his time, then he turns back to the television. This is not surprising in any way, but what is surprising is he's actually laughing. I don't believe I've heard him laugh like this ever.

"Where's Mom?" I ask, noticing her absence. She is normally the first person to greet me when I get home.

"What's that?" he halfheartedly responds.

"Where is Mom?"

Dad finally turns the volume down and turns back to me. "She is in Bristol with Julia, shopping again."

"Bummer. I wanted to spend some of my birthday money."

"I'm going to Bristol to work tomorrow. You can get a lift in with me if you want."

"I'll see how I feel in the morning. I might not be able to move after working today."

"Let me know in the morning then, love."

Did I just hear right? Love? Surely it slipped out of his mouth by accident. Or is the English countryside softening his heart?

"I'm going to have a shower."

"Good idea," he replies, turning the volume back up.

Sitting on my bed, I eagerly open the envelope from Trealla. I pull out an impressive blue piece of paper, but the only thing written on it is

Redeemable at Bramble Street, Bristol. What on earth has Trealla given me? It doesn't reveal much. There's no shop name, just the name of the street. I'm guessing it's some kind of voucher I can redeem. I'll just have to find Bramble Street in Bristol tomorrow and work it out for myself.

***

Dad and I pull up at the dock. Longshoremen are loading and offloading the boats as they pull in and out of the busy channel. Making our way along the dock, to buy my ferry ticket into town, we come across a man walking towards us, adjusting his tie.

"Good morning, Mr. Destinn," he says, shaking my father's hand, surprising me with his American accent.

"Morning, Maguire. Good to see a man of your age working on a Sunday and dressed the part."

"Thank you, Mr. Destinn. If you put the extra in, you get the extra out," he replies with an enthusiastic smile.

How can anyone be this happy to be at work on a Sunday morning? Especially an American who should be at home enjoying the summer.

"Hard work is the key, young man." Dad lights his cigarette.

"I've got plenty of hard work in me," he replies with a confident twist of his head.

"Let me introduce you to my daughter. Maguire, this is Isola. Isola, this is Maguire, one of my employees."

"Hello."

"Pleased to meet you, Isola." He politely lifts his hat.

Wow. His eyes. Or more to the point, his long, dark eyelashes make his eyes pop. I can't stop looking at them.

"Maguire has traveled here from America to try his luck in the English trade," Dad says, puffing on his cigarette.

"You came here of your own free will?" I ask. What kind of American would do that to themselves?

"Yes, I have. I arrived here a week ago."

And it shows in his alacrity. "That's a risky throw of the dice, coming this far for work."

"I'm sure it will be worth my while." He confidently nods at me.

"The voyage here will be well worth your while, Maguire. We look after hardworking men like yourself."

"I won't disappoint you, Mr. Destinn."

"You'd better not." Dad's tone resonates his expectation. "I'll see my daughter to the ferry and meet you at the office." Dad dismisses Maguire.

"Of course, Mr. Destinn. Good day, Isola." He smiles politely.

"Good day to you, too."

"I'll walk you to the ticket booth, Isola." Dad gestures to continue our walking.

"I'll be all right, Dad, I'm seventeen now, remember?"

"I know how long I've been feeding you for."

"Then, you'll know I'm old enough to walk by myself."

"Okay, then." He drops his butt on the ground and steps on it. "Here's some money for lunch. I'll pick you up at the Theatre Royal in King Street at two o'clock. Do you remember where it is?"

"Yes, Dad. I'll see you then." I quickly walk off before he changes his mind.

As soon as Dad is out of sight, I make my way to the long-haul ticketing booth. The ticketmaster slides open the glass door, looking down his nose at me.

"Good morrow. How can I be of assistance?" he says with little to no facial expression.

"Can you please tell me how much a fare will cost to America?"

"That would be subject to whereabouts in America you intend on traveling. It's a rather large country."

"Really!" That was rather a large serving of sarcasm. "I'll try for the East Coast." I try my best not to be ridiculing like him.

"Departing?"

"On the twenty-first of June next year."

"Return?"

"One way."

He flicks through the papers on his desk. "The *Sylvania Cunard* will be traveling to New York, with a seven-day crossing, at a cost of 118 pounds 10 shillings first class and an additional 18 pounds for a connecting boat to East Coast ports."

"118 pounds 10 shillings," I reply, shocked at the cost.

"Third class is 77 pounds, but not appropriate for a young lady traveling unaccompanied. Will I issue you a ticket today, miss?"

"No, I'm just inquiring for now."

"I'll see you when you save your pennies." He slides closed the door.

Looks like I'm in saving mode for the next year. There goes my shopping today. First things first. I'm attempting to call Sation again. Into the booth I go. The cold phone rests on my ear while I pray he answers. Damn it, I can't even get a ringtone. I slam the phone down and a lonesome tear rolls from my eye. I'm obviously doing something wrong with this international call. It looks like I'll have to continue to communicate via mail.

Wandering around the old neighborhood, near Christmas Steps, is right up my alley. The nostalgic part in my brain is on sensory overload, feeding on times gone by. Who's walked these cobbled streets over the centuries? What kind of merchandise or trades were exchanged in these old buildings? Spice, haberdashery, ancient grains.

I ask a man for directions to Bramble Street. As it turns out, I'm only one street away. With a tummy full of excitment, here it is right in front of me.

Half way down I pass a sign reading *Cartographer.* I don't even know what that is. Next, I pass a fruit store, a fishmonger, a silk fabric store and now a leather merchant. Surely Trealla doesn't want me to redeem my gift at any of these stores. A little further on I come across the pet shop Mom and Julia went to the first day we arrived. I realize I've walked down Bramble Street once before, only from the opposite direction. I look across the street to the cobalt-blue façade of Robust & Arabica. *The wine of the bean.*

Holding the piece of paper up in front of me, I see it's the same cobalt-blue color as Robust & Arabica. Trealla used color as a means of identification instead of numbers. Whatever is she up to?

Chapter Ten

Standing at the front of Robust & Arabica, I wonder, do I knock or walk straight in? Then Lizabethe walks past the window and notices me. Her purple dress and peach shawl grab my attention. I'd never wear those colors together, or add lush green earrings, but somehow she makes it look sophisticated.

"Hello, Isola." She beams a smile my way.

"You remember my name," I reply, happy that someone as amazing as Lizabethe remembers me.

"Of course, I do. You're the young lady who needed to make friends with England. By the look of things, you have."

"We're on talking terms now."

"Great to hear. Come on in and warm your bones, dearie," she says, opening the door wider.

The aroma of percolated coffee invigorates my senses entering her cozy residence.

"To what do I owe the pleasure?" she asks.

"I was given this piece of paper by a friend. I presume it's some sort of voucher I redeem here, going by the color of the paper and the color of the building. But I could be way off path."

"The color, the color. It's all about the color." She takes the piece of paper out of my hand, looking at it, shaking her head slowly as she reads. "Oh, that cheeky woman."

"Do you know Trealla?"

"You mean Pachamama?"

"No, I mean Trealla. A lady called Trealla gave me this voucher."

"Yes, I know Trealla, but I call her Pachamama, and going by this piece of paper, you know her too."

"Yes, we are friends."

"You're more than friends, dear. Trealla can obviously see you're awakening to the innate within."

"Yes. Apparently something within me is awakening. I was of the belief my heart exploded to life because I fell in love, but Trealla informs me it's something innate awakening."

"Trealla is right. Men aren't that powerful, dearie. It's definitely the innate that's responsible. The first time we met, I could tell your inherent nature had set out on its path to awaken. That's what led you here in the first place."

"Really?"

"Yes. Like I said last time, it takes someone with a distinct nature to stumble upon my residence."

"Who knows where my path will lead me next? I might be off to see the Wizard of Oz."

"No, wrong-colored shoes." She points to my black boots. "But then again, being at Avenlee makes you feel like you're living in a fictional wonderland, doesn't it?"

"Oh, it does. It's enchanting and Trealla makes it even more captivating."

"Yes, the heroine of horticulture has mastered that. Now, I'm sure you have been wondering what this crafty piece of paper entitles you to." She holds it in the air.

"The thought never crossed my mind."

"Nice one. As you can see, I have a lot of books in my home. That's because I'm a Storyteller."

"Okay." Where is this going?

"This voucher entitles you to hear the first chapter from any one of my books." She holds out her hand to her large and colorful collection.

"Oh," I reply, a little disappointed. Having a book read to me isn't really my idea of fun.

"Come stand in front of this bookcase so you can choose one."

I walk over and stand beside her.

"Now the excitement begins, but first you must agree not to question or look for logical explanation for what you are about to see."

"Unexplained circumstances are the norm for me nowadays."

"In that case, welcome to Imagination Station."

"Don't you mean Layleasta Station?"

"Someone's been reintroduced to their long-forgotten senses." She grins.

"Yes, and I have to reconnect with it."

"You must use your imagination as you would use any of your other senses. In fact, you're about to bring it back into fashion now, just as soon as you agree to abandon all logic and promise not to ask any questions."

"I promise."

"You must also never repeat to anyone what you're about to experience. This is for the innate at heart only."

"You can trust me, Lizabethe." What in heck is coming my way?

"Of course, I can. Our kind are trustworthy by nature. I just want to reaffirm with you these books are a private collection of tales that should never be shared with anyone but our kind. Now close your eyes, take a deep breath, and give this wheel a jolly good spin."

I reach for what resembles a miniature brass helm on the side of the bookcase and give it a hard spin. Next, I notice the books on the middle shelves start moving into the adjacent bookcase as if on a belt. If that isn't crazy enough, soon all seven shelves in front of me move like the first one.

Eyes bulging, I look at Lizabethe. She humbly smiles, then turns back to the bookcase. A noise sounds behind me. I turn to see every book around the room in motion. I look back at Lizabethe again. Still, she offers no explanation for why her entire collection of books is moving around her room in one continuous motion. Eventually, all the books slow down and finally stop moving.

"Wow! Did you see that?" I'm bubbling with excitement.

"Wait, there's more," a calm Lizabethe replies.

I watch one book from the bottom shelf somehow move up to the third shelf. Then two books from the top shelf drop onto the second. All seven shelves of books are now shuffling up and down within the bookcase, as if color-coordinating themselves. Back and forth, up and down, in and out, they move. My eyes can't keep up. The motion finally stops, and before my marveling gaze, the bookcase is color-coordinated perfectly, like the color spectrum of a rainbow. All the red books are on one shelf, arranged from the lightest shade to the darkest shade of red, as are all the other colors.

"That's astounding!" Lizabethe clasps her hands together.

"You're not wrong. Did you see all them moving? That's some kind of magic."

"I'm not refering to their motion. I'm refering to the volume of books. Normally our kind fill two or three rows, but lo and behold, you have filled every single row."

She steps towards the bookcase, closes her eyes, moves her head back and forth along the rows. She's murmuring and muttering as if amazed by whatever it is she can see through her closed eyes. Then she looks at me, shaking her head. "That's a profound collection of color."

I'm not completely sure if her level of fascination is solely attributed to the profound collection of colors in front of her. After all, her whole room is a collection of colorful books.

"Now I need you to select one book for me to read."

I'm still far too blown away by what I just witnessed to concentrate. It also doesn't help that no titles are written on the spines.

"Come on. Pick one."

"It would be easier if I knew the names of the books or what they're about."

"It's all about the color. Whichever color attracts your attention the most will be the one you're supposed to choose."

"Everything seems to be about color to you and Trealla."

"Of course it is. Color is the complexion of life."

"Okay, I choose the violet book on the top shelf." I point at it. "It's the first book that caught my eye when they stopped moving."

"Great choice."

"Can I take it off the shelf?"

"Well, I won't be able to read it to you if it's still on the shelf, dearie."

Flicking through the pages, I notice they're all blank. I look at Lizabethe, confused for the tenth time in the last five minutes. "Is this some kind of wisecrack? How are you supposed to read a book with no story inside?"

"Leave that up to me. I'm the Storyteller, remember?"

She holds out her hand for me to pass it to her.

"I know you're the Storyteller, but seriously, there're no words inside."

"Since when are stories only told with written words?" Lizabethe comments, then looks to the book in her hands. "Annabell Hennington, London, 1818," she says, as if she had read it off the cover.

Now I'm thinking Lizabethe doesn't have an eye dysfunction, but rather exceptional eyesight.

"Who is Annabell Hennington?"

"She is the lead character in this book. Going by the blurb, Annabell owned an apothecary establishment back in 1818."

"Apothecary. What is that?"

"An apothecary was kind of a pharmacy back in the olden days. Annabell would have mixed and dispensed her plant-based remedies to treat patients in her apothecary practice."

"That sounds like an interesting occupation."

"Yes, and a very rare one for a woman back in 1818. Now, choose a spot on the couch and make yourself comfortable. You're in for a treat," she says, taking a seat, too. "As you will have already figured, my collection of books isn't the kind you might stumble across at the local library. They're highly interactive in ways you could never imagine. As I read to you, you will inhabit Annabell's life as if it is your own. Every single one of her thoughts, senses, feelings and emotions you will personally experience."

My life just entered the next level of craziness. "So, you're saying, as you read Annabell's story to me, I'm pretty much going to be her?"

"Precisely."

"Do you know how absurd this sounds?"

"It sounds tantalizing to me."

She attempts to coax me into her whimsical world with her ambitious stare. Lizabethe is obviously talking her abilities up a little too much, because it isn't humanly possible. Nevertheless, I'm not about to throw my hands up and decline her tantalizing idea of entertainment. I smile back, welcoming more absurdity into my life.

"Read away. I'll add it to the long list of illogical events joining me on my path."

"Wonderful. I'll be honored to add to that list. You will need to close your eyes to block out your sense of sight so Annabell's existence can come to life. When the chapter is finished, I will tap you on the knee. Then you can open your eyes. But you can't open them before, else it will end."

My life keeps on getting weirder and weirder.

"Are you comfortable?"

"Very." I snuggle back in my seat.

"Good. Here we go. Close your beautiful blue eyes, surrender to your layleasta, and enjoy the story."

Chapter Eleven

Annabell Hennington, 1818. London.
Mi Se.

Following public demand and the gentle persuasion from my beloved husband, William, I, Annabell Hennington, opened an apothecary establishment on the first floor of our two-story apartment on the busy estuary's dock in London.

Much attention went into the design of my apothecary, making it appealing for my patients to visit in their time of need. The two large windows that curve out from the building I use to display my stunning sapphire-blue glass canisters, each labeled with their medicinal contents or plant oils. The front of the building's painted forest green, and large bold letters above the doors read: APOTHECARY EST 1818.

My two prized pieces of furniture are my brass Sessanta scales inherited from my grandfather, along with his loyal patients. He originally practiced medicine from this building before his passing. The second piece of furniture is a gift I received from William, a large apothecary chest made of maplewood. It has fifty compartment drawers storing my dried herbs, powders, spices, seeds and nettles. It's the finest piece of craftsmanship I've ever placed eyes on.

I established my apothecary in the year 1818, but my training began as a child watching my grandfather concoct remedies for his patients. Grandfather said that as soon as I learned to read, I reached for his farmer's almanacs and medical journals, preferring them over the latest Maria Edgeworth publication. In fact, the highlight of my year is the second Tuesday in September when the new almanacs are released. I would disappear for the remainder of September studying the coming year's moon phases, planting charts, spring tides and astronomy predictions.

As I grew older, my interest in plants shifted towards medical science. Unfortunately, my gender doesn't permit me to become a physician. But that didn't deter me from reading every medical textbook I could get my womanly hands on. Though, most of what I've learned came from the gentle voice of my grandfather. He taught me everything there is to know about plants and every disease they cured. I helped him grind down seeds, decoct roots in a big pot of boiling water and distill oils from plants. My favorite task was helping Grandfather perform the tincture extraction on echinacea plants we grew in our apothecary garden. Grandfather always told me, "Sing in the garden and the garden will sing back to you."

Now, twenty-five years later, I'm still tending to my apothecary garden, humming away to help it grow, grouping plants in rows according to their healing properties, just like Grandfather taught me. I've perfected extracting oil compounds from every plant I've grown. Now I have the finest quality oils in London that, amusingly, physicians come to acquire. I'm colloquially know as the Ethereal Oil Lady.

My husband, William, supports my professional pursuits, even though it is deemed inappropriate behavior for a wife to earn a living or heal the sick. Two hundred and fifty years ago, I'd be deemed a witch and burned at the stake. I'm sure William receives much criticism when he attends his glee club for polished Englishmen, but my William snubs the ignorance of those gleeful members and their pompous "Glorious Apollo" tunes. Being married to William makes me feel like the most blessed woman in London. He is my spoonful of goodness that wears off any foreign pesticides.

Nearly a month ago, William tumbled through the door in a qualmish state, his eyes puffy, body limp and feverish. I put together a potent elixir of clover, holy basil, boswellia carterii, peppermint and ravintsara, in hope to alleviate his fever. All day I heard people downstairs knocking on my locked door, but I didn't leave William's side. He became my number-one patient.

After a good night's rest, I'd hoped William might wake feeling better the next day, but he was in a worse state than the day before. I called for the doctor. He ruled out cholera, rampant across the world these days. But not even the doctor could diagnose his problematic state. He told me to keep on treating William's temperature with my elixir and hoped the illness would resolve itself.

Three weeks later, the doctor and I are at our wits' ends for a prognosis. William still is bedridden. His fever has dissipated, but unfortunately, so too his wellbeing. How can I not heal the man I love? I question myself, or, more so, disparage myself.

To find a remedy, I study all night, burning into the midnight oil. I limit my practice, closing the doors by noon, spending the rest of the day studying medical textbooks and anything I can get my hands on. One evening, I stumble upon an entry in my grandfather's textbook. The heading reads *Treatment for non-compliant illnesses.* There is an entry with all the signs and symptoms William's presenting with. Grandfather wrote "blood infection" next to it, and the treatment appears to be hidden in a plant called taka, growing in America. This plant's high levels of antibacterial properties seem to be my only hope. Unfortunately, it only grows naturally on American soil and nowhere else in the world. My hopes fade once again.

On the fourth Monday after William took ill, I hear a person persistently knocking at the door. Could they not see the "Closed" sign hanging in the window? I walk downstairs and peep through the curtain to see a gentleman, possibly a sailor, standing on my doorstep. He catches me looking and sends a warm-hearted smile. He doesn't look at all ill. In fact, his eyes are radiantly healthy and his smile could brighten the coldest evenings with their presence.

I open the door. "How do you do, sir."

"Well, thank you. I'd like to procure the fragrance coming from inside, to take home to my wife."

His American accent has a valorous tone and, as he mentions his wife, the thoughtful look in his prominent blue eyes makes me forget about my dreary predicament.

"Come inside." I beckon with my hand.

"Thank you, miss. I can smell it from the other side of the dock."

"I steam the essence in my apothecary daily. It's quite favorable to the olfactory system."

"I guess that's something to do with your nose."

"Close enough."

"What is it called?"

"*Lavandula angustifolia.*"

He looks at me, making no attempt to repeat its botanical name.

"But it's commonly known as lavender," I add.

"Lavender is a lot easier to pronounce. I've never been one to speak Latin." He grins.

His thoughtful gesture for his wife heartens me. I sense that, even though his exterior may be quite leathery, his heart is as soft as my cotton nightgown. I prepare a vial of oil, then cut a bunch of fresh stems from my garden and bind them in paper.

"How much will that be, miss?" he asks, smelling the stems.

"There's no charge today."

"Are you certain? I'm more than pleased to pay, especially given you weren't even open."

"You're the first person I haven't had to treat for an illness, which is somewhat refreshing, so it's my pleasure. I hope your wife enjoys it. The vial should keep for a while in a dark place. Take a vial of frankincense as well. Your wife can blend them together. When are you leaving?"

"I'm setting sail this evening. We are expecting our first baby in five weeks. I want to be home before the baby's arrival," he says with a smile three masts wide.

"I hope the wind is kind to your sails and you make it home in time. What work do you perform on board?"

"Everything. I am the owner."

"Maybe I ought to be calling you captain, then?"

"I'm not one for titles. Not even the seamen call me captain. Davy will be fine."

"Davy it is, then." I nod.

"What is your name?"

"Annabell Hennington."

"I'm pleased to meet you, Mrs. Hennington."

"You too. Can I ask, do they have apothecaries in America?" I wipe the broken pieces of lavender off my stone bench.

"They may, but I've never seen one in Georgia, where I'm from. The closest thing we have to herbal medicine is from the Muscogee and Seminole Indians. They have been treating themselves with herbs since long before white man's medicines came about."

"True. I have a patient I can't seem to cure, and I read some medical findings on a plant that seems to hold good merit in curing his blood disorder. However, the plant only grows in America and, if I remember correctly, it's a plant natives use. It's called taka."

"I pass by the trading post on my way back home. Maybe I can bring some back on my next haul to London."

"Aren't they savages?"

"To the contrary. It is of my viewpoint that the people writing these claims are the true savages. By nature, the Indians are gracious people of the land. Colonization has killed off more than half of them. And now the United States are invading Florida in an attempt to acquire it from the Spanish, killing every Indian in sight and displacing the rest farther south. Obviously, the Seminole and Muscogee fight back, but that doesn't make them savages. They're simply trying to survive."

"That's dreadful. I never knew that."

"Before I left Georgia, General Jackson arrived in Pensacola, turning Florida into disarray. I hate to think what's happened since I've been at sea. But I have good rapport with a few Muscogee clans. We often exchange goods. I've even employed a few men to work our horses. They would be happy to share their taka in exchange for goods."

"That's very kind of you, Davy, but the plant oils must be extracted and ingested immediately."

"If your patient wants to travel back to America on my boat, he's more than welcome to join me. As long as he's not contagious, that is."

"No, he's not contagious."

"Who is the patient?"

"It's my husband," I say, dropping my chin.

"I'm sorry to hear that. I will be making sail at high tide, heading to Georgia. I'm more than happy to have you and your husband aboard if you choose to join me. Look for my three-mast brigantine called *Makana*."

"Thank you for your generous offer, Davy. I'm just not sure if my husband is strong enough for the long journey, or myself for that matter. I'm petrified of the water. I can't swim."

"You don't have to swim alongside the boat. I'll let you on board." He cheekily grins, flashing his white teeth that stand out against his tanned skin.

"I'll think about it, Davy. Thank you again for the offer."

"I best be off, Mrs. Hennington. If I don't see you before tonight's high tide, all the best to you and your husband. Thank you for opening your shop. You brightened my day," he says, opening the door to leave.

Little did he know his amiable personality and contagious smile brightened my day more.

"I hope your wife likes her gift; it will be comforting for the baby as well."

"She will love her *Lavandula angustifolia*."

He pronounces perfectly. I knew he was more intelligent than he revealed.

***

Is this my opportunity to save William's life, or am I a fool to think he is strong enough to sail across the ocean? Then again, who am I fooling? I'm not even brave enough to step onto a boat, let alone cross the open seas on one. And what about my garden? I can't live without my garden, and my garden won't survive without me. Though, the thought that William may pass away here in London while a remedy awaits him in America, with the means to get there, encourages me to consider taking the voyage. Even though I haven't a clue where Georgia is.

For two hours I contemplate going and staying, changing my mind a thousand times. "Annabell, make up your mind," I say to myself.

I'm going. I'm doing this for William. I collect my finest herbs and elixirs, pack every vial of oil in my apothecary. I say goodbye to my beloved garden, singing to it one last time, then lock the door to my apothecary, blotting the tears rolling down my face. I feel awful for deserting all my patients and my garden, but I have to do this. I just have to. I walk away with William hobbling along beside me, hoping I've made the right decision.

I spot the *Makana* with its attractive timber bolsters running the perimeter of the deck. They look sturdy enough to put a great big barrier between me and the water's edge. Davy greets us on the dock. After I introduce Davy and William to each other, a deckhand escorts William below deck. I stand on the dock, absolutely petrified to step on board. Davy takes the case out of my hand. "What have you got in here, bricks?"

"No, glass vials with plant oils inside. I couldn't leave them behind. I planted, grew, distilled and bottled them. They're my babies."

"Your babies are welcome aboard." He smiles.

I nervously look at the waves rocking up against the ship, then look up and notice a round seashell carved into the timber next to the word *Makana*.

"I like that seashell. Is that what *Makana* means? Seashell?"

"No, *Makana* means gift. Seashells I'm just fascinated by, especially this rare one. It's a depiction of one I have at home."

"They are unique objects, aren't they?"

"Treasures from the sea, in my opinion. This one is called a cowrie. In real life, it has spots. You will find three different types of shells carved all over my ship."

"Why three?"

"I couldn't decide which one I liked the most."

"I'll keep my eye out for them."

The shells I like. The sea, however, is another story. I look down into the dark blue unknown and my body quivers.

"You appear worried, Annabell."

"I am."

"Annabell, let me reassure you, the crew and I are the best sailors on these waters, and the *Makana* is strong enough to brave the worst currents. You are in very safe hands."

"Thank you so much, Davy. That means a lot."

"I have cleared out the spare sleeping quarters for the comfort of your husband and yourself."

"You have? But how did you know I was even going to leave England?"

"I could see the courage in your eyes."

"All I see is fear." I look over the side of the dock in horror.

"There is nothing wrong with fear. As long as you are facing it and not running from it."

"I'm not sure about that. I'm going to be wearing a lot of lavender and valerian oil to calm myself."

"You will be fine, and you will smell a lot nicer than the sailors. The wind is blowing from the north as well, so that makes for good sailing conditions. If there is anything I can do to make the journey less frightening, by all means ask."

"There is something you can do, Davy. Can you please hold my hand while I step aboard? I'm rather nervous."

Chivalrously, Davy holds out his hand and, together with my heavy case of oils, we walk across the ramp onto his boat. As overwhelmed as I am, I somehow feel safe in Davy's presence and know he will provide a safe passage to America. I only hope the sea cooperates.

***

Three weeks into our voyage, I gain a small portion of confidence on board the *Makana*, even though I've almost run my lavender, valerian and chamomile vials dry. I've been eating sea pie with the sailors and listening to them sing sea shanties to pass the time. I've kept busy discovering the three different seashells and their names: Nautilus, Junonia and Kahelelani. They are so unique and beautifully crafted, but most importantly, they have distracted me from the place they originate from: the frightening sea.

I wake early one morning, before any of the sailors, and walk out onto the deck in my nightgown to gaze out across the sea, anticipating

Georgia in the distance while I hum away, but unfortunately the horizon hasn't yet brought forth any such view. While I'm here and feeling a little brave, I might take a small step towards the edge and run my hands over the seashells carved into the bolsters. Here I go.

"'Morning, Annabell."

Stepping back, I grab hold of the mast in reaction to Davy's unexpected advent.

"Davy, you startled me."

"Sorry, I didn't mean to."

My fright soon turns to discomfiture when I realize I've been caught wearing my nightgown. It also doesn't help that the salty breeze is blowing against my body, revealing even more of yours truly. Promptly, I feel it necessary to explain my debauched behavior.

"I thought I'd wake up before the other men and see if any land is in sight, but now I'm mortified you see me wearing so little. I apologize for putting you in this state of affairs, Davy." I cross my arms over my chest.

"Annabell, you have more clothes on than I. It's grand to see you about the deck alone. You must have found your sea legs."

"I won't go that far."

"Would you like me to hold your hand while you walk closer to the bolsters?" He holds his hand out for me to grab.

"Um, no, I'd rather you stay over there and let me do this on my own, thanks."

"I thought you'd say as much. I'll go about my chores, then."

I turn and face the sea and sing a little, like I do in my garden, to calm my nerves. I reach out to the bolsters and hear a loud thud, which startles me. Davy looks back at me, just as alarmed. Something isn't right for him to look this way. Oh, no! Could it be William?

Running below deck, I find William slumped on the floor, unconscious.

"William, are you all right? William, William, respond!"

He says not a word, moves not a muscle.

"Wake up, wake up, William." Tapping the side of his face creates no response, so I shake his frail, lifeless body. "Wake up! You have to wake up. We're almost there."

But I realize William is never going to wake from the death that has found him, and part of me dies with him.

"No, no, no, come back! Please, William, we're almost there. Don't leave me, my love. Please don't leave me."

***

Sometime later, Davy drags me away from William's body, consoling me while I uncontrollably weep.

We reach the shores of Georgia two days later. Davy takes care of all the funeral arrangements while I repent my decision to come here.

I lay William to rest the following morning. Davy escorts me back to the inn, then makes his way home to West Georgia.

Now I'm all alone in the world, with grief and guilt to keep me company. I failed the man I love. As far as I am concerned, I don't deserve to draw breath.

***

Ten months later, I'm still locked inside American shores, too fearful to cross the sea without a man like Davy to assure my safe return. The few times I have endeavored to return home to London, I get as far as the port and feel an overwhelming sense of guilt for deserting William's body, and so I return to the inn and cry myself to sleep, knowing I'm locked in Georgia for the remainder of my days.

It isn't long before my grief and guilt reach for whisky. Now whisky's fashioned me into an irrational woman. Overnight, I've established an American colonial thirst, consuming four tankards a day. Apart from laudanum, it is the most effective pain relief I can purchase. It's unpleasantly bold to taste but, at twenty-five cents a gallon, it is cheaper than wine and even milk.

This evening, six tankards haven't numbed my guilt. The ale has only evoked anger I have towards myself and that wretched taka that coaxed me here. I need to find this plant and rip out every one I see. I set out to find the Muscogee village with intentions to kill every taka plant I can get my drunken hands on. I'm going to take my pain out on this godforsaken plant that brought me here in the first place.

Hours later, in the middle of nowhere, I see what I presume to be fields of taka growing. I feel the taka under my feet and start kicking at it, spitting on it, and ripping it out. Crying my lonely whisky tears all over it. "Why? Why me? What did I do to deserve all this? Why couldn't you just let me save my husband? Why, why?"

I fall on the taka, exhausted from harboring ten months of sorrow. I've had enough of this misery. I wish it would end. I lie in the taka field in the dark of the night, hold my breath, and pray I die.

***

The slap of hands clapping together at the center of my chest brings me back to a cognizant state. Sitting up in tremendous shock, I realize it's the morning after. How have I came to be in such primitive conditions? I look down at my cut-up bare feet and begrimed garment. I have abandoned all moral qualities. Lunacy has definitely become me. I look up, frightened to see a native man gazing down at my desensitized virtues. Why isn't he running from the bad spirit in me?

But as I gain more consciousness, so too does the scornful voice inside my head, reminding me I don't deserve to draw breath while William lies in a cold grave. I am nothing but a puff of quackery, a widow by my own hand. I wish I'd never awakened. I wish this native man would pierce my chest with his arrow and let the vapor of death set me free. Then the penitence of my reality proves too astringent and I pass out.

Waking inside a canvas structure, I look up at seven poles leaning onto one another. The smoke from a small fire burning next to me seeps out through a hole at the top of the poles.

Am I dead? Is this what hell looks like? But then the sound of minor chatter in a language I can't understand sobers my deathly thoughts, and so too does my sore head. I peep through a flap in the canvas to see more structures dotted about the field. Then, to my surprise, the same native man pulls the flap open I'm peeping out of and we almost collide. Falling back in shock, I hear him laugh. Obviously, he finds this near-miss humorous.

"*Hesci.* Hello," he says, stepping inside.

"Hello."

"You want *owv*, water?"

"That would be great." Especially after all the alcohol I drank yesterday.

"Good for you, water." He passes me some sort of bladder to drink from. The tone of his voice holds warmth, and the felicity in his manner makes me feel unruffled by his fleshy appearance.

"Thank you." I smile.

"Mvto, thank you."

"Mvto," I repeat. I just learned my first native word. "Where am I?"

"You here, in Sisika's tipi." He taps the ground with his foot. "What do they call you?" he asks, momentarily shuts his eyes. Maybe he got smoke in them, or he suffers from astigmatism.

"My name is Annabell. What are you called?"

"Nakaho, Cvhocefkv Tos."

"Na-ka-ho," I repeat, breaking his name up into syllables, not even attempting to pronounce his surname.

"You English, I'm Muscogee."

"I'm a kind English person." I feel the need to express this.

"I know," he affirms. "Have you created, Annabell?"

"I don't understand."

"Your gift."

"You mean children? No, I don't have any."

He nods his head, as if to comprehend, but I'm not sure if we just got each other confused.

"Stand still," he says, then shakes his head and corrects himself. "I mean, sit still. I will be back." He seems slightly frustrated at his incorrect use of words. "I'm not using your language in a long time. I must practice." He then walks outside.

In his absence, my wondering gaze falls on what I assume to be a

Muscogee residence. A large hide covers the floor, softening the harsh elements. Bundles of dried sage and tobacco hang from the poles. Such primitive conditions make me feel like I've stepped back in time. I'm not sure what his plans are for me. I have a feeling it's death. The English are far from welcome here after the brutality we have caused. But if he's planning to kill me, why is he being so kind?

Nakaho walks back inside with an elderly woman. The furrowed lines in her face and her countenance clearly indicate the decades of wind and sun that have moved across her face. But regardless of her age, her eyes are as savvy as an eagle's. She steps closer, then flutters her eyes closed. Does she have astigmatism too? Maybe I should prescribe them infusions of chamomile and nettle. Unless fluttering the eyes is a custom they use to greet one another.

Nakaho appears much more approachable compared to this stern elderly woman looking, or not looking, at me. Awkwardly, I wait for her to open her eyes.

Moments later, she looks at Nakaho. "*Nubenlee*," she says in her native tongue, jutting her chin forwards.

She then grabs a shawl from a basket, then takes my hand and walks me outside and Nakaho follows on behind us. She continues pulling me along until we reach the outskirts of the village. It's apparent I'm not welcome here and the both of them are seeing to it that I leave.

"Where are we going, Nakaho?" I call back, trying to keep up with cuts hurting my bare feet.

"Sisika walks you to the *hvse* and you must follow." He follows too.

"*Hvse*?"

"The sun."

I really don't have an option. She is dragging me. Maybe she is taking me far away from the village so the children don't see me being killed.

Sisika finally stops, as does Nakaho. Nervously, I surrender to my fate, relieved to put this life to an end so I can join William. Still holding my hand, Sisika kneels onto the ground, pulling me down with her. Holding my pointer finger, she writes "Wakan" in the dirt. She stands back up and exchanges some words with Nakaho and walks back to the village.

Looking down at the word *Wakan*, I wonder if it means "Bury here."

Nakaho approaches me. This is it. I'm about to take my last breath. I close my eyes, cringing, praying for a quick death.

"Every morning before the *hvse*, the sun warms the changing woman. You must greet sun and in dirt you must write same word, until you know meaning."

"You're not going to kill me?"

He laughs so much he has to hold his belly. The last time I'd heard such mirth coming from a man was while listening to the punster sailors making merry mullocks at one another on Davy's boat.

"*Monkos*, we not killing you."

I ought to be relieved. Instead, I'm disappointed. Why can't he just put me out of my misery?

"If you're not going to kill me, then what are you going to do with me?"

"Nothing." He shakes his head.

I stand back up dusting off my knees. "What is all that stuff Sisika asks of me then, regarding the sun?"

"It's to bring balance. Through your feet, you must ground your energy on the changing woman and, from the sun and the *Ibofanga*, you will receive energy. These energies must flow through your body with your breath. This will bring balance and keep you in the circle of creation."

"What is *Ibofanga*?"

He points to the sky.

"What is the Changing Woman?"

He points to the ground.

"The *Terte*. The earth. We call her Changing Woman. She changes from cool to warm, from fertile to resting, from dark to light. She is forever changing and repeating nature in cycles."

"I understand. So, what is *Wakan*, then?"

"The meaning is for you to know. When you connect to *santi*, it will bring answers."

"*Santi*?"

"Your sense, *santi*."

"You mean a sense like smell and sight?"

"Your other sense."

Now I'm confused. "Does your culture believe a person has more than five senses?"

"Everyone has more senses. It's not culture, it's the nature of life."

"What are the other senses?" I ask, knowing there are definitely only five, but I'm curious to hear about the others.

"There are too many to say. The one you need to know now is *santi.* It is balance. You will find it between absence and presence."

This is clearly a cultural belief because I've never heard of any such sense in all my studies. But I'm not about to challenge his traditions. I've heard this culture has a lot of spiritual beliefs. "So is Wakan an Indian word?"

"There are no Indians here. Indians live east of the Indus. We are Muscogee, who live on the Changing Woman."

"It's a word from your native tongue, then?"

"It's a word to help you awaken to what's native within your heart."

"But I'm from London and far from native." How can't he see that?

"You will know when you know."

This is all getting a little too outlandish for me. Ten minutes ago, I was preparing for death. Now I'm trying to search my intelligence for an answer to a word, native to my heart, when all I know to be native in my heart is grief.

"Who is Sisika in your tribe?"

"She is one of great knowing of herbs, *heleswv.*"

"And who are you, Nakaho?"

"I am a *Romzeil*, a Storyteller."

"Oh, that sounds interesting. What stories do you tell?"

"Stories of the Ancestry of Creativity."

"Interesting." They're obviously traditional stories from his people and not the kind of stories I've grown up reading.

On our way back to the tribe, Nakaho walks me to the river where two women are standing. He talks to them, then walks off. One woman hands me a jug of foaming solution, the other a stack of clean clothes.

"Yucca," the first woman says.

Then she demonstrates for me to rub it on my body and points at the river, suggesting I need to bathe. My physical hygiene has fallen by the wayside since William's death. My once perfumed skin is now pungent, and this jug of yucca decoction is obviously used as soap by the Muscogee. But looking at the river, I shiver. Not only because I have to take my clothes off, but more so because I'm too scared to go into the water.

I kneel beside the river, naked, splashing water at myself. They look at me oddly, giggling. I guess I would look humorous, trying to bathe outside the water, but I can't get in. Being in water is like standing in fire to me. Neither of them are an option.

For the rest of the day, I sit watching them going about their daily tasks on the Changing Woman. The women sit talking while weaving baskets from some sort of palm leaf, and the men tend to the horses. Davy is right about how gracious they are. They walk about calmly, not stampeding in a mad rush to go hither and thither, like the monopolizing world of England. Even though the Muscogee are under attack from the United States, Nakaho reassures me we are safe here for now. I know they're keeping their distance from me just in case I'm harboring any disease. Nevertheless, they still take the time to smile as they pass by. I believe I've smiled more today than I have in the past year.

I notice Sisika approaching. I stand up, somewhat nervous. She smiles, then holds out her hand, showing me a colorful seashell necklace.

"It's delightful," I say, looking at all the beautiful tiny shells.

She nods in agreement, then moves behind me and ties it around my neck. She is giving it to me. What a kind gesture. Sisika is fond of me, after all. I put my hand on it, feeling the delicate shells and their smoothness around my neck.

"Thank you. *Mvto.*" Thank goodness Nakaho taught me this word.

"*Mvto, mvto.*" She holds my hand, shaking it, expressing gratitude towards me. Then she leans forward, resting her forehead on mine.

"*Cehecvkat hofones,*" she says.

The closeness is rather encroaching, however short-lived. She then turns and walks away.

Chapter Twelve

Nakaho returns on his horse in the evening to find me sitting in front of his tipi, clean, sober, and in my new native attire.

"Leave your head in the tipi. Come with your heart to the fire." Then he rides off.

I walk my heart over to the fire, leaving my past in the tipi, as I presume Nakaho is referring to. A large gathering of people assembles around the fire. Nakaho is being painted with red clay across his chest and yellow lines down his arms. He wears some sort of traditional jewelry around his ankles and wrists, making a percussion sound as he moves. Soon, everyone positions themselves around the fire. Nakaho sits me down beside Sisika. Sisika greets me with the nod of her head, then passes Nakaho a basket of bundled herbs and turns her attention back to the fire. I look around to all the happy faces illuminated by the glow of the fire. What does the glow on my face disclose? Can they see the former English medicine woman who healed hundreds of sick patients? Or can they see the one patient I couldn't save?

Two men, embellished in native trimmings, kneel down behind the two large buckskin drums. Then Nakaho and three other men, also wearing the same ceremonial attire, position themselves around the fire. Everyone falls quiet.

Nakaho yells out in his native tongue what seems a great declaration to the stars in the night sky. I can't understand a word he is saying, but the energy with which he expresses his message vibrates right to my core. He walks over and stands in front of me with his hand on his chest. Every eye turns my way.

"Let my thunder rain down on your heart. Until your heart thunders down on mine."

I'm feeling self-conscious about being the recipient of his passionate declaration. Then all four men draw a big deep breath from the night air, then thump at their chests, stimulating every heart around the fire. The ensuing sound comes from the three buckskin drums, and the dance commences. The four men move around the flames in rhythm with the drumbeat. A drummer starts to sing, and the energy becomes so infectious, I clap along with everyone.

The men's feet shuffle around the fire, kicking up the dirt. The mellifluent movement of Nakaho's body is captivating. He's utterly free and flowing. I never knew a body could move like this; I'm enthralled.

The longer I watch this sheer display of freedom, the more the ceremonial rhythm becomes hypnotic, as if I've been seduced into a trance. I'm as free as Nakaho looks. Happy tears flow from my eyes, telling me Nakaho's thunder is definitely raining down on my barren heart. But my heart bizarrely pounds a little too disproportionately. I feel it's about to spring from my chest and dance around the fire with these natives.

One last thump on the buckskin drum ends the dance, hauling me out of my euphoric trance and back to reality. *That was intense.* I grab at my heart and look around to see Sisika looking right at me.

"The drummer within you is awakening," she says, placing her hand on her heart. "Welcome back."

Sisika's English is as good as mine, if not better. "You know how to speak English?"

"And you know there is more to this life than you've been led to believe. Did you go beyond your body to another energy?"

"Yes. I've never felt anything like it before."

"I could see that. Next time this arises, follow the beat back to the drummer."

"The drummer?"

"Your heart is a drum. But a drum cannot play itself. It needs a drummer. Now you must find out who the drummer is, who is beating your drum to life." Sisika smiles, then stands up.

"What did you say to me earlier today when you placed your head against mine?"

"Long time no see." She smiles.

"I don't understand. I've never seen you before. And as for being your ancestor, that's impossible."

"Everything seems impossible before you awaken."

Sisika walks away, but the dancing continues into the night. I watch them stomping around in a circle and I want to join in, but I can't move properly yet. I don't think I've returned to my body fully; my heart is still full of unbridled joy. Who is the drummer keeping the beat? What could cause this euphoric experience, and what can possibly precede a heart?

Back at the tipi, astounded by what I just experienced, I lie for most of the night with my beautiful new necklace on, listening to my heartbeat. I try so hard to go back to that euphoric trance, but unfortunately, my heavy eyes win.

***

Tiptoeing outside the following morning, trying not to wake Sisika, I set out towards the rising sun. I have no shoes on, at Sisika's request. However, shoeless is my only option, given I'd lost them in the taka field in my drunken rage. That night, I didn't feel a thing on my feet, but sober and barefoot this morning is a different story. My delicate English feet feel every rock and prickle. I reach journey's end and plant the soles of my feet on the Changing Woman just in time for the first glimmer of light to touch the horizon. Its warmth penetrates my skin, waking me even more.

"Good morning sunshine." I close my eyes and breathe in its energy. Kneeling, with my finger I write in the dirt. *Wakan*. How many times am I going to write it before I work out what it means?

I make my way back to the village, enjoying the calming influences my new life has on me, when the ridiculing voice in my head returns to remind me just how undeserving of happiness I am. Within seconds, its pessimism strikes me like a rhumba of rattlesnakes, injecting me with insulting venom. If its words aren't crippling enough, the accompanying emotions reopen my wounds. I am undeserving of life. I couldn't save the man I loved. Even though I didn't kill him directly, I might as well have, given I didn't save him. He trusted me and I let him down. Six feet down. And now I'm nothing but a drunk.

I can't believe what I've done. I need to run. I don't deserve benevolence from these people. Nor their clothes, their smiles, their healing, nothing. If they knew the real me, they would have nothing to do with me. The right thing for me to do is leave. I need to find the one thing I do deserve. The one thing that will annihilate this voice in my head. Whisky. I crave it like my lungs crave air. I sneak out of the village and start running back to the life I know. These people don't need a woman like me here.

"Annabell! Annabell!"

I turn to see Nakaho chasing me. I run even faster. Within seconds, he is right behind me. I soon realize I have run in the wrong direction. Now I'm standing at a cliff with nowhere else to go.

"Annabell, stop. Is something wrong?" he pants, out of breath.

"Yes. My head."

"Did you hurt your head?"

"No, Nakaho."

"Did someone hurt your head?"

"Everyone's been kind. It's me. I'm undeserving of your consolation. I'm a bad woman, a crazy woman. Can't you see the death I hold in my heart, in my eyes? Just look at how you found me in my drunken rage. I'm a bad woman. I need alcohol. Or better still, I need to jump over this cliff. I can't do this anymore, I can't." Hysterically, I cry.

He places his hand on my shoulder. "Annabell, settle down."

"I can't." I shrug his hand off.

Nakaho steps towards me and stomps on my foot.

"Ouch!" I jump, grabbing my toes. "That hurt."

"It is supposed to."

I rub my foot trying to take the pain away. "Why would you do that?"

"To get you away from your head. Too much up there. Now, why are you leaving?"

"I don't deserve all of this. I want to go and drown my thoughts in whisky." I can't even stand still to speak I'm so agitated.

"You can run away, Annabell, and you can drink as much whisky as you like, but the bad woman you are running from will run with you everywhere you go." He gently places his hand on my arm. "The only place the bad woman exists is in your thoughts. She is not real. Free the thoughts and you free the bad woman."

"Nakaho, you're not listening to me. The things I did are real. If you knew who I really am, you would have nothing to do with me."

"You are human. Humans make mistakes. I've never met one that hasn't. You might have done bad things, but now you can do good things. So let me help you."

I shake my head at his optimism. "I'm beyond help."

"I would push you into the canyon if you were beyond help."

I turn my head and look over the cliff. "I have so many problems. Problems you can't help me with."

"I can, but you need to hear me."

I look back at him and feel his sincerity and wish I could believe him. "Can you talk louder than hate, guilt, and whisky? I doubt it." I shake my head.

"No, but I can talk softer than them."

Is he as deranged as me? How can softness overpower the loud, gritty hate in my head?

He places his strong hand over his bare chest. "You must come back to your heart and away from your head. Your thoughts will tell you either good or bad and take your energy. But in your heart, not a thought exists, only the sound it makes, *ba-boom, ba-boom*." He taps on his chest. "Be in your heart right now. It's a good heart. Be in this moment, not in the past. It's gone. Right now, in this moment, is all we have."

Nakaho caught my attention long enough to calm me. Taking a deep breath, I wipe my tears.

"Come back with me. I can help. If you think you don't deserve my help, that is just your head talking. I will not talk to your head. I will talk only to your heart. Your heart and I are great friends and it needs my help."

Nakaho silences my demons long enough to stop me from running off or jumping over this cliff. I now know if I'm ever going to survive, I need to let go of the Annabell I've become and surrender to Nakaho's help, and maybe even this drummer within.

I step back from the cliff, having come to my senses. Maybe the only thing I need to throw off this cliff is the contemptuous voice in my head, along with my past. I envisage emptying the past year of my life over the cliff and watch it fall through the air to the bottom of the canyon, never to be seen again. But my heart starts thumping with an indomitable pounding. It's the same feeling I felt in my chest watching Nakaho dance around the fire. The drummer is back, beating on my heart, but this time with a fist of iron, demanding I follow its lead.

"Nakaho." Breathless, I grab my chest.

"What's wrong, Annabell?"

"It's the drummer."

"Let it flow. Let go of your humanness and surrender to it."

"I am, Nakaho. But something else is happening. I can't feel my body, it's fading," I say, losing the strength in my legs. I drop to the ground and accidentally slide over the edge of the cliff.

"Annabell!" Nakaho shrieks, unable to grab me in time.

Falling through the air, I know my life is ending. Before I hit the ground, I need to meet the awaken. "I surrender, to the innate within."

My heartrate doubles, triples, combusts. Physical becomes trivial, inconsequential, all but dust. I'm awakening at last... *Bang.*

Chapter Thirteen

Isola Destinn, 1963. Bristol.

"That's the end of chapter one, Isola."

Lizabethe's voice startles me, then she places her hand on my knee.

"No, no, keep on going. I want to know what happens to Annabell."

"I can't. That's it for now."

"Please, Lizabethe. I haven't opened my eyes yet. I'm still Annabell," I plead, squeezing my eyes closed.

I hear the book shut, and Annabell's world instantly slips from mine. "*Arr*," I groan, opening my eyes. "That's not fair. I want to know what happened to Annabell. She just awakened, and I need to know what to."

"You will, in good time."

"Seriously, I can't just leave Annabell lying there, dying. I feel like I'm dying, too."

Lizabethe ignores me. She stands and puts the book back on the shelf, then sits back down. I can't believe I thought so little of her stories. Now I don't want her to stop. She definitely isn't talking up her storytelling abilities or her interactive books.

"In all seriousness, how did you do that? I was alive in London in 1818, wearing those vintage clothes, working in that amazing apothecary, sailing on that sea. I actually slept in a tipi. That was some kind of magic."

"No, there is no magic involved." She shakes her head, causing her long green earrings to sway about.

"You are one heck of a Storyteller, that's for sure. Is the rest of Annabell's book going to be as interactive?"

"Every one of my books reads in the same way. I have thousands of characters living on my shelves, waiting for a listener to give them life."

"I gave Annabell lots of life, and she gave me plenty in return. I could smell the *Lavandula angustifolia*, and feel the stems in my hands, although I'm not fond of grief. That is gut-wrenching. And by the way, whisky tastes terrible." I make Lizabethe laugh.

"Whisky does taste terrible straight, and yes, first chapters are difficult to experience. Second chapters are much more enjoyable. That's where the enchantment begins," she says with a wisp of excitement.

"I can't wait to hear the second chapter to find out what happens to Annabell. Oh, and how attractive was Davy?"

"He's a hunk. He reminds me of Paul Newman, with those gorgeous blue eyes and that swaying smile."

"You're right. He does look like Mr. Newman. So, when can you read the rest of Annabell's story? Tomorrow?"

"Nice try. I must inform you that, as interactive as my books are whilst hearing them, they are as equally interactive with wherever you are on your path in life."

"How so?"

"I guess you could say Annabell has the same distinct nature as us. So not until you awaken to who you are in this life will you be able to awaken to who Annabell is in her life. That's if Annabell survived her fall."

"Wow, you really weren't joking about your books being highly interactive. I can't believe I agreed to not ask questions. I have hundreds now."

"Let me explain this much, but you have to forget I told you," she whispers.

"I promise I'll forget."

"At the start of Annabell's chapter, I read out *Annabell Hennington, Mi Se*. Do you remember that?"

"Vaguely."

"To our kind, *Mi Se* is the word for our first chapter, sometimes referred to as the history of human thinking, when human thought creates our experience. It's one long historical thought process passed on from one generation to the next, holding us back from evolving. But when we do awaken to our inherent nature, we enter a realm that existed long before the thought of us ever did."

"And is that chapter two?"

"Correct. When you let go of your history of human thinking, you will move into a more authentic chapter of living, where you know who you are and don't think who you are. But for now, you live in your first chapter, just as Annabell was, up until the moment she fell over the cliff."

"Wow, this life of mine really is pushing at me to unthink myself, isn't it?"

"Yes, and for a good reason, dear. You don't belong with the historical thought society. You belong before it, outside it, beyond it."

"But I might not be able to let go and awaken. I tried not to think this morning. I lasted all of a second before another thought came racing back in. It's impossible to shut my brain up."

"It's going to take time, given you've spent seventeen years living unconsciously. Rather than trying to drop every single thought, you could try concentrating on one, for as long as you can."

"Okay, I'll try that, rather than going from one thousand thoughts to zero in one day."

"Little by little." She winks.

"So once I awaken and move into my second chapter, can I come back to this way of life?"

"There's no coming back. Nor will you want to."

The close-endedness of it makes me feel uneasy. "Can you stop yourself from awakening?"

"I guess you can prolong it. But why would you want to?"

"I'm not sure I want my life to change so dramatically. There's this guy I love and I'm worried if I awaken, then it will end."

"You would rather be with him than awaken?" she asks as if she has heard wrong.

"Yes, no one has ever made me feel like he does."

"That's a recipe for disaster. You need to love yourself more than you love him. You need to embrace your inherent self before you embrace anyone else."

"Not being with him is more of a disaster to me."

"My dear, it's best to awaken to your full potential and find the man who matches that, than the other way around."

"I've got a lot to think about, haven't I? In fact, I'm not meant to think. Oh, man, this is getting so complicated."

"You know, all this would be so much easier if you connected to your *santi*."

"That's what Nakaho spoke about with Annabell. What exactly is it?"

"I guess you could say it's like sleeping while you're awake. Legend has it, over seven thousand years ago, it was the most glorious sense known to mankind. All because it switched off your other senses and sat you in the sanctuary of stillness, in the absence of everything, and the presence of nothing."

"Absence of everything, and the presence of nothing. I'm confused."

"Activating your *santi* is like flicking the thinking switch off and the serenity switch on. You see, brains weren't wired to be turned on every minute of every day. That's why they were created with a complementary sense, which allows the brain downtime."

"And *santi* is the downtime?"

"That's right. Engaging with your *santi* allows your brain to switch off and your inherent nature to switch on, reconnecting you to your source of power. And in doing so, your entire mind and body move into a conscious state of equilibrium. But thanks to master manipulators of history, the world is a well-engineered brain factory, compulsively on the go. It's the greatest war ever won. They didn't even fire a bullet. They just removed the off-switch, which put the human race out of balance. Still to this day, people subconsciously feed the leaders their power in failing to stay connected with their own."

"Guilty," I admit, putting my hand up, making Lizabethe chuckle.

"We're all guilty of disconnecting from our source power." She picks up her water and sips.

"Do you have your sense of *santi* back, Lizabethe?"

"I sure do. I'm like a guru of *santi*. I can shut the worldly existence down in seconds."

"I'm the guru of the human thought society. I can't shut my brain up for a second. You no longer exist in your first chapter, do you?"

"No, I'm in the last chapter of my path."

"How many chapters are there?"

"Three in total, just as there're three chapters to every book in my collection."

"So, what happens in chapters two and three?"

"That's for you to discover."

"You're a tricky lady, Lizabethe."

"Highly intelligent as well."

"What chapter does Trealla exist in?"

"It's not my place to talk about another person's path. I have said enough. Trealla will be upset with me for saying as much as I have."

"She will?"

"Oh, yes, Trealla is adamant that nature should nurture one's journey and not another person's overactive tongue. That leans towards preaching and we're far from preachers."

"You are a Storyteller; I guess it only feels natural for you to talk away."

"Still, you have natural intelligence guiding you on your path and I trust it will awaken you to its extraordinary existence when it sees fit and not when I do. As Trealla always says, 'Nature knows best.' And trust me, Pachamama would know."

"Why do you call her Pachamama?"

"You can ask her, next time you see her."

"That's if I remember that word. My head is whizzing since stepping inside your door."

"You will awaken when you're meant to, and hopefully that's not much longer. Personally, I wouldn't mind indulging in Davy's gorgeous face again, not to mention his body."

"Same here. He is hot. I seriously need to be in his presence again."

"Then you seriously need to connect with your *santi* to help you awaken."

My birthday present has turned out to be the best present I've ever received, and the most superb story I've ever heard.

"Oh, no." Reality kicks in. "What is the time, Lizabethe?"

"I don't know. I don't own a ticking prison."

"My dad is going to shoot me. I have to go, but I'll come past next time I'm in Bristol."

"No worries, dearie."

"Thank you so much for reading the story. I loved it. Toodle pip."

"Toodle pip."

I bolt towards King Street, panicking Dad is going to go off his head for keeping him waiting. I reach the Theatre Royal puffing, but he is nowhere in sight. I'm in so much trouble.

"Isola."

I turn and see Dad at the curb. He crooks his finger at me, motioning for me to come to him, and so I nervously walk.

"I finished work early, so I thought I'd try my luck at finding you."

Now I'm confused. "What's the time?"

"It's around one o'clock."

"But it can't be." Annabell's story went for well over an hour.

"Going by my watch, it's ten past one. Is everything okay with you?"

"Yeah, I just thought I was late."

"No, you're not late. Where is your shopping?"

"I couldn't find anything I liked."

"You're better off saving your money for something important, anyway."

"You're right, Dad." Like a boat fare back to Fortier.

***

Trealla enters her kitchen, drawing her blind halfway, blocking out the afternoon heat, then hears a call.

"Hello, Lizabethe. I expected to hear from you," Trealla answers, slyly giggling.

"You're a very cheeky woman, Trealla," Lizabethe replies, bemused, peering out her front window on to Bramble Street. "You could have forewarned me before you sent someone that ambiguous to have a reading." Lizabethe makes her point loud and clear, looking out her window onto Bramble Street, unable to focus her attention.

"You don't need warning; you've been a Storyteller for hundreds of years," Trealla replies, with a hint of humour, turning on her coffee machine.

"Well, yes, but you could have at least given me the heads-up before sending someone as special as Isola my way. I knew she was gifted when she first came here, but not as gifted as I found out today. I'm out of breath just thinking about it."

"So, you'd already met Isola?" Trealla raises her eyebrows and tone of voice.

"Yes. I came home and found her warming her hands at my fire the first day she arrived. She thought she was in a bookstore and I was a customer."

"That's funny." Trealla laughs, placeing a cup under the spout of the machine. "So why are you in such a tizz? It's not as if she is the first Muklee drawn to Bramble Street."

"Because after reading to her, I now see how ambiguous she is. I've never met anyone so powerfully gifted, yet so humanly present. It doesn't make sense." Lizabethe paces back and forth, with her hand on her heart, flabbergasted, while Trealla casually takes the first sip of her cappuccino.

"I'm telling you now, Trealla, all the wisdom in the world won't unravel Isola's presence on earth. I doubt she'll ever awaken and create her gift in this lifetime."

"Have some faith in her. She's obviously more powerful than the human heart she chose to reside in, else she would never have chosen it in the first place." Trealla takes a less dramatic approach.

"I hope so. Isola is going to need it to break through her first chapter. I'm glad she has you guiding her. She's going to need it."

"Isola will be fine."

"*Mmm,* we'll see," she mutters. "I know I shouldn't say this, although I'm certain you already sensed something ancient about her but, by golly, you should have seen her ancestry, Trealla. It's stunning. Absolutely stunning." Lizabethe looks over to her special collection of books.

"When she first came here to Avenlee, I could see a rather colorful ancestry."

"Trealla, her ancestry is so colorful I thought a rainbow had exploded in my lounge."

Trealla smiles winsomely. "Wow! I just knew she was special."

"Oh, she's very special, very ancient, even archaic. I was wondering, Trealla, do you think she could be the One?" she says, tenatively.

Trealla almost spills her coffee, surprised by Lizabethe's foolish comment. "Don't be ridiculous, Lize."

"But look at her ancestry."

"That doesn't make her the One."

"True, but her ancestry dates back to Tyrian."

"So does mine, and I'm not the One." Trealla's heightened pitch reinforces her reply.

"I guess you're right, Trealla. Her ancestry just has me beguiled." Lizabethe falls back onto her couch.

"Very beguiled, I'd say, Lize. Don't get me wrong, I'm just as fascinated by how unique Isola is, but it's her fortitude that interests me over her ambiguity."

"You've taken a special interest in Isola, haven't you?"

Trealla places her delicate hand over her heart. "Anyone brave enough to choose a head and heart as powerful as hers intrigues me. And knowing her ancestry is as colorful as mine intrigues me even more. Can you imagine how powerful a woman Isola will be when she moves into her second and third chapters?"

"Maybe half as powerful as you."

"Thanks, Lize."

"You're welcome, Pachamama. I'd better be off, but remember, next time you send someone like Isola my way, please let me know beforehand."

Trealla shakes her head, gazing out to her fig tree. "I doubt there will be anyone as special as Isola gracing my valley in this lifetime."

Lizabethe smiles modestly. "True. But keep it in mind for the next life, cheeky woman."

Chapter Fourteen

After a tedious week at school, Saturday morning finally arrives. I spend all of two minutes concentrating on my breathing. Today, I have someplace breathtaking to be—Avenlee.

I arrive and see Trealla pruning the plant on her veranda while singing along with Dean Martin's "When You're Smiling."

"Hello, there," I gently say, not wanting to startle her.

"Ah, the little ray of light returns."

"Of course I've returned. I never wanted to leave."

"Someone's fallen in love with Avenlee, have they?"

"It was love at first sight, Trealla."

"Understandably so."

She gives me three kisses. I'm getting the knack of maneuvering my head from side to side, to receive and return.

"Why do Europeans give three kisses?"

"One's from Greece, one's from Spain, and the other from Austria."

"Really?"

"No, I'm joking. I've heard it's based on the notion of the three fates, with each kiss representing past, present and future. I've also heard it's an ancient custom that represents the sun, the earth and the moon. But I personally think Europeans just like to kiss a lot. I call it a triplet of kisses."

"Americans never kiss like that."

"Yes, I remember."

"Of course. I forget you're originally from America."

"So do I. That was many moons ago. Have a seat, Isola. It's beautiful out here today. I'll pour you a cold drink. You must be thirsty after your big bike ride."

"A drink would be great, thanks."

She steps inside while I walk out to the fig tree to have a rest on a seat.

Walking back out towards me she looks so pleased to have me here, which is comforting. "Here you go, hun."

I grab the glass of water. "Thanks. Oh, and I must also thank you for my birthday present. Wow! That was some gift. I'm still bewildered by the experience."

"I thought you might like it."

"Like it! I absolutely loved it. It's the most magical experience of my life, and I've been to Disneyland."

"It is quite fascinating the way Lizabethe's collection of books come to life. She sure is a gifted Storyteller."

"That she is. When I closed my eyes and stepped into 1818, I was blown away. I've never felt emotions like that in all my life."

She sits down beside me. "I was just as overwhelmed when I heard my first. I thought I'd gone insane, seeing things with my eyes closed and feeling another woman's emotions. I even contemplated going to see a psychiatrist afterwards." She chuckles

"That's so funny. I was thinking the same thing, and that was before I stepped foot inside Lizabethe's front door. I've been experiencing a lot of kooky things on this path of mine."

"Don't you worry. You're not going insane. You're perfectly normal. Everything around you just seems kooky for now. Trust me, one day the kooky will be normal and your present-day normal will be kooky. Enjoy the mystery of your first chapter, because next time you go to see Lizabethe, or a different Storyteller, to hear the second chapter, your perception of their stories will never be the same again."

"Are there other Storytellers like Lizabethe?"

"There's a scarce number of Storytellers who have special collections of books like hers."

"Has Lizabethe read Annabell's story to you?"

"I don't believe so." She shakes her head.

"Oh, you should read this one, Trealla. You'd love it. There's so much about plants and nature in it, and her essential oils were displayed beautifully, like yours. I can still smell them now. Oh, and you should have seen Annabell's apothecary garden."

"Wait until you see mine." She looks out the corner of her eye.

"You have one here?"

"Well, of course I do, love. That's were I make all my oils."

"Still, you have to go see Annabell's. I know you'll love it."

"Maybe one day I'll go visit Lize when I find the time."

"As I understand, it doesn't take long at all. Annabell's first chapter went for all of fifteen minutes, even though it felt like I was living it in real time."

"Really? It's been a long time since I've heard a story. I can't remember how long they take."

I'm sure she knows. She just doesn't want to elaborate.

"I'm happy you liked your birthday present, and it stirred up your imagination."

"Oh, it did. My *layleasta* had a jump start, thanks to you and Lizabethe."

"That's great to hear." She taps on my knee.

"Can I ask why she calls you Pachamama?"

Trealla grins, shaking her head. "Because she's a mischievous lady, that's why."

"What does it mean?"

"In Inca mythology, Pachamama is the fertility goddess who lives beneath the clouds and presides over planting and harvesting."

"So Pachamama is like Mother Nature."

"Yes, she is, but I'm not Mother Nature. I'm a guest walking in her earthly garden."

"That's a nice way to put it."

"We're all guests on Mother Nature's fertile home. Now, we'd best get a move on. We have a big day ahead of us. Let me show you to your room so you can put your bag away."

***

Trealla's staircase belongs in a hotel lobby, with its carved handrails and shallow, carpeted steps. The long hallway at the top of the steps is flanked by walls loaded with large photographs of trees. It looks like an art gallery rather than a hall.

"Who are the people sitting in these pictures?"

"They're called Green Seeds. They're the caretakers of the species of tree they're sitting beneath, holding their baskets. Their purpose is to keep their species of tree growing healthy and happy."

"Do they belong to some sort of gardening society?"

"I guess you could say that." She inwardly chuckles, but fails to elaborate.

"Do you have a species of tree you take care of, Trealla?"

"Not exactly. I am the caretaker of the ground they grow in."

"Gee, that's one heck of a job."

"It's not a job, it's an honor. It's the harvest of my heart to nurture the earth."

I point. "What tree is this one? I recognize it."

"This tree is the largest growing species in the world. It's called the Giant Sequoia, but its original name is Wawona, or *toos-pung-ish*. The Green Seed's name standing underneath is Washita."

"Look at her green eyes. They look like sparkling emeralds."

"Every one of these Green Seeds has green eyes," Trealla says as if it were completely normal.

"But how do they all have the same colored eyes?"

"I guess they were born with them."

I waste no time probing for a logical explanation. I move along to the next picture frame.

"Who is this lady?"

"That's Etta, and her seed is the *Prunus avium*, which is the sweet cherry tree. Her sister Ella is the Green Seed for another variety of cherry tree called *Prunus cerasus*, which is the sour cherry tree. If you ever meet them, don't get them mixed up. Etta gets very upset when her sweetness is confused with her sister's sourness."

"I'll keep that in mind."

"Etta and Ella are actually Lizabethe's sisters."

"Really?" I can't imagine having two sisters. "Oh, look, it's a hazelnut tree," I say, looking to the next picture,

"Yes, and this is the exquisite Sofia I told you about."

"She is stunning." I admire the woman's seductive amazon-green eyes and long, shiny dark hair. "Does Sofia still live in Italy?"

"Yes, six feet beneath the soil, wearing her wooden pajamas."

"Oh," I say, not sure how to reply to Trealla's "wooden-pajamas" analogy of death.

"Come along, Isola, you can look at the rest of these tonight. Let me show you to your room."

I follow her into a sunlit room perfumed by fresh flowers on the bedside table.

"This is lovely, Trealla." I place my bag down.

"I had a feeling you would like it. It's fresh and full of light, just like you. Now let's head outside and ground ourselves for the day."

"Can I first pick an oil to wear today?"

"Well, of course you can. Let's go see which one resonates with you today."

***

Outside, I follow Trealla, sniffing the frankincense on my wrists. I've picked well today. Trealla takes her shoes off and looks up to the sun, closing her eyes.

"What are we doing, Trealla?"

"We're plugging into the All. Take your shoes off and join me."

"Okay, what do I do?"

"Be just like a tree," she says, tranquilly.

"A tree." I look over to her, muddled.

"Let your energy fall through your feet into the earth like the roots of a tree, absorbing all the rich nutrients. Then let the life-giving energy from above trickle through you like a gift from nature. Now be still... When a thought comes your way, don't take it personal, just let it pass through like the wind passing through the branches of a tree. Now, breathe." She exerts her breath in and out, calming me even more.

Around five minutes later, Trealla takes a final deep breath in and out. "How did you go?"

"Oh, I need to be like a tree more often."

"Every morning, preferably. Now, we can get on with the day. Pop your shoes back on, love, and walk with me."

"Gladly."

We make our way into the garden, having energetically set our selves up for the day.

"So, did you come up with a theme?" Trealla jumps right in.

"I did. I've been inspired by Annabell. The lead character from the book that Lizabethe read to me."

"Tell me about this woman who inspired you." She looks across to me.

"Annabell lived in England and owned an apothecary. She grew all the plants, herbs, and spices in her garden that she worked with."

"So, it was a medicinal garden."

"Yes, her garden was very unique. She groups her plants according to their medicinal properties, with flowers like marigolds mixed through to keep the insects away."

"Sounds like my kind of garden. Tell me more," she says, directing me with her hand to turn right.

"Well, when I asked you what the couple was like who are joining hands, you said they're quite a spicy couple who complemented each other's differences and came together beautifully."

"Wow, you were paying attention."

"In knowing this, and experiencing Annabell's herb and spice garden, I imagined a garden that stimulates two different senses, yet complements each other's differences, just like the couple joining hands."

"*Mmm*, what two senses?"

"Taste and smell."

"Keep on going."

She sounds intrigued, thank goodness. "I imagined an interactive garden full of fragrant and edible plants paired together to create an interactive garden. Say, for example, we can plant tomatoes next to fragrant basil, and mint next to snow peas, and so on."

She turns her head my way. "And you were doubting your imagination. You've come up with a brilliant theme for the Sakrid. An embodiment of aroma and taste. It will be a flavor *festa*."

"Really? You're not just saying that to be nice?"

"I wouldn't be being nice if I lied to you, would I?"

"I guess not. Well, then, it's great to know you're happy with my idea. I spent all week at school planning it."

"Who said school is a waste of time? It's come in handy, after all."

"It has this week. I even managed to write Sation a letter in my English class."

"Time well spent, I say."

"I'm relieved you like my idea. I've been so stressed."

"A garden that interacts with our senses is a fantastic idea. We can even add complementary flowers to interact with people's sense of sight, and some musicians to stimulate the guests' sense of sound. My layleasta is running wild with ideas. It's going to take a lot of preparation to choose the correct plants that complement each other, not to mention getting them to flourish at the same time."

"This is where all your knowledge could step in, Pachamama." I smile cheekily.

"I guess Pachamama will have to. It's not a straightforward project."

"Do you think the couple joining hands will like my idea?"

"Well, given they're Green Seeds, I know they will."

"What trees do they care for?"

"Laurel cares for her *Cinnamomum verum*, and Cobiac cares for his *Malus baccata*, which is a species of apple tree."

"Apples and cinnamon complement each other." I smile.

"Why do you think I said your idea is fantastic?"

"Wow, I'm on the right theme trail, aren't I?"

"You sure are, love. I even think there're a few wild apple trees growing down by the river to eat from, and we can ask Laurel to bring some of her quality cinnamon."

"That's a great idea, Trealla. Rather than having toffy apples, the guests can pick apples off the trees and roll them into sugared cinnamon. That's very flavorsome."

"Before we get too enthusiastic about which plants to grow, an important step must be taken care of first: the soil. We need it as rich and fertile in order to get the results we want."

"Whereabouts are we to grow the garden?"

"Down past the Boulevard, towards the back of Avenlee. We're heading there now."

Trealla doesn't have to ask me twice. My stride increases, excited to see more of Avenlee. I've only seen a snippet of it so far, and my mind boggles as to what is to come. Trealla collects her wheelbarrow and we step onto a path that has a sign reading *Kore Forest.*

"I saw that sign on a different path last weekend, when I was looking for you."

"Oh, there are a lot of paths in this valley leading to the original Kore Forest. However, this path is the main one. Come have a look, you're going to love it."

Trees arch overhead, creating a tunnel effect as the well-worn path dips and wanders aimlessly into the rich green forest. Not only is this forest dramatically picturesque, it also exudes a romanticized atmosphere. Its evergreen charm makes me feel I'm walking into a fictional Sherwood Forest. Any minute now, Robin Hood's going to come walking along, hand in hand with his Maid Marian.

"This forest is old. Did you name it after a heroine or goddess?"

"It was named long before me. There are numerous Kore Forests around the world, and variations of the name, like Kali, Kora, Kauri and Kher. Legend has it the name derives from women linked to the Eleusinian Mysteries, but I know Kore is the name for the universal female spirit that roamed the vast lands long before our oldest known ancestors walked the earth."

"What are the Eleusinian Mysteries?"

"It was a gathering that historians believe it took place around 1500 BC in ancient Greece, but I know it predates that by thousands of years."

"Wow, that is a long time ago."

"Yes, a long time ago, when women were worshipped in ancient cultures as the all-pervading Kores of nature. Women who lived and nurtured these vast forests and were worshipped by all for their caretaking abilities."

"I love hearing all this history, but it's hard to believe women were once worshipped or owned land."

"Let me enlighten you on some buried history. Egyptian women were once in complete control of their lands, which descended from mother to daughter. There were even female pharaohs. Matrikadevis, a Hindu primal matriarch, governed her ancestral tribes, and Japan was called the Land of Queens. The powerful Kores and derivatives of that name can be found throughout ancient cultures, right back to the original aboriginals of the land. So, women once held their ground and were primary caretakers of this beautiful earth," she passionately says, brushing her hand gently across the face of a tree as she passes it.

"Wow, I didn't know that. I love it."

"In early civilization, people accepted that women who bear the fruit know best how to nurture and nourish life. Women were created with a womb and the ability to give birth to all that lived. And all that lived worshipped that which gave them life. So, women were naturally the custodial owners of the fertile earth and respected caretakers of all living energy. As was recorded in ancient text, all living kind suckled from the breast of the goddess."

"What happened then? Women don't own anything anymore and are hardly respected."

"That is a whole other story that I'm not getting into," she said, raising the tone of her voice.

"Please explain. You have tickled that nostalgic part in my brain that needs to know more."

She stops walking and turns to me. "I will say this much. Women have the greatest gift in the world, a fertile womb that creates and gives birth to life, and breasts to feed it. But somewhere along the way, this powerful gift made men feel inferior. The only way man could gain power over this gift was to dominate the species that have it. Now, a millennium later, we no longer worship the wombs of the world. Instead, we worship a male god, a father and his son, and the many denominations men took on in his greed to overpower the nature of life in female bodies. Women don't own anything because they can't fulfil their full potential in the nature of life. They don't own anything because they don't own themselves or their power. They're dominated by a society of wounded men who use their strength to control what they feel inferior too."

"Wounded men. I've never heard that before."

"Yes, some men are wounded, on a profound level. Their need to dominate comes from fear of inadequacy and the inability to connect to their role in the nature of life. These wounds inflict injustice to all because this fear puts everything out of balance. And balance in the the nature of life is everything. If only they could reconnect with their role in the nature of life and know how honorable and important their masculine role is, they would fear nothing of the feminine role and they would heal."

"So they have disconnected from their role in nature. That's sad."

"Yes, most of society has disconnected. Humans need to start honoring the nature of life in all. There is no superior sex, species, or race. Life is the greatest power, and that power is found in every human heart. Therefore, we are all equal. We just have different roles to fulfill to continue the cycle of life, peacefully. When we honor our role in ourselves and one another, we will live in harmony on earth again. Now, let's continue walking." She nudges her head forward.

"You're so wise. I wish I knew as much as you."

"When you know your innate self, all will be known. Now I could go on forever about the nature of life and my love for the Kores and the earth, but if I do, our new garden will never come about. Let's get a move on."

As we continue along the forest path, our conversation floods my mind, indulging my nostalgic personality. If I didn't love Sation, I'd dive heart-first into awakening and immerse in the truth of my kind. Trealla and Lizabethe are so intriguing. I've never met anyone like them.

Actually, I never knew women like this exist.

We come upon a small timber cottage with a front veranda and a flowering garden surrounding it.

"Who lives here?"

"No one at the moment. I use it as a little retreat. It's like my little getaway in the middle of the forest. I light the fire and cozy on up in the feather bed with a novel, listening to the rain tinkering on the tin roof. It's delightful, but so too is the Boulevard of Boutiques. Come along."

Further along the track, we cross over an old footbridge with a steady stream of water flowing under it. Moments later, the path opens to a quaint French-style province lined with ornamental trees and Parisian streetlamps arching over the road. I feel like I've stepped out of Sherwood Forest and into Paris in the 1900s.

"Welcome to the petite Boulevard of Boutiques."

"Oh, it's gorgeous. Never would I have thought this path would lead to a little French province."

"You just never know where some paths might lead you. Especially the natural ones." She grins, then continues walking into the Boulevard, pushing her wheelbarrow.

"It's so pretty and French-looking."

"That it is, *mademoiselle*. In ancient times, this part of the forest is where gatherings took place. Then around the year 1200, a little township was built, and it became known as the Kore Shire."

"How did it get its Parisian appeal?"

"About two hundred years ago, a French dame came here and spruced the place up, leaving her French touch on the Boulevard. It's been called the Boulevard of Boutiques ever since. This little province is now used for functions, fairs, and celebrations like the Sakrid. We will be using it for Laurel and Cobiac's Sakrid. All the guests will stay at the Bellisente Hotel, which is the double-story building up here on the corner."

I look over and read *Bellisente Hotel* painted in busy French script on the wall. The classy-looking hotel has flowerpots under the window sills and decorative lanterns adhered to the stone walls. A royal blue building with a lime-green vine crawling across the front wall catches my eye too. "Is that a hair salon?" I ask, after reading *Salon de Silver* on the side wall.

"No, dear. Originally, a salon was a gathering place for social exchange. People would meet and talk about contemporary literature and philosophies back in the fifteenth century. It was all the rage back then. We still host gatherings here from time to time, and book festivals."

"So, I can't get my hair cut here?"

"Definitely not, but you will find interesting things inside, like musical instruments, *La Carte de Tendre,* and plenty of paintings of *salonnières.*"

"Can I look through the window quickly?"

"Sure you can. Next time you're here, you can go next door to the apothecary too. Actually, we will be there most weekends."

"Fantastic."

Stepping under the veranda, I peer through the window and see a long corner bar and a grand piano. The walls are covered with paintings of all the salonnières, as Trealla mentioned.

"Can you see that gold frame with the map inside it?"

"Yes, I can."

"The next time we come back, you might find it interesting. It's called *La Carte de Tendre.* Written in the fifteenth century, it's an imaginary land of tenderness from a novel called *Clelie.* It's a map drawn from a woman's point of view, to educate a man on how to win her heart, or lose it, if he doesn't follow it. It was created to teach men gallantry and walk them in the direction of a woman's heart." Trealla smiles. "It was a hot topic of conversation in the Parisian salon days. But I guess a lot of things have changed in the dating world since then."

"I imagine they have."

"You still might find it interesting."

"The entire Boulevard is interesting."

"Well, hold onto that interest for another day, my dear. Our new garden awaits." She beckons with her head to walk on.

Trealla and I pass by all the different boutiques. I can't wait to see this street alive at a festival or the Sakrid. We reach the end of the Boulevard and the path weaves back into the Kore Forest. Five minutes later, we come to a hodgepodge paddock down by the river.

"Finally, we're here," Trealla says with her hands on her hips, looking around. "This is where we're going to create the garden."

How on earth are we going to make this area hitched worthy? I look around in doubt, then out of the corner of my eye, I spot an undomesticated-looking guy down by the river. He looks like a hunter in need of a shower and shave.

"Trealla, look, there's a man trespassing in your garden."

"Where?"

"There, look, look." I point. "How dare he hunt here? I hope he hasn't killed any ducks."

Trealla looks at me oddly. "Anyone would think you have never seen a man before."

"That's not a man. That's a Neanderthal. A trespassing Neanderthal."

"He's not actually trespassing. I asked him to come here and help us." She puts me in my place.

"You know him?"

"Yes, I do. We're going to need his muscles and horticulture knowledge."

"Knowledge. I doubt there is anything knowledgeable about him."

"Don't go judging a book by its cover. Come meet him, Isola, he's around your age. You might get along."

"I'm happy to stay here." I cross my arms.

"He's not going to drag you into the woods and eat you. He's my friend."

"I don't know about that. He looks a little too carnivorous for my liking."

She chuckles at me. "Suit yourself."

Trealla greets him with a triplet of kisses, which he fluently receives and returns, surprising me.

"Hello, love, how have you been?"

"I'm very well, thank you, Trealla." He smiles enthusiastically.

Wow. An American accent, and he has manners. I wasn't expecting either of those traits.

"Is this the spot?" He looks around, sizing it up.

"Yes, this is it. What do you think, Emerson?"

He scoops up a handful of soil, feeling it in his hand. Then, oddly, he brings his hand to his nose.

"I think it has potential." He nods numerous times.

"Great, that's what I thought, too. Wait until you hear about the garden theme we have planned."

"I have no doubt it's going to look Trealla-terrific." He smiles, then turns my way. "I see you have brought in another set of hands," he says, jutting out his strong jawline in my direction.

"She's more than a set of hands. Come meet her." Trealla takes him by the hand and walks towards me. "Let me introduce you to each other. Isola, this is Emerson and Emerson, this is Isola."

"Hello, Isola." He lifts his cap, unveiling more scruffy brown hair, and his dark brown eyes.

"Hi, Emerson."

"Isola just moved here from America," Trealla explains.

"Welcome to sunny England."

"Thanks."

"Dear Emerson lives over the mountain on the next property and has a wealth of landscaping skills and horticulture knowledge, along with a good dose of stamina." She pats his jacket, boosting his ego.

"Well, it looks like this paddock is in need of both of Emerson's skills," I reply. However, I wish we didn't need his help. I selfishly want to work away with Trealla on my own.

"Whereabouts in America are you from, Emerson?" I'm guessing, from his eager heartland smile, he's from the Midwest.

"Southampton. I know, it doesn't look it. I once surfed and had a killer tan. Now I garden in layers of clothing."

"I never would have picked you to be a wave slider from the Hamptons."

"I've molded to my surroundings. You'd have to be a California girl with that tan and long blonde hair."

"Wrong coast. I'm from the Sunshine State."

"A Floridian. And you moved here. Isn't everyone moving to Florida for the industrial boom?"

"My dad's lucrative gains in Florida are what brought us to the UK. But that's a tender subject I'm trying my best to get over."

"Sounds like a sore spot."

"Yes, it hurts every time I think about Florida."

"Well, I won't touch on it anymore."

Chapter Fifteen

Trealla informs Emerson of the garden theme and then all three of us get busy working. First, we clear the area of fallen branches and overgrown shrubs. Then, Trealla steps out a rough border while Emerson hammers in the pegs and ties the string line while doing juvenile things like trying to balance the hammer on his head. Now, he's walking on the chalk line pretending to walk on a tightrope. I'm doing my best to ignore his childish antics, but it's not easy. Luckily for me, it isn't long before we're digging over the dirt and Emerson slips into landscaping mode. Trealla isn't wrong. He does have a good dose of stamina. He's made more progress than Trealla and I put together.

We wind up the day, only making a small dent in the preparations. I've never worked this physically hard in all my life. I can't even find the energy to walk back to the manor, so Emerson's pushing me in the wheelbarrow. I drag my heavy legs up Trealla's grand staircase to my room and crash out hard.

***

Waking up to the sun shining in my eyes, I hear traditional Irish tin whistles, fiddles and a merry Gaelic voice. What the heck is going on downstairs?

I hop out of bed and every muscle in my body is making me regret working so hard yesterday. I enter the kitchen to find Trealla dancing to Irish music with flour all over herself. Here I am, in England, with an American-born woman who looks European and speaks Italian, listening to Irish music in her French kitchen. She is the worldliest woman I know.

"Top o' ye morning ter ya, me wee Leprechaun friend. Wud yer be wantin' County Galway's finest Oirish soda bread, then?" she says, turning the music down.

"I'd love some please, Trealla." I giggle at her accent.

"Yer canny be callin' me such tings. Why, Grace O'Malley is me name then. Oi cum from Connaught an oi tink they might be callin yer Molly O'Malley then."

"Molly O'Malley." I chuckle at my new name.

"We just after being called Grace and Molly O'Malley, den so 'tiz. Now be puttin dat green cap on yisser noggin an me bread 'ill be sure ter be sure, tasting even the better so."

"Are you celebrating something this morning?"

"Yes, dear. Tat I'm alive, tat's as good a reason I be needing."

"Fair enough."

So, with the traditional Irish melodies playing in the background, on goes my green cap and I know myself to be Molly O'Malley from Connaught, sitting across the table from Grace O'Malley, enjoying County Galway's finest Oirish soda bread.

Trealla pours a nip of Paddy's whisky into her glass of coffee then adds a dash of cream and takes a sip. She licks the cream off her lips, looking pleased with her brew.

"You better run along after breakfast and get dressed. Emerson will be here soon."

"He's here again today?" I gripe, slumping in my chair.

"Don't sound so thrilled, Molly O'Malley. The man knows lashings about gardening. You will learn a lot from him."

"I already have and that's to steer clear of hairy, immature nineteen-year-old boys."

My comment makes Trealla laugh.

"You'll get used to one another."

"Or we'll strangle one another."

"Let's get the garden planted first, then you can strangle one another. Now, before he gets here, we'd best go outside and ground ourselves to the earth like we did yesterday."

"Yay, let's go and be like a tree." I jump to my feet.

***

As we're putting our shoes back on, Emerson arrives, looking much the same Neanderthal way as yesterday. Trealla grabs a pen and piece of paper to write down all the plants we decide on today, and then we're off. Trealla's vegetable garden is the most obvious place to start finding aromatic and tasty plants. We go around detecting the heavily scented plants and adding them to the list, which so far consists of lemongrass, anise, hyssop and basil. Then we pick plants for their taste. Trealla writes down calendula, mint, passionfruit and oregano.

Trealla and Emerson hand me all sorts of herbs to taste. I've been rubbing leaves between the palms of my hands to release the aroma. Emerson breaks a stem from a plant and hands it to me.

"Here, try this, Isola. It tastes sweet like honey. We can add it to the list."

"What's it called?"

"Celandine."

I lick some of the yellow juice from the stem while Emerson looks on, awaiting my reaction.

"Oh my God. That's disgusting." The offensive bitterness screws my face up. I spit it out, trying to get rid of the pungent taste, while Emerson holds his belly in fits of laughter.

"What did you give her, Emerson?"

"Poison, that's what he's given me."

"I'm not that nasty. It's just a little bit of celandine," he says, with a prankster look in his eye.

"Oh, Emerson, that stuff's vile," Trealla says, placing her hand on my back to console me.

"Why is that plant even growing in your herb garden, then?"

"It's good for sore eyes."

"I guess I won't be getting sore eyes anytime soon," I grumble, still spitting.

"Here, have some parsley. It will take away the bad taste."

"I'll pass. You got me once. You're not getting me twice." I shake my head firmly at him.

"He's being serious this time, Isola. The parsley will help take the taste away," Trealla says.

She passes it to me. Cautiously, I nibble on it. Thankfully, it helps.

By the end of the afternoon, we have a rough list of plants filling both columns, but further discussion will have to wait until next weekend. It is late and I have to be home before dark. Turning seventeen hasn't granted me any moonlight time. My father is still honoring his role as commander of control here in England. Maybe even more lately, since his control over me is weakening now I'm spending so much time at Avenlee. He's definitely a wounded man.

***

I arrive at Avenlee the following Friday excited to spend my first full weekend here. Trealla and I are distilling bergamot tomorrow morning, then planting the majority of the trees in the Sakrid garden and, on Sunday, she is taking me to Bristol to meet with Lizabethe. All three of us are going to the flicks to see Elizabeth Taylor play Cleopatra. But first we have to get planting. We have three hundred and fifteen days until the joining of the hands, so it's going to be all-hands-on-deck.

***

Oh my, did those three hundred and fifteen days fly by, working at Avenlee. I've become Mother Nature's most observant guest, captivated by earth's procession around the sun and the changes that coincide. Such a simplistic forward motion results in such phenomena, it blows my mind.

Each day I spend with Trealla, I spend in awe, in balance, and grounded to my very core. Together, we experience the crisp sounds of winter, the evoking energy in spring, the balmy smell of summer and the harvest at year's end. Who would have thought the highlight of my week would be hanging out in a garden with a woman twice my age? A woman whom I now consider the heroine of my heart.

We've hosted three weddings in the garden of La Lilliana, an exhibition at the Bellisente Hotel, a literature festival in the Boulevard, and the massive hazelnut festival showcasing Trealla's homegrown nuts. I've worn every plant oil in her glass bottles, and I've slept in eight rooms at the manor. However, the room Trealla picked for me on my first night turns out to be my favorite.

With a lot of hard work, the Sakrid garden has turned into a masterpiece. I'm convinced Trealla tweaked the rate at which it's grown with her Pachamama magic. She bought several established trees, but as for the rest of the garden's growth, well, it is off the charts. All the trees are almost fully grown and bearing fruit.

Even Emerson is amazed at how quickly it's grown. He questioned Trealla a few months back, and she gave him the same nonsensical response. "Trees grow themselves." Well, yes, they do. But not at this rate.

I've accepted I won't get answers for everything that takes place at Avenlee and I've grown to enjoy the mystery of it. Speaking of mystery, I have written around five letters to Sation without receiving one reply, which is rather disappointing. Did he receive them? Or is my father keeping his replies?

Luckily, I've been too busy with Trealla to feel the full sting of Sation's silence. I have, however, kept in touch with a friend, Jane, back home. It's nice to catch up, but Jane doesn't know Sation or that we were even seeing one another. I'd kept it hush-hush, so I can't ask her to speak with him. Anyway, Jane is too busy writing about the awful assassinations back home and asking me if I've seen the Beatles. She presumes they walk down the street for me to bump into. The U.K. is a big place, Jane, and I live in a small town, miles from a major city. The only "Beatles" I see are in the garden at Avenlee.

Dad hates the fact I've become so independent. He's looked for any reason to cut back my time at Avenlee. So, I made sure I was home before the sunset and made certain all my grades were good, so he has no reason to stop me from going to Avenlee. Mom and Dad will be pleased with my exam results. I passed them with ease last month. I've almost finished senior year, which they call "final year" in the UK. Dad's been hassling me to choose a university. Um, sorry, Dad. I won't be here.

At times, Mom brought Julia out on weekends to visit. Julia spent the whole time looking for animals in the garden. Mom and Trealla also catch up through the week.

Lizabethe came to stay on the odd occasion. I find her whimsical personality so entertaining. It's fair to say not much gardening occurs on the weekends she visited. I listen to Lizabethe and Trealla tell stories of days gone by, wishing I'd been part of them. They speak of archaic cultures and historical structures I can't wait to visit. We laughed and danced to music down at the Boulevard. Lizabethe's playful approach to life may be fanciful to some, but it appeals to me. She has not a worry in the world and, if one presented, I'm sure she would pull a funny face at it and send it on its way.

Aside from these visitors, Trealla and me are the only ones at Avenlee. Oh, and how can I forget the annoying Neanderthal? Emerson's been here more often than not. Especially when we needed muscle in the mountains. We now tolerate each other, like Trealla said we'd grow to, or maybe I've just become accustomed to enduring his juvenile ways.

Surprisingly, I've learned a lot from Emerson, like if I want to yield perfect vegetables, I have to plant by the phases of the moon and sow the seeds at the right time of the day. So, if I intend on growing vegetables above the ground, like broccoli or tomatoes, I have to sow them with the rising sun, to bring them up and out of the earth. But if I want to plant a patch of potatoes or carrots that grow under the ground, then they have to be planted with the setting sun, as it sinks into the horizon. He even knows weird things like if his mom's cat is rubbing up against a tree, it means rain is on its way. His favorite saying is, "The higher the clouds, the finer the weather; the lower the clouds, expect shitty weather." Nine times out of ten, he's right. But the most important piece of knowledge I've picked up from Emerson is: never accept anything from him to eat. His celandine stunt left a lasting impression on my taste buds. Just the thought of that vile plant makes me wince, to this day.

It seems my history of human thinking dominates any chance of me awakening. Therefore, my second chapter remains a mystery and so, too, does Annabell's. I figure seventeen-plus years of thinking of myself as Isola Destinn is going to take just as long to unthink. Although I haven't given it my all. In fact, if I'm completely honest, I've done my best not to awaken. Apart from grounding myself every day, I make sure the human thought society remains a prominent part of my day. This hasn't taken my fears of awakening away. Truthfully, I feel like a ticking time bomb. At any minute, my final awakening can end life as I know it.

I've still grown as a person and made positive changes. I'm definitely no longer the resentful Isola, forced to leave Fortier. Now, I'm a reverent guest at Mother Nature's home, grounding myself and fulfilling my feminine role as a modern-day Kore. Trealla's ancient wisdom has me honoring the nature of life within me and all around me. I've learned about the heroines she named her gardens after, and other amazing women of the past.

It seems everything at Avenlee revolves around the sun, the moon, the stars, and color. On the odd occasion when a luminous rainbow appears in the sky, Trealla becomes overwhelmed with excitement, stopping everything she's doing to marvel at the triumphant, colorful arch in the sky.

Another colorful phenomenon to be admired at Avenlee is the seasonal changing of Rimsky birds. In the past year, I've watched Trealla's cute little birdies change from sky-blue to fall-red, from orange in winter to hot pink in spring, and now they have turned sky-blue again, just like the first time I walked down *la via dell'amore* a year ago. Which lets me know it is the season to sail on home to Sation. I know Trealla hoped I'd awaken in her valley and stay forever, and I gave it considerate thought, but looking at Sation looking back at me is still my favorite place to be.

Now, on the eve of Avenlee's event of the year, I'm laying in bed with a tummy full of guilt, unable to fall asleep. I decided months ago that disappearing from England without saying goodbye to anyone is my safest option. Everyone will try to stop me if they know, none more so than my father, and I'm not having him dictate my future.

So, I've decided to slip away without a trace and sail back to the man I love. Unfortunately, that means I sadly have to sail away from the woman and world I've grown to love.

Chapter Sixteen

The eagerly awaited day has arrived. Trealla and I are busy completing the final touches on the garden and hear crunching footsteps emerging from the Forest. We both look and see a transformed Emerson heading towards us, in a suave light-blue shirt and cotton pants. What's dropped my jaw, though, is the absence of his hair. Some barber had a decent workout to reveal this fresh-faced Emerson.

"Close your mouth, Isola, before you start dribbling."

"Surely that can't be the same hairy Neanderthal I've known for the past twelve months."

"It sure is. Wow, Emerson, you look amazing," Trealla comments as he enters the garden.

"Thanks. What do you think of my new outfit?" He turns in a circle of confidence, showing off his threads.

"I love the color of your shirt. You look classy indeed. Don't you think so, Isola?"

"It's about time you had a shower and shave, Emerson."

"Someone's already taken their smart-aleck pills this morning. You really are a—"

"Ah, ah, ah." Trealla swiftly cuts him off. "Must you two always be so belligerent towards each other? This garden is supposed to be a joyous, loving environment, especially today. Make me happy and be friendly towards one another."

"I can be friendly towards Isola, watch this."

Emerson reaches forward and scoops me up and over his shoulder like a sack of potatoes. Then starts running around the garden with me upside down.

"Put me down," I say, whacking my fists on his back.

"Not so sassy anymore, are you?"

"Put me down. This isn't being friendly."

"Yes, it is. See how much fun we're having?" He laughs, making the most of this moment.

"All the blood's rushing to my head."

He slows down and my head stops bouncing as hard. "I will put you down if you promise to be nice."

Trealla is too busy laughing to come to my rescue. I'm going to have to sort this out on my own.

"I promise I'll be nice," I begrudgingly reply.

He flips me over his shoulder and I topple onto my bottom.

"That was fun," he says, catching his breath, making Trealla laugh even more.

"Yes, I can't remember the last time I had so much fun," I gripe, giving him a rotten look.

"Now that you belligerent teens have that out of your systems, can you please be on your best behavior today?" Trealla pleads. "We don't want two people joining hands and you two strangling each other in the background."

"We will be on our best behavior, Trealla." Emerson takes the liberty of agreeing on both our behalfs. "Now, you ladies better run up to the house and get ready. It won't be long until the guests start arriving." Emerson acts sensibly all of a sudden.

"You're right, Emerson. I think I've completed everything I needed to. I've prepared the salon, opened all the windows in the hotel. I've told the little birdies to expect guests, and all the beds have been made at the Bellisente Hotel. Right, I think that's all I have to take care of. I guess everything's done then. Now take a moment to absorb what we've achieved. We turned a paddock into paradise." Trealla proudly takes in the picture-perfect view. "All that's left to do now is enjoy the celebrations."

She is right. I'm extremely proud of what we've achieved.

"We did good ladies, pat on the back to us," Emerson says with his chest held high.

"Yes, a huge pat on the back. Now, Emerson, I need you to head up to *la via dell'amore* and greet the guests when they arrive. That way, Isola and I can get ready."

"No worries, I'll head up to *la via dell'amore* now."

"Thanks, and please try to stay clean. You look handsome in that pressed blue shirt."

"I promise I'll be dirt-free for the day, Trealla. I'll see you ladies later. Remember what you promised, Isola." He winks at me and walks off.

As soon as he leaves, Trealla takes off her shoes and socks, prompting me to do the same.

"Let's ground ourselves in this delicious energy, then we can go get ready."

I'm definitely in need of some grounding after my joyride over Emerson's shoulders.

***

"Are you dressed?" Trealla asks, knocking on my bedroom door.

"Come in, I'm just putting my shoes on," I say, feeding the strap through the loop.

"Oh, Isola, that dress looks gorgeous on you. Pink really suits you."

"Thank you. You look extra beautiful in this orange outfit, and the oil you're wearing is divine. What is it?"

"It's a blend made from the garden of La Lilliana. Before we go outside, you can put some on, if you want."

"Yes, please."

"Now before we head outside, I need to inform you that Cobiac and Laurel are joining hands in the traditional Green Seed way, meaning it will be different from other weddings we've hosted at Avenlee."

"How different can a joining of the hands be, compared to a wedding?"

"Very different. Just be open to whatever comes your way. You're best off leaving your logical mind in this room and bringing your resourceful layleasta downstairs."

"Okay, I can do that." I sense some bewilderment coming my way.

Trealla reaches into her basket of fragrant gardenia flowers and places one behind my ear. “Perfect.” She smiles.

With her basket of flowers on one arm, and me on the other, we take our first step onto *la via dell'amore* to enjoy the event we have worked so hard to create. Halfway down, I make out around fifty guests gathered at the front gate. They're gorgeously dressed in garden-party outfits that are either orange, purple, yellow, blue, green or red.

“Gosh. How did they get so color-coordinated?”

“Every time we celebrate a Sakrid, we choose a single color from the rainbow to dress in.”

“Oh, no, that means I'm the odd one out. There's no pink in the rainbow.” I want to hide behind an elm tree in my fuchsia-pink dress.

“You look fantastic. Remember, pink is the color of love.”

“Yes, but I'm still going to stand out like a pink puff.”

“You're not the only one wearing pink today. Look up.” She points.

Hundreds of gorgeous pink-feathered birds ornament the trees. “But they were blue yesterday,” I say, confused.

“They changed color in honor of such a loving day,” she says, with her mysterious twinkle in her eye. “Remember, you left your logical mind in the room.” She reminds me to be open to anything and everything.

“At least I fit in with the animal kingdom's dress code.” I shrug my shoulders.

Walking towards the guests, I notice lots of them holding baskets.

“What do they have in all those baskets?”

“Most of the guests are Green Seeds, so they have brought their seeds and all the produce they have grown to share with everyone. You're in for a treat today.”

The guests soon notice Trealla walking towards them. They greet her with the joyful clap of their hands. I look closer and gasp, lifting my hands to my face, utterly blown away by the colorful light enveloping each guest.

“Isola, what's wrong?” Trealla asks, concerned.

“My goodness, Trealla. Am I seeing things?” I blink my eyes at this unbelievable sight. “They all have colorful, shimmering light evaporating from their bodies.”

"You can see them shimmering?"

"Yes, I can. Please tell me you can see it too, or else I've definitely lost my marbles this time."

"Well, yes, I can see it, but you shouldn't be able to. This is a second chapter aptitude. Have you had another awakening you haven't told me about?"

"Not that I know of." I shrug.

"Let me look into your eyes, Isola."

"No, I can't take my eyes off their shimmering bodies."

"It will only take a moment." She gently guides my face her way with her hand, then dives into my eyes. "You're still in your first chapter. You mustn't be far off awakening if you can see everyone shimmering."

No, I can't awaken now. Sation is almost in reach. "So, do you think I'll awaken today?" I ask, trying not to sound too negative about changes she's been waiting to see in me all year.

"Well, given you can see everyone shimmering, it could indicate you might."

There's no way I want to awaken now. I'm so close to my end goal. Luckily, I know how to prolong existing within my first chapter, by habitually overloading my head with hundreds of human thoughts. I'm definitely spending the rest of the day in my human head.

"What is this shimmering then, and how do they make it happen?"

"This is what a person looks like when they're free of their history of human thinking and living with an awakened heart. It allows them to diffuse their beautiful innate light and share it with the world."

"A light?" I look over to her, taking my sight away from this amazing phenomenon for a moment.

"Yes, their innate energy sparkles from within and scintillates through their skin."

"So, if I move into my second chapter, will I shimmer like them?" I ask, unable to believe I could be this magical.

"Yes, of course you will."

"What color will I be?"

"You will have to wait until your third chapter to find out. In your second chapter, you will illuminate with sparkling light, and in your third chapter, your sparkling light will gain a hint of color. So, you will have to wait until then to find out."

"How did I know you were going to say that?"

"Because you're a clever little Kore." She smiles. "Please don't mention any of this to Emerson. He can't see what we can, and we don't want our knowledge to become public knowledge."

This more than likely affirms Emerson isn't one of our kind. "I won't mention a word of anything to the Neanderthal, but boy, he's missing out," I say, looking at their sparkling essence scintillating from within, while Emerson stands right beside them, oblivious to it all.

"Do you shimmer like them, Trealla?"

Trealla takes in a noticeable breath and, as she exhales, a flint of light shimmers from the region of her heart, then another. Moments later her entire body is enveloped by a soft, shimmering light with tones of red.

"Oh, wow, Trealla," I say, taking a step back from the warmth radiating from her. Never would I have thought Trealla could get any more beautiful but, in this shimmering light, she is even more captivating. In awe of her light, I follow Trealla down *la via dell'amore* like a moth to a flame.

Trealla waves her hand, welcoming all the guests to come on in. As they step onto *la via dell'amore,* their sparkling lights fall through the air like colorful snowflakes, melting away on the ground.

The first couple make their way towards Trealla and me, each with a basket in hand. The woman's vibrant green eyes let me know she is a Green Seed of Middle Eastern appearance. She's wearing a bright saffron dress that hangs off one shoulder.

"My dear Trealla, it's been too long between visits."

"Much too long, Shamila. I'm glad you could both make it," Trealla replies with a generous hug. She takes a flower out of her basket and places it behind Shamila's ear.

"We wouldn't have missed it for the world," her partner says in a deep, resonant tone that seems to rumble from his boots. His dark brown eyes eliminate his chances of being a Green Seed.

"Hello, Zeke. It's so wonderful to see you again. Let me introduce you both to my dear friend who helped create the Sakrid garden. Shamila and Zeke, this is Isola."

"Hello," they both say, looking at me with interest.

"Hello. It's nice to meet you both."

"Sharmila takes care of the *Glycyrrhiza glabra*, which is the plant they make licorice from."

"I thought I could smell licorice." I sniff.

"Your nose serves you right, dear. Zeke and I have bought along a variety of licorice for everyone to feast on." Sharmila lifts the cloth covering her basket, revealing her treats.

"Oh I can't wait to eat your plant's sweet treats."

"Are you going to introduce my gift to your dear friend?" Zeke asks Trealla.

"Isola is still in her first chapter and won't comprehend how special your gift is, Zeke."

"Oh. Of course, sorry," Zeke retracts.

"Come along, Zeke, before you put your foot in it anymore." Shamila drags him away.

Before I can ask Trealla what all that was about, the next female guest is in front of us. Her fruity orange dress contrasts beautifully with her Polynesian tan. She looks like orange dipped in deluxe chocolate, which, in my opinion, is a delicious combination of flavors. Reaching forward, she wraps her arms around me, holding me like she has known me all my life. It probably should feel weird to be in the arms of a complete stranger, but oddly, it feels wholesome. I don't want her to let me go.

"You are a lovable ray of light, full of *mana*," she says, flashing her sparkling emerald-green eyes.

"Isola, this is Aunty Luana. We were talking last week, and I told her all about you," Trealla explains.

"Oh, hello, Luana."

"Please call me Aunty Luana. We're from the same *ohana*, meaning family," she explains.

This woman is so warm-hearted, I'm more than happy to be related to her. She is exactly how Sation described the Hawaiian people to be—happy.

"Avenlee is looking sumptuous as always, Trealla."

"Thank you. The summer season has brought the garden out in all its glory. However, we experienced the coldest winter on record this year. How is the Forest on the North Shore?"

"As harmonious as ever."

"Why don't you tell Isola about the seed you have the privilege of nurturing?"

"I nurture the koa tree. It's been grown on my island home long before humans have been living on the island. This is the instrument made from my tree. It's called a koa redwood ukulele." She holds the small instrument out.

"Elvis Presley has one of these on his *Blue Hawaii* album."

"Yes, he does. I'll play you a song later to make your heart smile."

"I'd love that, Aunty Luana." Little does she know, simply being near her glistening personality makes my heart smile. She is exactly like Trealla, only a Polynesian version.

One after another, the guests roll in with their charismatic personalities and color-coordinated outfits. And here I am, throwing off the color scheme. I meet Giselle, who brought along her basket full of fresh strawberries. I meet Azeil, who nurtures the earth like Trealla. Then Lizabethe comes along with her two sisters, Etta and Ella, each carrying a basket full of either sweet or sour cherries. Gillian and her partner, Matt, carry in a basket of cashew and pistachio nuts. Then along comes the handsome Sebastian with his basket full of passionfruits. He gives Trealla a seductive dose of European kisses, making her coy, which shocks me. Never would I imagine any man making the confident Trealla blush red. It's normally the other way around. I guess most men don't ooze sex appeal like this attractive, well-built man does.

The second-to-last guest shows the least amount of warmth, yet her presence summons the utmost respect. A Moroccan blue dress hugs her buxom figure and her dark complexion is as rich as a shot of coffee, but she sure could do with a spoonful of sugar to sweeten her up, or bitter her down.

"Welcome, Queenee," Trealla addresses her.

Instantly I know she is the Green Seed for the glorious maiden crabapple tree in the Pomona Garden.

"Hello, Trealla." She barely smiles.

"I imagine you've been looking forward to your cousin's big day."

"I have. I do admire a true-love apple."

"They go hand in hand beautifully, don't they?"

"True love will, always," Queenee replies, still not having smiled once yet. Then she turns to me.

"Queenee, this is Isola Destinn and Isola, this is Queenee Pippin."

"You have ancient decadence about you." She jumps straight to my appearance, without saying hello.

I think decadence is a good thing, although I don't know how to reply. "Thank you." I awkwardly lift my hand, waving the tips of my fingers.

"You're also the one who's been romping around my crabapple tree."

Oh, no. I'm in trouble with the Zulu Goddess. "Yes, I have. It's my favorite crabapple," I confess, wanting to hide underneath the layers of Trealla's dress.

Queenee protrudes her head forward, closes her eyes, then opens them back up, startling me with the whiteness of her eyes. She shows no expression, speaks not a word. Turning to Trealla, she passively grins, grabs a gardenia out of Trealla's basket, and walks off.

"My gosh, Trealla. That was intense. She definitely hates me and doesn't want me anywhere near her tree."

"Not one person here today has the ability to hate, and if she didn't want you romping around her crabapple tree, she would have told you long ago."

"How does she even know I've been near them? I've never seen her at Avenlee."

Trealla looks at me and winces. "I might have mentioned you like lying under her tree, humming."

"So, it's your fault I'm in trouble." I point at Trealla.

"You're not in trouble. Queenee beholds great wisdom and tradition. Sometimes those types of people don't come wrapped in bubbly personalities, but rather stern personalities that observe a lot and say the least."

"If you say so, Trealla."

I watch Queenee walk up the path, gazing over at her crabapple trees like a protective lioness looking out over her pride. She walks over to her tree and places her open hand on the trunk. I watch on.

"What is Queenee doing, Trealla, with her hand on her crabapple tree?"

"Traveling back in time."

"Huh. I'm confused."

"Second chapter Isola, second chapter." She offers no insight, only the chapter in which I'll find it.

"I thought you'd say that." I might just steer clear of Queenee today.

"Last, but not least, it's my forever and ever friend, Fairlee Maple."

At a guess, Fairlee stands all of five feet, wearing a full-length raspberry-red ruffled dress, accessorized with beaded jewelry running up her arms. On her head she wears a matching-colored pirate hat. She looks like a cross between a flamboyant Spanish dancer and a sixteenth-century pirate.

"Whit like are ye, Trealla?"

"I'm great, thanks, Fairlee. How about yourself?" Trealla rubs the side of her arm.

"A'm daein fine. It's been dunky's since a last saw ye."

"Way too long for my liking."

Fairlee greets me with a lively handshake. "Ma name's Fairlee. Whits yer name, lass?"

"Isola. It's nice to meet you," I say, letting go of her hand.

"A've no hurd that name afore, but ah like it. A've no seen any o' oor kin wae eyes as blue as thon," she says, stepping closer, staring right into my eyes.

"Isola does have beautiful blue eyes, doesn't she?" Trealla repeats, almost as though to translate for me.

"Michty me she does hae. Whit huv ye gifted the wurld then, Isola?"

"She hasn't yet, Fairlee," Trealla swiftly intervenes.

"Naw, thon cannae be richt." She tilts her head, looking confused.

"Isola is still in her first chapter." Trealla's tone cautions Fairlee not to step on nature's path.

What gift should I have given the world? Fairlee is the second guest to elaborate on some sort of gift-giving.

"Whit's fur ye'll no go past ye. Noo let me be tellin' ye whit ah huv bin giftin' the wurld. This green hert o' mines bin grawin the acer maple tree."

I look to Trealla for help, but she looks just as muddled. The only thing I understood is "acer maple tree." I figure she is the Green Seed for the maple tree.

"Noo do ye ken whit *acer* means?"

I shake my head. "No, I don't."

She steps closer. "It be Latin fur sharp, tha's how come thay gave it tae me, ah be the sharpest Green Seed thare is."

She may be the sharpest Green Seed, but she's also the hardest to understand.

"Your secret is safe with me, Fairlee."

"Ah ken it's safe wae ye. Ye ane o' us." She winks. "Noo Trealla, a've brocht ye ten jaurs of maple taffy, should be enough. Noo that's enough bletherin, a'll be gawin fur a wee dawnder doon yonder tae see mah maple trees." She salutes.

"You better be quick, Fairlee. It won't be long until the celebrations start," Trealla reminds her.

"A'll be on my way. Garden of Soteira I be, wae ma dear auld maplee. Lang may yer lum reek, Isola."

"Sorry, I don't understand."

"Never mind. A'll see ye when yer aulder."

She shakes my hand goodbye. "Aren't we going to see each other later?"

"Aye n efter ye will be aulder then whit ye are noo."

"True." I wave cheerfully as she walks off.

"There you have it, Isola. You survived the big introduction and the exuberant Fairlee."

"And the scary Queenee."

"Let's follow along behind everyone to the Boulevard."

Chapter Seventeen

The first time I set eyes on this sleepy Parisian province, I imagined it bustling with life. But never in my wildest dreams could I have imagine colorful characters like this bringing it to life.

All the keepers stand at the front of their boutiques, waving at the guests walking into the Boulevard. The keeper of the book boutique is eagerly shaking everyone's hand. He reminds me of Aladdin, dressed in a silky pair of puffy purple pants. The only thing he's missing is a magic carpet, but I won't be at all surprised if one appears. I'm prepared for anything to come my way after seeing everyone shimmering.

Guests start gathering in front of Salon de Silver and the Bellisente Hotel, two neighbouring buildings that are divided by a small street between them. Trealla, Lizabethe, and I make our way into the crowd. I stand next to my newfound relative, Aunty Luana, and she greets me with a smile.

"I'll be back in a moment, Isola," Trealla says, walking to the front of the gathering.

Trealla calls the crowd to attention. "Welcome to Avenlee, everyone. Please let us acknowledge, and connect with, the ancient land beneath our feet. Thank you for providing life for our physical bodies. For mothering us while we are far from home. For safekeeping our creative gifts and for cradling our ancestors. We are honored to share our energy with you and receive your energy in return."

And with that comes color, lots of color, shimmering from all the guests standing in the middle of the Boulevard of Boutiques. *Okay, this is nomal*, I try convincing myself, while freaking out by the amount of energy surrounding me. Trealla sends me a wink and stands beside me.

A few seconds later, everyone cheers, looking up at the second story of Salon de Silver. There, in the open window, Cobiac stands with tight sandy-blond curls and a delightful smile. It's all becoming real for me, seeing Cobiac in the flesh. He waves enthusiastically at all his guests and we wave back, equally excited.

Then the terrace shutters at the Bellisente Hotel open, making the white curtains come to life with the breeze. Laurel appears in a pale-mint lace gown, her hair pulled back into a French roll, revealing her pretty pearl earrings. Everyone gasps at her beauty, framed like a portrait. But unfortunately, Cobiac can't see her from the position of the buildings.

"That soft-mint gown's just gorgeous," Aunty Luana comments.

"It's beautiful, and different from your typical white wedding gown."

"You know, I never understood why women choose to wear ghostly white on their wedding day, when there are so many wonderful colors to pick from."

"I'll have to keep that in mind when I get married, Aunty Luana."

"My dear, you won't be getting married. You will be joining hands with your true love, which is much more meaningful than marrying a human."

"Well, I can't wait to join hands with my true love, wearing a colorful dress. However, I'm sure he will be human."

"I'm sure your true love can't possibly be. Your true love is one of our kind, and our kind is more than human." She smiles, then turns her attention back up to Laurel.

I will marry Sation, who is very human. No second or third chapter is changing that.

Cobiac holds up his hand, wanting everyone to quieten down.

"This is where we all get to help Cobiac and Laurel narrate their messages of love, given they can't see or hear one another. Listen, Isola, and you'll see what I mean," Trealla explains as the Boulevard falls quiet.

"Laurel, are you there, my love?" Cobiac calls from his window.

We all turn our attention to Laurel.

"Laurel, are you there, my love?" everyone calls out, perfectly in sync with one another. I can tell they have done this plenty of times before.

Laurel's face fills with joy at hearing everyone reiterate Cobiac's message. "Yes, I'm here."

"Yes, I'm here," the guests repeat.

"Laurel, will you honor my love and hold my hand for the rest of my life?" He smiles so cheerfully.

This time I join in narrating their love.

"Laurel, will you honor my love and hold my hand for the rest of my life?" we all repeat.

Laurel clasps both hands over her heart in response to his question. "Cobiac, it will be an honor to hold your hand and love you forever."

We all sigh, then repeat it. As soon as we do, Cobiac jumps up and down with excitement and we all cheer. I look back at Laurel and can't help but think if that was Sation, and I were in Cobiac and Laurel's situation, I wouldn't be able to resist. I'd run to Salon de Silver, into Sation's room, close the window, and join not only hands with him, but also lips, hips, and dangly bits. It's killing me watching them being separated from one another. Yet, I must say, this interactive play between them, involving us, sure beats sitting quietly on a church pew listening to a minister recite verses of holy matrimony.

The Boulevard falls quiet as we notice Laurel is no longer standing at the terrace window. She then appears at the hotel's entrance, looking at us briefly, before she starts running away.

"Trealla, she's changed her mind. She's running away. This is terrible," I say, distraught.

"She hasn't changed her mind. It's now time for Cobiac to chase after her and find her in the garden that we created. But first, Cobiac must wait for Laurel to start the countdown. Watch."

Everyone anxiously watches Laurel running away, until she stops at the end of the Boulevard, cupping her hands around her mouth. "Red, orange, yellow, green, blue, purple… Tyrian," she calls out.

All the guests repeat Laurel's color countdown back to Cobiac. As soon as we shout, "Tyrian," Cobiac bolts down the stairs and shoots out of the Salon, running after Laurel, who has now disappeared into the Kore Forest.

"Run, Cobiac, run," everyone yells, pointing him in Laurel's direction.

"Now we all get to help Cobiac find Laurel, Isola. It's like a big game of kiss-chase," Trealla says over the excitement.

The Boulevard turns into a stampede of guests chasing after Cobiac while he chases after Laurel. I even see the reserved Queenee running along after her cousin. Trealla and I make our way into the forest, leaving Lize and Aunty Luana dragging behind. Around five minutes later, we all start piling up on the path behind Cobiac. Luckily, the entrance is rather grand. Laurel stands inside the Sakrid garden, her pale-mint gown contrasting against the backdrop of exquisite passionfruit flowers. Cobiac picks an apple off the tree in the entrance and the deathly silence intensifies the tension.

"What's going on, Trealla?" I sense something important's about to happen.

"Do you remember the ancient Greek tradition of throwing an apple at your lover's heart?"

"Yes, I do."

"Well, the apple Green Seeds have their own take on this ancient tradition. Cobiac must throw the apple directly at Laurel's heart from more than seven meters away and she must catch it on her chest. Only if they achieve this will they be able to join hands. So their future is riding on his aim and her reflexes."

I now know what Queenee and Trealla were talking about earlier, when Queenee said she admires a true-love apple. "What happens if he misses her heart or if she drops the apple?"

"They will not be able to join hands and hearts for another year."

"That's a terrible tradition and way too much pressure to put yourself under," I say, feeling nervous for both of them.

"That's the traditional way that apple Green Seeds join hands."

Cobiac looks at his hopefully soon-to-be true love. Laurel looks at him, faced with the daunting task of catching the love Cobiac is about to throw her way.

"I can't watch this part." Lizabethe finally catches up to us in her snazzy high heels. "It makes me too anxious. Tell me when it's over." She covers her eyes.

"I might join you," I say, mirroring her anxiousness.

"Stop it, you two. Have some faith in them."

"I'm sorry, Trealla, but don't you remember the last time two apple Green Seeds attempted to join hands the traditional way? The apple hit the bride on the head and knocked her out cold," Lizabethe says.

"It did?" I respond, shocked this happened.

"Yes. That true-love apple turned into cider, sitting on the ground beside her."

"That was a one-off." Trealla attempts to downplay the terrible event.

"One-offs can happen once again. Tell me when it's over," Lizabethe says, keeping her eyes covered.

The anticipation is nauseating, but I have to watch. Cobiac is motioning his arm backwards and forwards, sizing up his target.

"Silence," Queenee calls out in her commanding voice.

With an estimated amount of effort, Cobiac cocks back his arm, then thrusts it forward, sending the apple sailing in Laurel's direction. The apple travels through the air as if in slow motion, reaching a height halfway towards Laurel, before descending in her direction. Laurel's facial expressions turns aghast under the mounting pressure. She cups her hands below her heart, focusing on the apple heading directly towards the center of her chest. The thumping sound of it hitting the palms of her hands and chest at the same time confirms this is indeed a true-love apple Laurel has caught exactly at the core of her heart.

Jubilant cheers erupt. We jump up and down, hugging one another, exhilarated by Cobiac's and Laurel's triumphant success. The jubilation is cut short when Cobiac motions with his hand for us to quiet down. He turns his attention towards his true love, who is still waiting patiently in the garden with her apple in her hand.

Silence once again falls upon the path, only this time it holds tenderness, not anxiousness. Cobiac walks through the entrance until he is an apple-width from Laurel.

"You are about to witness Cobiac and Laurel's first-ever touch. Never before have their hands met," Lizabethe whispers in my ear.

"You mean they've never, ever, touched one another?" I whisper back, shocked.

"That's right, never. I personally would have taste-tested his apples before I invested in a lifetime's supply, but I guess love knows love."

"*Shh*, you two," Trealla says.

We turn our attention to Cobiac and Laurel. They raise both their hands with their palms facing each other. Tenderly, they bring their fingertips ever so slowly and sincerely together until they hold hands for the first time. It's the most heartening moment of the day to me, reminding me of the first time Sation placed his warm hand over mine. The rush I felt as I looked down at his skin touching mine will forever be imprinted in my mind.

We all sigh, admiring the sight of love taking place right before our eyes as Cobiac and Laurel take their first kiss. Gratitude fills my heart witnessing such a rare, loving moment. They victoriously hold each other's hands up in the air for us to see true love has triumphed. Then both of them have a bite of the apple.

Trealla moves to the front of the entrance and calls for everyone's attention.

"On behalf of everyone, I wish to congratulate the both of you for finding true love in each other and for inviting all of us to witness the joining of your hands and hearts for the first time. It was aesthetically a pleasure to witness."

"And utterly nerve-wracking," someone calls out from the back of the crowd, making everyone laugh.

"Yes, it was also very nerve-wracking. Now I would like to introduce Avenlee's new garden, grown by Emerson, Isola and me. The intent of its construction is to treat your senses in an interactive flavor fiesta."

Everyone's humming, expressing intrigue. I just hope my theme is interesting enough for these delightful guests. I look over at Emerson's overcompensating smile and can tell he's as equally nervous as me.

"Does this mean we can eat from the garden?" Shamila asks, sounding a little confused.

"Yes, you can. We have grown fruits, herbs and vegetables next to one another that complement each other in smell and taste. There're tomatoes growing next to basil, strawberries next to passionfruit, snow peas next to mint, and so on. Or you can use your layleastas to mix and match whichever plant, fruit or herb you like. Even the pairing of the flowers and plant colors have been precisely chosen to create harmony for your sense of sight. We have champagne and strawberries on the entrance table. But if you wish to skip the champagne, you can pick an apple off the tree and roll it in the bowls of cinnamon sugar, because, as we all know, cinnamon and apples go hand-in-hand perfectly."

"What a great theme you have created, Trealla. Thank you," Laurel comments, and all the guests agree.

"Isola's layleasta came up with the theme for your special day."

Fifty pairs of eyes look my way.

"Thank you very much, Isola." Laurel smiles my way. "How kind of you to share your layleasta with us. It's gorgeous to look at and I'm sure it's going to be just as lovely to interact with."

"You're welcome, Laurel," I reply, feeling ever so proud of myself and also instantly relieved I didn't ruin her big day.

"Thank you, Emerson, for the energy you put into creating the garden," Laurel adds.

"No worries, Laurel. Great catch," Emerson says, making everyone laugh.

"Everyone, please step inside and enjoy," Trealla motions with her hand, moving to the side.

At first, everyone walks around, only looking, but it doesn't take them long to interact with the plants we'd paired together. Conversations flow with appetizing words as the guests taste-test twelve months of hard work. I put my hand over my heart and whisper, "Thank you, Annabell, for all your inspiration." Then I close my eyes and picture Annabell walking around her apothecary garden, singing and eating straight from her plants.

I'm realizing just how highly sought after Trealla is. All day people gather around her, conversing about everything green. Trealla is like an encyclopedia of nature's flora, happily answering everyone's questions. I can't understand half of what's being said. It's way too high up the garden path for me, but still, I can't help but admire Pachamama's wealth of knowledge.

I look over to see Fairlee sniffing a spearmint plant while taking a bite of the chili in her hand. Those two plants are definitely not planted side by side, but if anyone is going to test their taste buds, it's Fairlee. I notice Emerson pouring himself a glass of champagne. I think I'll get myself one, too.

"Putting up with each other looks like it's paid off, Emerson."

"It appears so, although I can't believe I didn't bury you under one of those trees," he says, pointing at the magnolia. "Lord knows I wanted to, but just imagine having to put up with you niggling away at your roots for the rest of time."

"You're a blooming fool, Emerson," I reply, listening to him laugh.

"Would you like me to pour you a drink?"

"That would be great." Wow, he's acting normal. "Hey, do you think there's anything different about Trealla and all these people?" I'm intrigued to know his opinion.

"What do you mean?" Emerson says, handing me my drink.

"I just thought they were odd."

"Maybe I'm used to odd characters, after hanging out at Avenlee for so many years."

"I guess so, but don't you think their green eyes and personalities are a bit odd? Not to mention the ceremony we just watched unfold."

"The ceremony was very unusual. However, plenty of people have green eyes, Isola."

"True," I say, looking over at the flamboyant Fairlee and her intense green eyes. "But don't you think their eyes sort of sparkle green?"

"I've never really looked at them that closely. I just figure they look healthy and bright. That doesn't make them odd, though," he says, finishing his champagne in two mouthfuls.

"So, in all your time here at Avenlee, you have never seen anything abnormal?" I drop my chin and look up at him, knowing he has to have.

"Maybe."

"Maybe?" I invite him to elaborate.

"Don't speak a word of this to anyone. Trealla will use my guts to fertilize her camellia trees. One day, I overheard Trealla talking in the garden. She was organizing a party for her Muklee friends, whoever they are. But the odd thing is, no one was with her. She was standing with her hand on her heart, having a full-on conversation with another person."

"Was Trealla talking to her plants or her birds?"

"Not a Rimsky bird was in sight, and Trealla was speaking as though someone was engaging in conversation with her."

"I guess that is a little abnormal then."

Oh, my goodness. He has no idea on what level of abnormal I'm referring to. Seeing characters out of novels behind your closed eyes, and seeing someone's essence sparkling from within them in bubbles of color, is the kind of abnormal I'm referring to.

Emerson pours himself another champagne. "Apart from that day, and the rate at which this garden established, I think you're the only abnormal and annoying person here at Avenlee." He nudges me with his hip, making me almost spill my champagne.

"Me? Annoying? You have got to be joking. If anyone is damned annoying, it's you, Emerson," I snarl. How on earth can't he see he's the antagonist between the both of us?

"Settle down. Don't go getting all angry. Remember, today is meant to be a day of love and happiness."

"You drive me bonkers," I say, taking a large sip of my drink before I wear it.

"You should know me by now, Isola." He winks.

"You're right, I should know better by now. At least now the Sakrid is finished, we won't have to spend time with each other anymore," I say, relieved.

"It has been a very challenging year, but we managed not to strangle one another, so congratulations to us."

He raises his glass and taps it against mine.

"We showed great restraint. What are you going to do with all your spare time?" I ask.

He shrugs. "I guess I'll still come help out at Avenlee. Trealla probably has another ten events lined up. But maybe I might fit in some camping and fishing. What about yourself?"

"I plan on swimming and soaking up the sun."

"You mean back home in America?"

"Yes, I won't be swimming in England."

"When do you plan on leaving?"

"Not sure yet." I swallow down my lie with a mouthful of champagne.

"Doesn't your family live here in Nolanberry?"

"That's even more of a reason for me to move back to America, to get away from them. Well, one of them in particular. I have other people to return home to, anyway."

"Really. What's his name?"

"Who?" I purposely avoid making eye contact.

"Come on, Isola."

"There might be a man," I reply, attempting to hide my grin.

"It seems an awful long way to go for a 'might-be man.'"

"Well, then, there is a man."

"Is he your boyfriend?" He nudges me once again.

"That's none of your business."

"Oooh, Isola has a boyfriend. Isola's going steady," he sings like a boy in fifth grade.

"Knock it off, Emerson, or else I'll tell Trealla you were listening in on her conversation with her Muklee friends."

"Nice try, Isola, but you wouldn't dare."

"Wouldn't I?" I smirk, hinting I might.

"You like me too much to see Trealla use my guts as fertilizer."

"Do I now, Emerson?"

"Yes, you do," he replies, putting his empty glass down, then starts walking away.

"I don't like you. You annoy the heck out of me."

He ignores me and continues walking away, knowing it will annoy me even more. He's so frustrating. I can't even tell him how much he annoys me without him annoying me in the process. Thank goodness this is the end of my relationship with the Neanderthal.

A few moments later, someone notices a beautiful rainbow forming in the sky. You would think they'd seen a pot of gold at the end of it, too.

They're all standing gazing up to it, chatting about all the vibrant colors. I guess they're quite beautiful.

A moment later, Trealla wanders on over, just as I finish my glass of champagne that, by the way, tastes terrible.

"Wow, that's the friendliest conversation you two have had," Trealla says.

"That's not true. We've spent most weekends talking to each other."

"No, you've spent most weekends niggling at each other. That conversation looked amicable. I even notice you both charging your glasses together."

Trealla obviously didn't see how our conversation ended. "We were actually congratulating each other on not strangling one another when we charged our glasses."

"I'd toast to that. Now, more importantly, are you enjoying your first Sakrid?"

"You're right, it's different from your traditional wedding. The guests alone set it apart in the most extraordinary ways."

"Speaking of extraordinary guests, would you like to talk to Queenee with me?"

"I'll pass," I reply, short and sharp.

"Oh, come on, Isola. She really is a very kind lady."

"She scares me. I think it's best I keep off her path."

"Just because she doesn't smile at you doesn't mean you should shy away from her. We should put ourselves in situations that enable us to bring a smile to someone's face and not always rely on someone bringing one to ours," she says, ever so sagaciously.

"Why are you always making me challenge myself?"

"Because you don't. When you start, I'll stop."

"If she bites me, it's your fault."

"See, Isola? You just brought a smile to my face. Now, let's go and bring one to Queenee's."

"Before we do, can you tell me why Queenee looked at me, then closed her eyes? A few of you have done it to me now."

"Some people can sense more with their eyes closed, than open."

“Really? That’s cool. Is it something to do with their senses?”

“No,” she replies, ending the conversation, making her way over to Queenee.

Queenee’s standing with the strawberry Green Seed, Giselle, admiring the climbing vanilla plant.

“Hello, ladies. Isola and I thought we would come over and indulge in these heavily scented vanilla pods. They were the most challenging plant to grow.”

“I was just saying to Queenee, I can’t believe you managed to get this vanilla plant to produce pods here in England. You really are gifted, Trealla,” the tall and elegant Giselle says.

“It wasn’t easy, Giselle, but as soon as it flowered eight months ago, I knew I’d have vanilla pods for today.”

Looking over to Queenee, I send a quaint smile, barely showing my teeth. I don’t want to appear over the top. To my surprise, she pleasantly smiles back, not only with her mouth, but with her eyes. The gentle look on her face melts my fears and makes me smile a little more. Maybe she really is a kind lady who just needs a little encouragement.

Then the delicate sound of Aunty Luana’s ukulele drifts through the garden. We all turn to hear her playing a Polynesian melody on her koa redwood ukulele. What a sweet-sounding instrument it is. Aunty Luana’s melodies resonate through the garden until the sun disappears behind the mountains.

As the daylight dwindles, so too does all the produce on the plants. The interactive garden is a huge success. It looks like an empty dinner plate that has been thoroughly enjoyed.

Trealla stands in the entrance and calls for everyone’s attention, shimmering right before my befuddled eyes again.

“Thank you, everyone, for sharing your gorgeous energy today. I think we can all agree the atmosphere has been delightful. Shall we make our way back towards the Boulevard, to say hello to all the Keepers? And please remember to call into the Photo Antiquary to have your photo taken for the Sakrid album. Also, make sure you visit the pastry parlor. Galien’s been busy baking for us. Let’s make our way back to the Boulevard to continue the celebrations."

Trealla shimmers her way out of the garden like a luminous human lantern for all to follow. Then, to my amazement, every third or fourth guest illuminates like Trealla, sending out their sparkling essence to light the forest path. The majority are green, yellow and orange with the odd red, purple and blue. The longer I look at them, the more I notice the Green Seeds' spheres of light have flickers of emerald green, just like their eyes. Then I notice Trealla and Azeil, who both nurture the earth, are shimmering with hints of red.

Does this have something to do with their gifts? Maybe every color represents a different type of gift.

I follow along behind Zeke without him knowing. I reach my hand into his sparkling blue essence and my skin turns warm and blue. For the first time in a long time, I want to awaken to the innate within. At times this mysterious world is too alluring to refute. I guess it's hard to deny something that lives inside, just waiting to enrich my existence in a way nothing else can. Will I be a guiding light in the dark for those who can't see?

As the long convoy of guests step under the charming Parisian streetlamps, their shimmers dissolve, returning them to their normal, abnormal selves. The piano's melody fills the night air, and the glamorous boutique lights create a winsome atmosphere. I'm now spending the evening in downtown Paris, 1920s style.

Everyone leisurely strolls about the Boulevard, socializing with one another. Lizabethe's two sisters take me on a tour of the boutiques. Our sense of smell leads us first to the pastry parlor to indulge in one of Galien's delicious treats. Etta's love of fashion then has us trying on dresses at the clothing boutique. Then her sister walks us to the book boutique. I've often stepped inside here to take time out from gardening. We treat our layleastas to a story that Habbib the Storyteller is reading. I know I'm not going to be transported to another era, given these books have words and illustrations inside.

After meeting Habbib, not only does he remind me of Aladdin, he even shares a story to a group of us about an Arabian prince who magically turned the stars orange to impress a woman he loved called Naranja. The story is fitting for his character.

We leave shortly after the story to have our photo taken for Laurel and Cobiac's album. The vintage photos of brides and grooms hanging on the walls steal my attention. But now it's time to make our way to the dining room.

Walking in, we are delighted to see all the Green Seeds' baskets elaborately displayed like banquets fit for the Greek gods to feast on. I dip my hand straight into Shamila's licorice basket. The smooth, soft texture of her original licorice sticks are to die for. I can't help but go back for seconds. Fairlee is pushing for everyone to try her maple taffy and, within half an hour, everyone is fairly up and grooving with the extra sugar kick her Scottish maple taffy delivers.

While everyone is dancing, I make my way to the vintage jewelry boutique. Looking through the windows, I see rings, bracelets, and pendants sparkling under lights. I'm twitching with excitement to finally be going inside.

"Find anything you like?"

I turn in fright to see Emerson standing behind me. "You scared the heck out of me, Emerson."

"I'm not that ugly, am I? Actually, don't answer that. You coming inside?" he says, walking through the front door.

There goes my peaceful look-around inside.

"Oh, wow." I'm bedazzled. I spot the meticulously dressed proprietor standing behind the counter in his monochromatic shades of orange.

"Hello to you both. I don't think we have met. My name is Mr. Ambrose." He introduces himself as if born with a silver spoon in his mouth. However, his welcoming smile softens his formal approach.

"No, we haven't met before. My name is Isola." I try speaking as eloquently as him.

"It's a pleasure to meet you, Isola. Welcome to the jewelry boutique."

"Thank you. It's exquisite."

"Charming it is, just like your eyes. Now, who is this young gentleman?"

"My name's Emerson. I live just over the mountain."

"How lucky you are to be neighbors with Avenlee. I presume you know Trealla well?"

"I've known Trealla for around four years now."

"That would have made for the most delightful four years of your life."

"Delightful and sweaty."

"Interesting combination," Mr. Ambrose replies, looking queasy at the thought of being sweaty.

Then the door opens and Sebastian, the passionfruit Green Seed, walks in, escorting a woman I haven't met. They look quite comfortable with one another, although what woman wouldn't look pleased with herself having Sebastian escorting her into a jewelry boutique?

"Feel free to look around, Emerson and Isola," Mr. Ambrose says, then attends to the attractive couple.

Emerson and I move a little further down the counter and continue looking at the display cabinets. I look back over to Sebastian, noticing the woman looking at the jewelry with her eyes closed. She must be one of those people who can see more with their eyes closed than open. I wonder if I can. I look at the cabinet, close my eyes… The only thing I can see is the back of my eyelids. I obviously don't have this rare ability.

"Mr. Ambrose, I found one, I found one! I can't believe it," the woman behind me gushes with excitement.

Maybe a little too much excitement to have found a ring or bracelet she likes the look of.

Mr. Ambrose quickly whispers something to her. Then the both of them look at Emerson and me. Whatever he said has something to do with us. I turn to the next cabinet, not wanting to intrude into their space, but as soon as I step to the side, I almost trip over Emerson, who is down on one knee, holding a ring up to me.

"Will you do me the honor of becoming my wife?

"Oh, Emerson, you're so embarrassing. Get up before they see you," I say, with more emphasis on my face than in the volume of my voice.

"Not until you say yes, my love," he says with such meaning.

As much as I want to laugh at him for perfecting acting like such a fool, I also don't want to encourage his idiotic behavior.

"Oh, Emerson, you are a buffoon, but an admirable one. Now get up."

"Is that a 'yes'?" He gives me a side eye.

"I'm leaving now. You're embarrassing me." I step around him and duck out onto the Boulevard, annoyed he ruined my time inside.

"My gosh, was that a compliment you just paid me?" Emerson asks, following me outside.

"Well, if you're fond of buffoons, I guess so, Emerson."

"I meant the admirable part, not the buffoon part."

"Oh, that part. I guess it was half a compliment."

"You can't give half a compliment, Isola."

"Half a compliment is better than no compliment at all, or what I've been calling you in my head all year."

"And what's that?"

"An annoying Neanderthal."

"Annoying Neanderthal," he repeats, with his hands on his hips. "You promised to be nice this morning when I had you tossed over my shoulder. I think you just broke your promise."

"No, you asked a question. I simply answered it. But you are an uncouth, uncivilized pain in the ass most of the time."

"You're going over my shoulder."

"You wouldn't dare, Emerson. I've got my dress on."

"I don't care about your dress. I'm an uncivilized pain in the ass, remember?"

Oh, no, he is serious. I bolt towards the party at Salon de Silver, attempting to escape him. I reach the salon and almost knock the French doors off their hinges, startling everyone inside. Then Emerson barges in, almost bashing into the back of me.

"Luks lik we huv another gam of kiss-chacey on oor hauns." Fairlee breaks the silence, making everyone laugh.

"No, I'm just proving to Emerson I can run faster than him."

"Ah, sure yer whaur."

My face turns bright red. Does everyone think the Neanderthal and

I are attracted to one another?

Slowly, I step back out the doors and make my way to the Bellisente Hotel, where a quieter group of guests is grazing. A few hours later, Cobiac and Laurel call it a night. Not long after, the guests do the same. I walk Lizabethe and her sisters to their room upstairs. On my way back down, I overhear a conversation two men are having at the bar.

"So, did you meet the woman Trealla is warmed to?"

"No, but I did sit next to her at the book boutique, she smelt great. Fancy her, do you?"

"She is stunning, but I'm a happily married man. I just can't figure out if she's one of our kind or not."

The younger man sounds rather confused by me. Well, join the club.

"I'm hearing you. I've never seen anyone as mysterious as her in all my lifetimes. Still, I have a feeling she's too powerful to be human," the older, wiser man replies.

"I'm leaning the other way, thinking she's too humanly powerful to be our kind. She is wearing pink, after all."

Then they both chuckle at my lack of dress sense.

"One thing is for sure, she's not a Green Seed, with those delightful blue eyes."

"True, I might just ask Trealla and put my curiosity to rest."

"You're dreaming, boy. Trealla never speaks on behalf of our nature. It's nature's way or no way with 'traditional Trealla.'"

"Well, then, I'll try looking into her eyes long enough and see for myself."

"Good luck with that. I'm sure you will see a Muklee looking back at you."

"We'll see."

Muklee. Muklee. What's a Muklee? It's the same word Emerson overheard Trealla say in the garden. Not only don't I know who I am, but neither do the people who are all-knowing. And what on earth is the older man talking about, saying he's never seen anyone as mysterious as me in all his 'lifetimes'? First, since when does anyone live lifetimes. And second, I'm far from mysterious. I'm just a woman in a pink dress.

Chapter Eighteen

Wow. Yesterday was out of this world. I doubt I'll ever experience anything like it again. Regrettably, it's time to say goodbye to Trealla and farewell to Avenlee for good. I've spent months trying to decide whether to tell Trealla I'm leaving. Eventually, I choose not to. It would be unfair of me to expect Trealla to conceal my disappearing act from my mom, and so it remains my secret. Well, my secret except for the ticketmaster, who looked down the end of his nose at me a month ago when I handed him 118 pounds and 10 shillings for a ticket aboard the *Sylvanis Cunard* for a seven-day crossing to America. But first, I have to survive saying goodbye to Trealla without any emotional telltale signs. I decide to get up and write her a goodbye letter while she is still sleeping. I pick up my notebook and a pen and head outdoors.

Dear Trealla,

As I write this letter under the shade of your fig tree, I look around, unable to find the words to express how grateful I am for everything you have opened my eyes to since opening your heart to mine. Never in my wildest dreams could I have imagined myself becoming the woman I am today, but thanks to you, the unimaginable happened. You truly are the heroine of my heart.

By the time you read this letter, I will have taken the next step on my path towards knowing who I am. Unfortunately, that next step is taking me away from you. As hard as it is for me to take that step, I must. For if my path originates from within my heart, it would be wrong of me not to go in search of what it yearns for, and that's Sation.

I will return to Avenlee and greet you knowing who I am, with the man I love by my side, and when you look into his eyes, you will know why I left everything I love here at Avenlee to bring him and me together and back to you.

I love you inside out, outside in.

Isola Destinn

"Good morning, love."

I fold up the letter. "Morning, Trealla. You had a big sleep in this morning."

She slumps down next to me. "I needed it after yesterday. What are you writing?"

"Just a letter to a friend, but I'm finished now."

"Is it a letter to Sation?"

"No, this is for a female friend."

"Oh, okay. Did you want to get dressed so we can have breakfast with everyone before they leave?"

"Sounds good."

Over breakfast, we all sit talking about yesterday's highlights. Everyone sounds like they've had a marvelous time. Avenlee's social event of the year has turned out to be the biggest event of my life. Emerson's transformation is even magical. I dodged the two men I overheard talking about me last night, just so they couldn't look into my eyes and see whatever it was they were talking about. However, I imagine all these eccentric guests have been watching me since the moment I greeted them with Trealla yesterday.

Later in the afternoon, the guests make their way back down *la via dell'amore* with their empty baskets, praising the three of us for creating such a memorable day. Now, it's just Trealla, Emerson and me at Avenlee, as it's been all year. Emerson decides to spend a few nights at the cabin in the Kore Forest, which is good because tomorrow when Trealla finds out I've skipped town, she is going to need someone to tell how much of a wretched disappointment I am. Given the adversarial relationship Emerson and I have shared all year, I know he'll be more than happy to join in on that conversation.

Emerson wishes me a happy birthday for tomorrow, then goes on his way and Treallа and I make our way back to the house. I can hardly look her in the eye, knowing I'm vanishing from her life. I feel so sick in my stomach for being dishonest with her.

"Is there something wrong, Isola?" Trealla asks when we reach the porch.

I swear nothing escapes her intuition. "Nothing's wrong. I'm just a little exhausted."

"You'd better get a good night's sleep. Tomorrow is going to be another big day, birthday girl."

"Yes, but nothing will ever top yesterday. Actually, nothing will ever top the past twelve months. Being here with you at Avenlee has been the most spectacular year of my life. I owe you a great big thank you."

"It's been a pleasure. My heart and garden are always open to you."

Oh my gosh, the guilt mounts. "We will never be strangers, Trealla. You're in my heart forever now." I reach forward, hugging her to hide the tears welling in my eyes. "I hope I haven't disappointed you in not awakening, especially with all the love and guidance you've shared."

"You will awaken when the innate within you intends to be known, not when you or I want it to. There's nothing to apologize for. As long as you live from your heart, the rest will take care of itself." She stops hugging me.

"My heart's open, Trealla."

"Good. Keep it that way. Now I still have plenty of events taking place at Avenlee for you to help out with, if you wish too."

"Sounds good, Trealla," I say, walking over to grab my bike while Trealla reaches inside the back door.

"Here is a present for you to open tomorrow. I'll give it to you now, just in case I don't get into town tomorrow. I have so much to tidy up here." She hands it to me.

"I'm guessing this isn't another voucher to visit Bramble Street," I say, given the size of the box.

"No, it's something I made for you."

"Thank you in advance. I'll open it tomorrow," I say, pushing it into my backpack.

"Good. You have yourself a happy eighteenth birthday." She smiles pleasantly.

"I will. Talk to you soon, Trealla."

"See you soon, love."

Peddling away from the most captivating woman I've ever known, I leave a trail of tears behind me. It didn't make a difference what chapters we're individually living or even whether I'm her kind. We simply have a heartfelt connection, regardless of anything and everything. The effect we've had on each other will last a lifetime.

Reaching the road, I place Trealla's letter in her mailbox knowing she won't collect the mail until tomorrow, then take one last look at the most spectacular view in the world and blow Avenlee a farewell kiss.

***

Eighteen glowing candles wake me, along with Mom, Dad, and Julia singing "Happy Birthday." Now it's time to make a wish, but honestly, I don't know what to wish for. All I've ever wanted is coming true today by sailing back to Sation. Maybe I'll wish for forgiveness in advance for breaking Mom's, Trealla's, and Julia's hearts and maybe for scratching the surface of my father's.

Breakfast is finished. It's time to say bye to Dad before he leaves for work. He reaches for his briefcase on the chair next to him and makes his way out of the dining room. For the first time in a long time, I feel the need to express some emotions. I follow him down the hall to the front door. I reach out, giving him an awkward hug to thank him for my birthday money. He reciprocates with just enough affection to not make me regret my actions. I'm sure he thinks it's the birthday joy making me reach out to him, but I can't leave for the other side of the world without giving him a hug. It could be the last time I even see him.

"'Bye, Dad."

"Goodbye, Isola. You have yourself a good birthday," he says, then closes the door behind him. Instantly, I feel hollow in the stomach. Walking back down the hall, I see Mom and Julia looking at me.

"What are you two gawking at?"

"The last time I saw you and your father hug one another, you were in second grade."

"What hug?" I play down our fleeting show of affection.

"While you're dishing out the hugs, here's one from me. Happy birthday, big D." Julia gives me a squeeze.

"Thanks, little D, love ya."

"Love you too."

"Now, my double D's, you'd better get a move on, or else you'll be late for school."

"I've have two free classes this morning, now that I've finished exams. I'll catch the bus later."

"Okay, then," she says, making her way to the front door. I follow on behind her and Julia.

"I'll see you tonight, Isola," Mom wraps her arms around me and I hold her a moment longer. I can't believe I'm doing this to her. She is going to be so upset with me when she finds out this is our last goodbye.

"I can't believe you're eighteen. It only seems like yesterday when I was holding you in my arms."

"Mom, you still are." I say encompassed in her embrace.

"Well, yes, but now your feet are touching the ground. Oh, but I love you just as much, sweetheart." She looks me in the eye. "Do you remember the first time we drove home from Avenlee and I told you the story about the wish Trealla and I made at the fountain in Paris?"

"Yes, I remember. Trealla wished for her beautiful garden, and you wished for love."

"Yes, but it's your love that made my wish came true. It's the love of a child I wanted more than anything in this world. You're my wish come true."

"Really, Mom? I thought it was Dad's love."

"No, it was the love of a child I wished for."

I wish she'd never said that, especially right now when I'm about to disappoint her beyond measure. Who would've thought following your heart could make you feel so heartless?

"Thank you for loving me, Mom."

"That's what moms do," she says pushing my hair out of my eyes. "We share our love and our lives with our children, who share their love and lives with us." She smiles, then kisses me on the forehead.

"Sorry for giving you a hard time lately." It's hard to speak around the unshed tears pooling in my throat.

"You're just trying to figure out who you are and aren't. And one thing you've never been is like others. I tried to make you fit in better, but I gave up pretty quick."

"I think you'll have more luck with Julia."

"Yes, that's true." She nods and steps outside with Julia.

"'Bye, Mom. Bye-bye, Julia." I could almost burst out crying.

"Ta-ta, birthday girl," Mom replies.

She closes the door and immediately the weight of guilt kicks in and I slide down the wall, unable to hold it up. That's our last goodbye.

For the first time in twelve months, I'm contemplating staying. How can I live with the guilt of hurting the woman who loves me the most? But, am I supposed to live with her for the rest of my life, just to keep her happy? What about *my* happiness? I have to eventually leave home one day, just like she did. I'd be going off to college next year, anyway.

Before I let my feelings get the better of me, I pick myself up off the entryway floor, grab a piece of paper and a pen, and write Mom a goodbye letter.

Dear Mom,

This letter will come as a surprise. I know my explanation will not make up for the sadness my actions will cause, but I hope one day you'll understand and forgive me for what I'm doing. I will be heading across the Atlantic Ocean as you read this letter, returning home to America, where I belong. I apologize for not giving you the opportunity to say goodbye, but I didn't want Dad to stop me and I couldn't bear seeing you upset. It would stop me from pursuing my future back home in Fortier. Please understand, Mom, that it's time for me to make my wishes come true and set out on my own path, just as all eighteen-year-olds do. As much as I've never quite fit into this family, I always knew I fit into your heart.

Love from your big D.

P.S. Please tell Julia I said goodbye. Tell her she can have all my clothes. I will be in contact.

I can hardly see passed the tears in my eyes. I place the letter on Mom's bedside table, then grab the small bag I've packed, all the money I've saved, and take my first step in Sation's direction.

Chapter Nineteen

I'm itching to get below deck and out of sight as I wait in the carpeted queue to board the ship. Dad's office is only a five-minute walk from here, and the last thing I want is to be caught in the final stages of my disappearing act. I hand my ticket to the well-dressed officer with a sigh of relief, virtually jumping on board, out of sight.

"Welcome aboard the *Sylvanis Cunard,* Miss Destinn. I'm sure your voyage will be most accommodating. The porter will see you to your room, and refreshments are being served in the main lounge."

The porter takes my bag and I follow along behind him. "You travel light, Miss Destinn," he says, leading me through the luxurious ocean liner that's been polished to the nines.

"It's easier traveling light. Can you tell me how long it will be before the ship pulls out of the harbor?" I ask, looking up to the chandeliers decorating the hallway with a warm glow.

"Everything is running on time and in shipshape Bristol fashion, so we should depart in fifteen minutes," he says, opening my cabin door.

"Great." I reply, looking around my decorative cabin with all its golden trimmings.

"Will you be needing anything else, Miss Destinn?"

"No, thank you. That will be all."

"Good day, miss." He closes my cabin door.

Twenty minutes later, the ship still hasn't moved an inch. It's now ten-twenty in the morning. I know Trealla won't be far off checking her mail, and Mom won't be far off returning home. Panic is setting in.

Curiosity has me up on deck to see what the holdup is. Hopefully it's not my father holding back the ship with his bare hands. Just as I step onto the deck, the sound of the foghorn blows. Finally, we're on our way. I've successfully escaped without anyone catching me. What an achievement.

"Goodbye, England. Thank you for your friendship. Look after my loved ones for me." I smile fondly.

"Isola! Isola!" I hear the faint sound of a woman calling.

I spot Mom and Trealla frantically running down the dock, with Emerson not far behind. I respect both of them too much to hide like a coward. I reveal the shame on my face, confirming I'm on board. The noise of the ship's engines is too loud to verbally communicate, but never have words been so unnecessary. The guilt in my eyes, and sadness in theirs, says it all. Knowing I'm the cause of their sorrow sickens me.

"Please forgive me. I'm so sorry," I cry out, but my words seem to hit the fog and bounce right back at me.

The distance between us grows dense with fog. Eventually, I lose sight of them, but the image of Mom breaking down in tears remains. Sadness drops me to my knees, but sadness quickly turns to anger. This is all my father's fault. If he wasn't such a controlling man, I might have felt comfortable enough to tell everyone I was leaving rather than disappearing from their lives. My fear of him fractures so many aspects of my life that I can never mend. I'm so angry at him.

"I hate you. I hate you. I hate you." I bang my fist on the deck.

"I'm sure the deck hates you, too." A man standing nearby attempts being comical.

"Go away and leave me alone."

"I've got nowhere to go. I'm stuck on this ship, like you."

"Well, if you won't go, I will." Wiping my tears, I stand and instantly recognize him. I can't believe my eyes.

"You're Mr. Destinn's daughter."

"No, you have me mistaken for someone else," I say, trying to wiggle my way out of being recognized by Maguire, my father's enthusiastic employee.

"I'm sure you are."

He is too intelligent for me to convince him otherwise. "Regrettably, I am his daughter. Promise me you won't stop this ship or tell him I'm on this ship." I know Mom hasn't told him yet, or else he would be running down the dock beside her.

"I could send him a message with one of my homing pigeons, but it seems they went on strike about thirty years ago. The old Morse code could be an option." He taps his finger on the railing, pretending to be sending a Morse code to my father. "Tap, tap, Mr. Destinn. Tap, tap, tap, runaway daughter found. Tap, tap, tap, aboard the *Sylvanis Cunard*. Tap, tap."

He is full of wisecracks, this guy. "Excuse me for not laughing along with you."

"Miss Destinn, how can I possibly inform your father you're on this ship when I'm on it with you?"

"You have a point." I'm clearly not thinking straight. I guess my mom will be telling him soon, anyway.

"This obviously means your father doesn't know you're heading back to America."

"No, he doesn't. I've run away. Although my mother just caught me escaping."

"He's going to kill you. Come to think of it, I would fetch a handsome reward for your return." He snickers.

"Don't you even think about it. I'll jump overboard and swim to goddamn America, if need be."

"I'm not going to do anything of the sort. So relax, woman. Anyway, if I'm not mistaken, aren't you old enough to be floating your boat in whatever direction you want?"

"Yes, exactly. I'm old enough to be doing just as I please." I have a feeling I can trust Maguire. He might be palsy-walsy with my father, but he is still his own man.

"I'm the last one to talk, anyway. I left home at fourteen," he says, running his hand along his jaw.

"Really, Maguire?"

"Yes, I've been independent from the get-go. Mom said I was born walking and talking."

No wonder he is so confident, having taken care of himself from such a young age. He is definitely not a *mammoni.*

"Were you born with those eyelashes too, or do you wear mascara?"

He laughs at my honesty.

"You're not backwards in coming forwards." He shakes his head. "No, I'm not into makeup. I inherited these long eyelashes from my old man. It's about the only thing he gave me before he took off when I was a kid."

Oh, I sense some tension there. "Sorry, I just had to ask. They make your eyes pop. So, what are you doing heading back to America, Maguire? Did you finally come to your senses?"

"I'm moving to Fortier to work for around six months."

"You're moving to Fortier?" Just when I'd escaped my father, I meet up with his protégé aboard my getaway vehicle. Great.

"Yes, your father has sent me to take care of a few business deals back home, so I'll be staying at your old house. What are your plans in America?"

"I plan on getting back to living my old life again. I miss Fortier."

"You miss your hometown," he repeated, apparently doubting my reply.

"Yes, I miss my hometown. I've been homesick ever since I left." I try to sound more convincing.

"I think you miss a little more than your hometown. You sure you don't miss a certain someone in your hometown?"

"No," I snap back, annoyed he's right. "I really do miss the sandy beaches and being able to swim all year round in the warm water. Then there's the beautiful island of Reefers." I soften my tone. "Some women are made for the earth, others for wide open spaces, and women like me are made for the ocean."

"That was rather poetic."

I can tell he's not buying into anything I say. Now I know why my father employed him. He's too switched-on to be led up the garden path by wordsmithery.

"You should be an ambassador of Fortier after that promotional spiel." He laughs, finding my inability to convince him amusing.

"It's none of your business why I'm going back to Fortier. I don't have to explain why I'm choosing to float my boat in this direction. I just am," I say, forthright.

"You're right. It's none of my business. You are your own woman, and a very confident one at that. I'm only teasing you. However, can I ask who you were hating on when you were thumping your fist on the deck?"

"My father."

"I've seen many businessmen doing the same thing in reaction to your father. He's never done wrong by me."

"That just means you haven't known him long enough."

"I've known him longer than my own father. He might be tough, but he's not that bad. He's just ambitious."

"Is that what you call it, ambitious? I call it insatiable greed, and that's the positive angle. Don't get me started on the negatives."

"Gee, I'd better not. I don't want to get you all fired up again, bashing the deck. She needs to get us to America before you sink her to the bottom of the sea."

"I was close to submerging her, wasn't I?" I huff, knowing how angry I must've looked.

"I might still get a life jacket ready just in case the angry woman returns."

"Best you do that, Maguire. We wouldn't want Daddy's henchman sinking to the bottom of the sea on his quest to impress."

"Oh, you're quick-witted, I give you that. You have a lot of your father's traits in you, that's for sure."

He is quick-witted himself and knows how to press my buttons.

"I'll be walking away after hearing that ridiculous comment. I have none of my father's traits," I say, winding up the conversation and leaving before he winds me up any more.

"Isola," he calls out. "Do you want to join me in the lounge for dinner?"

"Thanks, but I don't have much of an appetite, henchman." I smirk, then continue walking away.

"I'm not your father's henchman."

"And I'm nothing like my father."

***

Back in my 118-pounds-and-10-shilling first-class cabin, I wonder what the chances are of being stuck on a boat with Maguire. Worse, having to share the same small beach town with him back in America.

Falling onto my bed, I find out it has not an ounce of first-class bounce. I close my eyes, only to be traumatized by a flashback of Mom and Trealla's tear-soaked faces. That image is going to haunt me for a long time. I figure I deserve every ounce of this intolerable guilt, given I'm culpable for their sorrow.

I remember Trealla's gift. It's time to open it. Hopefully, it will cheer me up. Off comes the wrapping.

The envelope reads, "Happy birthday and thank you."

Oh, my goodness, there's a hundred pounds inside! This is so much money, so much money that I need. *Thank you, Trealla.*

I lift the lid on the box. Aww, it's a batch of freshly baked *Nico biscotti alla nocciola* and a small bottle of oil. The label reads *Garden of La Lilliana. Isola Blend.* She concocted oil for me. I twist the lid on the small blue bottle and inhale the aroma that captures my existence, instigating me to close my eyes and indulge in the tones of La Lilliana, a profound scent that she named after me.

My heart is full of gratitude. My gosh, I'm going to miss Trealla and Avenlee.

***

Two days into my voyage, I'm over eating sandwiches and hanging out in my cabin to avoid running into Maguire. I put my finest outfit on, dab on my beautiful *Isola Blend* and take a seat in the dining room.

Walking into the room, my eyes are taken by the mural painted on the ceiling of primordial sea gods and oceanic themes. Wow, that's very creative but how on earth did they paint that up there?

A waiter comes up from behind and helps push my chair in.

"Thank you." I turn and notice it's Maguire posing as a waiter. "Is my father paying you so little, you have taken up a second job?"

"Ah-ah, be nice, Isola. It's been hundreds of nautical miles since we last saw one another."

"True. Would you like to join me for dinner?" I ask, looking at his striking eye and lash combination.

"Thanks for the invite, but I've already eaten. May I recommend the Manhattan clam chowder as an appetizer, and baked Canadian ham with Cumberland sauce for the main course? You won't be disappointed."

I order the baked Canadian ham with Cumberland sauce at Maguire's recommendation. He has great taste in food. As I eat, Maguire's sitting at the bar, sipping his brandy. I feel so out of place and way too young to be sitting among all this finery. Everything from the cutlery to the artwork painted on the ceiling screams out luxury. Yet my eyes keep being drawn back to Maguire's mannerisms. He has this habit of swirling his ice around in his glass before every mouthful. Then at times he runs his hand along his jawline as if deep in thought, or deep into the history of human thinking. Spending time with him aboard this boat will help return some normality back to my life and keep my history of human thinking alive. Because one thing is for certain. Maguire is definitely not going to start shimmering or looking at me with his eyes closed. He is as human as a human henchman can be.

As I finish my meal, the waiter hands me a note. "From the gentleman at the bar," he tells me.

I thank him and open the slip of paper. *Would you like to join me for a drink?* I guess it can't hurt.

Maguire stands up as I take a seat beside him, which is impressive, especially after the primitive manners I'm used to enduring from Emerson. Emerson would have been more inclined to kick the seat out from under me for a laugh.

"What would you like to drink?"

I don't know what to order. The only alcohol I've ever tasted was a glass of champagne at the Sakrid. "I'll have a white wine, I guess."

My first sip is terrible. It tastes as horrid as the whisky Annabell drank.

"You don't like it, do you?"

I can't even open my mouth to say no. I'm still fighting it down.

"Wrong year and terrible vineyard," he observes.

"You know your wines, do you?"

"When you dine with mogul tycoons as often as I have, you soon learn how to talk their language and drink their over-exploited wines. I'll order you another drink. I hear the Applejack Rabbit or vodka martinis are good aboard *Sylvanis*."

I slide my wine to the side as the waiter serves my new drink, the Applejack Rabbit. I don't know what's in it or where it got its name, but it tastes like sweet, bubbly apple juice. I could quite easily drink it like soda.

"That perfume you have on is really nice." He sniffs, raising his nose.

"Thank you. It's oils from *Kingdom Plantae*."

"I've never heard of that shop."

"It's not a shop," I giggle. "It's from the earth garden."

"I believe you," he says, letting it pass right over his head. "So where are you staying when you get to Fortier?"

I haven't worked out that part of my journey. I guess a part of me naively thinks I'll fall straight into Sation's arms and then his bed.

"You don't even know, do you?"

"Is it that obvious? My only concern was making it onto the boat without being caught. I didn't consider where I'd rest my head. I guess I'll stay at a motel."

"You're courageous, I give you that."

"I don't think they would be calling me courageous back in Nolanberry right now. It will be more along the lines of a despicable, selfish villain. I bet they've banished me from their lives."

"They might be disappointed, but I doubt they will banish you from their lives. Why didn't you just tell them you were leaving to save yourself all this remorse?"

"I wanted to, but my dad would have locked me away if he knew I was escaping his command post, so I had no choice. I just hope Mom and Treallа will forgive me."

"Who's Trealla?"

"The most beautiful woman in the world."

"Really? You will have to introduce me to her if she's that beautiful."

"She's too beautiful for you, Maguire."

"Hey. Handsome is my middle name," he says, making his eyes go cross-eyed, pulling a funny face.

"You make me laugh." I chuckle.

"Or the cocktails are." He takes a drink. "Maybe we should call it a night."

"Gosh. How old are you?"

"Old enough to know you're a little drunk."

"And how old would that make you?" I look him in the eye.

"Twenty-two years young."

"Well, Mr. Twenty-two Years Young, I think I'll have another," I affirm, finishing my drink and sliding the empty glass towards the waiter.

"If your dad knew I was buying you alcohol, his blood would boil." He rubs his hand back and forth over his forehead, as if regretting this situation.

"In that case, order me ten more and send him the bill."

"You're trouble, girl," he says, shaking his head.

"I might be trouble, but I'm not a girl. I'm an eighteen-year-old woman now. I can stay out for as long as I like. I'm free," I say lifting my hands over my head, almost falling off my chair.

"Yep, you're definitely trouble," he says, turning his head, embarrassed.

"Excuse me, bartender. I'll have another Applejack Peter Rabbit, and old man Maguire will have a stiff, aged whisky."

I'm sure Maguire is regretting asking me over for a drink now, but I'm not.

"You know what I can't believe out of all of this? My father gave you the keys to stay in his house."

"It's not that hard to work out. First of all, he doesn't have to put me up in a hotel, so he'll save money. Secondly, it's been vacant for over twelve months, so it will be in need of some maintenance, so to kill two birds with one stone, he's sent me to take care of his business deals and also his handyman jobs."

"But you're not the handyman type," I tease him.

"Don't be fooled by the business suit. There's a handyman in me."

"There's a henchman in you, that's about all," I say under my breath.

"What's that, Isola?"

"I just said the garden is going to need an overhaul."

"Yeah, I'm sure you did."

The waiter serves his next glass of whisky and my Applejack Rabbit, only this time, he places a sliced strawberry on the rim of the glass for decoration.

"Have a look at that. It's a strawberry." Giselle the Strawberry Green Seed pops straight into my mind. "Do you know every strawberry has over two hundred seeds on it and they're the only fruit with seeds on the outside?"

"Really? You know your berries, do you?"

"I do. They like sandy soil and around six hours of sun a day, and they're the first fruits to ripen in spring."

"Wow, you really do know your berries."

"Yes, and guess what else... they're berry good for you."

"Two Applejack Rabbits later and you're a barrel of laughs."

"I've had three Peter Rabbits, I think," I say, hiccupping, knowing I should have probably stopped at one.

"Three too many, Isola. Maybe it really is time to call it a night after this one."

"I think you're right, Maguire."

Maguire places a twenty-dollar bill on the bar to cover the drink charges.

"Oh me oh my, have a look at that. American money." Never would I've thought I'd get excited about money, but I haven't seen American currency for over a year now. "I'm on my way home, Maguire." I wave the bill in the air as if it were the American flag.

"No, you're on your way to your cabin, little Miss Destinn."

Maguire escorts me out of the dining room and opens the door to my cabin. I fall onto the bed, as graceful as ever.

"Will you be all right, Isola?"

"I'm fine. I have three little Peter Rabbits to keep me company." I sit on my bed, a little dizzy.

"And I'm sure they will," he replies, standing at the door.

"Would you like to come in for a *Nico biscotti alla nocciola*?" I say in a drunken Italian accent.

"What on earth is a Nico… whatever else it was you said?"

"They're the best hazelnut biscuits in the world." I take the box of biscuits out of my case.

"I'll pass. Whisky and biscuits don't mix well. And by the way, now that you're heading back across the pond, you might want to start calling them cookies like an American and not biscuits like the Brits."

"This is true."

"Now to bed with you and your three Peter Rabbits. I'll see you tomorrow."

"Yes, Dad." Maguire once again shakes his head at me as he closes the door.

***

Lifting my head off the pillow, I wonder if I'm suffering from seasickness. *Mmm*, I think it's the liquid I drank, rather than the liquid I'm sailing on. I might just sleep this off.

The following day, I bounce out of bed knowing I only have three days to go until I'm home in Sation's arms. It's time for breakfast and, boy, am I hungry. I take a seat out on the deck, surrounded by my liquid love.

"Good morning, Isola. I'd love to join you for breakfast. I thought you'd never ask." Maguire boldly invites himself to breakfast.

"By all means." I hold out my open hand to the seat across from me.

"Thanks, but I'd rather sit beside you and have the same view of the ocean," he says, taking a seat.

"Suit yourself."

"Beautiful morning, isn't it? Yesterday was too, but I guess you didn't get to see much, stuck in your room."

"That nice drink you ordered me was a little too nice."

"Too much nice can be nasty the next day."

"Offensive, even."

"Have a look at this view. It's not every day you get to have coffee looking out to open blue seas."

"We are very fortunate." I keep looking towards the front of the ship for land to come into sight. Just like Annabell did on the *Makana*. "Tell me, Maguire, whereabouts in America are you from?"

"I grew up in Spillville but moved to Chicago to work."

"I've never heard of Spillville."

"You're kidding me. How haven't you heard of the famous Spillville?"

"What makes it famous?"

"Spillville is where the famous composer Antonin Dvorak wrote his renowned string quartet, 'The American.'"

"I've never heard of him, his string quartet, or Spillville. However, I have heard of Chicago."

"Everyone's heard of Chicago, Isola," he titters at me naivety

"How did you meet my father?"

"I was working for a shipping company, trading with your father. We met in Fortier and he ended up offering me a job."

"So, you know of Fortier then?"

"Yeah, I was there for about two weeks before I left to come to England."

"Wow, I didn't know that. So do your folks still live in Spillville?"

"My mom passed away two years back and my father took off when I was young, so who knows or cares where he is."

"So, we're both parentless in America."

"Yeah, I guess you can say that." He shrugs.

I'm definitely picking up on some uneasy feelings surrounding his father. I'd better change the subject. "Do you have a girlfriend in America to return to?"

"No, I don't, but I kind of left one back in Bristol who's not too happy with me or your father." His face turns strained, but it's better than the lost look on his face seconds ago.

"I know how she feels. My father has a way of dividing lovers, that's for sure."

"Slow down. Who's talking about love?" he said, holding up his hands.

He's getting all defensive about my mention of such intense emotions. But then he moves closer to me with a smug look.

"If your father has a way of dividing hearts, I'm guessing you have a lover in America you might be reuniting with."

"I gave myself away then, didn't I?" I sink back in my chair.

"You sure did," he laughs.

"He's not my boyfriend as such, but hopefully he takes one look at me and we can pick up from where we left off."

The server approaches us to take our order. "Would you like coffee or tea to start with?" she asks.

"I'll have a tea, please, and Maguire will have a coffee."

"It won't be long," she replies walking off.

"I knew there was more to your returning home."

"Aren't you clever?"

"It isn't hard to figure out a man is involved. People go to all sorts of extremes to please their hearts."

"I guess it's a little extreme," I hate to admit.

"Do I have to brace myself for a Hollywood love scene when we arrive? Are you going to run at each other with your arms wide open?" he mocks me.

"Um, no… He doesn't actually know I'm returning. We didn't keep in contact while I was gone," I say, knowing how crazy that sounds.

"Are you for real, Isola?" He sits up and turns to me. "And you thought I took a risk moving to England for work? Look at what you're doing. Did he tell you he would wait for you to return, when you last saw him?"

"I kind of didn't give him a last goodbye. I couldn't bear to put myself through a goodbye. So, instead, I just disappeared. Oops."

"Goodbyes really aren't your thing, are they?"

"What gives you that impression?"

The server places our drinks down on the table, and also a menu. I look to my right and see Maguire running his hand along his jawline, deep in thought. He plants seeds of doubt in my mind, making me wonder if I'm kidding myself to think Sation has waited all this time for me to return.

"I guess you'll find out soon how he feels," Maguire says, stirring a sugar cube into his coffee.

"Hopefully he's still into me."

"He would be a fool not to."

Is that a compliment or a comment? "Going by our last kiss, and the way he looked at me, I'm hoping he will still be interested."

"I think you will find most men can't take their eyes off you. Have you seen your reflection in a mirror?" he says, then takes a drink.

Okay, that is definitely a compliment. "That's nice of you to say, but he wasn't perving on me. There is more to it than that. I could feel the way he felt about me."

"Fair enough. I guess you will know soon where your fate lies with Prince Charming. I hate to mention this, but he hasn't been sent to Vietnam, has he?"

"Oh no, I hope not. What if he's been killed, and that's why I haven't heard from him?"

"Okay, that's a bit extreme. What if he just can't spell and that's why he hasn't written to you?"

"That's less dramatic."

"Yes, forget I mention the Vietnam thing. Let's go with he can't spell."

"Yes, let's. I don't want to entertain the possibility he's been sent to war."

"Let's order breakfast, shall we?" He picks up the menu.

I look out to sea. Is this extreme desire to please my heart an extremely foolish dream of mine? It's not as if Sation told me he loved me. This might be the biggest mistake of my life.

No, it's not. What Sation and I share is extremely real and worth all the effort I've gone to. I just hope he hasn't been sent off to Vietnam. If that's the case, I'll have to enlist.

Chapter Twenty

The restlessness I've felt since leaving America melts as the quaint township of Fortier comes into view. I've pictured this moment hundreds of times in the past year, but it's a million times better in real time. I've made the right decision in following my heart back home. The sight of Pattinson Pier alone soothes my heart, let alone what lies beyond it.

"Come have a look, Maguire, it's Pattinson Pier. Can you see it?" I point off to the left.

"I can. I think I can see your father standing at the end with a big stick that has your name written on it."

I push at his arm. "Don't ruin it for me."

"Relax, woman, I'm joking. On a serious note, given you haven't organized a place to stay, would you like to stay at your old house until you reacquaint with Prince Charming?"

He might have a dash of cheek about him, but he really is a thoughtful man.

"How about I show you to the house and if Sation doesn't sweep me off my feet today, I'll take you up on your offer?"

"Sounds good."

Maguire collects his luggage while I wait at the front of the queue, itching to disembark. The deckhand lowers the ramp onto the pier and gives us the all-clear. Finally, there's nothing standing between me and my desires. I've cleared the path to achieve everything I deserve, now I'm ready to receive. I step onto the pier and, simultaneously, my heart steps into overdrive. My vigorous heartbeat brings me to a standstill with one foot on the pier and one foot on the ramp. Maybe it's just the excitement of being home. Or is it the one thing I've been avoiding for the past twelve months?

"Excuse me, miss. You're blocking the exit."

Anxiously, I put my other foot onto the pier. *Thump, thump, thump.* My heartbeat makes its way to my throat. Oh no. I'm having my third awakening. *No, no, no, no, no.* This can't be happening. The knowledge I've kept at arm's length is now demanding acknowledgement, and it's more determined than ever to awaken me forever more. Adrenaline gushes through my senses, sending me into sensory overload. The exact euphoric sensation I experienced in Annabell's awakening is now here, calling on me. This can't be happening. Not now, when I'm moments away from Sation. With all my will, I think of every possible human thought. I think *I am human.* That I'm flesh and bone. I think, I think, I think, but the euphoria leans in and teases me its way. I run off the pier with fearful tears, unable to believe life could be this cruel to awaken me now.

But the second I step off the pier onto the path, my heartbeat slows down, way down. The euphoria dwindles to nothing, leaving my heart shivering and my nerves on edge. Taking a seat on the bench, I lift my feet off the earth, not wanting to be connected to anything natural that might call on the innate in me. Am I still in my first chapter? Have I thought myself out of evolving into my second? I don't feel any different. I'm still madly in love with Sation. I'm not shimmering, and I can't see anything with my eyes closed.

What a relief. I'm still my normal human self, thank goodness for that. Just when I've overcome every obstacle stopping me from being with Sation, the biggest one lies buried deep within me, ticking away like a bomb. I've been looking forward to grounding my feet on Fortier soil, and 'being like a tree,' to keep in tune with nature, but after this close encounter, I think it's best I revert to being in tune with the human thought society. I turn and notice Maguire walking towards me with a look of concern, carrying his luggage.

"Are you all right, Isola? A lady back there told me you look faint. Actually, she said, 'Your wife looks faint,' which made *me* feel faint."

I laugh at his facial expressions. Maguire obviously isn't the marrying kind. "I'm fine, Maguire."

"Are you sure? She is rather concerned about you."

"Honestly, I'm fine. Thanks, hubby."

"Not funny."

"The look on your face is," I say, relieved I've deflected my inherent nature, for the time being.

***

Fortier is even more beautiful the second time around, especially with my new appreciation of nature. Now I can name every tree I'm walking by. In fact, there're a lot more trees than I remember, or maybe I'm more aware of them now. Someone must have been busy planting all these trees a long time ago.

I left Fortier with a basic understanding of nature, but I've returned with a graduate diploma. Sation was once shocked I knew where north, south, east, and west were. Now I know the direction of Polaris, our northern star. The celestial education I received in the past twelve months far exceeds the twelve years I completed at school. Now, isn't that saying something?

I always knew I'd return to Fortier, but I never pictured myself here with a henchman three feet behind me. He looks so out of place in his business suit, carrying his luggage, with sweat rolling down his face. He doesn't belong in a countrified beach town, but I'm right at home.

Ten minutes later, here we are at Five Sycamore Street. Suddenly, I realize the tree in my front yard is, in fact, a maple tree. A Fairlee tree.

"So, this is the Destinn residence?" He takes in the view.

"Yep. A very overgrown yard. Luckily my father sent his handy henchman to tidy up."

"Knock off the henchman, will you? I'm nobody's henchman."

"What about Henchy then?" I smirk, but going by the look on his face, Henchy is not acceptable either.

***

"Your mom obviously forgot to cancel her Sears subscription," Maguire comments on the year's worth of catalogs piled up on the doorstep.

"It appears so."

With a little force, Maguire opens the front door. Stepping inside, we both inhale a year's worth of dust. Mom would die if she could see it in this musky, dusty state. Luckily, she was smart enough to cover all her furniture with sheets before she left. Walking upstairs, I remember back to my father dragging me down them, kicking and screaming, when I refused to leave. I gave him a workout that day. The tissues I cried into are still sitting on my bedside table. What's more tragic are the *Seventeen* magazines underneath them.

"This is your room, I take it?"

"It is." I screw my face up.

"I thought you'd be happy to be back here"

"I'm happy to be in Fortier, but I'm not too sure about this house. It reminds me of my father." Which isn't what I want, now that I'm finally free of him.

"You have it in for him, don't you?"

"We have it in for each other."

"At least your father stuck around. Mine was obsolete."

"True. Did you find yourself a room?" I turn my head to him standing beside me in the doorway of my bedroom.

"No, I haven't. It feels kind of odd being in my boss's house, as if I shouldn't be."

"How do you think I feel? I'm definitely not supposed to be here."

"Ain't that true?" He sighs and looks around. "So which room is mine?"

"Julia's room's next to mine, or the spare room's across the hall. Julia's room has a better view, though."

"I can't move into your sister's room."

"Why not? Julia's room is a lot bigger, and there can't be anything left in it. She carted everything across to England with her. Go look." He leaves to check them out. Moments later, he returns. "What do you think?"

"You weren't wrong. She really did take everything with her, apart from the mattress."

"She sure did."

"And you obviously didn't take a thing," he comments, looking around my room.

"Only my shitty attitude."

"I hope you left that back in England."

"I lost it in England."

"That's good to hear. Do you think your parents would mind if I moved the double bed from the spare room into Julia's room? I think I've outgrown a single bed."

"They'll never know. I doubt they'll ever come back here."

"You don't think so?"

"Maybe to visit, but never to live. They love it in Nolanberry. Which suits me fine."

"You really are Miss Independent, aren't you?"

"I guess so. I've happily been a loner all my life," I say, stepping back into the hall, desperate for some fresh air.

"You're leaving already?" Maguire asks, following behind me.

"Yes, I didn't come back to Fortier to be cooped up in this house."

"Where're you going?"

"Heck, you sound like my dad," I turn and say to him at the bottom step.

"I didn't mean it like that. I'm just making conversation."

"There's something I've been wanting to do for a very long time."

"Wow, this guy you have returned home for really does have you in a spin."

"Maybe." I grin. "Thanks for letting me stay here for the night. Make yourself at home."

***

I run towards the sea like a madwoman on fire, needing to put myself out. Yes, I can't wait to see Sation, but first I need the rush of my liquid love to saturate my skin, and cleanse all the absences I've felt within. "Hello, it's me. I'm back," I call to the sea.

But in all my eagerness, I'd forgotten to put my bikini on. Oh, well, skirt and singlet will have to do. I flip off my sandles and watch the water pool around my legs. The next incoming wave approaches and I dive straight in. "Ahhh." Finally, I'm home, where I belong

Like a captive dolphin being released back into open seas, I move through the water, finally free. Deeper and deeper I travel out of sight, but strangely, there's no need for air. It's happening again. Like when I dove off *Cybele.*

Swimming up to the surface, Pattinson Pier is off in the distance. How in heck did I swim out this far? I'm a good swimmer, but this is exceptionally good. Down I go, investigating this weird ability of mine. Minutes pass. My heart hasn't burst and my lungs haven't collapsed. Something's not right.

But surprisingly, I'm not alone, the siren is here. From the depths of the sea, her dulcet sigh sings to me, enticing me with her melodic humming to chase after the emotions she evokes in me. Without a thought, I'm gliding through the water at a momentous pace, in search of her origin, and the look on her face.

BANG.

Brought to a complete stop. The thumping pain in my head steals my attention. Out of the water I lift my head and see a person in a tin boat looking back at me in horror.

"Girl, you near on scared the melanin out of me. I'm 'bout as white as you."

I rub my aching head. "What did you hit me with?"

"I didn't hit you, girl. I be sittin' here fishin', mindin' my own business, then you gone and barged right into my boat. Given me an awful fright. I thought you were a shark coming to eat yourself some tasty rump."

"Oh, my head." I feel a lump the size of a tennis ball mounting.

"Whatcha doin' out in the middle of the ocean, anyway? And, by golly, how does someone your size swim so fast? I ain't never seen a person swim that quick before."

"I must have been caught in the current. That is, until I hit your boat." I look up to the silhouette of her body, unable to see her face properly with the sun shining behind her.

"I'll be damned, girl," she says, leaning towards me, peering at my face.

I recoil slightly. "Is it bad? Am I bleeding?"

"I'm not lookin' at the bump, although it be nasty. I'm lookin' at your irises. Boffum as blue as the ocean." She nods. "I been aksed to keep a lookout for you."

She leans down, picks me up by the arms with minimal effort, and drops me into her boat, like a weightless doll.

"You good," she says, but her inflection is confusing. Is she telling me I'm good or asking me if I'm good?

"You be lucky you hit my boat, girl. Who knows where you'd have ended up?"

My head pounds. "Can you please stop calling me 'girl'?"

"You are one, ain'tcha? Never seen breasts like that on a man before."

I'd never heard a woman speak so honestly before. "I am a girl, but my name is Isola."

"Yep, that be about right. *Salve*, Isola."

"Salve?"

"It's Latin for greetin's."

"*Salve* to you too then," I say, touching my aching head. "Hold on a minute. Did you say you were asked to keep an eye out for me?"

"Best believe it, girl."

My gut tightens. Hiring a spy to find me is just the sort of lengths my father would go to. In spite of my aching head, I stand. "I'll be off now." I turn to jump back into the water.

She puts her hand on my leg, pinning me back down on the seat.

"You trippin', Isola. Best you be sittin' back down."

"You're not taking me back to my dad. I knew it wouldn't take him long to put a hefty reward on my head."

"Your dad ain't no friend of mine, and I ain't after no reward."

"Then who told you to keep an eye out for me?"

"Pearl, my neighbor at Reefers."

"I don't know anyone called Pearl."

"Well, she knows you."

"How does she know me?"

"We're goin' there now. You can aks her yourself."

She grabs hold of the oars and starts rowing. I abandon the idea of swimming away. She'd probably just chase me. Besides, my head hurts too much to swim.

"It will take you ages to row to Reefers in this little boat," I grumble.

"You trippin'. Reefers is just behind you." She points over my shoulder.

To my surprise, there it is—a sea of crystal blue lapping the shore of the luscious green island of Reefers.

"Did I swim out this far?" I ask, confused.

"You a hot mess." She shakes her head. "I told you, you were on the move."

What in heck is going on? One minute I'm swimming at Fortier, then I'm breathing underwater. Next, I'm hypnotized by a sea nymph, and now I'm being taken by this woman to some other woman who apparently knows me. My life is a hot mess.

Turning back, I can't help but admire her dark, smooth skin, especially after spending the past twelve months with pale-skinned English people.

"Whatcha lookin' at?"

I look away, embarrassed she caught me staring.

"Out with it. What's amusing in my direction?"

"The color of your skin, and how smooth it is. I wish I had velvet-smooth skin like yours."

"Don't go wishin' for anyone else's skin but your own," she replies.

Suddenly I realize I don't know her name. "Sorry, I forgot to ask your name."

"My name's Stelina."

"Cool name."

"You gotta love whatcha momma gave you, nahmeen?" She pleasantly smiles. "Here we are."

Everything familiar comes flooding back. The gentle waves lapping up on the crisp sand, the fresh smell of the forest infused by the warmth of the sun, and the birds singing in the rich green canopy above. Paradise never looked so perfect.

With ease, Stelina drags the boat onto the shore, with me still sitting inside. She doesn't look overly muscular, but she sure has the strength of a man.

"Come with me. I wanna introduce you to Pearl. She be slap-happy to see you."

Even though I've been to Reefers many times, I've never seen the two beach houses we are walking towards. I guess I've never been this far around the coast before. One house is a humble-looking beach cottage. The other's older and stands on stilts, with a large porch.

"Pearl? Pearl, you home?" Stelina calls out, walking up the steps.

Who is this woman who, supposedly, knows me? I look through the front windows and see as many plants inside as there are outside.

"Pearl's around the back in the veggie garden, Stelina," a man calls out from inside.

"Wait until y'all see what I caught off the atoll today."

A man with gray hair neatly pulled back into a ponytail pokes his head out of the window.

"Catch yourself a big fish, did you?"

"Don't nobody catch 'em as big and bad as me, Ray." Stelina points at me.

The man turns in my direction. He looks surprised, but my attention is caught by the overwhelmed look on the lady's face walking towards me. Her hands reach for her face, then she pauses. But, as surprised as she seems to see Stelina's big catch of the day, I'm as surprised that I recognize her. It's the nurse who named me, who lives in my favorite beach house. At least now I know the name of the lady responsible for naming me. But more surprisinging is the inherent nature in her gracious brown eyes. The warmth of her heart steps another foot closer as she approaches, confirming to me dear Pearl is indeed one of Trealla's kind.

"Whatcha think of my catch of the day, Pearl?" Stelina asks, bouncing on her toes.

"I think it's not only a big one, but a very rare one." She smiles at me. "Hello, Isola. My name is Pearl," she says, formally introducing herself for the first time.

"Hi, Pearl. Looks like we meet again."

"Yes. When did you return from England."

Wow. Her memory hasn't failed her. "I arrived home today."

"And let me guess. The first thing you did is plunge straight into the sea." She looks at my dripping wet clothes.

"How did you guess?"

She shakes her head. "Some things never change."

"I wouldn't call it swimmin', Pearl," Stelina says. "Isola looked like she'd shot out of a cannon, she was movin' that fast."

"You look like you have been *hit* by a cannon." Pearl frowns. "What caused that bump on your head?"

"I whacked into Stelina's boat while moving at my missile pace."

"Ah, so Stelina didn't catch you," the man says through the window screen, stirring Stelina up and startling me. I'd forgotten he was inside.

"I plucked her out of the sea, Ray. That's as good as a catch, right?"

"Enough, you two," Pearl says, breaking up their tit-for-tat. "Isola, let me introduce you to Ray, my partner."

"Hello, Ray." I send him a little wave through the screen.

"It's lovely to meet you, Isola."

He reminds me of an old musician who's traded in his guitar and late nights for coffee and the morning paper.

"We'd better get you something for that bump before it gets any bigger," Pearl says.

"Okay. Bye, Stelina. It was nice to meet you."

"Best you believe it." She winks at me.

"You coming in for a cuppa?" Ray asks Stelina.

"I'm straight. I best be cleanin' the fish I caught today. I'll see y'all later."

"Come along, Isola," Pearl steers me around the side of the house.

"Is this your house, Pearl?" I ask, looking at the amazing view of the beach as I follow her magnetic trail of energy around the back.

"Yes, dear, this is my house."

"I thought you lived at Fortier in that grand old beach house."

"No, I just take care of that house while the owners are away."

"Oh."

The backyard is more or less the extension of the forest. There're no fences, only a vegetable garden sectioned off, which Pearl is now leading me through. She takes a seat on the garden bench, prompting me to do the same.

"You're one of them, aren't you, Pearl?" I come straight out and ask.

She gives me a suspicious side-eye. "One of what?"

"One of those people who is all-knowing of the innate within. I can see it in your eyes and feel the energy radiating from you."

She bends down and pulls out a small weed from the soil, putting it in her pocket. Then she turns back to me. "It appears you've made progress on your path while in England."

"Progress has definitely been made. I had the most extraordinary time."

"That's wonderful to hear. And now to answer your question, yes, I am all-knowing," she humbly admits.

"I'm not."

"I know that. However, I can tell you've had an awakening. I can feel it in your energy."

"I've had three. The third was earlier today on the pier."

"Three awakenings, and yet you still haven't awakened," she says, alarmed. "Generally, we have one or two and then awaken to our knowledge, but never three."

"Everyone except me, that is. Not that I mind. I'd like to stay in my first chapter. I'm happy hanging out with the human thought society."

"Normally, our kind are eager to let this human experience go."

"I admire the way your kind live and breathe. I truly do. But I'm happy being my human self."

"What makes you want to hold onto it so desperately?"

I want to say, *a man I'm besotted with, who means more to me than my second chapter*, but I don't want to sound pathetic to someone as evolved as Pearl.

"Actually, you don't have to answer that question. I've been around long enough to know the answer." She notices another weed and bends down to grab it.

"And what answer has time brought you to?"

"There's an element of comfort in controlling your life. Therefore, any hint of letting go to the unknown creates fear, making you cling even tighter to what you know. You don't free yourself because you fear what's required of you to become your true self, and so you safely remain the same."

"You're right, Pearl. I don't want certain things in my life to change out of fear of the unknown. I can't come back from your realm of living once I've gone there, can I?"

"No, you can't, but nor will you want to."

"Yeah. I don't know about that." I pause. "I think I'll stick with what's familiar."

She chuckles at my response. "Who you truly are knows everything, and I will not undermine its presence in your life by attempting to convince you to be or do anything else. Your nature obviously still requires you to be unknowing of its presence, given it hasn't awakened you fully. It's best we let it walk its path. After all, nature knows best."

"Yes, I'm walking a great path, now that I'm home."

"Let's see to this bump on your head before it gets any bigger. Some taka leaves should sort it out."

"Did you say 'taka'?" I look back at her, surprised.

"Yes. It's a plant my ancestors have been using for thousands of years."

"I read about taka in a novel once." Looking at the vegetable patch, I immediately spot the leaves. It looks exactly the same as it did in Annabell's story. I bend down and feel the leaves in my hand. The texture is identical. Annabell would have loved to have grown taka like this in England, to save her beloved William, and here I am with an abundance of it in front of me.

"If you have never seen taka before, how did you know the plant?"

"Oh, the novel I read was a very special interactive book that described it perfectly." Among other things.

Kneeling down beside me, Pearl asks, "A book you could hear and see with your eyes closed?" Pearl's interest in my comment shows in her wide eyes. She is obviously hinting to me that she too has been to see one of these special Storytellers.

"Yes. It wasn't your everyday book. That's for sure. Do you know Lizabethe?"

"No, who is she?"

"Lizabethe is the Storyteller who read the book with the taka plant in it." I explain.

"Oh, there're a number of special Storytellers who have the same collection of books like hers."

"Yes, that's right. They're hard to come across, so I've been told."

"They're very rare and very gifted. It definitely sounds like you had an insightful time in England. It mustn't have been all doom and gloom, like you thought it would be."

"The day I saw you at the house in Fortier, it was triple doom and gloom, but I made friends with an amazing lady who owns a garden called Avenlee, and she made it a pleasurable experience."

"I know of Avenlee," she said humbly.

"You do?" I gasp, happy to have someone to share my fondness for Avenlee with.

"Yes, it's a very sacred place among our kind, and so too is the lady who cares for it."

This conversation's getting better. Now I can also talk about my favorite person in the world. "In my opinion, Trealla outshines Avenlee. She changed my life for the better."

"That's pleasing to hear you have been in the company of this remarkable woman. It's also pleasing to see you back home."

"Thanks, Pearl. It's so good to be home. Reefers, just like Avenlee, has this natural mystic feel, like it escapes civilization and remains timeless. I can just be myself here."

"Yes, you can be your natural self here and nature will support that. Now, let me pick some taka leaves to put on your head." She leans over the garden bed, opening her palm over the taka. Then she motions her hand back towards her, as if to pull the scent of the taka to her face.

"What are you doing, Pearl?" I lean forward, never having seen this before.

"I'm using my senses to detect the healthiest plant." She continues wafting the scent towards her.

"You can detect that?" I'm amazed, watching her pick particular leaves she knows to be the best.

"Yes. I'll teach you one day, if you'd like."

"Cool." I watch on. "Is taka good for swelling?"

"Taka is good for a lot of things. My people have known of this plant's energy potential from the very beginning."

"In Annabell's story, she wished to use it to treat a blood disorder. She traveled all the way from London to Georgia to find it."

"Did you say 'Annabell'?" She stops what she is doing and looks back at me and smiles.

"Yes, Annabell. Have you heard that story?"

"I know the story of Annabell." She nods.

"That's amazing." I bring my hands together, excited we share the same fictional interests. "What chapter did you read up to? I've been dying to know if Annabell survived her fall."

"You'll have to wait until you move into your second chapter to find out if she survived. Now, take a seat while I place the leaves on your forehead."

"Yes, Nurse."

Like Trealla, Pearl is obviously unwilling to divulge information before nature does. I watch her bruise the leaves to release the properties. The taka smells just like it did in Annabell's story when she stomped all over it in her fit of rage. I look up at Pearl's soft, caring eyes, smiling, thinking she has known all this time I'm one of her kind, maybe even since the day I was born.

"Pearl, why did you ask Stelina to keep an eye out for me?"

"Because I knew when you turned eighteen, you'd return home, just like you said you would," she replies, putting all her concentration on treating me.

"Well, yes, but why is it so important for you to ask her to keep an eye out for me?" I push for an answer.

"Because you're special. And that's all I'll say."

"Special to you, or special in general?" I probe for more insight.

"Both. Now wait here a moment. I'll run inside and get some ice to put on your head as well." She disappears inside, dodging any further questioning about my specialness.

I thought Trealla was tight-lipped, but Pearl is even tighter. There's no budging this woman for trade secrets. I've found more rattling circumstances and eccentric people to live among. In fact, they were here all along. I just failed to notice them. Now, three awakenings later, they're coming out of the woodwork, in full view.

Chapter Twenty-One

Inside the tidy kitchen, Pearl swings open the freezer door and pulls out a tray of ice cubes.

"Oh my goodness, Ray. I'm so overwhelmed. She returned. I could just thank every star in the sky."

Seated at the table, Ray wraps his large hands around a mug of tea. "Well, you've been asking every star in the sky to look over her. You might as well thank them. Are you okay?"

"I don't know what I am at the minute." Pearl spreads a dish cloth on the table, empties the trayful of ice onto it, and ties the cloth into a bundle. "I'm so glad Stelina got Isola out of the water."

"Stelina did you proud. I was so happy to see her standing on the veranda. You should have seen your face." Ray smiles, slightly giggling to himself. "I thought you were going to pass out when you realized it was her."

"I nearly did, just like when she was born. This moment has been a long time coming, Ray."

"You don't have to tell me." He lifts his mug and takes a drink. "She hasn't awakened yet, has she?"

"No, Ray, and she has no interest, either. It's so frustrating. She is so gifted and doesn't even know it."

"She has a mind of her own. Which isn't a bad thing. Keep calm, Pearl. She'll awaken soon. Maybe it's a good idea you keep her out of the sea, just in case it lures her away like once before. It would be a shame to see all that creativity go to waste now."

Holding the ice-filled cloth, she heads for the door. "I'd rather die than see that happen in this lifetime."

***

Pearl returns and peels back the taka leaves, assessing my treatment. "It looks better already, but I'll still put this ice on it for good measure."

"Thanks, Nurse Pearl."

"Pearl will be adequate," she says in her matriarch tone, holding the tea towel of ice to my forehead.

"Ouch. That's cold."

"You will get used to the coldness soon. Now, I'd love for you to stay longer, but the last ferry back to Fortier is due to leave in twenty minutes."

"That's okay, Pearl. I can swim back. I move like a fish in the water nowadays. You should see me."

"You're no more a fish than I am a Cuban circus clown. However, now that we're on the subject, I have a very important matter to discuss with you."

"Fire away, Pearl. I'm all gills." I smile, making light of my new talent.

"I'm being serious," she says in an authoritative tone. "I need you to stay out of the sea."

"For how long?"

"Indefinitely."

"Indefinitely?" I chuckle. "That's not possible. My head is feeling much better, if that's what you're worried about."

"That's not it." She gives me an earnest look. "It might sound impossible, but it's very important you stay out of the sea."

Pushing the ice away from my head, I stand, restless about this conversation. "I've waited over a year to be back in that water. You can't ask that of me."

"I must, Isola. I'm sorry, but you just have to trust me on this one."

"Tell me why."

"I can't," she says, dropping her head.

"You're asking me to stay away from something I love, and you can't even give me a reason why?"

"Well, actually, I'm not asking you to stay out of the sea. I'm insisting you do."

Now I'm very restless. Actually, more like agitated. "If you want me to stay away from the only place I truly belong, then I need a good enough reason why."

"The reason is because..." She pauses for a moment, with an awkward look in her eyes. "The reason is because you love it so much, it could kill you."

"You can't be serious, Pearl. I'm a great swimmer. How on earth could loving something so much kill me?"

"I don't know. It just could."

"I'm sorry, but this is way too absurd to agree to. You're not even sure of why you're insisting on it yourself."

She steps towards me. "I know we've only formally met today, and what I'm saying might sound absurd, but I need you to trust me."

"But you don't understand. I'm a great swimmer. I really am, I swam to Reefers today."

"I know how confident you are in the sea. I've watched you swimming all your life."

"Well, there you go. Nothing's happened to me so far."

"Now things are changing."

"The only thing changing is the state of my happiness." I've been looking forward to swimming with Sation. It was our favorite thing to do and now she's asking me not to. "If you knew how much I loved the water, you wouldn't ask this of me. The sea is my liquid love. I feel so peaceful in it."

"I'll welcome you into my world as a replacement, and you'll be surrounded by love in this forest." Her sincerity shines from her gentle brown eyes, but the forest will never cut it.

"That's so kind of you, but nothing can replace the feeling I get gliding through water." Especially with Sation.

"Don't underestimate the magic in this forest," she says, leaning towards me, hinting to a magical life I'm yet to discover.

"Is it really that important to you?" I reply, feeling the need to be guided by her innate knowledge. She has obviously presented on my path for a reason and clearly knows things about me that I don't.

"I wouldn't demand such a thing of you if it weren't. These awakenings you are having are restructuring your existence." She places her hand on her heart and once again gives me a gentle, wise stare. "I need you to promise me you won't go into the sea."

I drop my head into my hands at this absurd promise I'm faced with. Out of respect for her and the notion she may very well know more about the sea's deathly consequences, I'll come to an agreement. After all, I've come home to live my life with Sation and not flirt with death.

"In pain and suffering, I promise to stay out of the sea, for now. But it's going to kill me."

"Not as much as it will if you swim in it," Pearl responds, looking directly at me. "How about for now, instead of swimming, you spend time here on the island. There is a life existing on this island as old as the stars, and the legends it beholds will entertain your heart."

"Now that sounds rather intriguing, but do you know how much time I planned on spending swimming? I might have to move to the island to fill in that much time," I joke, letting her know I planned on spending every single day in the sea.

"I don't mind how much time you spend here, and I know Stelina would like your company. There's only a four or five year age gap between you, so you'll have things in common."

"You and Stelina might not mind, but the old lady that owns the island might object. She hates us Fortier foreigners coming here."

"I'll have a word with her. She won't mind a bit."

"I don't know. I've heard she's rather unwelcoming."

"Don't you worry about her." She shakes her head, reassuring me it will all be taken care of.

"Well, that will be a great big challenge for me, spending every day on an island surrounded by my liquid love."

"There will be enough love and adventure on this island to keep you happy. Just you wait and see."

There will be enough love and adventure in Sation's arms to keep me happy and I guess I can always swim in his tropical bule eyes.

***

My conversation with Pearl replays in my mind on the ferry ride home. Does she know about the humming I hear under the sea? And is this what could potentially kill me? Surely not. Her voice boasts of loving peacefulness. I decide I'll have another talk with Pearl about this promise. But first I need to find those tropical-blue eyes to dive into.

As the ferry approaches the dock, I meet with my first challenge in the form of Pattinson Pier. That pier seems to entice the innate out of me. If I step onto it, I could potentially awaken, which is the last thing I want. But I've just promised Pearl I won't go into the sea. What a mess I've gotten myself into now. How the hell am I going to get to dry land without my heart bursting through my ribs? It's decision time. I'll try my luck with the pier first.

Making sure I'm the last person to exit the ferry, I purposely dominate my existence with brain activity and nervously place one foot on the pier, waiting to see if I'm going to be bombarded by the innate dream-killer. Thankfully, nothing happens. Down goes my other foot onto the pier. I pause. Still nothing. I let go of the rail, putting the full weight of my body onto the wooden planks. My heart remains cool, calm, and unchanged. This obviously isn't the time for my fourth awakening. *Phew.* The pressure is on. I need to find Sation before I awaken and it's all ruined.

"Isola Destinn! Is that you?"

Whipping around at the sound of Nick's voice, I turn to see him sitting at the end of the pier with several other men, with fishing rods in their hands. He jumps up and rushes over to me. His familiar smile makes me feel warm inside. Finally, I'm back home with my people.

"Nick. Oh my God, what a surprise," I say, looking at the men he is fishing with, praying Sation isn't among them. Our first rekindling moment needs to be perfect, and this is far from it. After a quick scan, I sigh with relief that he isn't here.

"I can't believe it's you, Isola," Nick says, giving me a hug.

"I can't believe you're fishing."

Nick chuckles. "I got roped into it by my old man. It keeps him happy. When did you get back?"

"About three hours ago."

"And look where you're returning from already. Reefers." He holds out his hand towards the island.

"You know me all too well," I chuckle, knowing he's right.

"My God, Isola, what is that on your head? It hurts to look at." He moves closer to take a look, showing concern.

"Oh, I swam into a boat, but it looks worse than it is. So anyway, how have you been? Are you still living inland?"

"I lasted four months and ditched the boondocks, much to my mom's despair. I hear you performed a sneaky disappearing act." He raises his eyebrows, nudging me as if I'd successfully performed a magic trick.

"I'm not big on goodbyes." I wince at my lack of social skills.

"We all gathered that, but look at you now." He steps back, taking in the full length of me. "You're all grown up and ladylike."

"England had a maturing effect on me."

"Remind me never to go to England." He winks. "I do like that you still don't wear shoes, you bohemian beach babe."

"I have matured, but I still love to feel the sand under my feet." He jogs my memory to collect my shoes on the beach where I took them off earlier.

"Actually, Isola, I did do something mature while you were gone. I got my own pad, just up the street here."

"That's very grown up of you."

"Yeah, I moved into a house with a friend of mine a couple of weeks after you left."

"Good for you, Nick."

"You remember my friend Sation?"

"Yes, I remember Sation." Good heavens, I remember the sound of his breath leaving his lungs.

"We moved in together."

"Really?" I struggle to keep my voice casual. "That would be a party house, with you two living together."

"Nah. Sation's away at the moment, so it's been rather quiet."

"He is?" *Oh my God, he's been conscripted to Vietnam.*

"He's on a work-slash-vacation in Canada for two weeks."

I heave a sigh of relief. *Thank goodness for that.* However, two weeks isn't what I want to hear. Just as well I've grown patient over the past twelve months.

"I hope you're enjoying the house to yourself while Sation's gone."

"I've got the old man visiting this week, so it worked out. Are you back for good, Isola, or just visiting?"

"I'm back for good, but my folks are still in England."

"Whereabouts are you staying?"

"For the time being, I'm staying at my old house with a guy from England, but it's just until I make other arrangements."

"Really? He's a lucky cat."

"He's just a friend, or to be exact, a housemate. So don't go jumping to any conclusions."

"Yeah, right." He rolls his eyes.

"I'm serious, Nick. We ran into each other by chance on the ship back to America. He works for my father. There is definitely nothing going on. He's like my dad's protégé."

"Okay, then."

He accepts my reply, I think. I hope. "So, have you hooked up with anyone special?"

"Well, believe it or not, I've been going steady with a chick for about six months now."

"Six months? Heck, I don't know whether to believe you or not."

"I know, it's crazy right. She's throwing a birthday party for my twenty-first at her house this coming Saturday. You should come."

"I'll definitely be there." Especially now that I have all the freedom in the world to stay out as long as I want.

"Great. Oh, and bring your housemate along. It's going to be quite a bash."

"He can stay home. He's too stiff to get into the Fortier flow."

"We'll give him a few drinks and unstiffen him."

"If you insist."

"Nicolas! Nicolas, your rod's on the bite," Nick's dad calls out.

"I better get back to the fishing. I wouldn't want to miss a bite," he says, rolling his eyes in his dad's direction. "I'll see you Saturday night. Ten Milson Street. Bring your party hat."

***

Do I knock on my own front door or walk straight in? As much as it's my old house, Dad gave Maguire the keys, not me. I'm just the homeless runaway he's been kind enough to take in for the night, or maybe for two weeks now. I guess I'd better knock.

Maguire opens the door. "Isola, you're home."

"Yes, I am, Henchman."

Before I even get the chance to walk in, he closes the door on me, locking me out. I think I overdid the henchman title. I knock again. Moments later, I hear footsteps walking back towards the door.

"Who is it?"

"Funny one. Open the door."

"Is that Miss Destinn, daughter of Mr. Destinn and ambassador of Fortier?"

That rascal. I can't even get upset at him, given I need to stay here tonight.

"Yes, that's me. Now can you let me in? You've had your fun."

"First you have to call me 'Boss.'"

I can just picture the smirk on his face on the other side of the door. "Can you please let me in, Boss?" I say in sufferance.

"I can't hear you."

He is going to pay for this.

"Open the door, Boss!" I yell.

The door swings open. "Welcome home, Isola, come on in." He greets me like a bellman at a fancy hotel, irritating me even more with his formal disposition.

"You're good, Maguire, I give you that."

"Why, thank you," he smirks, stepping to the side. "What happened to your noggin?" His facial expression takes on my pain.

"I ran into some tin."

"And hard, by the look of it." He looks at it from all angles.

"It's really not that bad. A lady I know put these special leaves on it and the swelling's gone down heaps."

"Fair enough. So, no luck with the prince on his noble steed?"

"Don't go there, Maguire," I say, walking upstairs, listening to him snicker.

***

What a day it's been since first stepping onto Pattinson Pier. I experienced an awakening which I fortunately smothered in thoughts. I rediscovered my extraordinary ability to breathe underwater and reacquainted with the dulcet humming in the sea. I met Pearl, Stelina, and Ray. Next, I consented to a ridiculous promise to stay out of the sea. I find out Sation's in another country and, to finish the day off, I've ended up back at Five Sycamore Street with a henchman in the room beside me. What a heck of a day. Looks like kooky-crazy is becoming my norm.

Knock, knock, comes through my bedroom wall.

"What do you want, Maguire?"

"Good night, Isola."

"Nigh night, Henchman." I get the last giggle.

Chapter Twenty-Two

Waking up to "Running Bear Loved Little White Dove" echoing from the shower is a far cry from waking up at the tranquil Avenlee. Throwing back the covers, I put my bikini and dress on, and make my way to the beach. I smile, knowing I have this view of blue to wake up to for the rest of my life. Bliss.

Stripping down to my bikini, I step closer to the water. As it pools around my feet, my promise to Pearl pokes me in the eye, stopping me from taking another step forwards. I'm so angry about making such a ridiculous promise. The sea is right in my reach, but I can't touch it. Why did I do this to myself, and why is Pearl making me?

"Why, Pearl, why?" I scream out to Reefers. I throw my dress back on. I'm going to see Pearl, via the ferry this time, to make her revoke this unreasonable promise.

***

The ferry docks at Picolo Pier. Within minutes, I'm knocking on Pearl's door. It appears neither Pearl nor Ray are home. However, I can hear music playing at Stelina's.

"Hello, are you there, Stelina?" I call out over the music.

"Who is it?"

"It's Isola. I met you yesterday."

"Come on in. I'll be just a moment."

I've walked into what looks to be a museum of geographic maps hanging on the walls. Wow, I wasn't expecting this. The old maps have navigational paths trekking across the land masses. The oceans have charts of longitude and latitude, emphasizing the depths and currents of the water, with little old decorative ships dotted about. However, I'm unable to familiarize myself with the abstract land masses and names written on them. Stelina comes in as I step closer to investigate. I sit on the sofa as if I've been patiently minding my own business the whole time.

"Well, look who I have sittin' in my clapboard cave." She smiles.

"It's a very interesting clapboard cave." I look around.

"That it is. You didn't have to take your shoes off to come in." She looks at my feet.

"I didn't put any on this morning. I rarely do."

"That's interestin'." She looks down at my feet again. "You put some beautiful oils on though." She lifts her nose in the air, sniffing. "I can smell ylang ylang, orange, lavender, maybe even a hint of geranium."

"Good nose."

"Good blend of essences, all 'em smell good together. So, did you have a bo-peep at my maps?"

"I did have a little look, but I couldn't understand the names of the places."

"Noneum? Not even America or England?"

"Where is England?" I look around on her walls.

Stelina points her finger to the wall behind me. "It be there."

"Oh, I see. My goodness, does that say Avenlee?"

"Best believe it does."

"Avenlee is a beautiful valley on the outskirts of Nolanberry Village. I actually spent a lot of time there when I lived in England."

"No need to explain Avenlee to me, girl."

"You've been there?" I say, amazed.

"I visited the majestic Avenlee a very long time ago. Truth speakin', I rowed a boat across the seas to every place marked out on these maps."

"All of them?"

"Yep, allum."

"Now I know why you have toned arms and the strength of Hercules," I joke along with her improbable statement.

"I'm being one hundred with ya."

"What's one hundred?"

"Honest, one hundred percent."

"Oh, I understand." I look back to the maps. "That's pretty impressive. It must have taken you forever."

"Where there is passion and persistence, anythin' is possible, nahmeen?"

"You mean hard work."

"That's right."

"All these places look kind of important. Are they cities?"

"I can't elaborate a lot 'cuz you're still hangin' out in the human hemisphere." She swirls her hand up around my head. "They be archaic names to places rich in energy. Places a special type of individual once walked across the earth to sink their feet into."

"So, they're special destinations."

"You got it, girl."

"Who are the special individuals?"

"Legend has it they be energetically in sync with these places, creatin powerful magnetic currents on earth. But unfortunately, the illusion of ownership took hold and ended their roamin'."

"What is the illusion of ownership?"

"It is a triflin' belief in a man's head, that he owns the earth. When the first man drew a line in the dirt, declarin' ownership of it, it ruined everything. That belief in ownership-initiated defense, sparkin' control, activatin' greed. And the more lines drawn, the more powerful the illusion became. Robbin' every human of their desire to move about freely. The saddest thing of all is, all man will ever own is his share of the illusion and another man's freedom, of which robs him of his own."

Stelina blows me away by her thought process and knowledge.

"Mother Nature be regrettin' extendin' that invite out to us. She be shakin' her head at our highly evolved stupidity. It's hard to believe *Homo sapiens* means 'wise man.' Ain't a lot of wisdom in killin' one another over dirt, that be here to give us life."

"So, is that why there're no lines on these maps? Because they were drawn before the illusion of ownership was created?"

"That be right. All 'em drawn when folks were free to walk without comin' across one illusion line of ownership. Now we have fences dividin' houses, lines dividin' states and checkpoints dividin' counties, it's a goddamn shame."

"So, does that mean Avenlee is old enough to be one of those special places?"

She looks up as if to be thinking how best to respond. "I'll put it to you this way. Avenlee has stood the test of time, and also the illusion of ownership, by bein' a designated place for, for..."

Stelina stops explaining, as if she suddenly remembers this information isn't for my unawakened ears.

"Designated places for what, Stelina?"

"For all 'em who ain't like others."

"You mean those who have innate natures?" I turn my ear in her direction.

"Yes, those who have a natural somethin'-somethin' goin' on." She moves away from her maps. "Let's take a seat on the couch."

"You're one of them, aren't you?" I ask, sitting down.

"No, there only be one a me that all 'em are like, right?" She grins.

"Don't confuse me. I'm new at all this."

"Well, then, yes, I do have an innate blueprint."

I just knew it. I'm getting good at detecting their kind. "Are you in your second or third chapter?" I'm curious to know.

"Around two years back, I awakened," she says, sitting tall, filled with pride.

"Has your life changed much from your first chapter to your second?"

"By golly, it has. It be a whole new role of the dice."

"Really?" I try dumbing down my apprehensiveness.

"Indeed, there's no better feelin' than unpackin' a lifetime of thinkin', and then followin' the beat of your heart back to the drummer."

"I haven't heard that expression in a while, the drummer." I quickly think back to Annabell's night around the fire.

"Wait until you personally meet the drummer. There ain't nothin' sweeter, not even pop." She shuffles with excitement in her seat.

"I've had a few awakenings." I quietly drop this information in her lap.

"Get a move on, girl. How many you be needin'?"

"No more. I'm happy living the way I do."

"It dun work like that. When the truth comes knockin', sister, it will answer on its own behalf. You won't have a say."

"We will see about that." I lean back in my chair, knowing I have this under control. It might have the power of intelligence but nothing can out-power true love.

"Yes, we will. You make me laugh." She chuckles. "Just enjoy the next awakenin'. It be your last."

"How the heck can that be enjoyed? It's like having a heart attack."

"You just ain't got to the sweet spot yet. You have to ride the wave as it builds, and then POW. You're surfin', girl, all the way to ecstasy island."

"I'm more than happy living in my first chapter. This is my sweet spot." I tap my finger on the armrest.

"You're a stubborn one, ain'tcha?"

"Strong-willed, I call it." I wink, owning my determination.

"What will be, will be. Now, what can I do you for? I probably should have aks that at the start."

"I came to see Pearl, but she's not home. So, I thought I'd pop in to say hello. Pearl told me yesterday I'm welcome at Reefers any time I like."

"I spoke with Pearl shortly after you left. She said you be kickin' it here with us. I must warn you, I'm dead honest. Although I can't tell you, what I can't tell you. Nahmeen?"

"You mean you won't step on nature's path?"

"Correct, but the rest be straight up one hundred."

"I already gathered that."

"That's good, 'cuz by golly, are you in need of some straight up."

"Well, in that case, do you know why Pearl made me promise to stay out of the sea?"

"Nope, I don't, but Pearl knows things about ya I don't, so listen to her and take an 'L'. Pearl would never steer ya wrong, right?"

"Are you sure?"

"Yes. Pearl is a stoic woman, speaks few words, and doesn't get involved in anyone's business. But if she gives you advice, it's for your own good. You should think yourself lucky she cares so dearly about ya."

"I'm very grateful. It's just not easy for me to stay out of the sea when I've spent the past year looking forward to being back in it. I love being in the water."

"It wouldn't be easy for you, I see ya, but some things are taken from us because we ain't supposed to be holdin' onto them, right?"

"Is that what taking an 'L' means?"

"Yes, accept your losses. So, best you let go and see what else takes its place. It's called surrenderin'."

"*Mmm*, surrender. I'll give it a go."

"I have somethin' else you might enjoy. Somethin' Pearl will be happy for you to dive into. Come." She motions with her head to follow her.

We walk out of her map room and instantly I'm taken by surprise. Her clapboard cave looks like a rainbow exploded and permeated the furniture and fixtures. Everything from the chairs at the kitchen table and the crockery drying in her dish rack are multi-colored. Her house is a mirror image of her colorful personality.

I follow Stelina into a large room filled with records. On the far wall is a great big solid timber cabinet with a Zenith record player inside. All teenagers dream about such a piece of furniture.

"Welcome to my love of music." She places her hand over her heart.

This hand-over-heart thing definitely has some significance to it. I've seen too many of them do it now.

"Gosh, this is some collection of music. I'm never leaving this room."

"It's been my passion for the past five or so years now. Our kind need to listen to music. It's important."

"I was just about to ask why, but of course you can't tell me." I beat her to the disappointment.

"It's funny watchin' someone else tormented by the same cryptic world I once lived in," she giggles.

"Ha, ha, that's not funny."

"Is for me. One day you'll laugh at someone in suspense of the truth and see how entertainin' it is, too."

"I won't be that cruel."

"Think of it like you're readin' through a mystery or suspense novel and the answers are about to be revealed in the next chapter."

"It will be the last mystery or suspense novel I ever read."

"More of a reason to enjoy the adventure before it ends, right? Now, would you like to pick yourself a couple of records for us to listen to?"

"I'd love too. How many?"

"Three or four will keep us entertained for a while."

Flicking through the records in the A section, I come across singers I've never heard of like Art Blakey, Al Jolson, Anita O'Day. I move away from section A to B and again, all I find are unknown singers like Bill Monroe and Bea Booze. Finally, I spot the Beach Boys' new single, "I Get Around." On the B side is my favorite Beach Boys track, "Don't Worry Baby." Yay, I've found a song I know and love. Tucking the record under my arm, I move on to section C, then D, and so on. Around ten minutes later, I have a few records to listen to.

"Let me see whatcha picked. Phil Phillips, The Four Tops. Doris Troy, and The Beach Boys. By golly, I expected you to pick The Beach Boys, but not these other artists. Are you sure you don't got a little doo-wop in you?"

"I might. Who did you expect me to pick?"

"Maybe Ricky Nelson, The Rollin' Stones or Bob Dylan."

"Bob Dylan yes, Ricky Nelson maybe, but not the Rolling Stones, and thank God you didn't say the Beatles."

"Not a fan."

"I don't see what all the hype is about."

"You've picked yourself some fine music, Isola. I actually went to see The Four Tops when they were called The Four Aims. Great quartet they are. Levi Stubbs has one of the baddest baritone voices in the business."

Stelina really knows her music. "Who's your favorite singer or band?"

"I got hundreds, from all eras of time, but at the moment, I'm listenin' to Patsy Cline and Sister Rosetta Tharpe. Oh, and I can't get enuffa Sam Cooke. That man be sexy and soulful all in one. Gives me soulspiration, maybe even sexspiration," she giggles at herself.

"Soulspiration? Did you make that up?"

"Ain't nothin' been said that ain't been said before. Now, which song will we play first, Little Miss Doo Wop? Phil Phillips, 'The Sea of Love?'" she suggests.

"I've changed my mind. I want to listen to Sam Cooke now. Have you got 'Bring it on Home to Me'?"

"Best you believe I do, sister."

Stelina drops the needle onto the vinyl and turns the volume up as loud as it goes, just the way I like it. Grabbing hold of my hand, we dance around the room, appreciating such a fine song.

"How 'bout I pick your favorite song off the Four Tops album?"

"Okay, go for it."

She runs her gaze down the list of songs, then lowers the needle onto the track, which happens to be my favorite, "Baby I Need Your Loving." We end the day listening to "Don't Worry Baby," capping off a great day with my newfound friend, Stelina, and our love of music.

When it's time for me to catch the ferry, I tell her good-bye. "Can you please say hello to Pearl for me and tell her I came to see her?"

"Sure, I can. I'm goin out fishin' tomorrow. You wanna kick it with me?"

"I'd love that, although you might have to handcuff me to the seat so I don't jump in."

"Aain't no way you'll escape my reach. Don'tcha worry about that."

"I'll see you tomorrow then."

"I look forward to it, Little Miss Doo Wop."

***

I walk inside the front door to see Maguire sitting at the kitchen table with a pen in hand, working away like Dad. He is so preoccupied chewing his gum, he hasn't even noticed me. I creep up behind him. "Boo."

"I knew you were there all along," he replies, unruffled.

"You did?"

"I saw you walking past the window before you even got to the front door."

"Looks like I'll have to practice my sneaking-up skills."

"Someone sounds like they've had a good day. It wouldn't have anything to do with a man, would it?"

"Not at all. I found out Sation's away for the next two weeks."

"So, I'm stuck with you?"

"Funny one. I can get a motel room. It's no problem."

"I'm joking. You stay as long as you want. It's your house, after all."

"Thanks, Maguire. I'll see what plays out." I notice a gum wrapper on the table. "Is that Bazooka you're chewing?"

"Yep, it's my childhood treat. I've been looking forward to it the whole way home."

"Mine's Raspberry Razzles. I'll have to treat myself to some. So, what did you get up to today, Maguire?"

"I came downstairs and cooked you breakfast this morning, only to find out you had already left the house."

"Oh, that's so sweet of you. I feel terrible now."

"I didn't think you would be up and out of the house that early."

"I wasn't planning on being up early, but I had to escape your singing."

"There is nothing wrong with warming up the vocal cords first thing in the morning," he says, rubbing at his throat.

"So, you're going to sing like that every morning?"

"I sure am. Something would have to be wrong for me not to wake up singing. I've been doing it all my life."

"This is going to be torturous." I roll my eyes at the thought of it.

"I take requests, if it makes it easier," he smirks.

"Staying with you is going to take some getting used to."

"I'm sure we'll manage. What did you do today, go for a swim?"

I wish. "No, I went to Reefers to visit a friend. What did you do after you cooked me breakfast?"

"I worked all day," he says, looking at all the paperwork covering the kitchen table.

"On a Sunday?"

"Yes, on a Sunday."

"You need to stop being so work-oriented and start having some fun." I try to encourage him to lighten up.

"When you work for your father, there's little time for fun."

"Yeah. My father paid for the word *fun* to be removed from the dictionary."

"I'll get out and have some fun when all this work is complete." He throws his pen on the table.

"Come to think of it, I ran into a friend of mine yesterday. His twenty-first birthday party is this Saturday and he told me to bring you along."

"I guess it couldn't hurt."

"Do you want to check with my father first? I don't want to be leading his henchman astray."

"Stop calling me damned henchman, you little snitch."

***

Maguire knocks on my wall like he did last night, and so I knock back.

"Any requests for tomorrow morning's wakeup call?"

Oh this man is going to give me a run for my money. Rather than let him know he's irritated me, I pretend to be sound asleep.

Chapter Twenty-Three

Sure enough, it's seven o'clock on the habitual dot and the wisecrack henchman wakes me again singing "Running Bear." I feel like attacking Maguire like a grizzly bear. I might as well get up now.

I'm making extra eggs for Maguire this morning, given he cooked breakfast yesterday. As I pour the water over Maguire's coffee, the aromas take me straight back to Robust & Arabica. Gosh, I miss Lizabethe and that gorgeous private residence of hers.

A few minutes later, Maguire comes shuffling downstairs bare-chested, surprising me with his masculine entrance. I turn my ogling eyes away from him before he catches me checking him out.

"Good morning, Isola," he says, putting his shirt on.

"'Morning. I've made you breakfast."

"Aren't I lucky?"

"It's the least I could do to repay you for cooking me breakfast yesterday," I say, lifting the eggs out of the pan onto a plate, then passing it to him.

"This looks great, thanks." He takes a seat at the table, tucking into his eggs. "So, did you like your wake-up call this morning?"

"I'm surprised you didn't pick a different song."

"I've had that song stuck in my head all damn week. I can't stop singing it."

"Thanks to you, neither can I." I pour myself a glass of milk and sit down at the table.

"Have you let your parents know you're alive?" he asks with his mouth full.

"No, I haven't yet. I did leave them a letter before I left to let them know where I was going."

"Still, you should call your mom. She'll be worried sick about you."

"You're right, I'll try calling her today," I say, dreading hearing her sad voice.

Ten minutes later, Maguire places his knife and fork down on his plate. "Thanks for breakfast. It was good."

"You're welcome."

"You do know I was only joking about cooking you breakfast yesterday?"

"Are you kidding me?" He laughs at my goodwill. "I feel like hitting you over the head with my plate now."

"Well, I better be off then." He grabs his briefcase and heads for the front door, having gotten me good. "Have a good day, and thanks for breakfast." He chuckles again.

I anxiously walk over to the phone and pick up the receiver. As soon as I hear the dial tone, I hang up. It's too soon. I need more time to prepare for the abuse I'm bound to hear screaming down the receiver. Maybe I'll leave it to tomorrow, or better still, next year.

***

The kind ferryman gives me a welcoming smile as I step aboard. He's been running the ferry service for as long as I can remember. I doubt there's ever a passenger to transport most weekdays, but still he carries out the morning and evening service with a smile.

I arrive at Pearl's to see her standing barefoot under a huge tree fern with her eyes closed. The serene look on her face lets me know she is grounding herself to the island energy. I have no doubt it would be a daily ritual for her, connecting with the earth while standing under the ancient forest canopy. That blissful feeling from Avenlee is no longer part of my life. I'm into thought energy now, the kind that keeps me connected to the human thought society and Sation existence. I step quietly past Pearl, not wanting to disturb her.

"Isola," her peaceful tone stops me. "When you're finished fishing, come back and see me. And stay in the boat, no swimming." She closes her eyes and drifts back into the earth.

"Hey, Stelina."

"Ah, Little Miss Doo Wop returns. Let's go catch us some dinner. Do me a solid and carry that bucket o' bait."

She picks up the rods and we make our way down to the boat, which is all of a two-minute walk.

"In you get." She motions with her head.

"You jump in and I'll push us out. Surely, I'm allowed to get my feet wet."

"While you're with me, ain't no water touchin' that white hide of yours. Now jump in."

Out past the atoll, Stelina rows her little tin boat, keeping a close eye on me the whole time. It seems the overdue friendship I've longed to have with an interesting woman around my age steals my attention from the water. Although I wouldn't mind cooling down from this searing heat.

We get to chatting about Sation, then Stelina tells me some dating stories of her own. She isn't embarrassed to kiss and tell, either. I can't stop laughing, listening to her experiences and idioms for fraternizing with the opposite sex, especially when she used the words *Libidinous Rumpus* instead of saying "sex."

Our five-year age gap doesn't seem to be an issue, and neither does the fact that we're living in different chapters. The subject of our kind hasn't come up, which is cool. We are just two women in a boat, on the sea, in the sun. There's one conversation I will take away from today and that is Stelina's take on love.

In her opinion, what humans perceive to be love is nothing more than the interaction of hormones, engineered by the intelligence of life to draw man and woman together to continue the cycle of life, and in doing so, it rewards us with orgasmic pleasure. But Stelina's personal definition of love isn't physically or sexually driven at all. In her opinion, love is the purest and most powerful form of energy, living in one person seeking itself in another, and in its unification, it becomes even more pure and powerful. I like her view of love, but personally, I like the hormonal interaction the most.

***

"Are you there, Pearl?" I call out through the screen door.

"I've been here all day on tenterhooks, waiting for you to return," she says.

She doesn't ask whether I've been in the water, but I feel compelled to confess. "At the start, I felt the urge to dive on in," I tell her, "but once Stelina and I started talking, I forgot all about the water."

"That's great to hear."

"Yes, and so too are Stelina's stories. I've spent most of the day laughing."

"I hate to think what came out of her mouth." Pearl rolls her eyes, knowing just how liberated Stelina's tongue is.

"What do you want to see me for? I haven't got much time before the ferry leaves."

"Yes, of course. I want to check the bump on your head," she says, taking a look. "It's a lot better. There's no mark at all."

"Taka leaves have worked wonders." I smile.

"They do every time. Stelina told me you were here yesterday, looking for me. Is everything okay?"

"Everything's fine. I came to ask you a question, but Stelina gave me the answer I needed to hear."

"Oh no. Maybe you should ask me anyway," she says as though daunted by what reply Stelina might have given.

"No, trust me, you would approve of Stelina's answer."

"If you say so." She looks unconvinced.

"Yes, it was an appropriate response. Well, I'd better get a move on else I'll miss the ferry."

"Feel free to visit whenever you like. I need to walk you through the rainforest and introduce you to its natural powers."

"I'd love that."

***

Maguire and I play happy housemates for the rest of the week, sharing all the chores and living spaces. We eat our turkey TV dinners on the couch and take turns running to the store. Listening to his long-distance phone calls to his girlfriend back in Bristol is rather awkward. I feel sorry for her, knowing how much she must miss him. But after hearing Maguire talking to her, I can tell he isn't interested in pursuing their relationship, as he has already told me. Half the time he drags his feet to answer her sometimes daily calls. It's clear to see their long-distance romance has a fast-approaching expiration date.

I make the dreaded phone call to Mom. After the initial awkwardness, it isn't half as bad as I presumed. However, she is still upset I didn't tell her I was leaving, to which all I can do is profusely apologize. When I ask her what Dad's reaction was to my leaving, she says, "Let's not talk about that, dear." I guess I already knew the answer, anyway.

I confess to Mom that I returned home because of a man I'd fallen in love with. She is completely understanding, but still she emphasizes I could have told her I was leaving. Mom's happy I'm staying at the house with Maguire. I'm surprised she hadn't been told. I was certain the henchman would have leaked my whereabouts to Dad by now. It looks like he's not as stuck up my father's backside as I'd thought. The call ends with a promise I'll write to her weekly.

***

"Are you ready, Isola? Your friend Nick will have turned twenty-two before you're out of the house," Maguire calls from downstairs.

"I'm just putting my shoes on." A few minutes later, I come downstairs to see a look on Maguire's face that is hard to interpret.

"Well, say something, Maguire, even if it is a wisecrack."

"You look beautiful."

What a gentleman. "Thank you, Maguire. You really can't go wrong with a black dress, and a sparkling pair of earrings. You look good yourself."

"You really can't go wrong with a black shirt, pair of jeans and my sparkling personality."

"Oh, yes, the sparkling personality is hands-down a winner." I cheekily grin.

"There is one thing you're missing, Isola."

"What's that?"

"An escort," he says, holding out his arm for me to grab hold of, proving his maturity once again.

I smile at his chivalrous gesture and link my arm through his.

When we arrive at the party, I seek out the guest of honor. "Happy birthday, Nick." I give him a kiss.

"Have a look at you, Isola. You're a knock-out."

"Nick, stop it. You're embarrassing me. Let me introduce you to my, my… my housemate, Maguire." I struggle to find the right title to give him.

"Nice to meet you, housemate," Nick jokes in response to my stupid-sounding introduction.

"Likewise, Nick, and happy birthday." Maguire holds out his hand to Nick, who shakes it.

"Can I get you a drink, Maguire?"

"Yeah, I'll have a root beer, thanks."

"No worries. I'll just go grab us both one."

Maguire turns to me with a troubled look on his face.

"'My… my housemate.' What was that all about?"

"Sorry, Maguire. I just got all choked up on how to introduce you. Henchman would have described you perfectly, but I know you would have disagreed with that." I give him a sassy wink.

"Here you go."

Nick returns, saving me from Maguire's backlash.

It didn't take long for Maguire and Nick to get to man-chatting. I soon realize Maguire is just as socially friendly as he is the confident businessman. He hasn't lost all his social skills working for my dad. I leave them to talk and catch up with a few girls I know.

"Isola, where have you been? We haven't seen you in ages."

"I've spent the last year in the U.K."

"The U.K., that's a gas," Paula says. "Did you go see the Beatles?"

Are the Beatles the only band anyone my age listens too? I can't believe how limited women's musical interests are. "No Beatles for me. I spent most of the year in the country." I dare not add, in a garden.

"I bet you're glad to be home, then. Is your boyfriend from the country, and does he have any friends?" Paula asks, gazing over to Maguire.

"He's not my boyfriend, we're just friends, he traveled back from Bristol with me to work in Fortier for my father. But he's originally from Chicago."

"You mean you're not an item?" Paula's eyes light up.

"Hell no. Like I said, he works for my dad."

"How exciting! He's single?" Carol, who has been standing here quiet the whole time, jumps up at the mention of a possible love match.

"He is all yours, Carol." I step back, clearing the way.

"No, I saw him first, Carol." Paula's now staking her claim.

"You have to introduce me to him first. Imagine that, me going steady with an attractive English businessman from Chicago." She blushes.

"Chicago's in America, Paula." Carol corrects her.

"It is?" Paula looks at me for confirmation.

"Yes, it's in Illinois." This goes to show, not everyone knows where Chicago is. "I'll leave you two to fight over Maguire. I'm going to the bathroom."

I've heard enough. I'd rather listen to Maguire talk than talk about him. But as I'm walking back to where I'd left them, I only see Nick.

"Where did Maguire go?"

"He went to the toilet and to grab another beer."

"I thought the party might have been a little too much fun for him and he left."

"I can't believe you think he's a stiff. He's a great guy."

"You reckon, Nick?" I say in doubt.

"I do, and I also think he would like to be more than your housemate."

Nick nudges me.

"Nick. Don't say that." I grab him by the arm, giving it a little shake. Fearing someone might have heard, more importantly, Maguire. "Did he say something?"

"No."

"Well, then, how do you know?" I ask, lowering my voice.

"I'm a guy. Trust me, he does."

"Well, I don't want him to have the hots for me. I'm not interested in him, period."

A woman approaches Nick. "There you are, birthday boy. I've come to have a dance with you." Her smile is as positive as Doris Day's.

He puts a hand on her shoulder. "First, let me introduce you to a friend of mine. Isola, this is my girlfriend, Jenny."

"Hi, Jenny."

"Hello, Isola." She smiles generously at me, and then leans forward to give me a kiss on the cheek.

She has such a beautiful warmth about her. Not the innate kind, but it's admirable all the same.

"It's nice to meet you, Jenny. I hear you've stolen Nick's heart."

"Not as much as he's stolen mine," she says, looking into his eyes.

It's great to see Nick has found a woman as full of life as he is, even if she is noticeably older than him.

"Are you here on holidays, Isola?" She shows interest in me, which is nice.

"No, I'm home for good, thank goodness."

"Isola has even brought a guy back with her." Nick nudges me with his shoulder.

"Is that the guy I hear the girls talking about?" Jenny jumps in and asks.

"See, I told you, Isola. You better snap him up before someone else does," Nick adds.

"His name is Maguire, and we're just friends. I'd be more than happy if one of them snaps him up. Now please, Jenny, take Nick to have that dance before I hit him over the head on his birthday."

"Come on, birthday boy, your cupid skills aren't required here. Isola is intelligent enough to find her own lover."

Jenny winks, then drags Nick over to the dance floor. I spot Maguire walking back towards me with a big grin on his face. However, as he approaches, I feel awkward after hearing Nick say Maguire is sweet on me.

"I thought you ran off on me, Isola."

"I just got chatting with some friends. So anyway, what's with the smile?"

"You wouldn't believe it. A woman just came straight out and asked for my phone number."

"That was a man, not a woman," I say, straight-faced.

Maguire looks over to her, horrified. Then I burst out laughing, giving up my joke. "Oh, you got me good, you little snitch."

"The moment presented and I ran with it." I chuckle. "You need to lighten up anyway. But in all seriousness, it doesn't surprise me a woman asked for your number. You hold every woman's eyes tonight."

"Really?" he modestly replies, running his hand along his jawline.

"So, did you give her your number?"

He shakes his head. "No, I didn't."

"Why not?"

"Because I can't remember it. And anyway, I have one woman who already calls me enough. I don't need another."

"Sara," I say, in an annoyed tone.

"Is it that noticeable I don't want to talk to her?"

"A-ha." I nod generously.

"I wish she'd get the hint. I should have made more of a point of ending it before I left," he says, in a regretful tone.

"Why didn't you, then?"

"Well, I did, kind of, but given we were only seeing each other for about two months. I just presumed it would fizzle out. But now I have to talk to her more than I did when I lived in Bristol. I bet you she's calling me right now, wondering why I'm not answering the phone." He shakes his head, frustrated.

"Well, just tell her straight out you're not interested and be done with it."

"I did, but she didn't accept my decision. She's one of the most persistent women I've ever known."

"Good luck with that."

"I'm going to need it. Just as well as we live in different countries, else I'd have her bashing down my door every day," he says, lifting his beer to his mouth, having a drink.

"I'll let all these women know they'll have to wait a moment longer before they can bash your door down."

"I don't want any of them bashing on my door."

"A bit frigid, are you?"

"Do I come across as frigid?" He gives me a steadfast look.

"No… not at all."

Oddly, we continue looking at each other longer than we should. Then the music stops, and all the lights go out on the party.

"Looks like it's time to sing happy birthday," Maguire says.

Thank goodness for that. From out of the darkness, a deep voice sings, "Happy birthday to you." Everyone gathers around Nick and joins in, singing as we watch the twenty-one flickering candles heading in Nick's direction.

As the cake draws near, the flickering afterglow on the person's face carrying it reveals the warm blue eyes I've sailed home to reunite with. Sation's presence devours my existence just like it did the first time I saw him. He looks over at me, surprised to see the sea has returned me. Our paths have finally realigned. Everyone continues singing "Happy Birthday" while we gaze into each other's eyes, lost in the presence of each other.

Nick blows out the candles and the glow disappears from Sation's face, giving me a moment to take a much-needed breath. Someone turns the lights back on and both of us are still standing frozen in time, unable to take our eyes off each other, like old times.

"Sation! You came back for my party," Nick bursts out, giving Sation a firm pat on the back while Sation juggles holding the cake in one hand.

"I wanted to surprise you, buddy," he says, still looking at me over Nick's shoulder.

"Looks like Prince Charming has surprised you too, Isola," Maguire comments, nudging me from my trance.

"Surprised is an understatement," I mumble back, totally infatuated by Sation's arrival.

Sation sets down the cake and steps in my direction. I brace my eager heart from jumping out of my chest to greet the man it's traveled thousands of nautical miles to be with.

"I think I might know you," he teases.

"I think I might know you, too."

"You're that fisherwoman who left Fortier over a year ago, although you have changed. I hardly recognized you."

"I'm still the same girl you used to know," I say, trying to control the smile on my face.

"Doesn't she look fantastic?" Nick says, interrupting our long-awaited reunion.

Sation grins. "She always has."

"The guys have been asking me who is the hot babe in the black dress, but I told them Maguire had already beaten them to it."

Nick teases me once again. This time I feel like knocking Nick out for suggesting someone's snapped me up in front of Sation. I need him to know I'm very, very single.

"Maguire is my friend, Nick. I'm single," I affirm, making sure Sation knows I'm very available.

"Lighten up, Isola, I'm just playing with you." Nick nudges me, but I'm far from impressed.

"Have you moved back to America for good, Isola?" Sation asks.

"Yes, I moved back into my old house last week."

"Couldn't stay away from Fortier, eh?"

"No, I couldn't. It has a certain kind of attraction that called me back," I reply, flirting, looking into his unforgettable blue eyes.

"Is Jessie here, Sation?" Nick asks, scanning the crowd, which instantly raises suspicion in my mind. "Oh, there she is." Nick looks over my shoulder and beckons to someone with his hand.

I turn to see who this Jessie is. It's the woman with porcelain skin, who once before induced a jealous rage in me. Looking back at Sation, wanting him to reassure me all is not what it seems. But the repentance on his face says it all. The girl who meant nothing to him obviously means something to him, and the truth wells in my eyes.

She walks over and wishes Nick a happy birthday while Sation and I stand there, paralyzed by the awkward situation we've found ourselves in.

"Jessie, I can't believe you and Sation are here," Nick says. "What a surprise."

"We couldn't miss your party."

Hearing her talking on behalf of Sation torments me. Before her presence sucks the last ounce of life out of my annihilated heart, I step away from this horrific scene.

"Isola, where are you going?" Nick calls out, stopping me from taking another step.

I blink my eyes to blot out my tears, then I begrudgingly turn back with a brave look on my face, as if nothing has happened.

"Let me introduce you to Sation's girlfriend. Isola, this is Jessie, and Jessie, this is a friend of mine, Isola."

"Hi," is all she says, and I reply, "Hello," not that she really bothers to listen.

Here I stand in arm's reach of the man I've waited over twelve months to reunite with, only to be introduced to his girlfriend.

"Do you two know each other?" Nick asks, making me engage in more conversation with her when neither of us wants to.

"I don't think we have ever met, have we?" she asks, as if I am supposed to remember on behalf of both of us.

"No, I don't recall meeting you, although I have seen you around," I reply, looking at the crippled expression on Sation's face while he stands between his past and his present.

"How was your vacation anyway, guys?" Nick asks.

"I guess you could say it was very eventful." Jessie replies as she flashes her left hand around in front of us.

It takes me one second to notice just how eventful their holiday had been and another second to realize I'm in love with a man who is engaged to another woman.

Nick erupts into a fountain of congratulations. "Sation and Jessie are engaged," he announces.

While everyone gathers around to congratulate the happy couple, I stand choking on the blood gushing from my pulverized heart. I slip out the side gate into the darkness, carrying my heart like a wounded soldier who's bleeding to death. I've broken so many hearts to conquer Sation's, my heart's just been added to the casualties.

I stumble down to the beach, bawling, dropping to my knees and vowing never to love another man for as long as I live. One is enough to last a lifetime.

Chapter Twenty-Four

At three a.m., I return home. Maguire is slumped over the kitchen table, still wearing last night's clothes. The sound of the door wakes him, and he jumps to his feet.

"Isola. I've been looking for you all night. Are you okay?"

I ignore his sympathy and continue towards my room.

"Isola, please talk to me."

If I open my mouth, I may vomit my broken heart all over him. Nothing he can say will comfort me, anyway. My true love never truly loved me and I have to suck that up like poison, or as Stelina says, take an 'L'.

***

I've barely left my room in weeks. Self-preservation's given rise to reclusiveness. I can't even bring myself to visit Pearl or Stelina. I doubt they would want to see this negative woman I've become, anyway. There's nothing natural or flowing about me, apart from my tears.

I can hear Maguire on the phone to Mom now. The other night when she called, he informed her of my unfortunate circumstances, which only prompted her to phone twice as often. Each time she calls, I hear Maguire telling her the same thing he told her the night before.

"It's no use, Mrs. Destinn. She won't leave her room. I've tried all your suggestions."

Then he would come and knock on my door, asking me to come and talk to her. I'd pull the covers back over my head, wishing they would both give up and leave me the fuck alone. And tonight will be no different. I can hear him coming up the stairs now.

"Enough is enough, Isola. You're coming with me."

He barges into my room. I can't believe his bravado.

"I'm not going anywhere."

"Oh, yes you are." He drags me downstairs to the kitchen, letting my hand go to pass me the phone.

"Talk to your mother," he demands.

I send him a filthy look and take the phone from his forceful hand. What is it with people thinking they can just pick me up and take me wherever they think I should be? I have a brain and I can make my own decisions. I should have bitten him like I bit Sailor Kipling when he dragged me out of the sea.

When I hold the phone to my ear, Maguire steps out of the kitchen, giving me space to talk to Mom.

"Isola, are you there, sweetheart?"

Her soft voice reduces me to tears and now I can't stop crying, all over again. Mom doesn't say another word. She lets me go for it until I eventually calm down.

"Mom," I whimper.

"Yes, darling."

"I love him so much. But he doesn't love me."

"Come home, Isola. Please just come home. I hate knowing you're this upset."

"I can't. I have to be near him. Even if he doesn't love me, I still love him."

"Who is this man, anyway?"

"His name is Sation. He grew up outside of Fortier on an orange grove, so you wouldn't know him."

"Well, I know he's a fool to let you go."

"No, Mom. I'm the fool to love a man who doesn't love me. I can't believe this is happening." I slump down in the chair.

"Oh, Isola, I can't bear to know you're in this much pain. Please come home and I'll look after you. We can go to Avenlee together to take your mind off this heartless man."

"I'm too embarrassed to come back, knowing how I just disappeared without saying goodbye to everyone, and even more so now, given it was all in vain."

"What you did was very spirited, regardless of the outcome. He's the one missing out, and one day he'll realize this."

"No, he's too in love with another woman to miss me, all because I had to move to goddamned England. This is all Dad's fault. If I'd stayed here in Fortier, I'd still be with Sation."

"You don't know that. He may have chosen her over you regardless if you were home or not. I know it's hard to believe, but Sation has made room for the right man to come into your life. Just you wait and see."

I can envisage Mom shaking her finger at me.

"I don't want another man. I want him. I love him. I need him. My life is nothing without him," I rant.

"Settle down, Isola."

Mom is right, I have to calm down or else I'll have her over here, dragging me back to England. I take a deep breath, attempting to control my emotions.

"Now, listen, I know you love this man and it seems like you'll never get over him, but one day you will, and you'll forget he ever existed."

Mom is being sweet, but honestly, in a thousand years they will be able to dig my bones up and still find traces of love for him alive in my DNA.

"Maybe I just need some time, Mom. I'll be all right."

"Of course. Time heals all wounds."

I take a much-needed breath in and out. "I'm sorry for hurting you when I left, Mom. Especially if this is how it made you feel."

"You may have left my side, but you never left my heart."

"Yes, but I caused it pain."

"To the contrary. You actually reminded me of how unconditional my love for you is. To love selflessly is a mother's honor."

"You're so beautiful, Mom. I miss you."

"I miss you too, darling. Now please let me book you a fare back to Nolanberry. Then I can take care of you."

"Let me think about it."

"Okay, darling. You think about it, and in the meantime, I want you to get out of the house. You don't belong inside. You need to be out in the sunshine."

"I will, Mom."

"I'll call you in a couple of days to check in on you, so answer my call," she stresses.

"I'll answer. I love you, Mom."

"I love you too. Now get outside, my wild child."

***

Maguire returns at night, when the flooding of emotions have run their course. He definitely made him self scarce earlier. Who could blame him? I don't even want to be near me. I knock on my bedroom wall to thank him before I fall asleep.

"Isola, is that you?"

"Who else would it be, Santa Claus?"

"Hallelujah, the sassy Isola I know is back," he says, chuckling.

"Thank you," I say sincerely, acknowledging all his support.

"You're welcome."

"Night, Maguire."

"Good night."

***

After knocking on Maguire's wall last night, it seems I've granted him permission to revive the early-morning shower concert. He had respectfully restrained from singing while I was grieving, but it's all trumpet-playing this morning. Oh and he's making up for it with his version of an Everly Brothers song, "When Will I Be Loved." I'll give him one thing, he has a good voice.

I open my door and see a bag of Rasberry Razzles on the floor. How sweet of him to remember and also go out of his way to get them for me. Best I go make him breakfast.

He comes downstairs looking momentarily shocked to see me out of my room, watching television. Without making a fuss of it, he goes about his business, as if the last few weeks never happened.

"I almost forgot what you looked like, Maguire." I attempt to make light of my hermit behavior.

"I'm still the same handsome henchman you remember me to be."

I can't believe he referred to himself as the henchman, just to put a smile on my face. He really is a sweet man.

"Yes, you are indeed a handsome henchman," I mumble, wrapped up in my dressing gown on the couch.

"Did you notice my handsomeness step up a notch since I purchased my new bike?" He seems eager to boast about his new toy as he puts on his shoes, getting ready for work.

"So that's whose bike I've heard roaring up the street? I thought it was the neighbors'."

"No, it's your housemate's. Steve McQueen has moved to Sycamore Street with his new Triumph Bonneville." His energy exudes excitement.

I guess this is his way of having fun and spending all the money he makes. "Does this mean you're staying in America for good?"

"I don't know what my plans are, but if I go back, I'll just sell it."

"True."

"How about when I get home this afternoon, I take you for a ride? We can go grab a soft-serve at Dairy Queen. It's about time you broke free from your shackles."

"I'd rather stay in and hide from the world, but thanks anyway."

He walks over to the couch were I'm sitting. "Where is the courageous Isola I met on the ship coming here?"

"She lost her shine in a sparkling engagement ring."

"No, no, it just momentarily blinded her. Her courage outshines any sparkling ring."

I look up to him, ready to make another excuse to remain small, wrapped up in this dressing gown, hiding for another five years. But I know being small, blind, and hiding isn't what a powerful Kore would do. She'd go buy her own sparkling engagement ring and marry the courage inside herself. "I'll think about it," I say, subdued, looking up to him, not wanting him to think I've gone from hermit to heroine in two seconds.

"No thinking, just doing." He gives me a stern eye, pushing at me even more. "I'll be home at five. Be ready."

***

At Mom's request, I'm leaving the house, hiding behind my glasses and wide-brimmed hat. It's time to take in the view of the sea. Hopefully, I don't run into anyone I know, especially a certain someone I love.

It seems every man, woman, and child are here, escaping the heat. The sea breeze is going to have to satisfy me, given the water's out of bounds. I roll out my towel and look up to the sun. Mom would be happy if she could see me. Am I better off going back to Nolanberry empty-handed, with my head hung in shame? It would be easier to move on, rather than be tortured by random sightings of Sation holding hands with his fiancée. But what if I return to Nolanberry and Sation and Jessie split up and I'm not here to claim him back? Then I'll regret it.

"Isola, is that you?" a female voice asks.

"Yes, it's me," I answer, trying to adjust my eyes to the bright light.

"It's Sally and Meg, from school," the polite-spoken Sally says.

I sit up. "Sally Timons and Meg Curtis. I remember you. How are you both?"

"I'm well, thank you, Isola," Sally replies, dressed in a Mary Quant-style garment. She's fanning her face, looking way overdressed to be at the beach, but she has always been fashionable, rather than functional.

"I'm boiling hot. I've got to cool off," Meg says, taking off her miniskirt to reveal her shoestring bikini, looking much more comfortable, although her hair is so heavily set and sprayed, the breeze hasn't moved it.

"We saw you at Nick's party, but you left before we got to say hello," Sally comments.

"We figured you took off with the hot guy you brought. Good catch, that one," Meg adds.

"Well, yes, that guy would be a good catch, but we're just friends." I am happy they assume Maguire is the reason I left and not the announcement of Sation's engagement to Jessie.

"We girls are going to a dance on Friday night. You should come. Everyone will be there."

"I'll think about it, Meg. I'm not sure what I've got going."

"Well, give me a call if you want me to pick you up," Sally offers.

"I will, thanks."

"It was great to see you again." Meg smiles. "I never thought I would, after you disappeared to England."

"Sorry about that. I'm not a big fan of goodbyes. Well, long-term ones, anyway."

"Fair enough. Hopefully, we see you on Friday night. Bye, Isola," Megs says.

"Call if you need a ride," Sally adds, then they walk off down the beach.

"I'll try to make it. Bye."

I watch them meet up with their boyfriends further down the beach. Do I really want to hang out with friends and pretend to be having a good time when I feel miserable? Socializing with the girls was never my thing, anyway. I'd rather study the oceans of the world or walk through the forest at Reefers than talk to girls about boys, because that's all they ever do. Do I really want to be part of that crowd now? I don't dress like them or think like them. They probably look oddly at the way I dress. Well, I know Sally would. She is dressed up in something I'd wear to a wedding.

It occurs to me I should visit Stelina and Pearl. My dress sense is much more suited to their way of life: natural, light and flowing. However, they probably think I've dropped off the face of the earth by now. It's been over a month between visits. I reason that my current state of affairs would only disappoint them, anyway. Maybe my absence is better than my presence.

***

"Let me help you with your helmet, Isola," Maguire says. He stands close as he feeds the strap through the loop. This is the closest I've ever been to Maguire, or any man, in a long time, apart from when he dragged me downstairs to talk to my mom. I won't say it feels awkward. It's just different.

"What is the sweet smell?" He sniffs the air.

"Rasberry Razzles. I've nearly finished them all. Thank so much."

"My pleasure."

"I can't believe I've let you talk me into getting on this bike. I'd rather ride my dusty old Sting-Ray and meet you at Dairy Queen."

"Relax, it only goes one hundred miles per hour. You'll be all right."

I step back, pointing my finger at him. "If you go that fast, I'll kill you. I mean it."

"I'm joking. Come back so I can finish fixing your helmet."

I obey, then Maguire jumps on the bike and gives it a stern kick-start. "Jump on," he yells as he taps the seat behind him.

Lifting my leg up and over, I hold lightly onto his jacket. This all seems kind of strange.

"You'll have to hold on tighter than that, Isola," he yells over the engine.

He reaches behind himself and grabs my thighs, sliding me closer. Now I'm really feeling out of sorts with my legs spread on either side of him. Our friendship just took on a new level of closeness.

"You ready?"

"I think so."

"Don't worry, you're in good hands."

Taking off causes me to tighten my grip. Oh my God, my stomach just jumped into my mouth. I need to distract myself before I totally freak out. Closing my eyes, I hum my ocean melody, but it's not working. The bike's way too loud. This isn't brave of me. This is stupid of me. I'm interested in calm things, not heavy, manufactured chunks of steel that travel at ridiculous speeds. What was I thinking, agreeing to this? I know I need to be a brave Kore but there are other ways to bring out my courage than frightening it back to life.

By the time we get back I swear never to get on another bike as long as I live. There was not one ounce of enjoyment in it for me. I make my way up to my room and spend the rest of the evening brushing out the tangled knots in my hair from all that wind. Never again.

Chapter Twenty-Five

Friday night has arrived and I'm stepping right out of my comfort zone. Mom would be proud. I called Sally during the week and asked her to pick me up for the dance. I'm eighteen, after all, and supposed to be out and about, wearing splashes of makeup and socializing on the dance floor. I've even bought a new minidress to try and fit in with the crowd. But waiting in the driveway now, with all this makeup on, I feel so overdone and restricted in this figure-hugging dress. Fashion is so uncomfortable. I can't even walk properly in these heels. How on earth am I going to dance? I hear Maguire's bike revving up the street. I was hoping I'd be gone before he got home.

"Jesus, is that you, Isola? What did you do with the ball-and-chain around your heart?" he says, lifting his helmet off his head.

"I traded it in for some dance shoes. I'm going out with some friends."

"About time. Do you need a lift?"

"Definitely not. I'm never getting on that triumphant piece of terror again. And I've done my hair up so I can't wear a helmet."

"*Mmm*, I can see that." He looks at my hair-do. "So, you plan on walking to this gig in those heels, do you?"

"No, I have someone picking me up. Here she comes now."

Sally pulls the car up to the curb with the music blaring. Meg's in the front passenger seat, waving, excited to see me.

"See you later, Maguire." I give a little wave.

"Will you be home tonight, Isola?"

I smile at him as I open the rear passenger door and slide in. "Not sure, but don't wait up for me, Dad."

***

The hall is dimly lit and packed, which is great. I feel so out of place, but not for long. When I left for England, everyone danced the stomp and drank soda pop, but things have definitely changed in the year I've been gone. Now everyone's doing the twist and drinking whisky sours. Illegally, of course. Sally's boyfriend gave us some drinks before we came in and mine's gone straight to my head.

I'm having so much fun. I've already decided I'm coming back next Friday night. I never realized how much I love to dance and it's been fun catching up with all my old friends

Halfway through the dance party, those drinks I had earlier get the better of me. My head's spinning. I'm calling it a night.

Stepping into the fresh air, I realize just how drunk I am. I have to walk this off. Wandering along, slightly disoriented, I realize I'm in Malus Street and about to pass by the grand beach house Pearl looks after for her friend. A thought comes to my drunken mind. I'm going to run barefoot across the lawn while everyone's in bed. I've wanted to feel this lush green lawn under my feet my whole life, and I've got a belly full of courage to help me do so.

I slip my shoes off and step onto the lush lawn. It holds me present, making me feel at ease, connected to the earth again. I miss this feeling, the feeling of being whole. The feeling I gave up to be with Sation. I should have stuck with the earth, with being like a tree. I hate to say it, but it feels better than when I used to ground myself at Avenlee, or maybe that's just the alcohol.

I might as well creep around the side of the house to the front garden, there's a beautful apple tree I wouldn't mind standing under. I've come this far, I might as well keep on going. The apple tree reminds me so much of the big crabapple in the Pomona Garden. Trealla would love it. Gazing up the trunk, I lose my balance and topple onto my back. Unhurt, I drop my shoes and my dignity, content to lie on the cool ground.

Sation will never throw an apple my way now. Sadness rushes back at me with double the emotional punch, and the reality of it hurts like hell.

I put him before my family and my friends. I even put his love before my inherent nature, fighting off awakening at all costs. There I was, freaking out I was going to awaken on a daily basis, for nothing. It was all for nothing. I would have been better off awakening and moving into my second chapter. Maybe I should surrender now that I have nothing left.

***

An object hits the side of my arm, waking me. Then another, only this time on the side of the head. Am I dreaming? I open my eyes and realize I'd fallen asleep, or more like passed out, under the apple tree last night and the objects hitting me are rocks.

"Isola! Isola!" A voice calls from the beach.

I rub my eyes. It's Stelina, hopping up and down over the beachfront fence, waving at me. Horrified at my drunken state, I run towards her before the owner of the property sees me.

"My gosh, Stelina, what time is it?"

"Time you woke up to yourself. Whatcha doin', sleepin' in someone's yard? You're lucky the owner didn't catch you and have you arrested for trespassin'."

"Relax, Stelina. Remember, they're only illusionary lines of ownership."

"This ain't no laughin' matter."

I suddenly realize I'm barefoot. "Oh, no! I've left my new shoes under the tree."

"Bad luck now," she says, dragging me by the hand along the beach.

"Slow down, Stelina, my head's aching."

"What's wrong with your head and why you dressed like this?" She looks me up and down. "You look a hot mess girl."

"I went to a dance and had one too many drinks."

My answer brings Stelina to an infuriating standstill.

"You listen here, Isola. Humans use alcohol to escape their head. We don't. We be stronger than that. And where the hell you been? Pearl and I ain't seen you in over a month."

Stelina is clearly annoyed with me, but her opinion is now annoying me, especially at this volume. "I'm not interested in being one of your kind, and I haven't been able to find my way out of my house, let alone to Reefers. Sation's engaged to another woman."

"So, you go wipe out on grog," she says, placing her hands of her hips.

"There's nothing wrong with having a drink," I snap back, defending myself.

"No, not at all. You look radiant, healthy," she replies with not an ounce of pity but with a tone of sarcasm. "Ain't you sick of feelin' weak?"

"I have a broken heart, Stelina. What am I supposed to do?" I stamp my foot on the sand, annoyed.

"You could've chosen other things than drink all that booze and fall asleep in someone's yard. I'm sure Trealla taught you how to ground yourself to the earth. Did you ever consider doing that?"

"My God, Stelina. You've obviously never had a broken heart."

"Ain't nothin' broken in your heart, girl. The problem's comin' from a little higher up. If you spent more time witcha feet on the earth, you'd realize your thinkin' is the only thing broken. Don't nobody gotta tell you how nasty you're acting right now." She shakes her disapproving head at me like I'm a child.

"Oh, this is all too much for me," I say, throwing my hands up in exasperation.

"That's because you still don't know who you are. All you know is, you're not his lover. I'm no fool, girl. I know you been fightin' awakenin' because you're too worried your love for Sation doesn't exist in your second chapter. I know you'd rather find a life in Sation's existence than find the life within your own. Now you don't got neither. You're lost. Just look atcha." She again looks me up and down. "You look like all those gutless women, lost without a man holdin' your hand. Too weak within yourself to stand on y'own two feet. I'll tell you what, I feel sorry for men, havin' to hold all you weak women up."

"Well, if you're so smart, Stelina, why don't you tell me who I truly am, given I only see myself as the pathetic woman Sation doesn't love?"

"There you go again, 'specting someone else to help you find yourself. It's hard to believe this is what women have amounted to. We once nurtured every livin' thing to its glory. Glory." She raises her hands in the air, infuriated. "Now we can't even care for ourselves. If y'ask me, Sation and his fiancée done you a favor. Maybe you might let go of him now and find the innate Isola."

"That was nasty, Stelina." I let her know that comment hurt.

"No, watchin' you trying to be human is nasty. Triflin' nasty."

"There's nothing wrong with being human."

"No. Not at all… if you are one." She storms off, kicking up the sand behind her.

"I *am* human," I yell out to her. "Look at me. I'm a gutless, weak-hearted woman playing my part in the human thought society. I've accepted that. Why the hell can't you?"

She turns back around. "You go on accepting that for yourself, and in ten years, let's see how happy you are with all that creativity lyin' dead inside you. It be a recipe for depression."

I walk towards her, mad she doesn't understand what I'm going through. "I can't lose him, Stelina. What's so fuckin hard to understand?"

"That you turn from the person who love you the most." She points her finger at my heart. "You here to free the innate, to create your gift. A gift to last hundreds of years. Not cook dinner for a man."

"This is so unfair," I vent in anger.

She shakes her head and walks off.

What a morning this has turned out to be. I wake up to a few home truths, at a volume exceedingly hard for my alcohol-soaked head to equalize.

Yes, I should have made more of an effort to visit her and Pearl. Especially after the connection we'd made. But the longer I left it, the harder it is to go back. Which I guess is the exact same way I feel about the innate within me. I feel too disconnected to go back now.

***

I've almost reached home and can see Maguire in the driveway, washing his motorbike. Great. Here we go.

"You must have had fun last night. You've danced your shoes off."

"Yes, I had fun. You should try it some time." I roll my eyes at him, listening to him snicker.

I seriously can't be bothered listening to him. I've heard enough criticism from Stelina to last the rest of the day. I'm going up to bed.

A few hours later, I wake up to a quiet, empty house. Finally, I have it to myself. It's time for a long, hot shower. Naked, I step out of my room into the hall. I'm halfway to the bathroom when I see Maguire reach the top of the stairs.

"Oh, shit." I run to the bathroom with my hands covering my behind.

"Nice butt." He laughs.

Today can't possibly get any worse.

***

It is strangely quiet this morning, which is rare. Extremely rare. Have I slept through Maguire's early-morning shower concert? I place my ear to the wall and can hear Maguire snoring. He's slept in. I have to make the most of this opportunity. How can I get back at him for waking me up by singing at ridiculous hours of the morning? I get an idea.

Struggling to contain my giggling, I fill a large cup with water. I creep into his room to see him sprawled out across his bed in his boxers, sound asleep. My God, he has a fine body, although he could do with a tan. *Here goes…*

The cold water hitting his skin causes a big reaction.

"What the hell!" he says, half asleep, jumping out of bed.

"Morning, Maguire."

"You're gone, girl."

He leaps towards me. I drop the cup and bolt out of his room, but I get only two feet down the hall before he has a hold of me.

"Why did you do that?" he demands, turning me to face him.

"For the look on your face. It's priceless," I gasp through peals of laughter.

"The look on *your* face is going to be twice as funny in a minute."

He lifts me up and carries me towards the bathroom as I try wriggling free. But it's no use. He's too strong. He turns on the cold water in the shower and tries to detach me from his body to push me under the water. I'm clinging to his bare skin, dreading the freezing cold water touching me, but in all the commotion of our bodies pushing up against one another, I'm kind of liking it. Maybe a little too much. And going by the look in his eyes, he might feel the same. I'm convinced he's about to kiss me. Oh, my, he *is* going to kiss me. Nick was right. He has the hots for me.

I let my guard down, and Maguire lets go of his end of the pheromonal tug of war, but he pushes me under the freezing cold water. I fall flat on my butt, doused in cold water. He stands back, laughing, looking at my soaking wet nightie clinging to my body, revealing how cold I am.

"Good morning, Isola. Nice to see you up, bright and perky."

He laughs, then walks off, leaving me in the freezing cold shower with my perky nipples wishing him good morning. I can't believe I thought he was going to kiss me, and I contemplated letting him.

***

After a long week of innocent flirtatious remarks and second glances between me and Maguire, Friday night is on my doorstep. Just as I'm getting ready, I hear the phone ringing in the hallway. I rush to pick it up, thinking it might be Sally.

"If it's Sara, I'm not home," Maguire calls out from the yard.

Maguire's been avoiding Sara's calls all week now. The second I answer the phone and hear her accent, I can't help but be playful. "Maguire, Bristol is on the phone for you," I call through the window screen, covering the end of the receiver.

He comes inside, grunting, while I wave the phone at him, knowing he doesn't want anything to do with her, which makes it even funnier. He takes the phone, covering it with his hand.

"Where are you going?" he hisses.

"To do the Watusi," I say, shaking my butt as I walk away, enjoying the fact he's curious to know where I'm going.

This time I'm sticking with the dance floor rather than trying to keep up with my friends' special drinking abilities. Waking up sick is enough to ensure I remain alcohol-free.

Halfway through the night, I'm dancing to "Wooly Bully." Suddenly two hands grip my hips. I know who it is from the smell of his familiar cologne. I push myself back into him, moving my hips to the beat until he twirls me around to face him.

"Who would have thought you could do the mashed potato, Maguire?"

"Who would have thought you'd have the hots for the henchman?" he replies with the sexiest smirk.

He is right. He's grown on me. He takes the lead, spinning me around on the dance floor, holding my gaze in his. If his lips move as well as his feet, I'm in trouble. And if he takes the lead with my heart like this, we're both in trouble. The end of the song has him spinning me into the crowd, leaving me wanting more. I need to calm down, way down. It's time for a bathroom break.

"My God, Isola, you two look hot out there," Meg says, following me into the bathroom.

"Did we?"

"Hell, yeah." Her head retracts back.

"Oh, Meg, I don't know what to do," I say, looking in the mirror as if hoping to find the answer reflected there. "How can I get involved with him when I still have feelings for another guy?"

"Does this other guy have feelings for you?" she replies to me in the reflection of the mirror while reapplying her lipstick.

"No. He's probably lying in bed right now, feeling his partner." I look at myself saying that and see how ridiculous I look and sound.

"Well, hello, sister, you and your housemate need to make a playdate. And by the way, who is this other guy?"

"Just someone I met in England. But I guess Maguire's the man in my reach now?" I lie again, too embarrassed to admit I'm in love with a guy who's in love with another woman.

Meg turns to me. "You would be mad to pass up a man with eyes like his."

"Best I go look back into them."

"Best you do."

She nudges me out the door.

"Have you got a French letter?" she asks, putting her lipstick back in her bag.

"What's a French letter?" I ask, confused.

"Where've you been, Isola? A French letter is a condom. Get with the times."

"Gee, Meg, let me get to first base with him before we touch down."

"You two skipped over first base on the dance floor."

"Good God, am I really going to do this? Kiss him?" I pause before opening the door.

"Yes. Good God and I insist you kiss."

***

Maybe I should've had a drink, I feels so nervous walking towards Maguire.

"Would you like to come and have another dance, Isola?"

I look to the dance floor than back to him. "I was thinking about getting out of here."

"You're not going anywhere yet. We haven't done the twist."

My insides have been doing the twist since he first grabbed hold of me.

The next song comes on. Maguire shuffles with excitement, and half the crowd makes their way to the dance floor.

"This is a cool track. You know it, don't you? They're from the U.K., The Honeycombs."

"Um, no, what's the song called?"

"'Have I the Right.'"

I turn my ear to listen. "The right to what, Maguire?"

"To hold you."

"No, you don't." I laugh, having fooled him. "Of course, I know the song. It's hit the billboards. I just wanted you to ask, to hold me."

"So can I?"

"No," I reply with a sassy smile.

Maguire shakes his head at me, takes my hand, leads me onto the dance floor, and here we remain, dancing, flirting, and having fun for the rest of the night.

The cab drops us home. Walking upstairs, he's one step behind me the whole way. Any second he's going to grab hold and spin me around like on the dance floor. Especially after spending the whole night teasing the hormones out of one another.

I reach my bedroom door and linger for a moment, not knowing where to go from here. Everything is quiet now. There's no music, no crowd, just our hearts breathing. He steps closer, his chest now touching my back. I have to turn and kiss him. I just have to. His breath on my neck is sending me crazy. As I turn, he steps back and continues walking to his room. He opens his door, takes one more look, then steps inside, leaving everything that makes me a woman pulsating. He seriously isn't going to leave me hanging here like this, is he? But he does.

I don't get why he won't kiss me. Maybe he wants me to follow him into his room, or maybe he is waiting for me to invite him into mine. My God, I'm so confused and aroused all at the same time. I'll play it safe and not make any advances, just in case I'm reading this all wrong, but my word, he's got me turned on.

Chapter Twenty-Six

"Wooly Bully," I hear Maguire singing down the steps. The memory of dancing to it last night returns the rush I felt when he grabbed me from behind.

It's evident from our first glance that the chemistry between us has shifted.

"Good morning, Isola."

"'Morning," I reply, trying my hardest to hide any telltale signs I have a crush on him.

"How was that dance last night?" He acts as if he hadn't shown up.

"I guess the atmosphere was a lot more entertaining than the Friday night before."

"Really. How so?"

"I found someone to dance with."

"Sounds like fun. Was he a good dancer?" He looks me in the eye.

"Yeah, he has a few good moves."

"Did he lay one on you?" he asks, looking over those long, adorable eyelashes of his.

"No, I mustn't be his type. He missed his chance now. Last night's been and gone," I say, attempting to sound unfazed. I walk into the kitchen to wash my plate at the sink.

He follows and stand behind me, like last night. The rush is so overwhelming, it has me closing my eyes.

"I'd say his chances are still running high, wouldn't you?"

I slightly lean back into him, forbidding myself to turn around. "Aren't you going to be late for work?" I play it cool.

He lowers his face, resting it on the side of mine, pausing.

"You smell so good." He inhales.

Our bodies draw closer to one another. Now there's no space between us.

"You're right. I'd better get to work." He steps back.

My comment was meant to tease him, not urge him to leave.

Again, he walks off, leaving me hanging. Oh, my God. What is he trying to do to me?

Surely, I'm not imagining all this. He just confirmed he likes my scent. Surely, he's interested in how I taste? It's delightfully frustrating, I must admit. But enough is enough. Kiss me, Maguire, kiss me!

***

It's ten o'clock and Maguire still isn't home from work, which isn't uncommon, but given I've been thinking, needing, and wanting him all day long, it feels like forever. I feel pathetic sitting up so late waiting for him. Not that I know what I'll do when he arrives. This is stupid. I'm going to go to bed, but I'll leave my bedroom door open in case he wants to come on in.

Not even five minutes after I fall asleep, the sound of his bike roaring up Sycamore Street wakes me. I listen to him close the door and walk up the stairs. Now he's stopped outside my bedroom door. Is he going to make a move? Please make a move. His shadow disappears from my doorway and my hopes crumble again. My God, what is this man trying to do? Kill me with sexual suspense?

Now I'm waiting for him to knock on my wall to say good night, but the only night I've ever wanted him to, he doesn't. I guess he thinks I'm asleep. Oh, but I'm not. My hormones are wide awake. I guess I have two choices. I can lay here all night wondering, or I can step out of my comfort zone and make the first move.

"Please don't let me regret this," I say, throwing back my covers.

Tiptoeing down the hall, I'm busy convincing myself I'm doing the right thing. I push open his door. Immediately, he sits up, looking at me with a blank stare. Oh, no, I'm regretting my actions already. But then he pulls the sheet back and holds out his hand.

Now he's taking the lead, laying me down in his bed, pulling me close, holding me in his arms. His hands move all over my body and I can't help but feel my way around his. I don't think I've ever felt this aroused. If he doesn't kiss me soon, I'm going to burst.

"Your skin, your lips," he says, shaking his head. "I can't hold back anymore. I have to kiss you."

And kiss me he does.

His touch is passionate and slow. We roll back and forth on top of each other. At one point, we almost fall out of the bed, lost in the heat of it all. This is hands-down the sexiest night of my life and we aren't even having sex.

***

"How did you get in my bed?" Maguire teases, snuggling up to me in the morning.

"Don't you remember inviting me in?"

"Nope, but now you're here, you're not going anywhere." He kisses me, pulling me closer. "Actually, last night when I saw you standing in my room, I wasn't sure if you were going to throw cold water on me again."

I can't help but giggle. "No, this time I came to throw myself on you."

"You can throw yourself at me whenever you like. I'll never get enough of kissing you. You have the softest lips. They drive me wild."

"I also have the worst case of stubble rash from kissing you." I gently touch my chin.

"Sorry, gorgeous. Had I known we would kiss, I would have shaved. Here, let me kiss it better."

He lightly kisses my lips and face. He makes every inch of me feel worth kissing. I'll proudly wear his pash rash all over me.

"Can you believe this, Maguire?" I look him in the eyes as our foreheads rest on one another.

"Believe what?"

"I kissed you. The henchman."

The mention of the word *henchman* triggers him into work mode.

"Oh, shit. What time is it?" he says, grabbing his watch beside the bed. "Oh, no, I'm late for my meeting." He jumps out of bed, scrambling for his clothes.

"Do you want me to call my dad and see if he will give you the day off?"

"Oh, no, I've kissed the boss's daughter." He says bringing his hand up to his head. "He's going to kill me."

"He's not going to find out. Now come back to bed and kiss me some more."

"You're going to get me fired, woman," he says, leaning over the bed, pausing in his mad rush. "I can't believe you're lying in my bed and I have to leave. It's just not right."

"Why didn't you make a move on me earlier?"

"I've wanted to. I just didn't want to cross any lines with your father."

"That man is never having control of my future relationships again."

"I can't believe I held back as long as I did. I've wanted you since I saw you passionately bashing the deck with your fist."

"Really."

"Yeah, you've got guts, you're determined. I like that in a woman."

He gave me one last kiss, then took off.

Maguire is the last man on earth I thought I'd kiss, but now that I have, I don't want to stop.

***

Seriously, these emotions are sending me crazy. I've changed clothes ten times. I don't know where to stand or whether to kiss him or whether I should act like nothing has happened. My head is reeling. And now he's about to walk in the door.

"What have you done to me, woman?" he says, virtually dropping his briefcase. "I can't get you off my mind." He walks over, clutching my face in his hands, kissing me ever so passionately. I've never felt this wanted in all my life.

"The more I kiss you, the more I can't stop," he says. "You're like a box of Cracker Jacks. The more I eat, the more I want."

"I also come with a fun surprise." I wink.

"What's my surprise today?" he asks, kissing my neck.

Then the high-pitched ringing of the phone interrupts us. It's hard to ignore, especially knowing who's most likely on the other end.

"That's Bristol on the phone for you." I turn my head.

"Jesus. How many more times do I have to tell her it's never going to work? This is the last time." He storms off to answer the call, and by the determination in his stride, he is going to make sure it is the last one she ever makes.

***

Our blissful kissing sessions have grown longer and stronger over the past three weeks. I've only slept in my bed three times, last night being the third. But waking up to Maguire singing "Baby, I Need Your Loving" makes me want his loving.

The steam-filled bathroom hazes my stark nakedness. Maguire stops singing, wipes the water from his face, then runs his eyes over everything he's only felt in the dark. Holding out his hand, he invites me into the shower. He stands to the side, watching the water run over my skin. Eventually he starts kissing me, as passionate as ever. But it's not enough. It's time, we both know it.

The shower's left running, a trail of water behind us. His body weight I welcome between my open legs. But simultaneously, someone lays their knuckles on the front door.

"Damn it, they're going to knock the door down in a minute. Don't move, gorgeous, I'll be right back."

He turns off the shower and wraps a towel around his hips.

"Hold your horses, I'm coming," he calls out after they knock again.

What are the chances of someone knocking on the door just when I'm about to engage in *Libidinous Rumpus*? I know he'll be doing his best to get rid of whoever is interrupting our first lovemaking session. But a few minutes have passed now and I'm wondering who's keeping him. I wrap a towel around myself and start walking downstairs.

"Where is Isola?"

"I think she's still in bed, Mr. Destinn."

"That would be right."

Chapter Twenty-Seven

My heart's no longer pounding with hormones, it's pounding with panic. Poor Maguire's downstairs with only a towel around him. I can't go down with wet hair, just in case Dad puts two and two together. I grab the hair dryer from the bathroom, creep back into my room, and start drying my hair in the closet. Five minutes later, I put a pair of old pajamas on and walk downstairs as if I'd just woken.

"Dad." I act surprised to see him. I glance over to Maguire, attempting to hide his guilt, knowing what we would be doing right now if he hadn't answered the door.

"Hello, Isola."

"Hi, Dad. I didn't expect to see you this morning."

"I thought I'd surprise you, just like you surprised your mother and me on the twenty-first of June."

And there it is, my dad's first dig at me.

"Well, surprise, surprise," I reply, as if we're both even now. "What are you doing in Fortier?"

"I had business to take care of on the East Coast, so I thought I'd call in to check up on a few things."

"You're by yourself?" I look beyond him for Mom.

"Yes, your mother and sister are home."

"That's a shame." I stand there awkwardly, not knowing what else to talk about. "I guess I'll put the kettle on."

"I wouldn't mind a coffee after traveling all night. Maguire, you can go put some clothes on," my father says, looking him up and down.

"Yes, of course, Mr. Destinn."

The three of us sit around the kitchen table, trying to push through the constricted conversation, until Maguire and Dad talk about the business deal Maguire has been working on in Fortier. Maguire jumps into henchman mode, sounding just like my father. It all sounds like one big moneymaking feast, full of all the delusional trimmings. I feel like screaming out, "Guys, it's paper that's been cut into rectangles you're putting all your worth into." Instead, I play footsies with Maguire under the table, much to Maguire's disapproval.

Maguire heads upstairs to get ready for work, leaving Dad and me sitting alone together at the kitchen table.

"Your mother would love to be here now," he says, looking around the kitchen.

"Yes, she did love this house." I turn in my chair looking around so I don't have to look at him directly.

"I mean to see you, not the house. She hasn't been the same since you up and left, especially the way you did."

It took him all of one minute to purposely make me feel like crap. Little did he know the only reason I left the way I did was because of him.

"I guess I know how she feels."

"And how is that possible, Isola?"

"When you made me leave Fortier, I lost out on love, too."

"It's my understanding he doesn't love you at all and is engaged to another woman."

His insult rips at my heart. "It was love, and I'd be with him now if you hadn't shipped me off to the other side of the world to squeeze more money into your wallet."

"I moved us to England for the sake of the family."

"You never did it for the sake of the family. You never considered anyone's feelings but your own. Mom, Julia, and I were more than happy living here in Fortier." I no longer feel the need to shrink in his company or hold my tongue back.

"Yes, but happiness doesn't pay bills, Isola."

"And money doesn't hold families together."

He closes his book firmly. "I did it for your own good," he snaps back.

"My own good… well, don't expect me to thank you. Happiness might not pay bills, but money can't buy a family. Your bank account might be rich, but your heart is poor." I stand, having had enough of this conversation and the company, and start walking off.

"You're a spoiled brat. That's all you are."

I turn back to him. "Spoiled brat. I've never asked you for anything, apart from letting me stay here in Fortier, but you couldn't grant me that."

"Well, in hindsight, I wish I had left you here. My life has been a lot less complicated without you in it."

"The feeling's mutual," I say, storming out of the house, trembling.

Why can't he be kind and loving like other dads? Why can't he ask me how I've been, or give me a hug instead of putting me down and telling me how much better off he's been without me around? He has treated me like an enemy my entire life. I don't deserve it. I'm a Kore and deserve respect. The only nice thing he's done is let me stay in the house. However, I know that's Mom's doing.

***

The following morning there's no kiss good morning, no singing in the shower, and not an ounce of harmony flowing through the house. It's once again turned into a command post for the reigning king to control.

First thing in the morning, they're at it again, making more and more money. It's sad to witness my dad buying into his share of ownership, and even more sickening to watch Maguire agreeing with my dad to win his approval.

For everyone's safety, I decide to keep a safe distance from my father while he's here for the next couple of days. The thought has crossed my mind to visit Pearl, but I'm too embarrassed to show her what kind of woman I haven't become. I think I'm best off staying away, too, especially after my heated argument with Stelina. Instead, I'm going to head down the street and pop into the record shop.

"Hey, lady."

"Hello, Nick. Buying a few albums, are you?" I comment, looking at the ten or so albums in his arms.

"No, I work here now." He puts the stack of albums down on the counter.

"Really? It's the perfect job for you." I give him a fist bump.

"Yeah, I get to listen to music and make money at the same time." His loud speech boasts with enthusiasm.

"Win-win. Let me know if any vacancies come up. I have to start looking for a job and I love music."

"Will do. What's with the smile? You seem rather happy."

"What smile?" I grin a little more. "I'll say this much. Maguire grew on me."

"I told you he was keen on you. Jenny told me you and Maguire were the talk of my birthday party."

"I doubt that. I'm sure the newly engaged couple were the talk of your birthday party," I overstate.

"No, that was the shock of the party," he says with his eyes slightly bulging.

I attempt to stop my mouth from gaping open. "Really?"

"Yes, no one ever expected they would get together, let alone engaged. She's a pushy woman, so I guess she got what she wanted."

She also got what I wanted.

"Sation's not the same guy he used to be anyway, or maybe he's just grown up and I'm still running amok." Nick laughs. "I've moved out of the bachelor pad and settled in with Jenny, though. I guess that's a mature thing to do."

"Yes, it is."

"I thought it was best to give Sation and Jessie their space, and I like hanging out with Jenny. She's a really cool chick." His admiration for her is easily noticed.

"Yes, she seems it. I'm really happy for you, Nick."

"Looks like we're all shacked up now." Nick chuckles at the absurdity of it. "So, are you going to come to the engagement party?"

"No, Sation and I aren't really friends, and I've only met Jessie once."

"Garbage. Sation thinks you're a top chick. He asked if I'd heard from you when you were in England."

"Really?" It's nice to know I at least crossed his mind.

"I know you and Sation were once an item, Isola." He directly gazes at me. "You don't have to hide it."

"How do you know that?" I don't admit or deny it, but I'm sure I look shocked.

"Sation disappeared for months after you both met."

"I thought we kept that under wraps." I'm sure the smugness shows on my face.

He chuckles. "So did he."

"Anyway, that's a thing of the past. We have both moved on now. I doubt I'll be invited to the engagement. Jessie and I really didn't take a liking to each other at your party."

"That's just Jessie. She's a bit stuck-up, and anyway, you're definitely invited because they've left the best man in charge of the party and I'm inviting you and Maguire."

"Jessie is letting you organize her engagement?" I ask for clarification.

"Sation and Jessie are having their formal engagement with their well-to-do families at some posh restaurant out of town. But they're also having an informal party for all their friends and that's the party I'm organizing. So, you have to come. Actually, I'm meeting Sation here soon to go through the details."

"Sation's coming here?" My voice lightly gasps.

"Yeah, soon."

I have to get out of here with this sudden onset of anxiety. "I'll let you go then. It was good to see you, and congrats on the job."

"It's always good seeing you. Drop in and say hello whenever you want. I'll keep my ears out if there're any jobs available."

"Great. Say hello to Sation for me."

"Will do."

***

Given Sation's in the neighborhood, I'm avoiding the street and taking the beach home. Come to think of it, I'm not going home. It's time I went to Reefers. I miss Pearl and I'd love to take her up on her offer to walk around her mystical rainforest. If I hurry, I should make the lunchtime ferry.

But as fate will have it, the man embedded in my heart is now embedded in my sight. I knew this would eventually happen, and now here it is. He's walking towards me. My breath comes to a stumbling halt. There's no escaping his warm blue eyes now. It's just him and me, the sand and the sea.

"It's been a while since you and I stood alone on this beach." He heads down Reminiscent Road, given we've no future to converse over.

"It's been a while since we stood anywhere alone together." My voice shakes as I struggle to maintain eye contact with him. Looking directly into his eyes will bring back all my unmet desires.

"Did the guy you live with tell you I came to see you?"

"No, he didn't. When did you come to see me?"

"The day after Nick's birthday party. I wanted to explain why, why..." He stumbles for words, shifting his weight from side to side.

"You know what, Sation? It really doesn't matter anymore." I stop him in his tracks.

"It does matter, Isola. Let me explain."

"I don't want to hear why you don't want me. I should've known you weren't interested when you failed to reply to my letters."

"What letters?" He looks at me, squinting.

"The letters I sent you while I was in England."

"I'd moved house, Isola. We sold the orange grove. I didn't get any letters."

"And your mom never passed on your mail?"

"No, she didn't. What did you write?"

"What does it matter? I obviously don't mean anything to you." I cross my arms, looking away.

"Stop it. I couldn't take my eyes off you." He dismisses my statement.

I turn back to him and give him a smug grin. "Yes, I remember the way you looked at me. But I guess Jessie remembers you looking at her the same way, and at the same time."

"No, Isola, I was very loyal. Half the time you were so casual with your approach, I wondered if you were even interested in me."

"Interested in you? Are you kidding me?" I uncross my arms, enraged. "I was mad about you. I just didn't want to come across as a needy schoolgirl, cramping your style."

"Isola, you didn't even say goodbye the day you left for England. I came to look for you, but you had just disappeared." He throws his hand out in front of him as if to throw fault back my way. "That hurt like hell, not getting to say goodbye."

"I'm not good at goodbyes. And no, I didn't throw myself at you, but I did make love to you."

"I made love to you, too." He points his finger directly at me. "But still… still you couldn't say goodbye. I never wanted you to go to England in the first place."

"And I didn't want to get back to find you engaged," I yell.

"You were gone, Isola, gone." He lifts both hands over his head, irritated. "What did you want me to do?"

"I wanted you to wait for me like I waited for you," I shout, wishing I could rip out the pain in my heart.

"I'm sorry, but I thought you'd be gone for good."

"No, you hoped I would, so I didn't find out the woman who meant 'nothing' to you means the world."

"Jesus, Isola, I only got with her to take my mind off you. I'm sorry I moved on, but I thought you would have too."

"I didn't, but I'm trying my hardest to now." I turn to the sea to calm down, wanting this knot in my throat to go away. My short-term absence in his life created his long-term absence in mine, and it hurts like hell.

Sation grabs my hand, taking back my attention. I look into his eyes, gutted I won't spend the rest of my life staring into them.

"I promise, when I was with you, I had nothing to do with her. You were it for me." He holds my hand a little firmer in an attempt to convince me, lowering his voice, bringing our argument back down a notch.

"Unfortunately for me, you have something to do with her now. It's as simple and painful as that."

He lets go of my hand and kicks at the sand.

"I should have waited. I should have. But I was going through a hard time." He paces back and forth, rubbing his clenched fingers over his skull.

"Hard time. Hard time!" I scoff. "You clearly haven't been doing it hard." I reply, frustrated by his comment.

"My mom died just after you left." He turns directly at me, clutching at the aching in his chest. "I know all about hard times, Isola."

That set me back on my heels. I fumble for the right words to express my sympathy, but there are none. "I'm so, so sorry to hear that, Sation. I feel terrible. Here I am, hammering you with my broken heart when yours is shattered."

He looks me directly in the eye, jaw trembling with grief. "I lost the two women I cared about the most, and I didn't get to say goodbye to either of you. I needed you more than ever, but you were gone, and Jessie reached out to me."

"Ignore everything I said. That's not important now. What happened to your mom?"

"A car accident," he says, fighting back tears. His downward gaze tells of the heavy burden he holds in his heart.

Without a second thought, I reach out, holding his heartache like it is my own. Dropping my losses that are far inferior to his. We fall into each other's comforting arms. Both grieving our fate, and the woman who gifted him life. I wish I could take away his pain and mine, but I guess this is our lot in life.

"I'm sorry I didn't say goodbye, Sation. I should have, you deserved that. I just couldn't deal with the pain." I regret my actions.

We let go and step back from one another, different people from moments ago.

"It's all right. I understand all about pain now, Isola, and how hurtful goodbyes can be."

"More than both of us." I acknowledge his suffering. "I'm sorry for yelling at you. I guess I just need time to get over losing you, you big hunk." I gently smile at him through the sincerity of my heart.

He draws a noticeable breath in, then exhales all the tension. "I'd still like to be friends, Isola."

"I don't think that will work until I don't want to be your lover," I say, making him laugh.

"You let me know when we can be friends. Until then, chin up, beautiful." He places his open hand on the side of my face, holding me. I turn into it, wishing it was his face. I place my hand over his, so just for one moment there is nothing between us. We are skin on skin. Then, I let go.

He drops his hand and the moment's gone. "I have to go. I'm meeting Nick on his lunch break and I'm late."

"Okay, I guess this is goodbye." I fidget at the thought of it. But more than ever before, I'll have to brave this one.

"Take care, Ke aloha."

"Oh my God." My hands reach for my mouth, shocked he held onto those words. "You remembered."

"I'll never forget you."

I gasp in air, pulling on all my strength not to burst out crying. We should both be walking away. We've said our goodbyes, but neither of us move. We are stuck in everything that could have been that never will, all the while gazing into each other's eyes.

"You're going to have to walk away, Sation. I can't." My voice quivers.

Still, he continues staring right back at me. His body's at a standstill, yet his eyes are rapidly searching mine.

"I'm glad I got one of you back," he says, watery-eyed, then walks away.

There goes my favorite place to be, and it burns deep down in my soul. He stops further down the beach, takes one last look at me as I hold both my hands at my heart, then he walks out of my sight.

***

Maguire is in the kitchen when I get home. I was going to go to Reefers, but I'm so mad, I have to have it out with him. He thinks he's being cute, blowing me a kiss across the room, hiding his affections from my dad. But I'm certainly not sending one back.

"Why the hell didn't you tell me Sation came to see me?" I give him a scornful stare.

He doesn't know where to look. No doubt he's searching his dignity for a valid response.

"I didn't want you to get any more upset than you already were," he replies, trying to entice me to lower my voice with his tone, but I'm too wild.

"No, you didn't want me to be near him. Admit it." I throw my index finger at him, demanding the truth.

"Yes, I didn't want you near him," he admits, without a tone of remorse. "He's no good for you, but regardless of that, you wouldn't even leave your room."

"You knew I would have left my room for him, and that's why you didn't tell me."

"Keep your voice down, Isola. Your dad will hear you."

"I couldn't give a shit if my dad hears me."

"Jesus, settle down. I'm sorry I didn't tell you, but I couldn't stand seeing how upset you were over some guy who clearly didn't give a damn about you."

"You don't know he didn't care for me. You know nothing about him."

"Any man who let you get on a boat and sail away from him doesn't deserve a place in your life. I don't need to know him to know that." Now he's the one throwing his index finger around, asserting his belief.

"He had no choice. I had to go. You know how powerful my dad is."

"Well, then, why didn't he sail to England to be with you, just like you sailed halfway around the world to be back here with him?"

"Regardless of whether he deserved a place in my life or not, I deserved to be told he was asking for me."

"Why are you speaking to Maguire like that?" Dad walks in the room.

"You mean the same way you have spoken to me most of my life?" I say, giving him an evil stare. I feel like attacking him for ruining my relationship with Sation.

"It's all right, Mr. Destinn." Maguire tries playing down the situation.

"No, it's not all right, Maguire. Isola, stop being so goddamn rude and apologize to Maguire."

I glance back at Maguire like the good little girl my daddy wants me to be and sarcastically reply, "Sorry, Henchman. Next time I'll remember to use my manners, if you remember to pass on messages."

"Isola, come back here," my father yells as I walk away.

"Being near you is the last place I want to be in this world." I slam the door with as much force as I want to punch my dad in the guts.

***

"Isola, wake up, wake up."

I sit up, half asleep, looking at Maguire sitting on the end of my bed. "Go away, I'm still sleeping." I lie back down and pull the covers over my head.

He gives the covers a shake, adamant I wake. "I want to talk about yesterday."

"I'm so mad at you about yesterday. Just go away. Dad will hear me yelling soon, and I'll have to apologize again."

"Your dad's gone out to get the paper."

I throw back the covers. "Well, in that case, I can yell. Get out of my room." I point at the door.

"What have I done so wrong?"

"I'll tell you. I'm forever being told what to do. My entire life has been dictated by others just to benefit them. I'm sick to death of people making decisions on my behalf because they think they know what's best for me. And that's exactly what you did in failing to tell me Sation was at the door." I explode like a shaken bottle of soda that Maguire unfortunately popped the lid on. He takes a step back from the bed, probably wishing he never walked in here. "I won't have it anymore. I have a brain and I can make my own decisions. I'm a goddamn Kore and I'll walk my path." I slam my fist down on my bed.

"What's a Kore?" He looks at me, confused.

"Never mind. Just leave me alone."

"I'm sorry for not being honest with you. But I won't apologize for wanting to protect you, which is where I was coming from. I've felt the need to protect you ever since I saw you upset aboard the ship. It's just who I am, it's what I do. I protect the people I care about, and I care about you." He takes a breath from his wordy explanation. "I promise I won't make any decisions on your behalf ever again, especially now I know how much it upsets you. You're the best thing that's ever happened to me and I can tell by the way you look at me you feel the same way. So, I'm asking you, not telling you, please don't let this ruin what we have."

"I need to make my own decisions." I point at my chest, determined to hold my ground. "This is my life, mine."

"I understand, you're a free-spirited woman. I should have known better than to decide for you." He takes my hand in his and kisses the back of it. "I have to tell you something quick while your dad's out. He wants me back in Bristol."

"Are you kidding me?" My eyes protrude forward.

"No, I've finished doing the due diligence here in America and he needs me back there. I told him I'd think about it."

"I can't believe you. I can't believe you would even consider it."

"Hold up. Hear me out. I'm not going anywhere you're not. But if you want to go back to Bristol, I'll accept his offer. If not, I'll find a new job here in Fortier. I've got two weeks to answer him."

"I'm not going anywhere." I put my foot down.

"Well, then, neither am I. I'll find a new job here."

"You've spent years working towards this job. You love what you do."

"I love you more."

Oh my, did I just hear right? "You love me?"

"Yes, yes I do," he affirms.

"You're crazy."

He chuckles. "Your wit drives me crazy in love with you."

I shake my head, grinning profusely. "I'm so happy to hear these words come from your mouth."

"They didn't come from my mouth. They come from my heart."

Grabbing his face in my hands, I kiss him until I'm out of breath. My feelings aren't far off, but now's not the time to say it back. I'll wait for my dad to leave, so I can scream it out loud. I have one fine man in my reach and I'm never going to place one moment of absence between us and risk losing him like Sation. I've learned my lesson there.

Chapter Twenty-Eight

Smiling with relief that my dad is leaving, I watch him and Maguire through the curtains, shaking hands goodbye. I can't bring myself to see Dad off. Our relationship, or lack thereof, has never been more intolerable. I guess he can't get money out of me and I can't get love out of him. Why we were ever paired as father and daughter is beyond me. And how dare he attempt to tear another man away from me? He's never doing that again.

Maguire watches Dad drive away in the taxi, then walks back into the house with the sexiest look on his face. "Now, where were we?"

"I believe I was laying in your bed. Wet."

"*Mmm*, I'll take your word for it."

He scoops me up, carries me to his room, grabs a French letter out of his drawer and lays me on his bed, taking my clothes off, until all I'm wearing is my jewelry.

"You might not be wet, but I think this is where we left off," he says, kissing my neck.

Oh, I'm wet, and he's just about to find out.

"You have no idea how bad I've been wanting you, Isola."

I look him directly in the eyes. "Show me."

Deep, slow, inside he goes. I gasp at the sensation. Every inch of how badly he wants me, I relish, lifting my knees a little higher.

He's in total control, putting my nerves at ease, looking in my eyes to perceive the pleasure. If his busy hands aren't on my breasts, they're on my butt or ardently holding my face.

But it's all going way too fast. I can feel the end is near. Attempting to slow it down fails. Oh my, oh my, the end is here.

***

Throughout the following month, we are bound to each other like the gods had willed it. My body moans with pleasure day and night, sometimes even midday. The level of intimacy increases, and my level of clothing decreases. But after the highest of highs, I need sleep, and my girl below needs a reprieve.

"I'm off to bed, Maguire," I say, lifting his arm off me as I get up off the couch.

"I'll be up soon."

"Tonight, I'm sleeping in my bed. Alone. I seriously need one night of uninterrupted sleep."

He looks up, giving me a side eye. "Yeah, sure."

"I'm serious. I need sleep."

"Well, sleep and stop wanting to make love to me."

"I think it's the other way around." I walk off, and of course he starts following.

"Seriously, we won't have sex. We can just cuddle, Isola."

"As if that's going to happen," I say, walking into my room.

"Oh, come on, Isola, you're breaking my heart." He grabs at his chest.

"No, I'm getting some sleep. Now get to bed," I say, closing my bedroom door.

Not even ten minutes later, Maguire's knocking on the wall. "What are you doing, Isola?" he calls out.

"Trying to get to sleep."

"I know what will help you fall asleep."

"Have some willpower, Maguire. It's one night."

"Willpower? My willpower wants to make love to your willpower."

I can't help but laugh, lying here in bed.

"Come on, Isola. I need you."

I want him just as bad, but seriously, can we not go one night without each other?

"Maguire."

"Yeah."

"Meet me in the hall."

Colliding into each other's arms outside my bedroom door seems like a fair compromise. It appears the thought of going without makes us want it even more. Moments later, I'm on all fours. The next, Maguire's inside me. We move in tune with one another, as natural as the twirling wind of a hurricane. Craving the fury, our bodies stop at nothing, other than self-defeat.

We lay beside one another, out of breath but extremely satisfied, looking up to the ceiling, holding on to the internal explosive feeling.

"Thank goodness you gave into your willpower. That was hot." He turns his head and looks at me.

"Yes, it was, and now I'm off to bed. Good night, Running Bear." I kiss him, then crawl back to my bedroom. But of course, he's following in line again.

"No, Maguire." I firmly point my finger again.

"Yes, Isola."

"I gave into sex, not our sleeping arrangements. Our bedrooms are out of bounds for the night."

"So, you just used me for sex?"

"Yes." I smirk and continued to crawl away. "I'll see you in the morning." I push my bedroom door closed.

"You're a heartless woman," he calls out, falling back on to the floor.

"No, I'm a sleep-deprived one. Now get back to your cave, Running Bear."

"If I must, my white dove."

***

The following night, Maguire places the mail on the kitchen table after his bike ride.

"There's a letter addressed to you, Isola."

"Is it from Mom?"

He looks at it for a moment, then turns it over. "No, it's not from overseas. Here, open it."

He passes it to me, and I peel back the flap and pull out the card.

To Maguire and Isola.
You're invited to celebrate Sation and Jessie's engagement.
Please join us on the fifth of January at Poppy's Restaurant, Reefers.

I can't read the rest. I put the invite back in its envelope, about to throw it in the bin. Why did they choose my happy place to celebrate their happy moment? He of all people knows how dear that island is to me.

"What is it, Isola?"

"Junk mail."

He picks it up off the table and starts reading it. "I guess we're not going?"

"You can, but I'm definitely not."

"How about on the fifth, I take you out on a date instead? Let's ride up to Daytona Beach for the weekend."

"That's nice of you, but really, I've accepted what is and I don't need to go anywhere to escape their celebration. Right here with you is the only place I want to be."

"Really?" he says, grabbing hold of me.

"All I want is you."

"You've got me. All of me," he says, reassuring me with an affectionate hug that eventually ends with his hands on my behind, as always.

"Did you say all of you, Maguire?"

"Yes, I'm all yours."

"How about all of you comes and jumps in bed with all of me?"

"I'm the luckiest man alive," he says, affectionately rubbing his nose on mine. "Let's jump in the shower together rather than bed."

"Only if you sing to me."

"And your request is?" He tilts his head at me, awaiting my reply.

"Surprise me. I'll be up soon."

"I still want to take you to Daytona Beach some time," he says, walking upstairs.

"Sounds good to me. Let's go this weekend," I call out.

A few minutes later, I hear a knock at the door. I open the door to see a woman standing before me.

"Hallo. I'm not sure if I huv the correct 'ome or not, but does Maguire Beriman live 'ere, too?"

Her slight Bristol accents with its rhotic R and extended O's is a giveaway, but the sight of her gobsmacks me.

"Yes, he does. Come in."

"I've spoken to you on the phone a few times. My name is Sara," she says, with the typical lack of facial expression.

"Yes, we've spoken a few times."

"Bleedin' 'ell its hot ou' 'ere, init?" She fans her face with her hand.

"Very. I'll just run upstairs and get Maguire for you."

"That be proper good."

I turn to see Maguire standing behind me in absolute shock, staring at Sara's round belly with what I presume is their unborn baby growing inside. Just like that, my world falls apart.

"Hi, Sara," he says, trying to drag his eyes away from her stomach.

"Hallo, Maguire." She leans in, giving him a kiss on the lips, which he awkwardly receives.

"This be gert lush," she says, looking around the living room.

"Yes, it is." His eyes glaze over the room, too dumbfounded to collect a thought.

"I'll leave you two to catch up." I need to get out of here as quickly as possible. The same sickening feeling as when I saw Jessie's engagement ring is back.

"I'll talk to you both later. Bye, Sara."

"No, Isola." Maguire snaps back. "Sara and I will talk upstairs. You don't have to go."

His eyes plead with me, knowing when I walk out the door, I might never return.

"It's okay, Maguire. I told Meg I would catch up with her tonight," I say. Another lie. I walk to the door, giving him and his growing future some space to reunite.

"Bye, Isola."

"See you, Sara."

"Isola," Maguire says, trying his hardest to get me to stay with his intonation.

But nothing's keeping me here. I walk out of the same door Maguire's future just walked through.

Staggering along the windswept beach in the dark, unable to hold up my harrowing reality, the sand bares my weight as I crash down on my knees.

Our relationship will never work now. Maguire's going to be a dad, and he has too big a heart to walk away from the responsibility. Especially given his father walked out on him. It's over. And just to add to the drama, it's starting to thunder.

Running from the beach, to the protective branches of the apple tree I once slept under, I curl into a ball, sobbing, unable to believe my future's been pillaged on me again.

Hours later, a car pulls up and two doors close. The house lights turn on, shining out to the garden. Jumping to my feet, making myself pencil thin, I peek around the tree to see if I'm in the clear to bolt. But my sights stop me in my tracks, possibly killing the remainder of me. Through a bedroom window, Sation and Jessie get into bed. Sation kisses Jessie goodnight, then turns out the bedside light. Not only does she have the man I love, she also lives in the house I love.

Despondent and damaged to my very core, I'm slapped by the hand of cruelty once again, only this time, I'm not getting up. The price I've paid for loving has resulted in too high a deficit. All that's left is the sea. And here it is, only yards away. Tempting me with its soothing ebb and flow. Oh, but that's right, Pearl's taken the sea out of my reach, too.

Heavy-hearted, I return to the beach, and hum the sea's dulcet melody over and over again like an insane woman, using its feeble vibrations to fill the lonely spaces loving has created in me.

***

Waking from my cataleptic state, I realize the morning tide's risen up the shore and washed me out to sea like a lifeless shell. Technically, I haven't broken my promise to Pearl. I didn't go into the sea, the sea came to me. And right on cue, I hear her. The sea. Her dulcet melody hums to me. It won't be long until she summons me with her alluring tone. Before it's too late, I must get out. Or, will I stay?

The sacrifice I've been avoiding, fighting and flirting with, for over a year now, demands a decision. I've been holding onto what I want rather than what's meant to be. I've hated my father for controlling me, yet I'm just as guilty in controlling my predestined path. As Stelina said, watching me be human is nasty. She's right. It's time to become my own resolution, the heroine of my own heart. It's time to step away from the history of human thinking and take a walk down an unknown path, to the innate residing within.

As if the sea knows I'm about to walk away, she hums a little sweeter. This will be the last time I hear her. I lower my chest into the sea, letting my sadness indulge in her serenity. I wonder what the intent is in her eyes and where she resides. I dip a little lower, one last time, and then a little lower again. I have to see her, just once. Under I go.

Isola, get out of the water. You made your decision, my inner voice says.

But the lilt in her melody is too beautiful to turn from. Her pure resonance I need to experience, just a little longer.

What am I doing? Stop swimming. Get out of the water. Okay I'll swim back and get out. But she won't let me. I'm fighting against the current of her voice, kicking with all my might, struggling to ignore her melodic voice resonating louder and louder. *Stop singing to me. I'm going back. Stop, stop.*

Battling my way back, I break through the surface, kicking like mad. My head is above the water, but still she tugs at my heart, refusing to let me go. Oh my God, she won't let up.

Fight it, fight it. I reach shallow waters and run along the bottom of the sea, trudging through the breaking waves, raging against the sea. The next incoming wave pushes me along. I wash up on the shore beyond, fatigued, breathless, and in absolute shock.

What the hell just happened. Pearl's right, I can't go back in. I don't know where her humming will take me.

Trealla once said to me, "Who might you be in the absence of thought, and how much are you willing to let go of, to find out?" Now I'm willing to sacrifice everything and surrender to the life existing in me, long before the thought of me ever did.

I'm a Kore, a guest on this magnificent earth, connected to the nature of life flowing through me. With my bare feet on the ground, being like a tree, I live and breathe the innate in me.

My heart rate doubles, triples, combusts. Physical becomes trivial, inconsequential, all but dust. My final awakening is here, at last.

Chapter Twenty-Nine

Isola Destinn, 1964. America.
Mi Seola.

Within the lines of this body, the sound of its beating heart, I live upon this earth ensouling Isola Destinn's heart. I'm not a human being. I'm a soul, being human, the innate light.

As I approach Pearl standing in her forest, our pre-eminent life forces shimmer to life, elevating our friendship beyond the world of flesh and bone. I'll never see Pearl or myself as I previously have. Our physical bodies are now superficial wrapping to a far greater life living within. Trealla was right when she said, "When you stop thinking, you start knowing, and then you start living." I've never felt more alive and less human in all my life.

"So, this is who I've been my entire life, and you knew all along?"

"Yes, dear. The day you were born, I looked into your little eyes and saw an exquisitely gifted soul looking back at me."

"You must have been blown away."

"Indeed, I was. The soulful energy flowing from your tiny heart was so powerful, it sent your mother into shock. She couldn't even think of a name for you." Pearl chuckles. "But I knew exactly what was going on. The miracle of an Anithian had just been born."

"What does that word mean, *Anithian*?"

"You don't know?" She tilts her head towards me.

"Am I supposed to?"

"You're awakened, so yes, you ought to. Second chapters are the domain of our Anithian souls."

"Anithian, Anithian. It kind of sounds familiar." I scratch at my head.

"When did you awaken?"

"Earlier this morning."

"Your soul obviously needs more time to dismantle that rather dominant human body it chose to reside in, which comes as no surprise to me."

"So, what does Anithian mean?"

"It's the name of our ancient creative souls, which differ from human souls. Anithians descend from far beyond the stars with an exorbitant ability to create."

"Create what?" I wrinkle my nose.

"Our Anithian souls into gifts, to live independent of our physical bodies on this beautiful earth."

This must be the gift Zeke and Fairlee were talking about when they presumed I'd created mine. "So, our souls turn into gifts, is that right?"

"Wow, your soul certainly is taking its sweet time to enlighten you."

"Yes, but I can shimmer just like the rest of you," I say, freeing the light of my soul.

"You have that part figured out, that's for sure." Pearl waves her hand through my soul's light. "You have no idea how happy I am to see your essence shimmering. I've waited a very long time for this moment."

"Eighteen years, I guess."

"Yes, for eighteen long years I've watched your soul wander this earth, leaving a trail of light everywhere you walked." She smiles with such happiness. "Let's take a seat on the veranda and I'll explain the universe inside that wild heart of yours. I think we're in for some rain soon, anyway. I can smell it coming." She lifts her chin, detecting the rain through her nose.

The sky darkens as I follow Pearl out from under the forest canopy, towards her house. This shimmering is going to take some getting used to. I feel like sparkling fairies are flying around me. Pearl settles into her seat, like she's in for the long haul, and I sit across from her, trying to control my amateur soul from shimmering of its own free will.

"Let me walk you back to the beginning of your soul's evolution."

"Good idea."

"Because an Anithian soul is formless, it requires a physical body to create itself into the form of a gift. So, it chooses the perfect characteristics in a human to achieve this. Unfortunately, when we're born, our Anithian knowledge is overshadowed by our humanness, then society places more distance between our knowledge. This first chapter is anciently known as *Mi Se*."

"Is this what you also refer to as the history of human thinking?"

"Exactly. It's our most challenging phase. Life never feels right, living in the human domain. We are wild at heart, living in controlled environments. We are full of ancient wonder, searching for the place our souls feel most alive. We know something's missing, but we never quite work out what, that is, until our souls' vibrational frequency rises and consciously awakens our existence. It floods every cell of your body with enough energy to defuse your humanness and awaken you to its soulful presence on this glorious earth. In this moment, you finally know who you truly are."

"That's exactly what happened to me. I let go and my soul rushed through my entire body. I was everything and nothing, at the same time. Formlessly existing in the most serene place I've ever found myself to be."

"*Mmm*, it's called eternity."

"Well, eternity is more serene than under the sea, and for me that's saying something."

She smiles winsomely. "So, this is the end of your first chapter. You're no longer a Muklee, an unawakened Anithian. Now you're embarking on your second chapter, a phase where your soul is free to come to life."

"Ah, so that's what Muklee means." I smile.

"Yes, but you are no longer a Muklee. You're awakened to the innate within. Well, almost."

"Yeah, almost." I nod.

"Don't worry, your soul will gain more strength. Then it will take you on a voyage of discovery into our extravagant existence, beyond this one dimension of time. You're in for a treat." She flashes her eyes at me.

"Can't wait." I eagerly rub my hands together. "I'm so glad I finally surrendered. It explains so much."

"I promise you, the sacrifice of your human existence is your soul's triumphant victory."

"This victory has come at a price, though." I raise my eyebrows at the extent of troubles I've gone through to get to this point.

"No, you never gave up anything you weren't meant to be holding in the first place. Now, the next phase in your Anithian life is the most stupendous occasion, when your soul creates its gift. Which moves you into your third chapter, anciently known as *mi sunez*. Your soul will then live independently upon earth where it's longed to be, freed amongst all the soulful gifts living hidden in plain sight. This is your soul's ultimate quest, to enrich the earth," she says with such zeal.

"So Anithian gifts are everywhere."

"Everywhere. Hanging in the Louvre. Dancing around a fire, invoking hearts. The soulful voice singing on the radio. Ornate lovers inspiring fairytales. Fictional muses in ancient novels. Growing in exquisite gardens, or simply the soulful feeling in an untouched native homeland. Our souls' gifts are everywhere. You just need to use your soul-sight to discover them."

"And I've been walking around blind for eighteen years. I really don't belong to the human world, do I?"

"No, you belong to the Anithian kind, the kind that gives to the human world. And the type of Anithian you are will determine what your soul creates."

I cock my head in her direction, keen to digest more information. "So, there are different types?"

"There're seven that create seven different gifts."

"What is my gift?"

"Not until it is created will you or anyone else know. However, there's a roundabout way to find out, by narrowing down what type of Anithian you aren't. This will come with time. The most renowned Anithian is the artistic Nubenlee. They're our famous musicians, painters, writers, dancers, actors and so on. The Nubenlee enrich the human world with soulspiration, filling every gift and room they enter with energy as rich as the sun. We also refer to them as having a heart of gold, because the color of their soul shimmers golden yellow."

"So, do all seven Anithians have their own color?"

"Yes. Each one is a different color of the rainbow. Speaking of rain, here it comes."

Large raindrops randomly hit the decking. Pearl drags the pots away from the house and places them out into the open to catch the rain.

"Here, let me help you," I say, dragging over the largest pot. "I love it when the morning sky turns dark with summer rain like this. It creates such an invigorating mood."

"It's the kinetic energy in raindrops. But let's save that for another day. I'm just going to get some water to drink. I haven't spoken this much in years." She giggles.

Pearl seems to be radiating with invigorating energy herself. Has my soul brought her an extra dose of excitement, or has she always been this radiant and only now, with my new perception of energy, I can detect it? Maybe it's a bit of both.

Pearl returns with two glasses of water and takes a seat. However, she also places a small drawstring bag on the table beside her.

"Here you go." She passes me a glass. "Now, where were we?"

"We were talking about the Nubenlee."

"That's right. Our inspirational artists, who fill the world with their soulful attributes."

"Is it possible I could be a Nubenlee?"

"I can't see why not." She shrugs her shoulders.

"Wow, this is exciting. What are the other types of Anithians?" I ask, taking a drink.

"We have Native custodians, who are typically indigenous women, anciently known as Alizarins. Their souls are energetically identical to a specific place on Earth called their native homeland. They don't create material gifts like the Nubenlee, but when their feet connect with their homeland, the dual energies harmonize, creating powerful currents of energy, enriching everything growing around them. Hence why they don't often wear shoes."

"That must mean Trealla is an Alizarin, given she walks barefoot often."

"Correct, and Avenlee is her native homeland. Actually, it's our oldest native homeland in the world. Our kind seek its energy more than any place on the earth, but we will discuss that later." Pearl unlocks her ankles and slides her bare feet under her seat. Obviously, Pearl's an Alizarin, too. Which also makes me think it's possible I could be one. I hate wearing shoes.

"It's all making sense now. This is why I got such a kick of energy when I first arrived at Avenlee, and why everything grows so prolific there."

"The soulful energy currents vibrating in that valley could power the whole of England, so yes, that's what captivated your soul. Next, we have Viridis, also known as Green Seeds."

"I met plenty of Green Seeds at Avenlee, carrying their little baskets of goodies around."

"Avenlee is a Green Seed sanctuary, and those baskets of seeds they carry are like badges of honor. It's a tradition they've held for hundreds of thousands of years. You will even see depictions of Viridis with their baskets in ancient stone carvings, like the Olmecs and also the Assyrians of ancient Iraq. Those baskets have baffled historians for centuries." She snickers to herself, then takes a sip of her water. "Anithians could answer so many ancient mysteries."

"So, what exactly do Green Seeds gift?"

"Viridis dedicate their prolific souls to one particular seed, and anywhere they plant that seed, their soul remains with the tree. Their soul's energy protects and provides rich nourishing energy, ensuring the tree's existence on earth is bountiful and never becomes extinct. They can also place their hands on their trees and travel back through their growth over the years."

That's possibly what Queenee was doing in the Pomona Garden at the Sakrid.

"Next, we have the highly sought-after Lazelees or Artisans of Love."

"Sounds interesting. Tell me more." I eagerly sit forward in my chair.

"Their souls are the most exquisitely loving, loyal and protective of our kinds. But first you must understand that in every Artisan's formless state beyond this human experience, they energetically harmonize in a sphere of love with another Anithian called their Anoi. When they both come to earth to live, they are separated. But an Artisan can't go without their Anoi. So, Artisans voyage to the end of the earth to find their Anoi, and when they do, they bestow their loving souls in the most endearing ways, and this returns them to their sphere of love again."

"Oh, my heart. They sound divine."

"Yes, and if you're lucky enough to have an Artisan as a soul counterpart, you're guaranteed to receive pure, insatiable love. Some Artisans have been so skilled in the art of love, their lives have become legends and passed down as the greatest romance stories, mythologies, and fairy tales of our time." She expresses her delight with her hand on her heart.

"My goodness, Pearl, how do I find myself an Artisan of Love?"

"You don't. Artisans find you. That's their gift, to make you their destination, but that's only if you are an Anoi." She taps her finger on the table, to clarify the difference.

"So then how do you know if you're an Artisan's Anoi?"

"Well, personally, I don't know because I don't have one, but I've been told that when you look into their eyes, eternity exists."

"That just gave me boost jumps."

"What are boost jumps?"

"You know, goosebumps." I giggle.

"We are both learning things today." She shuffles in her chair. "This is another reason why you need to evolve from your first chapter, because there's a soul counterpart out there awaiting your love. He might not be an Artisan and you his Anoi, but every Anithian has a soul counterpart to connect with."

"So, my soul has a counterpart, and that counterpart could possibly be an Artisan?"

"Yes, we shall wait and see."

"What color are Lazulee souls?"

"Iridescent blue."

I think back to Zeke's vibrant blue shimmer. He must be an Artisan of Love and Shamila must be his Anoi. If only I'd known all this back then.

Pearl stands and looks up passed the veranda roof, while the raindrops land on her face. "Those rain clouds are dark. This storm's here to stay," she comments, then sits back down, drying her face. "Next, we have the whimsical Romzeil. They gift their creative souls through the unique art of Storytelling, taking Anithians into another dimension of time. The lady who read Annabell's story to you is a Storyteller."

"So that's why her books are so magical. It's her Anithian gift."

"Yes, a gift that is highly regarded among our kind. They're also lucky enough to be born in their second chapter and retain their knowledge. This is another way of narrowing down what type of Anithian you are, because if you're not born awakened, you're not a Storyteller. Just like if you don't have emerald-green eyes, you're not a Green Seed."

"I can definitely cross Storyteller off my list, given it's taken me eighteen years to awaken, and only recently."

"That's true. Now, the next type of Anithian is a Guardian, or anciently known as a Naranja. Their protective souls look after all Anithian gifts, as well as Anithians themselves. They're often archaeologists, conservationists, and antique collectors. Some even own museums or libraries to keep Anithian gifts safe, hence why you may also hear them refered to as Keepers. I should also mention there are two types of Guardians. The first being the one I've just explained, and the second is a Native Guardian. They help Alizarins protect their homeland and the animals on it. You will be able to identify a Native Guardian by their rich orange shimmer and from the warm protective energy their souls radiate."

"I remember meeting a Keeper at Avenlee. His name was Mr. Ambrose. He is obviously a Guardian of jewelry."

"Yes, and the jewelry would have been made or owned by Anithians."

"So that's what's so special about all that jewelry."

"Yes, it holds the energy of our souls. Now, moving on to the last

Anithian of our kind, which is our greatest mystery. The seventh soul has never revealed itself and remains unknown. Some Anithians are of the opinion it hasn't taken human form yet. Some Anithians are audacious enough to think the seventh soul lives within the animal kingdom. But truly we don't know."

"That is a great mystery." My mind casts out thoughts of intrigue.

"Yes, the greatest in the Anithian world. Alongside your rather dominant human life." She smiles.

"Am I really that human?"

"I've never met an Anithian as human as you. Your untamed soul definitely set itself a challenge in this poweful young heart of yours. But don't you worry. Your soul has ignited. You can look forward to creating your soulful self into a gift, and that gift can help awaken you in your next life."

"Next life," I reply, with a sizable tone of intrigue.

"That's another part of your existence I must inform you of," she says, as though she's been keeping this important knowledge until the end. "After your soul creates itself into a gift, you continue living and eventually die, as everyone does. But because your soul is eternal, it can return to live another life by ensouling another body. Then it starts the Anithian journey all over again."

I internally pause after hearing this last snippit of Anithian knowledge. There is nowhere to go in my brain to find the logic. I feel there is only a whole new existence I must make room for.

"Um, okay, so, so basically…" Oh my goodness I can't even speak. I look at Pearl bewildered, as she looks back at me waiting for me to articulate my thoughts. "So basically, you just blew my mind," I fumble out, making Pearl laugh.

"Oh, dear, Isola, just take a deep breath."

"I'll take five." I overexert my inhalation and exhalation. "That's out of this world. So, this soul within me is eternal and can come back and live again and again and again?"

"Correct. Your soul can return as many times as it likes, creating as many gifts as it chooses. Your soul's energy will already be existing here in the form of a gift, from a previous life. These gifts also help us awaken."

"Are you for real?" I lean inward, wide-eyed.

"Yes. Say, for example, you're a Nubenlee who's written a famous song. Chances are, when you return in your next life, you will hear the song playing. The moment your soul identifies its energy, it creates an awakening. So, our previous gifts act as tokens to awaken us in the next life or, as we call it, the afterlife. You will hear the term *afterlife* often now."

Just when I'm grasping the intricate details of this new existence and the different types of Anithians, the plot deepens.

"So, I've possibly lived before this lifetime, and I will possibly live after this life, too?"

"Yes, more than likely." Pearl nods.

Pearl gives me a moment of quietness, to let the knowledge of my eternity sink into my consciousness. The more I learn from Pearl, the more I realize how foolish I was to think I'm human. And knowing my soul's energy could already be living here on earth ignites my curiosity even more.

"Do you know how many times your soul has been here, Pearl?"

"Around twenty times now."

"Oh my goodness, really? I wonder how many times my soul has lived?" My sight goes out of focus as I look out, pondering this question.

"A lot, I'd say."

"Can you tell?"

"Yes, with age or lives comes wisdom, dear. I also know because our souls have crossed paths in another life."

"Are you serious? That's amazing," I say, bubbling with intrigue to hear my soul has lived before.

"Our souls crossed paths around a hundred and forty-five years ago."

"A hundred and forty-five years? That's crazy." Again, I'm looking out into the ether trying to take all this in. "So, I was soulfully alive a hundred and forty-five years ago?"

"Yes, and it will astound you to know I'm still existing from that lifetime."

An overwhelming silence drowns the conversation. Pearl just became the oldest person I know.

"You're a hundred and forty-five years old? That's astounding."

"No, I'm one hundred and fifty years old. We met a hundred and forty-five years ago, when I was five."

"Wow, you're old. But you don't look it," I quickly add, hoping I haven't offended her.

"Being an awakened Anithian means you don't waste your energy stuck in your head, thinking and wrinkling your life away. Therefore, you save a heck of a lot of energy to use on living longer. We physically age around two to three years every ten years."

"That's amazing. So, I'm going to look eighteen for a long time?"

"Yes, the soul is a youthful elixir. Less thinking, less wrinkling." She smiles.

Now I know why Trealla looks so much younger than my mom. "No wonder you got a shock the day I was born."

"Oh, boy, did I get a surprise to see you had returned, and to a labor ward I was working on. You, of course, have a different body in this life, but I'd identify your mysterious soul no matter how different you physically look."

"Do I have a mysterious soul?"

"My oath, you do. It doesn't give much away."

"Tell me about it. It's not even enlightening me on much," I say, making Pearl laugh.

"Well, as elusive as you soulfully are, I'm grateful that we've crossed paths again. Even if this lifetime is completely different from the last."

"How is it so different?"

"In many ways, but the biggest being last time we met, you were the adult, and I was a child."

"That's hard to picture. How did we meet?"

"You went to see an Anithian Storyteller who told you the story of another life you had lived, and when you walked out, you caught me listening in."

"Hold up." I lift my finger, pressing pause on her next bomb shell. "Did you just say Anithian Storytellers tell stories of other lives your soul has lived?"

"Yes, I was getting to that. Our lives are recorded within our souls. This is how I know I've lived around twenty times, from reading back through my Anithian ancestry with a Storyteller."

Instantly, Annabell Hennington's story changes from being a fictional novel with an interactive twist to an all-revealing autobiography of my soul's ancestry upon earth. This means Lizabethe lives among thousands of Anithian lives, and some are mine.

"Are you okay, Isola?"

I fall back into my chair. "I'm just in a bit of shock to know that I was Annabell in real life. At least now I know why I could feel every one of Annabell's emotions and senses as if they were my own. My soul actually lived them in real life. Come to think of it, if I was Annabell and lived in 1818, that's around a hundred and forty-five years ago. So that means you're from that life. You must have been a five-year-old girl from Nakaho's tribe."

"Great detective work." She winks at me.

"So, then I've also returned to the same country and state where I previously lived."

Pearl remains silent and only nods her head slightly, not wanting to give much more away.

"Are Sisika and Nakaho still alive?"

"Not from that lifetime. Maybe in their next."

I have a million questions running through my overactive brain and I don't know which one to fire at Pearl next. "So, was your tribe an Anithian tribe?"

"No, not at all. Nakaho, Sisika and I are Anithians born to the Muscogee."

"And then along came me, the prudent Englishwoman." I chuckle at my conservative past.

"Yes, you definitely stood out. You're lucky Nakaho found you."

"Very true."

I think back to Annabell's story. I remember being married to William. Voyaging across the sea on Davy's boat, desperate to find some taka. Then, just as the first chapter ended, Annabell lay on the bottom of a canyon, possibly dead.

"Pearl, this is terrible. At the end of my first chapter, I'm a brokenhearted, deranged woman who fell from the top of a cliff and could have possibly died. I'm feeling somewhat unsuccessful in my life of Annabell Hennington."

"There's no use being upset. Nothing can be changed. You were a Muklee and beguiled by your humanness."

"Yes, but poor Annabell, poor me. I can't believe I had to lose my husband. I had nothing but guilt and alcohol running through my veins."

"Keep in mind, Isola, maybe that's what had to happen for her to finally awaken. We sometimes go through these difficult situations to force us to let go, and that's when the transformation occurs."

That's exactly how I awakened. My life had to turn out badly to make me let go. However, remembering how Annabell hit the bottom of the canyon, I doubt she awakened to anything except a grave. But on second thought, I don't remember meeting Pearl in my first chapter, which means I must have met her in my second. Therefore, Annabell must have survived her great fall in order to have met Pearl.

"How do Storytellers do that? That's magic."

"Your soul records and stores the ancestry of its creativity, like a grand old Anithian library. And Storytellers have a unique gift to tap into our soul's ancestry, via our eyes, so we can traipse back through time. It's a form of energy memory."

"Wow, that is unique, the ancestry of creativity. Actually, those are the stories Nakaho told Annabell he'd read. This means he was an Anithian Storyteller."

"Yes, a Romzeil."

"Of course! And this also means my soul has been recording my life up until now."

"Correct, and you will probably read this life in future lives."

"I seriously need to start living better, if every moment of my life is being recorded. I also need to hear Annabell's second chapter and find out about the woman I was. I might even be back here for a reason. Can you tell me what happened to her?"

"No, that would be un-Anithian of me." She shakes her head. "I've already said more than I should have, and regardless of that, it would only be my opinion of Annabell's life. Like I said, Annabell didn't give much away apart from love, so you're best-off hearing your ancestry from your soul via a Romzeil."

"Well, then, it looks like I have to find one."

"That might be a problem. Because you started hearing Annabell's story with Lizabethe, you must finish hearing the story from her."

"So, I have to go back to England?" I say, hoping I'd heard wrong.

"You will. Only under special circumstances will a Storyteller loan a story out. In the meantime, I suggest you visit the Storyteller here on the island. That's if you're interested in doing some soul searching through your ancestry."

"There's a Storyteller here on the island?" I point down at the ground, surprised.

"Luckily for us, there is. His name is Natoli, and he's a very sought-after Storyteller, too."

"I've always been interested in history, and whose better to know than my own? This is going to be so exciting to know all the gifts my soul's created. Where does Natoli live?"

"On the North Shore."

"I thought the North Shore is inaccessible."

"If you know the way, it isn't." She gives me a smug look out the corner of her eyes. "Natoli holds the wisdom of the world under his cap but chooses to laugh about life instead. It's believed his Anithian ancestry runs well into indigo, or possibly even the Tyrian collection of books."

"What is the Tyrian collection of books?"

"Anithians use the seven colors of the rainbow to color-sequence their lives on earth. Each color is broken down into around twenty shades, which represent twenty lifetimes. So, the more lives your soul has lived, the more colors you will have in your collection of books. They begin in red and progress into orange, yellow, green, blue, indigo and then Tyrian. So, if an Anithian has indigo or Tyrian in their collection, it indicates they're the oldest of our kind, which means their soul has possibly lived more than one hundred lifetimes."

"One hundred lifetimes? Are you serious?"

"Yes, but this is very, very rare."

"That is very, very old, and this color archiving system is a clever way of recording history."

"We do this because we are eternal. We could return to live in other cultures or eras of time, so we need timeless ways to record our ancestries. And given the colors of the rainbow are universal and never change, it makes perfect sense to use them as a method of organization rather than numbers or alphabets that constantly change." She pauses and takes her last mouthful of water. "I think we'll leave it there. You've taken in a lot of information for one day."

I remember being able to choose from multiple shades of books on Lizabethe's book shelf. If I'm not mistaken, Annabell's book is rich purple. Lizabethe was even stunned by the number of books I had to choose from. So maybe I'm an old soul, like Natoli. All this insight creates even more questions.

What kind of Anithian am I? What have I created in other lives? Why have I returned to the same place I previously lived? But most importantly, what am I here to create in this life?

"I can hear your cogs turning from over here."

"You should hear how loud they are in my head."

"Now that the rain's stopped, go take a walk through the forest or on the beach. Let your soul breathe in some fresh air. It will do you a world of good."

"Good idea."

"Before you go, I've got something to give you."

She grabs the small bag off the table, loosening the drawstring. Then takes out a necklace of shells. She walks behind me, putting it around my neck.

"Is this Annabell's necklace?" I clutch at the hope.

"It sure is. It belongs to your soul."

"I remember when Sisika gave it to me, and later that night she said, 'Welcome back from my ancestor.'"

"Sisika must have known you in a previous life and was welcoming you back."

"Stuff just keeps on getting older, the more I walk this path. The village where you and Sisika lived, is it near?"

"It's about an hour's walk from Fortier. But that's all I'll say. You need to find out about Annabell's life for yourself."

"Fair enough. Thank you, Pearl. You have obviously looked after this for a very long time."

"I'm glad it's back with its rightful owner." She pats me on the arm.

"And look, it even matches my ankle bracelet. It's beautiful."

"Just like you. Now go take a walk. I've run out of words. I'll see you later."

***

I look out to the horizon and feel as eternal as the sea. Two years ago, I questioned if I was even alive. Nothing really moved me. I guess a part of me was dead. The most spectacular part, as Trealla once said. Now it's time to create my gift and find out what type of Anithian I am.

How do you want to live in this world? Soul, show me the way.

Out of the corner of my eye, I see a little tin boat sailing towards me. It's Stelina. Taking a breath, I exhale, sending my shimmering soul beyond me. Stelina's face lights up as she shimmers in return. Standing up, her boat rocks with excitement. Off balance, she falls into the water, swimming towards me, her soul ablaze. Oh my goodness, she is going to take me out with one enthusiastic swoop. I brace myself as she wraps her arms around me, inundating me with love and a firm, soulful squeeze.

"You made it, soul sister. You're awakened."

I give a modest shrug. "Nothing to it."

Chapter Thirty

Benjamin McCall, 2011. America.

Eleven months ago, I dropped my head into my hands after Rose the tutor left, accepting responsibility for this story. Now, in utter disbelief, I hold in my hands the manuscript I've written. I did it. I have an imagination after all! I can't wait to tell Rose.

I also have an insight into an ancient world within this world that I can't get enough of. Even if it's only fictional, Anithian knowledge and creativity have given me a whole new perspective of the world and my existence within it.

Rose is right. Writers don't write great stories. Writers surrender to great stories and the stories write themselves. I've been so inundated by Isola's story since surrendering to her, my hand couldn't keep up.

I kid you not. Some days, I didn't eat. I haven't seen my mates in months. I have no idea of the value of my bitcoin. Heck, I make Emerson look like a clean-cut Neanderthal. I'm as wooly as him. But boy, do I have a cracking story, as well as a sore ass.

Now I understand what Isola meant. This story isn't intended for humans. It's meant to bypass the history of human thinking and speak to the soul.

Could these soulful Anithians exist in plain sight amongst us? Are there Native women harmonizing with the soul of the earth? Do Storytellers and their Anithian libraries exist? Is Bramble Street real and Avenlee an actual garden? Are the songs I listen to sung by the Nubenlee? Do the oak trees outside my window contain the soul of a Green Seed? I hope so.

Isola has an ancestry of creativity, and a soulful gift I need to know about. But I won't find the answers to any of these questions until I write some more. Just when I thought I was finished, Isola awakens and creates a whole new beginning.

Leaning back in my chair, feeling rather proud of myself, I look to the waves carved into the walls, noticing the seashells at the bottom that I've overlooked until now.

"What the heck!" Jumping out of my chair, unable to believe my eyes, I rush over to the wall and slide the cabinet to the side, exposing the wall. The same three seashells carved into the *Makana* are carved in my wall. They are exactly the same as Annabell described them. What in the world is going on? Surely this is just a mere coincidence. But what if it's not?

Racing outside to the front of the house, I jump up and down trying to grab hold of the tall branch pushing against the wall, blocking my view. Taking the branch in my hand, I hold it out of the way and look up at the wall.

"I'll be damned." Staring back at me is a Cowrie shell and the word *Makana*. Letting go of the branch, I lean back against the oak tree, flabbergasted.

Everyone has a story to tell. But I have a story telling me. *Anithia* has only just begun.

About the Author

Lee Lehner is the author of adult magical realism novels. Her passion for storytelling is at the heart of her unconventional characters and the rumination they provoke. Lee's imagination draws attention to esoteric worlds, ancient female wisdom, and desirable men who enjoy a good chase. Lee attributes her earthy nature to growing up barefoot in Australia, where she resides today, devoting her time away from writing to meditation and indulging in the essence of plants.

Acknowledgements

First and foremost, my eternal love and gratitude to my son, Mitcheil. This story exists because of you. I gave you life, but in truth, you have given me more. Thank you for holding the dream for me from the very beginning. I take great courage in knowing I have your unwavering support and love. I'm honoured to be your mother.

My warmest appreciation to Isaac and Kaia, for enriching my heart with love. One day you will both read this book and understand the importance of awakening to the innate within. I'm excited to see what you create.

I am forever in debt to my parents, Gilda and Karl. Thank you for your constant outpouring of unconditional love and support, especially while writing the books. Our daily allotment of coffee brought about conversation I will treasure forever.

My love and gratitude to my beautiful sister, Tahlia, for standing by me through my struggles, successes and early drafts.

Special thanks to my fiancé, Tory. Your love and companionship I truly appreciate. Thank you for sharing this wondrous journey of parenthood.

My gratitude to the following people. Margaret Love, for sparking my fascination with history. Belinda Reid, for your holistic shot of humour and friendship. Alexandra Bebenek, for your divine presence in my life. Angela Edginton, for your bottomless friendship. Robin Kuipers, for encouraging me to get publishing. Michael Lehner, for all your love. Lyla, Bodi and Benji, for bringing so much joy to my heart. Davina Horvat, Silvia Bradley, Danielle Dale and Emma Dickson, for years of friendship.

Thank you to the following people who shared their knowledge and support. Rebecca Richards, Velvet Tea, Jennifer Sharp, Arnot Hutcheson and Helen Williams.

The final result would not be what is without Jasmine Sullivan's diligent proofread and edit suggestions.

Finally, thank you to the woman behind the scenes, there are no words.

Lightning Source UK Ltd.
Milton Keynes UK
UKHW010633031222
413194UK00005B/363